Father's Day

Father's Day

RAMONA MICHELE GREENE

FATHER'S DAY

This is a work of fiction. All of the characters, names, incidents, organizations, and dialogue in this novel are either the products of the author's imagination or are used fictitiously.

iUniverse books may be ordered through booksellers or by contacting:

iUniverse
1663 Liberty Drive
Bloomington, IN 47403
www.iuniverse.com
1-800-Authors (1-800-288-4677)

Cover art, "George and Debra", by Ramona Michele Greene.

ISBN: 978-1-4917-7558-5 (sc)
ISBN: 978-1-4917-7559-2 (e)

Library of Congress Control Number: 2015914074

Print information available on the last page.

iUniverse rev. date: 10/22/2015

This book is dedicated to my own father, Royce Garner. You gave me the tools needed to be happy in life and taught me the value of hard work. I miss you, Dad.

Aknowledgements

One would think that one's second book would be easier, but that isn't necessarily so. The writing may be easier, but the production and publishing is even more daunting because you know what's ahead. This makes the people who help me along even more important in their roles.

First of all is my dear, hard-working husband, Jeff. I could not do this without his encouragement. He continues to surprise me with the support I so desperately need. I love you, Jeff.

A natural second is Cathryn Major. Once more enduring the repeated readings it takes to properly edit a book, she has done so without a single complaint. Thank you for your hard work and cheering me on, Cathryn!

A big thank-you goes to Rebecca Lucas for acting as a secondary editor. She has the uncanny ability of catching typos and flubbed phrases more than anyone I know. Thanks, Becky, for giving my book that final polish!

And thank you to all my family and friends for your constant support!

Chapter One

Chaos had erupted in the intensive care unit at St. Luke's Hospital. A solemn group of people watched fearing the worst as nurses walked briskly in and out of the ward. One person noticed with curiosity that the nurses were smiling—even giggling—as they left to go back down the hall.

"Wait a minute everyone. I don't think it's what we suspect," he told the others. George left the group to go to where his sister-in-law lay dying—or so he thought—from a flu that she had picked up on their recent visit to Japan. The little room was filled with nurses attending to Shelly along with a doctor studying her heart rate. Also, to his surprise, lay his brother on the floor with a nurse attending to him.

"What happened to him?"

"Oh, he just fainted," the young nurse cheerily replied. "He got a little excited when the doctor told him—"

"That Shelly wasn't going to die on us, after all," the doctor finished for the nurse while giving her a stern look. The nurse took it as a reprimand and to keep her mouth shut.

"Oh, wow," George said looking at Shelly and nonchalantly stepping over his brother's long legs to get to her bedside. He looked down at her and noticed with both amazement and alarm that she meant more to him than his own sister. He would have been very sad if she had died. He smiled at her and asked, "Shelly? Shelly, dear? Are you going to be okay?"

She mumbled and moved her head, but that was enough reaction to make him happy.

"It'll take a while for her to fully recover, but we're hopeful," the doctor remarked. Robin then made a noise that attracted their attention. "Meanwhile, you can take care of your brother."

George came over to his younger brother and squatted down beside him. "Hey, you all right, mate?" He patted Robin on the cheek. Robin sat blinking, trying to remember what happened. "Come on. Let's go tell everyone she's going to make it!"

He helped him up and Robin noticed his elbow hurting from his fall as he straightened out his glasses. He stood rubbing his arm, still in shock from what the doctor told him. He went over to his wife and brushed back her long red curls. He kissed her on the cheek and whispered something to her, making her give the hint of a smile. He then followed his brother out to the waiting area.

The family members waited with great apprehension as to what was happening with Shelly. As they watched the brothers emerge, they were confused by George's smile and Robin's dazed look.

"She's still a bit out of it, but she's gonna make it!" George announced. Everyone cheered, but George's wife, Debra, immediately asked Robin, "What's the matter, honey?"

He opened his eyes wide and surveyed them all, trying to figure out how to tell them his news. They began to worry, but waited patiently. "Shelly is…uh…she's—."

"Spit it out, Rob," demanded George.

He looked at his brother and said, "She's pregnant."

"What?!" the crowd answered.

Robin finally smiled. "Yeah. We're going to have a baby."

"Oh, my God!" Rachel screamed, so happy for her friends.

Everyone took their turn hugging and congratulating Robin.

"This is strange," remarked their cousin Terry after they all settled down. "Everybody knows except the girl who's pregnant."

And with that, Robin lost his smile and put his head down. "I'd better go see to her." He left the group to be with his wife.

Rachel then smacked Terry in the arm. "Wha'?" her boyfriend asked, getting an ugly look from everyone. "Oh. Sorry."

Debra and Rachel then began to talk to each other about this mind-blowing news, leaving George to talk to Terry. "Talk about a twist of fate," he said as Terry smiled and nodded. "No wonder he fainted."

"He fainted?" Terry asked with relish.

"Yeah… Hey, so what's the deal with you and Rachel?" his cousin asked, being curious as to why Terry had not gone back to England as planned.

Terry suddenly turned bashful. "Well, I kinda got addicted to her."

"Uh-huh."

"So, uh, what do you think about lettin' your dear cousin stay a bit at your place?"

"Depends on what you mean by 'a bit'."

"Just until I get me own flat."

"You're moving here?" he asked with astonishment.

Terry smiled. "Can you handle me living in the same city as you?"

George gave him a wry look. "Why do you think I moved to America in the first place?" he joked. "So, what are you going to do here? I hear the petrol station is hiring."

"No, thank you," he replied with a grin. He then explained his job offer to play with a Miami soccer team.

"Sounds like a bit of a risk," George said with concern.

Terry glanced back at Rachel and lightly said, "It's worth it," and flashed one of his famous smiles.

"Wow, well, this is fantastic. So what? You going to marry her?"

"Uh, not so quickly. We'd like to get to know each other better first. That was the whole problem. We haven't been able to be normal."

"You two? Normal? Never happen," he said, shaking his head.

"I can't believe this!" Rachel told Debra for the seventh time. Debra simply laughed. Rachel was completely astonished and, oh, so relieved.

Meanwhile, Robin had gone back to be by Shelly's side. He wasn't able to be celebratory yet. He still felt she wasn't out of the woods and he wasn't going to be convinced of it until she was alert and back to her cheerful self.

The doctor, however, was more hopeful. He watched Robin for a moment then said, "She's going to be fine. Her temperature is gradually falling. We don't want it to go down too fast or she'll go into shock, so she's doing just as she should."

"What did you mean a while ago when you said there might be complications?" Robin asked, not really wanting to know the answer.

The doctor didn't feel like getting into it right now; he felt they should focus on Shelly's recovery, instead. Nevertheless, he replied, "Well, a temperature like what Shelly has been through can cause birth defects at such an early stage in development. Now, that doesn't mean it's for certain, it just increases the chances."

This didn't keep Robin from wanting to know the facts. "What kind of defects?"

"Facial, cardiac… Again, that can happen with a perfectly normal pregnancy, but you shouldn't worry about anything unless you have something to worry about, understand?" He gave Robin a very stern look.

"Yes, sir."

"And it's definitely something that your dear wife doesn't need to know about anytime soon. She needs some recovery time—she doesn't need worries. She'll have to handle that soon enough."

Robin nodded obediently.

"By the way," the doctor said before making his exit, "don't be surprised if she's a little forgetful at first—she may have had a little swelling." He tapped his head. "So, take it easy with her."

Robin said, "Okay," then made a motion showing his exhaustion with the whole situation, but then turned to his wife and smiled. There she was, living and breathing and fighting for her life. He felt he should talk to her more and cheer her on.

He caressed her and kissed her, leaning over her trying to contemplate what his life would have been like without her. "Shelly? Darling? It's Robin."

She gave her head a funny tilt and opened her eyes enough to focus on him. She tried to smile.

Terry's words echoed in Robin's head, and he wanted to clear this matter up as soon as possible. "Dearheart, I hope you can understand me. You know you've been really ill, don't you?"

She nodded.

"Well, the doctor gave me some news that I just have to tell you." He waited a second to make sure this was registering. "We're going to have a baby," he said happily.

A strong look of confusion came over her and she started to breathe harder.

"Do you understand?"

"A baby?" she whispered.

"Yes! You're pregnant, sweetheart."

She swallowed and blinked her eyes, trying desperately to figure out if this was reality or a dream.

Robin laughed and hugged her. He had done what he could; it was just going to take time for it to sink in.

The doctor came back in and told Robin that he ought to let Shelly rest for a while.

"When can she come home?"

"Well, let's make sure she's completely recovered first. I'd like to keep her overnight, just to make sure she's stable. You can call us in the morning to check on her progress. Meanwhile, I suggest you get some rest yourself."

Robin reluctantly agreed. He thanked the doctor profusely and went back out to his family to tell them that Shelly needed her rest. The girls hugged him once more and they all took their leave. Robin went home, immediately falling asleep on the couch.

When George and the rest got back to his house, they were feeling too jovial to sleep. Instead, they sat in the living room discussing the strange turn of events. Once the topic died down, Terry and Rachel began to get the feeling that they were about to be laughed at by George. Oddly enough, it was Debra who first said something.

"So, are you going to tell us what is going on with you two?" she giggled.

They all started to laugh and Rachel relaxed. "Okay, here's what happened." She went on to explain how she had moved back home to Puerto Rico and Terry chased her down. Debra and George listened with interest and expressed their happiness for the young couple.

"I really thought that was it—that I was never going to see him again. Then, there he was—in Puerto Rico!"

"What had you done—call her family?" George asked Terry.

"Yes, once I accepted this position. I had to find her, and Shelly had given me her number there. So, after hours of trying to figure out how to call Puerto Rico, I got a hold of her father and had a talk with him."

"I bet he put you through the wringer, didn't he?" asked Rachel with a giggle.

"Oh, yes."

They laughed at his expression.

"How did you do it?" she asked.

"I just had to explain to him how much I needed to have you in my life." He looked down in embarrassment.

It got quiet, but then Debra broke the silence with the exclamation, "Well, this is just fantastic! Now what?"

"Well… George said I could stay here until I can get my own place—if that's all right with you."

"Yes, of course. And you, Rachel?"

"Shelly said I could move into her old studio if I came back. She always second-guesses me—it's very annoying." At this point, Rachel lost her smile and her voice began to quake. "You know, I just don't know what I'd have done if she had died." Here, she cried, still shook up from nearly losing her dear friend.

The family was immediately reminded that it was Rachel who had known Shelly the longest. Terry rubbed her back and said, "It wasn't her time, love. Shelly's got a lot of miles left in her, as I hope we all do. She needed to stick around so George can be the mean old uncle he was always meant to be."

This made everyone chuckle and Rachel smiled again and took Terry's hand and held it. Then she laughed at a thought. "What's so funny?" he asked.

"I was just thinking how unhappy Robin was when she brought home that dog. What's he going to do with a *baby*?"

They all laughed at this notion. To imagine the 'master of order' trying to be a father gave them plenty to kid about. Robin changing a dirty diaper was just too funny to imagine.

But, they weren't giving him the credit he deserved. Robin awoke the next morning feeling completely rejuvenated. He had his coffee and a shower and showed up at the hospital bearing balloons and flowers. He was determined to celebrate.

When he got to the hospital, he had a bit of a shock not finding Shelly where he'd left her. An easy explanation came from the nurse stating that they had moved her to a regular room. He swiftly set off to find her, hearing that she was fairly awake and coherent now.

He popped his head in to find her sitting up and trying to work the television remote. "Hello, hello!"

"Robin!"

He quickly put down the flowers and kissed and held his wife for a very long time. She really was together and it did him good to see her back to normal. She still seemed a little 'hung over' he felt, but she at least understood what was going on.

He sat on the bed, brushing back her hair, thinking how unreal it had all seemed. It was hard now to imagine that he had almost lost her.

She was extremely happy to see him and immediately asked him, "Is it true? Am I really pregnant?"

"Yes, my love, you are."

She placed her hand over her mouth and gave a chuckle. Then, she looked at him with big blue eyes and was unable to say anything. She threw her arms around his neck and cried. She couldn't believe it was true. She had all but lost hope for such a miracle.

It felt so good to Robin to hold her again and he was unsure what to say. He wondered if she knew how close she came to dying. "Do you realize—" he started, but then stopped himself.

"What?"

"Never mind. I just…I'm just so grateful to have you in my life."

"Same here." She looked at him feeling that some sort of change had taken place. There was almost fear in his eyes. It made her uncomfortable. She figured it was just the stress he had been under and the news of the baby that had thrown him off balance. Hopefully, he would soon be back to his old self.

"Oh! I thought I'd tell you. Rachel and Terry are back together."

Her mind raced. "Terry?"

"Yeah, Terry." He then recalled the doctor's warning. "My cousin, Terry. You know—he went out with Rachel and they hit it off, but then they couldn't decide who was moving where?"

Her eyes moved from him to all over the room, racking her brain trying to remember.

He felt sorry for her and said, "Don't worry, love. The doctor said you might have a little amnesia. You'll probably recall him when you see him."

She felt like she had been asleep for years and was trying to catch up to all that was happening. She held her head in her hands like a college senior on her last exam.

"Please, dearheart, don't worry," he pleaded. Need to change the subject, he thought. "The doctor said you could go home today as long as your temperature is stable."

"Really?" she asked eagerly. She was anxious to go home to familiar surroundings. Maybe she wouldn't feel like such an alien in a lost world.

He leaned over and hugged her once again. "Yes, babe, I'll take you home."

As he held her, she could never remember such a reassuring feeling.

Late in the afternoon Shelly was released much to Robin's relief. He brought her gratefully home and held her arm as she ascended the steps to their house. She came in and looked around with the same odd expression she used to give when she first started coming over to the great manor. "It sure is dark in here," she said softly.

"Sorry. Been gone all day, so all the lights are off." He turned the light on to the living room and she followed in, making a beeline to the curtains. She pulled back the drapes to expose the setting sun. He smiled at her knowing she was getting back to the Shelly he loved. "Do you need rest?" he asked, watching her sit down on the couch.

"Are you kidding? I'm tired of resting. Talk to me and get my brain going again."

He happily complied. Besides Shelly, the topic of the day was Rachel and Terry, so he told her of his visit to George's that day and what all they had to say.

"By the way," she interrupted, "I remember Terry now. He just popped into my head."

"Oh, good." He smiled and went on with his story. "Yes, I asked him what made him chase her down."

"Oh, yeah?"

"Yeah. He said Rachel was the only person he ever knew who could get high on the smell of rain, so he figured he'd better do all he could to keep her."

"Ha-ha. That's true. I've seen her. She says it reminds her of crayons."

"Crayons?" he laughed. Then, for the first time since her illness, she really laughed. Robin stopped talking and just studied her. He knew he had to put all this in the past and to get on with the living rather than dwell on the dying that never happened. He looked at her rosy cheeks and then it really hit him: they were having a baby.

She cocked her head at his stare and asked, "What's up?"

"You realize we're having a baby?"

"No, not yet. It hasn't sunk in."

"It did me, just now."

She smiled. "Wow."

His eyes got big and she laughed. "So, which room shall we put it?" he asked.

"Don't call the baby an 'it'. I mean, we're not having a curio cabinet. Say 'he' or 'she', but not 'it'."

He laughed. "Very well. Where shall we put him?"

"How do you know it's a *him*?"

"Why, you silly cuckoo!"

Shelly laughed heartily at capturing him in this trap.

"Well, it's certain I brought the right woman home… Come on. Let's go upstairs and take a gander at the rooms."

"Actually, I'd love to take a bath."

"Oh! Of course. I'm not thinking. You did just come out of hospital, didn't you? I'll run you a bath."

"Great. Uh, not too hot."

"No, dear. You've had enough heat for a while."

"And will you wash my hair? I love it when you wash my hair," she asked sweetly.

"Yes, O Queen. Your wish is my command." He gave her a bow which made her smile. She loved her silly Englishman terribly.

They walked up the stairs, he behind her, and when they got to the landing she turned to the right.

"No, darling. This way," he corrected.

"Oh, yeah. I always get so turned around in your house."

"*Our house*, dear."

"Right. Our house."

She came into the bedroom and sat on the bed. Robin got the tap going in the tub and came out to notice her thoughtful look. "What is it, love?"

"Well…I was wondering…"

"Yes?"

"The house will always seem like 'your house' to me until it has some of me in it."

"Ah! Well, of course it will… Never really thought about it, but it does seem a bit too masculine for a lady."

"Don't get me wrong. I love it. Every corner reminds me of you—"

"But no corners of your own?"

"I've got my dressing room, but could we brighten up bits of the rest? Like the kitchen and living room, perhaps?"

"I don't see why not."

"Don't worry. I'm not going to put floral toile all over the place, just, you know, splashes of color here and there."

"I understand. This is your home now, and I'm so glad you're here in it with me. I just couldn't imagine…" he trailed off, shaking his head.

"Imagine what?"

"That…that you wouldn't want to contribute some of your taste into it." This was the second time he kept himself from mentioning the fact that he almost lost her. He simply didn't want to discuss it.

Shelly studied his face, wondering if that was what he was going to say. Something told her not to ask. She really wasn't aware of her near-death experience, so in ignorance she blew off his odd behavior. She gave him a kiss and took her bath.

They got her all cleaned up and they enjoyed a cup of tea on her favorite leather couch. She was feeling quite normal, and began to mull around ideas in her head on decorating the living room. She would love to paint it yellow and wondered how he would take it. She looked at him and noticed his far away expression. She felt a little qualm of worry thinking maybe he wasn't ready for this child. "Robin?"

He jerked back to reality. "Yes, love?"

"Are you okay…about this baby?"

He knitted his brows, wondering what made her think he wasn't. "Well, of course! I'm extremely happy."

"Then why do you seem so unhappy?"

"Oh," he chuckled. "No, dear. Just dreading this tour and having to leave you here."

"Hey, I'll be all right. I'm going to be very busy in this house. How do you feel about yellow?"

"Ha-ha. You do whatever you like—whatever your heart desires." He leaned over and kissed her.

They chitchatted for a while longer until they were both sleepy. They made their way to the bed and immediately fell asleep.

Robin jolted in the middle of the night reliving the moment he awoke to find her with that horrible fever. He caught his breath and reached over to her. Her skin was cool, and she smiled at his touch. She was fine. Robin, on the other hand, wasn't. He lay awake for some time with a thousand thoughts tearing through his mind. He eventually got up and went downstairs to tinker with his piano.

What a good friend that piano was. It had helped him with so many problems and never complained about the time of day or night he called upon it. He looked at it and felt somehow he was being unfaithful to it. Shelly, and now the baby, were more important than his music—something he never thought would happen. He began to realize how much stronger she was than him. Between the baby and finding out about her real father, he couldn't see how Shelly could be so calm. She amazed him. And now here he was, trying to figure out if he wanted to quit or not. Quit. It finally hit him what he was thinking. That was the whole problem. He didn't want to leave Shelly's side. He got scared at the concept of leaving the business and wondered if he was overreacting. He really couldn't see over the next year or so. He was so torn what to do. One just can't cancel an entire tour. The responsibility of all the people who depend on him for all their jobs weighed heavy on his conscience. And what about George? Oh, what a mess. He began to play louder without realizing he was doing so. He was in a Beethoven mood, and wondered if he could clone himself like the man in a movie he had seen. It seemed like the only way out. He simply couldn't be in two places at one time. He played a very low E chord, and in doing so, woke up Shelly. He then realized how loud he had been playing and looked upstairs to find his wife looking down on him with her eyes half-opened. "Sorry, love," he apologized.

She came downstairs, and without saying anything, gave him a hug. Then he looked at her as if he'd seen her for the first time again. He got down on his knees, put his hands on her hips and gave a loving kiss to her belly. It wasn't until that moment that Shelly realized she was having his baby. She began to swoon and he held her tight and quickly asked, "You okay?"

"Oh, Robin," she said hugging him. She began to cry, but he could tell it was a cry of joy, and he gave a smile and held her dearly.

The next day Robin welcomed in his cousin and Rachel. Terry found Shelly up and about and looking quite like her old self, other than she hadn't quite regained her 'luster'.

Shelly was extremely happy to see her friend, and Rachel was likewise. She followed Shelly into the kitchen as she got some water to drink, leaving the guys to talk in the living room.

"I can't believe this, Shelly."

Shelly gave her a look, letting her know that she couldn't either. After the ectopic pregnancy she had had, she was led to believe that she would never get pregnant again.

"You're going to be a mommy!"

"I don't think anyone believes it. Like they say, 'when you least expect it'."

"Reminds me of Terry. I never thought I'd find the man of my dreams in George Parker's swimming pool."

"So, he's the man of your dreams?" Shelly asked with a smile.

"He must be. He flew all the way to Puerto Rico to get me."

"This is just so wild how our lives have changed because of this crazy family of Englishmen."

"No kidding. I never thought I'd like a Brit."

"Ha. They're addicting. Next thing you know…" Shelly patted her tummy to finish her sentence.

"Believe me, I'm in no big hurry for that."

Shelly leaned against the kitchen counter, glowing. Rachel realized that now that she had Terry, she was no longer jealous of Shelly, and she was happy for that fact. She didn't care if she was jobless, homeless and had no general purpose in life; she had Terry and she felt fulfilled. This reminded her of what she came there to ask. "Uh, Shelly?"

"Yeah?"

"Did the offer of the studio still stand?"

"Oh, yes! I'd love for you to take it over. It means so much to me, but it really is impractical now that I have one here. It'll be like keeping it in the family. I'll get you the key. I think it's on Robin's keys." She went out to rob him of the set and came back to find Rachel surveying the kitchen. "Oh, I'm going to repaint it."

"Halleluiah."

"I mean, I like red, but this is too much. I'm thinking about giving it a Tuscan look with a faux finish."

"You really wouldn't have to repaint it then, just give an effect over this. You know, with sponges. Then stick some garlic and grapes and stuff everywhere," she replied waving her hands about.

Shelly handed her the key and asked with delicacy, "Where's Terry staying?"

Rachel squirmed a bit. "Well, he told George he was going to get his own place."

"And?"

"And, what?"

"And do you want him to?"

"Shelly, you know more than anyone how I stand on that issue. I reamed you about it before *he* proposed," she said, pointing her thumb towards the living room.

"Looking back, I really don't see that it matters that much. You end up spending all your time together, anyway. You just have to trust him in the end."

"Well, it's simply an issue of independence."

"Do you want to marry him?"

Rachel looked down in thought. She looked up to reply, "Yeah, I do. It's just that we didn't want to jump into anything so quickly. We just want to be normal for a while."

"Now I'm abnormal."

"No, I mean— Dammit, Shelly, you always do that!"

"What?" she asked laughing.

"You're definitely back to your old self again."

"Abnormal?"

"Yes!"

They both laughed. It did Rachel's heart good to see Shelly back at it.

Meanwhile, the guys were having their own conversation. Terry explained his job opportunity and Robin listened with interest. He perked up when Terry told him that he very nearly signed up with a major London team.

"You gave up playing with the Gunners to move here to be with Rachel?"

Terry took this defensively rather than complimentary as Robin meant it. "So? I heard you nearly killed yourself when Shelly ran away on you."

Robin's eyes flared up and he wanted to smack him so bad that it was all he could do not to. Instead, he quietly said, "How dare you?"

"Sorry," he apologized once he realized how it sounded. "Berk."

"I'm sorry! Look, I'm just a bit nervous about it all, okay?"

Robin sat fuming and Terry wondered how he was going to get out of this one. He always seemed to be putting his foot in his mouth when it came to his two older cousins, and he couldn't understand why he did it. He felt inferior to them, and was ready to point out any of their weaknesses.

D'Artagnan the young Doberman came by, wanting to get on the couch. Robin got up to take the dog outside, giving Terry a minute to think. When he came back, Terry said, "Robin…I would have done the same."

This softened Robin up a bit. "You really need to watch your mouth," he said sternly.

"I know. I have such a large one."

"Yes. And if you tick Rachel off, she'll leave you high and dry, mate, and you'll be stuck in America. If you intend to try to have any sort of relationship with her, or anyone for that matter, you had better grow up."

Terry felt as if he was listening to his father again. Robin's defensiveness of her surprised him. However, Terry felt like he was a different person when it came to Rachel. She brought out a side of himself he never knew existed. He ran his fingers through his blonde curls.

The girls came back in, and they all sat down amicably.

"Oh!" said Rachel suddenly, "Debra said she wants to have a dinner for you two Saturday, if you're up to it," she finished, looking at Shelly.

"Umm...*Chez Debra*. Yeah, I'll make it."

"You know, I think Debra wants to be a chef again."

"Did she mention it?" asked Robin curiously.

"Sort of. Let's see...what was it she said? Oh! She said she missed working—that she felt like she should be doing something. When did she quit?"

"Shortly after they married. That would have been...six years ago. Maybe seven."

"Seven year itch," chimed Terry.

"Uh-oh," replied Shelly.

"Yes and my brother doesn't understand the concept of working unless you need to," Robin remarked with a small chuckle.

"To go from insanely busy to not must be weird."

"She keeps busy, but I suppose there's some sort of adrenaline rush to working a restaurant."

Everyone hummed a 'yeah' under their breaths and went on to discuss general topics, enjoying each other's company. It was agreed they would meet at George's that Saturday.

Chapter Two

In the next couple of weeks that followed, Rachel moved into Shelly's old art studio and went back to work at the glass studio, the Parkers worked on their upcoming tour, Terry had several meetings with his new employers, and Shelly continued to heal as Debra watched the craziness around her.

She really did feel she was missing out from the rest. Until one day, fate turned around for her. She was at one of her favorite pastry shops when she ran into an old friend she had gone to cooking school with.

"Jenny!"

"Debra! Hi!" she replied, giving her friend a hug.

Debra took a look at her and remarked, "Looks like you've got something in the oven other than pastries!"

The lady affectionately rubbed her well-rounded belly. "Yup! Will and I are finally going to have to grow up!"

"Oh, don't do that!" Debra laughed.

"Say, are you working right now, or are you too busy being a celebrity's wife?"

"Ha-ha. Well, I am a lady of leisure these days," she answered with regret.

"Hmm. Would you *like* to go back to work?"

"Why do you ask?" Debra could tell the lady was contemplating something.

"Well, I sure can't be a mommy and run that crazy café. I've been looking for someone to sell it to. Will's business is doing really well, and all we've got right now is the house payment."

"I can't imagine you retiring."

"Well, I thought the same of you… Oh, I might eventually get back to it, but not right now. That'd be impossible. So, you interested?"

A little fire lit in Debra's heart. She definitely was tempted, but she knew how George felt about the subject. It wasn't that he was old-fashioned, but he had such a crazy schedule that when he was home, he wanted her there as well. He never appreciated her love for cooking as much as his own for playing music. That was the only issue that really bothered her about him. "Well," she began to answer, "I need to talk it over with George."

The two women chatted for a while and the friend gave Debra her number. "Now call me, okay? I'd rather sell it to someone I know who will take care of it than a total stranger. It's rather like giving away my favorite puppy."

"Yes, they become endearing, don't they? A bit of a love-hate relationship."

"Ah! So you do remember?"

"One never forgets," Debra laughed.

Debra bit her lip in deep thought on the way home. How would George take it? She really didn't know. She couldn't see him completely standing in the way of her happiness. He would probably grumble considerably, but eventually give in.

She turned the car around. She couldn't wait for him to come home, so she would see if she could steal some time away from him at work.

She got to the office and was greeted by various employees that she knew. She went down the hall to his office and peeped in, afraid of disturbing him. She saw a girl that she was unfamiliar with talking to George. She had an abundance of blonde hair and cleavage. She caught something strange in the tone of the conversation, and listened in.

"You're sure your wife doesn't know?" asked the blonde.

"Yes, I told you. No one knows."

Sounded like something out of a situation comedy.

"Well, don't you think you should tell her?"

"Not yet. I've got it all planned out. Trust me, okay? Now, did you get the airline straightened out?"

"Yes, yes. Here it is," she said, handing him what looked like a flight plan.

"Good… Well, I hope I can pull this off," he sighed.

"I have every faith in you."

"I couldn't have done it without your help, dear… Now, we'd better get back to work."

Debra was taken aback. She didn't know what to make of the conversation. She thought hard. If it had been around their anniversary or holiday or something similar, she would presume it had to do with a surprise for her, but it wasn't and the tone in his voice was not of his usual cheeriness. Her heart raced, and a million things ran through her mind.

"Hi, Deb!" a voice called, scaring the life out of her. She looked up and smiled at her brother-in-law.

"Hi, Robin, how are you?" she replied, slightly out of breath.

"Doing all right. Are you okay?" he asked, looking at her oddly.

"Oh, fine! Just thinking about something," she laughed carelessly.

"All right then," he said doubtfully. "He's in there," he nodded towards George's door.

"Oh, okay, thanks," she stammered. Robin smiled with suspicion and walked away with a shake of his head.

She knocked softly on the door and heard her husband say, "Come in!" He looked up to see her and quickly got up to meet her. The blonde looked on with a big smile. "That's all for now, Suzi." The woman took her leave.

"Who's that?" Debra asked.

"Oh, my new secretary." He looked at her expression and smiled. "She's not as dumb as she looks… I'm still recovering from Maria leaving, but I think she's going to work out fine. She gets to the brass tacks of things, which I appreciate, as you know."

"Oh, that's good."

"Now, my dearest," he said, grabbing her hand, "to what do I deserve the honor of your presence?" He asked the flippant question with tension in his voice.

Debra delicately went on to tell him about the friend and her café. "George, I know you haven't been too keen on my working, but I sure would love to go back. I miss the people and the craziness of it all. What do you say?"

George looked at her and genuinely felt sorry for her. Had he really been stifling her natural ambitions all this time? "If you really want it that badly, who am I to stop you?" He wrapped his arm around her and gave her a kiss. He then went back behind his desk and started to mess with the papers upon it. She watched him shove the flight plans under a folder swiftly. She couldn't help but notice the serious look on his face.

"What's the matter?"

"Nothing. I said if you want it, get it."

"No, there's something else bothering you."

"Well, to be honest, this tour is driving me crazy before it even starts, and Robin's behaving like a zombie. I don't know what the hell his problem is. He's about as helpful as a grapefruit. He's constantly on the phone to Shelly, and he's got the concentration abilities of a two-year-old."

Debra had to smirk about this. "Well, honey, you have to understand what is happening to him. He just found out he's going to be a father."

This remark seemed to light a spark in George's eye. "Yes, well, some men don't get that sentimental about their children," he replied with what could only be called spite.

She wondered what made him say that. Who was he referring to? "Well, you ought to know Robin by now."

George finally cracked a smile. "Yes. True. My sappy brother."

"Gotta love him!"

"I do, I do. But, damn! I wish he'd at least show some effort. It's like he doesn't even want to do this tour!"

"I tell you what: Why don't we invite them over for dinner and you can pick his brain?"

"Sounds good," he said after some thought. "Friday?"

"Great. You'll ask him?"

"Yeah," he answered as he moved more papers around the desk.

"Well…I guess I'll see you later then, honey."

"Okay, babe." He gave her a peck and walked her to the door.

She left, feeling very confused. She really was bewildered by the whole thing.

It was eight o'clock that same evening when she got a call from George. "Hey, sorry, babe. I'm still stuck here. We can't seem to finalize Vegas. Hopefully, I'll get out of here soon, though."

"Oh, okay, honey. Be careful coming home."

"I will. See you."

"Bye."

She sat down on the couch looking vacantly at a magazine when the phone rang again. It was Shelly. She was very pleased to have someone to talk to, and Shelly's bubbly personality was just what she needed. After some preliminary chitchat, Shelly asked, "Was it Friday or Saturday we were supposed to come over? Robin can't remember."

"Oh, Friday."

"Thanks. He is getting *so* forgetful lately."

At this point, Debra could hear the man in question holler out, "Hey!"

"Robin's home?" she asked Shelly.

"Yeah. He's been home for a while. Do you need to talk to him?"

"No, no. That's okay. When did he get home?"

"Let's see…around 6:30."

"Oh."

"Why?"

"George is still at work. I just presumed Robin would be there, too."

Shelly giggled. "He said George sent him home because he was being an idiot. Is everything okay? He said George was a bit on edge today."

"Well, to be honest, this tour is starting to get to him."

"Oh."

She could tell Shelly was mulling this over in her mind. Maybe her husband wasn't as concerned? She said good-bye to Shelly, reminding her once again about Friday.

George made it home at a quarter past nine. His edginess had turned to exhaustion and he fell asleep as soon as his head hit the pillow by 10:30. Debra lay by him wondering what was going on, but refused to concede to her thoughts that anything was actually *wrong*. His quick agreement for her to purchase the café disconcerted her. Why did he not even put up an argument? Was he grateful she had something to keep her occupied? She tossed and turned for a couple of hours, but eventually gave up the fight and got up to go downstairs to fix herself some chamomile tea. As she blankly dipped her teabag up and down, she heard the doorknob rattle. It was Terry.

"Hello," she greeted quietly.

"Hello," he answered curiously. "What are you doing up so late?"

She shrugged her shoulders. "Couldn't sleep."

"Everything all right?"

"Oh, yes. Just have a lot on my mind… Guess what."

"What?"

"I'm going back to work!"

"Really? Where?" he asked happily.

"A friend of mine is selling her café."

"And you're buying it?"

"Yup!"

"Wow, that's fantastic! Congratulations. Uh, you are happy about it, aren't you?" he asked, studying her expression.

"Oh, yes! Just a bit overwhelming, that's all." She was alarmed by her obvious transparency of her emotion, and tried to focus on him. "So, did y'all have fun tonight?"

"Yeah. We just hung out at the studio. I helped her move some stuff around. Shelly's a bit of a packrat. She still has stuff there. You ought to have seen Rachel shootin' off in Spanish every time she'd open a cabinet to find more rubbish." He chuckled fondly at his girlfriend's antics.

Debra laughed at this vision, which made Terry smile. "Those two are polar opposites, aren't they?" she asked.

"Well, to tell you the truth, I haven't had much of a chance to get to know Shelly."

Debra thought for a second. "She's very special. She leads a simplistic life, which is good for Robin."

"Yes, his mind is a bit of a mare's nest."

"She keeps him grounded—no, *focused*."

"Boy, he would have been a mess if he had lost her." He shook his head appropriately. Terry had the unnerving habit of brazenly, but truthfully, summing things up, but Debra took it coolly.

"Undoubtedly. You never know when it's going to be all over."

There was something hidden in that remark, but Terry wasn't sure if she was thinking of herself or if it was directed at him. His relationship with Rachel was at that delicate stage, and he was hypersensitive about it. "Well, uh, I guess I'd better get to bed—meeting tomorrow and all that. Goodnight, then."

"Goodnight, Terry," she replied with a soft smile. She seemed to bounce back to her usual self immediately.

It was Friday. Debra set out to get some groceries she needed for the night's dinner with Robin and Shelly. It was a hazy day, unusual for that time of year in Miami, and as she drove down the expressway, she caught a glimpse of the odd steel-blue color of George's car at an auto sales lot along with the vision of a man who looked like it could be him, but with a blonde. She thought for a moment, telling herself that she was probably imagining things. As she continued to drive, she came upon the neighborhood of the M.P.'s office. Curiosity got the best of her, and she pulled in.

She immediately found Robin going through some mail. "Hello!" he greeted. "He isn't here."

"Really?" she continued to look around. "Is his secretary here?"

"Blondie?" he laughed. "No, she isn't either. I presume they went to Martin's about those contracts. Just got here myself. Shelly wasn't feeling too well last night and therefore I was up as well." He gave a yawn to make his point.

"Oh! I hope she's going to be well enough to come over tonight," she asked with grave concern. "If she's not, just let me know. We certainly can have it some other time."

"Oh, no. She'll be fine. She's usually okay by the evening. I'll check on her later—I'll ring her to make sure, though."

"Okay, great," she said with her usual smile. "I'll see you tonight, then."

"Yes, ma'am… Uh, shall I tell George to ring you?"

"No, that's okay. I just happen to be in the neighborhood."

"Fine then. See you tonight!"

That evening, Debra set forth to the enjoyable task of cooking dinner. She had a lovely pork roast already simmering away in the oven and she was working on a polenta and some vegetables. Her mind went deep into thought. She couldn't put two and two together about George without getting an answer she didn't like.

A loud hissing sound emitted behind her while she was preoccupied cutting up the broccoli. She griped at herself for forgetting to turn the heat off her polenta and wondered how she could make such a silly mistake.

She was able to save the dish and sat down at the kitchen table. She felt like an idiot. She faced the fact of what she was suspecting of George. If she were wrong about him, she would be overwrought with guilt. Otherwise…

She wondered what was making her think of such an awful thing in the first place. They had a good relationship, for the most part. The only thing she felt they were truly guilty of was not communicating enough. Why did it seem that this was made clear to her so suddenly though? When did this realization take place? Then it hit her—Japan. When she and Shelly went there to see the boys' concert and she saw how happy Shelly and Robin were together, she felt something was missing in her own marriage. She also realized her depression was made worse by not seeing her son at Christmas. She missed him terribly, but knew a sixteen-year-old boy needed his father. Still, it wasn't right for her ex to keep him from her just to take him skiing. They lived in the state of Washington, so he could have done that on any weekend.

Debra's mind continued to reel, and she felt that if she didn't confide in someone and ask for advice, she was going to blow—but with whom? When you're married to a celebrity, you really can't trust anyone to keep a secret of some vague suspicion. Only someone in the same situation would understand. "Of course!" she thought to herself. "Shelly."

Could she rely on the flighty artist that everyone had grown to love? Would she be able to understand her situation considering what an ideal marriage she had with Robin? Ah, but she had had a bad marriage previously as well—one, in fact, where she had been cheated on. It seemed that Shelly fit the bill perfectly. She decided to ask Shelly's advice.

Debra was able to finish the meal without any more accidents just in time to say 'hello' to her husband who came in. He seemed distracted and upset. "What's the matter?" she asked nervously.

He threw down his keys and wallet onto the island counter and shook his head. "Every time I think I have one date settled, something happens to another. Our booking agent is about to have a nervous breakdown and my stupid *git* of a brother told our road manager the wrong date for Chicago—argued with him even—and now he's threatening to quit. I wished he wasn't such a control freak. We go through road managers like toilet tissue!"

Debra couldn't help but giggle.

"It's not funny."

"No, dear. I know it's not. But one can't help laughing the way you talk."

He cracked a smile. "Sorry. But I think I'm going to give him a piece of my mind tonight."

"Oh, please don't make it too uncomfortable—for poor Shelly's sake."

He looked at her oddly. "Oh, because she's pregnant?"

"Yes."

He took a deep breath. "Very well. I'm still going to have a nice little chat with him, though."

"As you should," she said to placate him.

"Where's Terry?"

"More meetings. He's got plans with Rachel, so they won't be here."

"Just as well. It could get bloody."

"Ha. In what sense do you mean that?"

He smiled back and replied, "Both. It could get bloody awful and I could punch him in the nose—easy enough target."

"Now, George."

"*Now, George*," he mocked. "All right, all right, I'll behave."

His attitude lightened up somewhat and she studied him, gathering up the courage to ask a question. "I stopped by today, but I missed you."

"Yes, Robin said you did. I was at Martin's, naturally."

"Oh, really? You know I could have sworn I saw you over by Sun Motors while I was coming from the grocery store."

George almost seemed to flinch, but he kept his cool. "Huh. Must have been my twin."

"Yeah. I guess so."

So that was it. She raised the opportunity for him to say what he was doing there—for he obviously was there—and yet no reason was given. She went back to her dessert.

There was a definite tension that night at the dinner table. The brothers sat at opposite ends of the table, the ladies on the sides. Debra concentrated on Shelly to distract herself from the pensive vibrations George was putting out. "How are you feeling?" she asked her sister-in-law.

"I'm doing all right, now anyway. This morning was pretty rough, though," she said with a grin of embarrassment.

"Have you seen a doctor yet?"

"No. To tell you the truth, I don't know where to go. I certainly don't want to go back to that quack."

"Maybe you should go visit mine, I'm quite fond of him."

"Yes. All the ladies are," broke in George.

"Oh, he's not bad to look at, then?" Shelly asked. Robin cleared his throat quite intentionally, making her laugh.

"The good thing is that he'll listen to you," continued Debra.

"Sounds good to me."

"Fine. I'll give you his number later."

A lull of silence fell on the party. Robin was completely unaware of the stare his brother was giving him. Instead, Robin's face became clouded and he began to rake his fork through his polenta like a Zen garden.

Shelly caught this action from the corner of her eye and gently nudged his leg with her foot. He startled and smiled at her. She needed to say something. She thought for a moment. She looked at Debra and said, "Well, Rachel has moved into the studio."

"That's terrific!" Debra said with relief. "How does she like it?"

"Oh, great. It's going to take her a while to get completely moved in, considering she's got her belongings all over the place. She's got stuff in storage, in Puerto Rico, our house…"

"Our house?" Robin asked.

"Yeah. Did you forget Chuckie?"

"Oh, yeah. She wants him back, then?"

"Ha-ha. You kinda like him, don't you?"

"Well, he is interesting to watch." He wasn't about to admit he liked the little guinea pig.

"That he is. Especially when you feed him."

"Don't worry, you'll have another little one to feed soon," Debra said cheerfully.

The couple both opened their eyes to their full extent making George and Debra laugh. Then all became silent once more, and Robin stared at the ice cubes in his water. This time, everyone noticed him. He looked up, surveying everyone. His eyes fell on Shelly. She looked so lovely in her deep forest green dress with her red curls softly cascading over her shoulders. He smiled at her, and then said out loud, "I have an announcement. Unfortunately, it's not going to be a good one, but I have thought long and hard about this." Everyone was riveted. They really had no clue what was coming. "I've decided to quit the business, or at least, the performing."

Not a word.

"I mean, I can produce, or write, or—"

"Teach?" Shelly asked surprisingly.

He looked at her with wonder. "Yes. I guess I could."

George got up, threw his napkin onto the table, and went outside to the patio.

"Excuse me," Robin said to the ladies, and followed him out.

Robin's heart pounded as he walked up to George, who stood staring at the pool. He didn't turn around, but knew Robin was there.

"Listen, I'm sorry, George. I know this is quite a shock to you, and I can't blame you for being angry."

George shook his head. "Not as much shock as a realization of my fears."

"What?"

"I had a feeling you were going to do this. The way you've been acting lately—I saw it coming. I just couldn't believe it."

"Look... You have to understand... I'm feeling overwhelmed by all that has happened lately—"

"*You're* feeling overwhelmed?" George got up right into his face. "Let me tell *you* what is overwhelming: Eighty-four employees who depend on your success to get them a paycheck—that's what—and that's only the immediate staff; forty-five towns expecting us to show up and entertain them. Let's see, an average of four thousand seats a city, well, that's a lot of fans—"

"I know, I know! Jesus, do you think this is easy for me? Do you think I haven't rolled those numbers in my head already? My wife nearly died, dammit! And now she's pregnant with a child we had had no hope of ever having. Do you think I can leave her here and go on the road and concentrate on what I'm doing? I can imagine neither leaving her nor giving those 180,000 fans a half-ass concert because I can't give them my all."

George was slightly taken aback by this. He had never seen Robin get this upset and definitely never heard him speak about something so passionately before. Could it be that Shelly had awoken a side to him that had lain dormant for years? He felt he needed to compromise. "All right. Can we meet in the middle on this? Is there no way you can at least do the tour? We're talking *three months*, Robin. And I can have Debra call on Shelly every day to make sure she's well."

Robin looked at him with pitiful eyes. "You're right. Yes. I'm being hasty, I know… God, George, you just don't understand." He sat down on a patio chair, his elbow on the table and his hand on his head. George began to feel sorry for his brother and tried to imagine what it would be like to lose Debra. The thought made him shudder, but it made him realize that Robin nearly did lose not only his wife, but a baby as well—Oh God, he thought. That's it. They had already lost a baby. He hated himself for forgetting.

He came over to him and put his hand on his shoulder. "Rob, look…if you really can't do it, just say so. I understand."

Robin looked up at him with a look of fear. He really didn't know. "Can I give you my answer Monday?"

"Of course," George said quietly.

While this conversation was taking place, the girls were trying to recover from Robin's announcement themselves. Shelly hoped Debra wasn't mad at them and that it wouldn't affect her relationship with her. "Debra, please know that I knew nothing of this. I had no idea he was even thinking about it!"

Debra quickly smiled. "Don't worry about it. Robin's just looking out for you. It's rather nice, really," she said with a sentimental note. "I mean, he puts you before everything else in his life."

Shelly picked up the odd tone in her voice and felt something else was bothering her. "Is something wrong?"

Debra's usually sparkly eyes began to turn red. She uttered out a reply. "I think… I think, maybe, George is having an affair."

"What?!"

At that moment, the two men came back in and Debra got up and went into the kitchen. Shelly sat with her mouth still agape.

"You all right, babe?" asked Robin.

"Uh, yes." Shelly tried to recover herself. "Is everything settled?"

"For right now." He reached over and grabbed her hand.

Debra came back in, dry-eyed and carrying a cake.

Shelly was still stunned. She looked back and forth from one person to another. She started to swoon as if the room was spinning on her.

"Darling, what's the matter?" Robin asked impatiently. He knew something was definitely wrong, for she began to turn quite pale.

"Well, first you, then—," she dropped off. She passed out, and Robin quickly grabbed her to keep her from falling.

"Shelly! Shelly!" he cried. He picked her up to take her to the couch. "*This* is what I'm talking about!" he exclaimed to George.

Debra got her some water and Robin gently patted her cheek. George stood watching all this with concern, his arms crossed and breathing hard.

Shelly woke up, wondering what happened. "You tell me!" answered Robin. She instantly looked at Debra and saw her panicked expression. Then she looked at George and back to Robin.

"Uh, just too much at one time. Maybe it's because I didn't eat that much today and then I did just now." She seemed to be rambling. She tried to get up, but Debra stopped her.

"It's best if you just lay there for a little bit."

She easily complied.

Debra took George back into the dining room to help clean up the dinner plates. They took them into the kitchen and she started a pot of coffee.

"Is that normal?" he eventually asked her.

"Oh, yeah. She'll be fine. I imagine Robin's news shocked her. She didn't know he was going to do that."

"Really?"

"Yeah."

"Huh… He really is a stupid git."

Debra chuckled and shook her head at him.

"What, uh…what did she mean while ago?"

Debra's stomach knotted up. "When?"

"She said, 'First Robin, then—'. Then what?"

"Oh. I told her about the café."

"Oh." He thought this was a silly thing to get excited about, but women will get excited over the most unlikely things.

Debra hated lying, but now wasn't the time to get into it. He helped her bring the coffee and cups into the living room. She brought the cake plates in and found Shelly up and talking to Robin.

"Okay now?" she asked Shelly with a warm smile.

"Oh, yes. Thank you."

Everyone quietly took their coffee and cake.

"So, what do you think?" George asked Shelly. Her eyes got big and wondered what he meant. "You know, about her café?"

She looked at Debra who gave her a look she understood. "Oh! I think it's great." She hoped this was the correct answer, since she had no idea about it in the first place. "Where is it located?" she pleasantly asked her.

"In the Pavilion Mall," replied Debra.

"Oh, that's nice there."

Debra was relieved Shelly picked up on her hint and continued to chat about her new project for a while with them. George was tickled to see how excited she got about it.

The conversation did well to lighten up the tense atmosphere that evening. They went on to chat about other things until Robin and Shelly decided it was time to go home.

As they walked to the car, Shelly muttered to herself, "God, what a night." He helped her into the car and her mind began to go back to Robin's announcement. It was starting to bother her the more she thought about it.

It was a quiet ride home. Robin could feel her getting angry with him and then he began to feel angry with her for doing so. He finally spoke.

"What? Are you upset because I've decided to give up show business?"

She turned to give him a vicious look. "I fell in love with you for you, not because you're a superstar, and you know that. I couldn't care less what you do for a living. I'm pissed because you decided to tell George right then and there without even discussing it with me first!" Her accent flared up, and her voice cut through him like a knife. He almost seemed to wince from it.

"I'm sorry. I'm still not used to having to answer to anyone but myself."

Did he mean she was being the nagging wife? She could feel her mind reeling. "Well, ultimately it is your job and none of my business—but wait! It is my business because I'm the reason you're quitting. I don't like it, honey. I don't like feeling like Helen of Troy."

He, of course, had never stopped to think how Shelly would feel about it. Any simple-minded woman would have been thrilled to find out her husband would sacrifice his career to stay home with her. But Shelly wasn't simple-minded, and she reminded him so by making him feel like he was playing Paris to George's Hector—choosing the love of his life over his brother and country. Nevertheless, he was ready to defend himself. "Look, you have to understand what I'm feeling right now. I almost lost you and the baby, and I want to be here in case you need me. I want to play my proper role."

As he stopped for a red light, Shelly was left with a look of shock. "What…what do you mean you almost lost me?"

Robin turned to see her expression until the person behind him honked to tell him that the light had turned green. He really didn't know what to say. Start from the beginning, he figured. "Well…when you were sick…" he drew in a breath from the horrid memory of it all, "you very nearly died." He worried what this would do to her already fragile state. Instead, she sat dumbfounded.

She opened her mouth to say something, but nothing came. Her mouth shut, and she simply breathed hard. She put her hand to her forehead, and he feared she would start crying, but nothing. He pulled up to the house, and helped her out. "Are you all right?" he asked.

She looked up to him and put up her arms to hold him. He held her and kissed her cheek. She stood back, gave him a sad, blank look and said, "Do whatever you like, babe." She shook her head. "Do whatever you like." She turned around and went into the house.

He worried about her and watched her all night, but she was silent. She didn't know it, but he caught a tear rolling down her cheek as they lay in bed. He knew he had better think this thing through and not make anymore rash decisions. He felt bad for insulting her intelligence, but he really did want to stay here with her. He didn't want to leave her side.

He rolled over on his side and cupped his hand around her cheek. She turned to look at him and knew what he was thinking. She had no desire to be a china-doll and wanted to remind him that she was a woman of strength. She leaned over, putting her fingers in his soft hair and kissed him. He, in turn, grabbed her curls and gave her a breath-taking kiss that reminded her of one he gave her so long ago. He wanted to be reminded of who she was, so she did so. He was extremely grateful. Shelly was human once again. Maybe he could think a little more clearly now.

Chapter Three

The next morning Shelly awoke wondering if last night was just a bad dream. It all seemed so surreal, like some freak parallel universe. *Did Robin really quit? Did Debra actually say what she did? Did I really faint?* She tried to settle her mind. She looked over to Robin, who was still asleep, and quietly got out of bed. It was 9:00, and she wondered if it was too early to call Debra. She decided against it as she stood next to the kitchen phone. Oddly enough, it rang, scaring her half to death. She quickly picked it up, not wanting it to wake Robin. It was her mother. The woman was giddily happy for the arrival of a grandchild, and she began to call Shelly on a constant basis.

"How are you?" she asked.

"Oh, fine," Shelly replied with a heavy breath.

"You don't sound fine."

"The phone scared me. I was standing right next to it when it rang."

"Oh. Well, I just thought I'd call and see how you were."

"Oh, *I'm* fine," she answered with a slight bitterness.

"What do you mean? Is Robin all right?"

"Well, he's thinking of quitting."

"I didn't know you could quit being a superstar."

Shelly usually got upset when she called him a 'superstar', but this time she took it in stride for the joke it was intended to be. She simply laughed, "I guess *he* can."

"Why?"

"I don't know. Being overprotective of me, I suppose."

"Overprotective? Why should he be?"

"Well, Mom," she really didn't know how to put this without getting her too upset, "when I was in the hospital… well, my fever was worse than I thought."

"What…what do you mean?" The tone in her voice changed dramatically.

"I, uh, I almost died."

"What?!"

"Yeah." Silence. Shelly wondered what she was thinking. "Mom?"

"Huh? Uh, yeah… God, Shelly."

"I know."

"Um, I have to go," she said with a quavering voice. "I'll call you later, okay?"

"Okay, Mom. Mom?"

"What?"

"I'm okay now."

"That's good."

Shelly sat at the kitchen bar after saying good-bye to her mother. This morning seemed to be a continuation of last night, and she considered going back to bed to make it all go away. She could feel her morning sickness coming on again, so she fixed herself some tea and sat down in a deep, soft chair with a chenille throw. She drank her tea and fell back asleep.

Robin eventually came down to find her in her repose. He smiled at her and sat down quietly on the couch. He thought hard how he could compromise between Shelly and George. As much as he loved Shelly, he owed George so much. It was always his brother who encouraged him to become who he was, and he felt he was being unfair to him.

He got up and went to the den to call George. "Good morning."

"Good morning," George drowsily answered.

"What say I come around this afternoon and we talk?"

"Fine with me, I have no plans. Terry will be here, though."

"That's fine. I think I've come up with an idea."

"Oh?"

"Yeah."

"Brilliant."

"After lunch?"

"Sounds good."

"Okay, ta."

"Later." George hung up the phone, pleased that his brother was at least trying to figure out a way to make everyone happy.

Robin came back into the living room to discover his wife awake and smiling. "Hallo!" he greeted.

"Hello," replied the smiling face.

"How are you?"

She rolled her eyes around, trying to assess herself. "I'm okay, now."

"Good!"

She looked at his warm, sad eyes, wondering how she got to be so lucky. She was instantly reminded of Debra and how things had gone awry for the sweet lady. She then asked her beloved, "How would you like an omelet?"

"Mmm! Sounds wonderful. What made you think of that?"

"I was thinking about Debra."

"Why were you thinking of Debra?"

"Uh…her new café." That reason seemed to come in handy lately.

"Oh, yes. I'm glad she got it," he said, plopping onto the couch. "She needed an outlet."

"Yup, and we need breakfast." With that said, she got up and went into the kitchen. Robin followed her in like a puppy.

His mind trailed off while she was cracking the eggs, wondering what kind of mother she was going to be. Loving, he thought, but unorthodox. He laughed imagining the baby crawling around in little overalls.

Shelly caught the laugh and asked, "What?" He told her of his funny thought and she laughed asking, "And what kind of father are you going to be?"

"I've really no clue."

She stopped whisking the eggs and studied him for a second. "Patient…and always teaching him something." She turned back to the stove to pour the eggs.

He beamed with the idea of being a father and couldn't believe how lucky he was to have Shelly in his life. He looked up and saw the bright curls he loved. This reminded him of something. "You know, we need to make some plans."

"For what?"

"To visit your father in Ireland. We ought to before you get too far along."

"Oh. Father Father?" she asked with a nervous laughter. The thought of meeting her birthfather (who, after-the-fact, joined the priesthood) made her a nervous wreck.

He laughed. "Yes, indeed."

"But, what about your tour? Are you really going to quit…just like that?"

He got up from the barstool to get the plates down for her. "Well, I've been thinking."

"That usually proves dangerous."

He pretended to hit her in the jaw. "Pow… No, dearest, I've come up with a plan that I'm going to propose to George today."

"I didn't think that was legal."

"Would you—"

"Sorry. I'm in a flippant mood today."

"So it seems. Anyway, I think a mere delay would suffice. I mean, the first few months for you are the, uh, riskiest. What if I put off part of the tour until later, so as to make sure you're, you know…"

"Good and pregnant?" she retorted with a gesture of her fist.

"Ha-ha. Well, comfortable in your pregnancy."

"Well, it does make sense. The first trimester is the scariest."

"I'm still going to miss you like hell," he said laying his hands on her shoulders and kissing her head.

"I know. Same here. But I've got plenty of work to do, that's for sure. "I've got to start working on the nursery, and there's redecorating to do." She surveyed the room, thinking up ideas.

"Now, I don't want you climbing ladders and all that, do you understand?" he demanded.

She was about to tell him not to worry, but she turned to look at him and realized he was being dead serious. "Yes, I will take care," she complied.

"Good. Now, let's eat!"

"Sounds good to me!"

They ate their breakfast eagerly, lingering at the table with the toast afterward.

"So," Robin said at length, "do you *want* to see your father?"

She sat her orange juice down. "Yes…yes, I do."

"Good! What are you going to tell him?"

"I have no idea. I just hope it's not too much of a shock for the poor man."

"I'm sure it's going to be."

Shelly smiled to herself.

"What?"

"I get to tell him that not only is he a father, in the biological sense, but that he's also going to be a grandfather."

Robin laughed. "Ta-da! Instant family."

"Really." She watched him get another cup of coffee. "I thought your mom was going to go into hysterics when you told her we were expecting."

"She very nearly did," he laughed. "This will be her first grandchild, finally, at the age of seventy-four."

"Yes." Shelly got very quiet, and Robin took notice.

"What's wrong, love?"

"Your mom was so kind about…you know."

"The first time?"

"Yeah." The memory of their first loss still leaving a sting with them both.

"I'm very fortunate to have my mother. She didn't lecture me at all. Are you concerned what your new father is going to think when he finds out?"

"I really don't think he needs to know."

"Well, I don't see how you can keep it a secret. I mean, there could be something said about what a miracle this one is from someone, and he'll wonder why it was said. I don't think it's good to start off a relationship with secrets. He'll love you, no matter what."

"You think so?"

"Oh, yes."

"He needs to see the good and the bad, huh?"

"No one's perfect, and I certainly don't think he'll be disappointed in you." He gave her a smile for encouragement.

"What if this had happened to your own daughter, how would you feel?"

The question shocked him, but it was a good question and he knew it. "Wow. Well… I'd probably do the guy in who put her through it."

"Well, you're pretty safe then, considering his vocation."

Now Robin worried about what the man would think of *him*. Would he instantly be protective of his newfound daughter? "Oh, dear. That is a can of worms."

"Precisely."

"I guess we need to wait to see what kind of temperament he has. He may just take off his collar and take me out back and teach me a lesson."

"Ha-ha. I highly doubt if he could reach to hit you in the jaw."

"Never underestimate an Irishman when he's mad."

She laughed and got up to put the plates up. She stood at the table for a second.

"Are you all right?" he asked.

"Oh, yes. I was just wondering. How do we do this? I mean, do we call him up and ask to set up a meeting, or just pop in on him, or what? Write him some long letter of explanation?"

He thought for a second. "I think it's best if we just go to him and tell him in person."

Shelly felt relief in the 'we' part. She knew she couldn't do this alone. Truth was, Robin was always a curious creature, and he wouldn't miss it for the world. "Very well, let's do it!"

He smiled, and went to the desk where he put his information on the man. He came back looking at the papers and said to Shelly, "It has the name of his parish, but no phone number."

"You've decided to call him?"

"I don't think we should jet off to Ireland without making sure he's there first," he laughed.

"Oh. Well, we can probably look it up on the internet."

"Okay. I will leave that to you."

She laughed at his uneasiness about the computer, and went to the task. She came into the little room he deemed as her 'office'. It basically was a room in which she could put all her paperwork to keep it out of the rest of the house. Robin stayed sitting on the couch in the living room finishing his coffee. He had no desire to be in the messy little room with that confusing machine.

She came back in with a print out of phone numbers. He helped her figure out how to call Ireland, scribbling down several digits. He had written thousands of autographs in his time, but nothing he had written had ever given someone more of a charge than when he passed that number to her. She sat staring at it.

He tried to encourage her. "It would be a good time to call. It would be late afternoon there."

She shook her head ever so slightly. "I don't think I can."

"Do you want me to?"

She nodded.

"Very well." He smiled at her, picked up the phone, and dialed the long number.

Shelly watched and listened as Robin talked to whom she deduced was some sort of secretary. Robin grabbed the pad of paper to write on while saying, "Oh, really?" He jotted down some information and proceeded to give many thanks to the person on the other line. He hung up, smiling an odd smile. "Well, how about that?"

"What?"

"He's at a conference."

"Oh," she said with disappointment.

"In New York City."

"What?!"

Robin simply chuckled.

"He's in America?" she said in a daze.

"Yes, dearest. It almost seems destiny, as if he were coming to you." She stared at him momentarily. "So, what about it? Shall we go hunt him down? The lady told me his whereabouts," he said, holding up the pad.

Shelly finally cracked an uneasy grin. "I guess so."

"He's going to be there until the 16th, so we've got a bit of time. I need to talk it over with George as to when would be a good time to sneak away. It's going to have to be a quick visit, I'm afraid."

"I'm just glad you can make it at all. I would be too intimidated to do this alone."

"Well…we will go and see your father, and everything will be fine." At least, he certainly hoped so. He gave his wife a kiss and then went on to read his newspaper.

It was later in the day, and George, Robin and Terry sat at the crescent-shaped bar in George's sunroom eating peanuts and drinking pale ale. Robin gave his idea to George about delaying the tour and then bit his lip with anticipation for the answer. Terry got a kick out of not being the one this time waiting to hear George's opinion of him.

But, George was understanding and considered the fact that they really weren't having any luck trying to get organized with the tour anyway, and beyond that it probably wasn't good marketing, a setback was almost welcoming. Robin went on to tell George of the trip to New York they needed to take.

"Wow. New York, huh?" asked George with a strange look.

"Yeah." Robin returned his gaze with the knowledge of the irony.

"Is there something about New York I should know?" asked Terry, feeling quite out of the loop.

"Let's just say it's not Robin's favorite town," George replied, still looking at his brother, knowing the city held bad memories for him.

"Oh." Terry figured he'd have to get the story out of George later.

"Yes, well, anyway, so that's it. We're going to find Fr. O'Connor and introduce him to his daughter. I hope to God this doesn't stress Shelly out too much, but she really wanted to go and who am I to stop her?"

"She'll be all right, Rob. It's got to be terribly exciting for her."

"True. The person she grew up thinking was her father was not a very nice person. Maybe, hopefully, this one will be a better replacement."

"From sinner to saint?" kidded Terry.

"Yes, quite…

Chapter Four

It had been settled that Shelly and Robin would leave the following weekend. Shelly was a nervous disaster before then and driving everyone around her crazy. Robin would occasionally banish her to her studio to settle down. The little building had a calming effect, and she would always find something to do there.

The day came for them to leave, and Shelly was calling everyone to say good-bye and to hear words of encouragement. She thought before calling Debra. She was still in shock of Debra's suspicions about George and frankly couldn't believe it. But, people are different when it comes to their mates, so who knows? She very well could be right.

Debra answered the phone with her usual cheerfulness, other than sounding a little tired.

"Are you okay?" Shelly asked.

"Oh, yes. Just been busy trying to get ready to take over Jenny's restaurant. How have you been?"

"Fine, thanks. I have my first appointment with the doctor next week."

"Oh, how exciting!"

"Oh, yeah. I'm thrilled."

"Ha-ha. You'll be fine. Is Robin going with you?"

"I couldn't stop him if I tried."

"Good! I'm happy to see him looking forward to it."

"Yes. Yes, he is… Uh…is everything all right with you two?" she asked delicately.

"Well…I…I don't know," she said with a crack in her voice. "I mean, maybe I'm imagining it all, I just don't know."

"You're going to have to talk to him eventually. Otherwise, it will just fester inside you."

"Yes. You're right, of course." Debra was anxious to change the subject. She had a feeling of guilt about the whole thing. "So, it's your big weekend, huh?"

It was Shelly's turn to get nervous. "Yup," she answered simply.

"I'm sure everything will work out. He'll love you. How could he not?"

"Robin laughs at me because I keep saying 'poor guy' over and over again. I really do feel sorry for the shock I'm about to lay on him. I think it would help if he weren't a clergyman. It wouldn't make him so innocent in my mind."

"Ha, yeah, I guess so," she laughed. "Well, you are his responsibility in a sense. He should know about you. He would *want* to know about you."

"Yes, I guess that's true. I never thought about it that way. I mean, I'm not a child anymore, but he did put me here."

"Exactly."

"Well, I'll be glad when it's all over."

"That's understandable, but hopefully you'll have a good time and enjoy each other."

"It's got to be better than the last time I went to New York."

Debra remembered that very visit very well. "Oh, yes. I'm sure it will. And for heaven's sake, make Robin take you shopping!"

Shelly laughed heartily. "Now *that's* something to look forward to!"

Debra gave her suggestions of places she needed to see and gave her a bit more encouragement and rang off. Robin came in and told her, "Are you going to sit on the phone all day, or are we going to New York?"

Shelly smiled and quickly got up to hug him. She kissed him and he reciprocated eagerly. She giggled at his carrying away and mocked, "Are you going to kiss me all day, or are we going to New York?"

He gave her a wry look and a long kiss. He was all hers, she knew it, and she was grateful.

The next morning they awoke in a hotel room overseeing the fantastic New York City skyline. They had had a rough night of it. Shelly tossed and turned, and Robin would wake up with every flip.

Shelly's morning sickness returned with her nervousness, so Robin simply ordered coffee and toast from room service. He buttered his toast while looking at Shelly who was subconsciously stirring her coffee. "Everything's going to be okay, you know," he said without much hope of cheering her up.

She looked up and softly smiled. She was so happy he was with her for this, but didn't know how to express it. She chose not to say anything at all.

A couple of hours later they were on their way to the center where Fr. O'Connor was having his meetings. They hoped to catch the man as he left for lunch. They inquired at the front office as to his whereabouts, and were directed to the building where they could find him. Robin held Shelly's hand as they walked down the long halls. The doors were still shut to the room that they needed, but they could hear voices behind them.

"Well, I guess we'll just wait here," Robin said, leading her to a bench that sat in the hall. Shelly was trembling, and Robin felt helpless not knowing what to do for her. He put his arm around her and did his best to console her. He worried she might faint again like she had the other night, but she held strong.

The voices became stronger, letting them know the meeting was breaking up. Shelly stood up and Robin stood behind her with his hands on her shoulders. The door opened. Various men in clericals came out along with some suits, all vaguely looking alike, until a clerical came out with the reddest hair thought possible on a man. Robin felt Shelly's blood turn to ice. The gentleman turned around to see them and Robin stuttered, "Father O'Connor?"

"Yes! Hello! How may I help you?" answered the man with a thick Irish accent and a bright smile.

Robin felt Shelly start to swoon and gripped her shoulders.

"Oh, dear. Is your lady all right there?"

"Uh… Let's get her seated." Robin sat her down all the while Shelly simply stared at the priest.

Robin gathered his wits and shook the man's hand introducing himself and Shelly. He was completely taken aback by the similarities of the two. "Is there a place where we can talk?"

"Well, yes. Let's go back in here. They won't be using it. Everyone's at lunch."

"We don't want to keep you from your lunch, but it is rather important."

The man wondered what the young couple wanted and how did they know him.

They got Shelly into the conference room and she continued to stare at the man.

"Well, not often do I get to talk to someone with the same red hair as mine," kidded Fr. O'Connor. Robin had to stifle a chuckle. "Now, what can I do you for?"

Robin looked at Shelly. He wasn't going to tell him. He gave her a nod and she blinked, looking at her husband for the strength she needed. He gave her a gentle smile and she turned to the priest. "Do you…do you remember Patty Harrison from Corpus Christi, Texas?" she finally got out.

The man's expression drastically changed. He opened his eyes wide, studying Shelly and realizing just how much she looked like him. "Yes. Yes, I do," he finally said.

"Well, she's my mother."

"Oh, is she then?" His voice began to crackle. Robin felt that he was beginning to get the idea.

"Yes, well…" Shelly wished she could just blurt it out, "I just learned that her husband wasn't my father after all."

"Is that so?" The man began to fidget.

"Father O'Connor, you knew my mom before you became a priest, there's nothing wrong with that, but I felt you should know… That I wanted to know you…" Shelly began to cry.

Tears began to well up in the man's eyes and he simply said, "Oh, my dear Lord," and he rubbed his brow.

Robin put his arm around Shelly, wondering what the man was going to tell her. He was afraid of his denying her—that would break her. He reprimanded himself for not thinking of that earlier, but this had to be done. How could anyone say that Shelly was not his daughter? The similarities were just too uncanny.

But, the man simply stared at the young woman with clouded eyes. There was no denying—this was his daughter. He muttered to himself, "I have a daughter? Oh, my sweet Jesus." Then he looked up to her and the volume in his voice got louder. "I have a daughter!" He stood up and pulled Shelly up to her feet and held her hands. With nervous laughter, he hugged her and they both cried.

Robin was relieved. He got up and excused himself. He figured they needed their privacy. He wandered around the halls, wishing he hadn't stopped smoking—he sure could have used a cigarette right about now.

"My girl, believe me, I had no idea," Fr. O'Connor told his newfound daughter.

"Yeah. Mom kept it a secret for a very long time."

"I can't imagine how painful that must have been for her. She should have told me!"

"I know. I think she was afraid of Dad and what he'd do if he found out, so she just kept it to herself. Course, huh, he had his suspicions." She unknowingly fiddled with her hair.

"Was he a good father to you?" he asked with worry.

She turned her eyes away. "Oh, well, you know, average, I guess."

He knew she wasn't being completely truthful. He had dealt with enough abused children in his line of work to know the signs. He felt horribly guilty, but remained curious about her mother. "How are your parents?"

"Oh, Dad died when I was ten. Mom is fine—she's still in Corpus."

"Really? She raised you on her own then?"

"Well, with the help of her parents. We moved to their place after he died. Of course, she has her own place now. She has her own home decorating business that does rather well."

"Ah, good, good." His mind began to travel back to long ago and he studied her with a smile. "You know, you look just like my mother did at your age."

She was dumbfounded. She hadn't stopped to think about the extended family she had that she knew nothing about. "Really?"

"Yes. Yes, you do. Maybe one day you can meet her."

Shelly gave a big smile. "I'd love to."

The man shook his head. "I can't believe this." A look of confusion came over him. Shelly was still unsure of how he stood on the matter. But then he continued, "Just when I've resolved to the fact that I will always be a priest and never have a family of my own, the Good Lord gives me a daughter from nowhere."

"Actually," Shelly said with a grin, "you've got more than a daughter."

"What do you mean? Oh! Your husband, yes, and a son-in-law, too. He seems like a nice man. English, is he?"

"Yes, he is—but, well, we also just found out we're going to have a baby."

This almost seemed to be too much for the man to digest. He sat back in his chair for a second without saying anything. "You mean...I'm going to be a grandfather as well?"

"Yes, hopefully."

"Well, my goodness... Congratulations, I should say... I don't know exactly what else to say... I'm stunned by all this."

"I know—too much at one time. I knew this would be too much for you. I'm so sorry." She shook her head. She could see the tears in his eyes, and she felt the odd sensation that she knew was inevitable all this time. However, he deserved to know the entire truth.

"No, no, dear. This is...wonderful. Yes, wonderful." He continued to study her sweet face and was astounded by the miracle of it all. "This is truly a blessing. I have a family!"

Shelly regained her smile. "Yes. Yes, you do." An idea came to her. "Hey, let's go find Robin, and we'll treat you to lunch."

"Oh, you don't have to do that."

"Yes, I do."

"Well, I don't want to put you out."

"Father, we're rich."

He laughed heartily, and she wondered if it was because of what she said, or the fact she called him 'Father' and meant it in a different sense than how he was accustomed to hearing.

They stood up and hugged again, and set forth to find Robin. "He *will* wander off when he's bored," Shelly grumbled.

They eventually found him outside admiring some unusual plants.

"Take us to lunch, honey."

"No problem. When do you have to be back, Father?" Robin asked as they walked back to the street.

"Oh, not until 2:00. Only one more meeting, and that's it. Then back to Ireland." Shelly's smile quickly faded. Now that she had found him, she didn't want him to go. Her father noticed her change and asked, "What's the matter, dear?"

"Just wished I had more time with you."

"I do, too. Of course, you can always visit me in Ireland, and I'll be back in the States in August."

"Really?" she said anxiously. "Where?"

He gave a wry smile that threw Robin off guard it was so much like Shelly's. "San Antonio."

"What?!" exclaimed Shelly.

"Texas in August, eh?" Robin said dryly and gave a wicked chuckle.

"Ah, it'll be warm, won't it?" he asked slowly nodding his head, knowing the answer.

"Warm, yeah." Robin muttered, "I still remember melting into a puddle on an outside stage in Houston in '88. We would play anywhere in those days."

"I meant to ask you, son, why I recognize you. Weren't you on the telly, or something?"

"I've been on the telly, but I'm just a singer."

The man stopped walking and looked at him. "Here now, you're one of those, uh, Ministers of Parliament, are you not?"

"Yes sir, I sure am."

"Hee-hee," he giggled, looking at Shelly. "No wonder you said you're rich."

Robin gave her a look and she gave him an apologetic look back.

"I do like some of your songs." The priest saw Robin's look of surprise. "Don't think I live in a cloister, son. It's a priest's job to know what is influencing the public."

"And how do you think our music fares?"

Shelly got nervous all of a sudden. She hoped she would faint to distract them, but no such luck.

"From what I've heard, it's fine. You seem to have a fairly good outlook on the world. There are a few songs that are a bit depressing, though."

"Life isn't all milk and honey, Padre."

"Ah, that it's not, my lad. That it's not. I guess I just prefer to focus on the good because it gives me a more positive outlook overall. A, uh, mental conditioning, so to speak."

"Understood. But sometimes, you have to admit, a bit of wallowing in self-pity is good for the mind, if not the soul."

"Ha-ha! How true! No one likes pity from others, but, oh!, how we like to feel sorry for ourselves. Well, we have different means with the same outcome, I suppose. I encourage people to think positively, and you encourage them to express themselves and get it out of their systems."

"Yes, exactly. Whatever works, I suppose... Do you think we confuse them?"

"Ha, well, that's a question I'm not sure if there is an answer. Very possibly, though!"

"Maybe they can figure it out considering which one of us is speaking."

"Or singing, in your case."

"Ha-ha. Yes."

"Maybe it's the music that makes the difference."

"Hmm. Sounds like a subject for a thesis. 'Does music make life more or less tolerable?' Hilarious."

"Uh, excuse me professors, but could we eat? I'm hungry and so is the baby," Shelly interrupted.

"Oh, sorry," the two men said and walked along side her, one on each side.

They had gotten to the street and Robin hailed a cab. Shelly was relieved that the men ended their conversation on an amicable note, but it had made her a nervous wreck. She did have to laugh at herself, though. She saw the same conviction to the occupation in both men, and thought it funny that she indeed did marry a man like her father—even though she had never met him.

Robin treated them to a small restaurant he had been to before that he was fond of. It was cozy, and he felt they could have some privacy there. They sat in a booth enjoying the food, atmosphere, and company. Shelly felt she could grow very fond of her new relation, and thought about the fact that he was a priest. She asked why he became one, and he gave the usual answers to such an inquiry. Her face turned rather sad and Robin noticed. "What's the matter, dear?"

"Father, can I ask you something on a professional level?"

"Well, of course."

"Why," her voice cracked, "why is it that there is always something wrong?"

"What do you mean?"

"Why is it that there always has to be something wrong—that things can't be perfect for at least a while?"

The man knitted his brows and asked, "Do you have an example?" trying to get to the heart of the problem.

"Yeah, I do. We thought we couldn't have children— and that's a whole other story—and now, we actually are and…and there's a chance it may…" She trailed off, closing her eyes.

"It may what child?"

She looked up nervously at Robin with tears about to fall. "It may have a problem because of an illness I had."

"You know?" Robin asked with astonishment.

"You knew?" she asked back.

The couple stared at each other and then he held her.

Fr. O'Connor remained silent, shocked to see this breakthrough. They quickly settled down and Shelly dried her eyes. She apologized to her father and he replied, "No, no. That's okay. I'm just sorry you're having to go through this. But, one thing you've got to remember is not to worry about something that hasn't happened yet. And when it's time to worry, you put your trust in the Lord to help you deal with it. The Lord doesn't hand you anything you can't cope with, and I think you're a strong enough person to handle whatever may come. Is it for sure that your baby will be hurt?"

"No."

"Well, see? You already said that you didn't think you would get to have a baby, and now you are expecting one, so you don't know what other miracles may come your way. You need to concentrate on taking care of yourself and doing all you can to be a good and healthy mother. You may very well be worrying about nothing."

"You're right, of course." She looked at Robin. "I'm sorry."

"Nothing to be sorry about, love. It's understandable considering all you've been through," Robin replied. "Whatever happens, we can handle it—together. You've got to know that." He held her hand and she smiled. He then wiped a tear from her eye and said with a grin, "You know, you ought to use waterproof."

This did the job of making her laugh. "Okay, I give up. How can I be a pessimist with you two?" She turned to her father and said, "I promise to have more faith in the situation."

Fr. O'Connor went on, "It simply doesn't do to worry about something that hasn't happened or may never happen. Your baby will be loved no matter what, and that is what it needs most. Don't just have faith in the Lord…have faith in yourself and in your husband."

"Yes, sir," she meekly replied. He seemed to take to being her father quite easily in his little lecture. She chalked it up to being a priest and very used to telling people the way it is.

Robin wanted to chuckle watching him handle his usually stubborn wife with ease, but instead simply said, "Well, that's settled. Maybe we should eat now?" He was worried about Fr. O'Connor's schedule.

"Yes, yes…" the priest agreed. He picked up a piece of bread and broke it, and as he did so, his face clouded.

"What's wrong?" they both asked.

"I haven't been thinking. I haven't been thinking about the implications of this at all."

"What do you mean?" Shelly asked.

"What is going to happen to me when they find out?"

"Could you lose your priesthood?" asked Robin with concern.

The man's mind rambled. "I really have no idea. I mean, Shelly's grown, so I don't know how they would handle this. Do you think, well, could it be possible to keep this to ourselves?"

"As long as you're all right with that."

"I admit that doesn't sound like something a priest would say—to withhold the truth—but I really fear for my job. He looked at Shelly with astonishment and slowly said, "How can this…be bad? How can this not be what is meant to be? I cannot feel that I should be punished for something I did so long ago, for I have already served my punishment by not seeing you grow up—by missing out on your childhood…"

The man looked as if he was going to get angry at her mother for keeping Shelly secret to him, so Robin interrupted, "No, Father, there is no reason. Let's just keep it in the family."

The man uneasily agreed, but he did feel guilty about the whole thing. He really felt he had some praying and thinking to do, and wouldn't do anything until he had done so. However, he was determined to enjoy his meal with his newfound family.

They did enjoy the rest of their meal on a lighter note. Robin noted, however, that the two red heads were completely fascinated with one another and couldn't help but observe their counterparts for similarities to themselves.

When it was time to take Fr. O'Connor back to the center, Shelly was very sad to say good-bye. Robin, however, was very happy for her and knew how this meeting would fill a void in her heart that he couldn't fill himself.

They promised to meet up again in August, and they exchanged addresses and phone numbers. "Shelly," her father said, "thank you so much for finding me. I had no idea you existed, and I can't tell you what a blessing you are to me." At this point, he lost his words and gave her a hug.

"I'm glad I found you, too, and you need to thank Robin for encouraging me to look for you."

He shook Robin's hand. "Thank you. Thank you very much, indeed. Keep taking care of…of my girl." The words felt too odd for him to say.

"Certainly. Take care, Father."

"Have a safe trip," Shelly added.

"And you as well! God bless you both."

The man went back into the building, leaving Robin and Shelly alone. "I do hope he'll be all right," lamented Shelly.

"I do, too." Robin wrapped his arm around her and started the walk back. "Well…what would you like to do now? We are in the Big Apple."

"Golly. I have no idea. Any suggestions?"

Robin looked down at the pavement. "There's one place I'd like to go to again—there's something I need to do there."

Shelly resisted the urge to ask what, due to the odd expression on his face. He was in deep concentration. She simply complied and they left.

They hailed a taxi and Shelly grew curious when Robin requested the driver to take them to the Waldorf-Astoria.

Chapter Five

It was earlier that same day when George woke up and told Debra that he had some work to do at the office. She said good-bye to him after a quiet breakfast, and wondered after shutting the door why he had to go in so early on a Saturday.

She sat stewing around remembering what Shelly had told her. She did need to get this off her chest whether or not she was correct in her accusation.

She found plenty of busy work to do for her restaurant of which she was going to take over very soon. She tried to concentrate on that task to keep her mind from rambling. Fortunately, George wasn't gone that long. He came in smiling and inquired what she had been doing. She gave a brief description of what all she had done and he seemed pleased.

She looked at him with love and sadness, and nervously asked, "George?"

"Yes, dear?"

"What…what has been going on?"

He seemed to fidget. "What do you mean?"

"Honey, I *know* I saw you at that car lot with Suzi, and, well, it just seems you're trying to hide something."

"What is it you think I'm hiding?" he asked with a grave face. He wanted her to come out and say it, but she wasn't falling into that trap.

"I don't know," she said looking at him with cobra-like eyes. "Why don't you tell me why you're lying?"

If she hadn't been so serious, he would have laughed and told her the truth of what was really going on, but instead she was on the defense, as if she could easily believe the worst-case scenario. "I can't believe were having this discussion. Are you actually accusing me of having an *affair*?"

Now that he said it, it scared her. If she was wrong, this was going to be detrimental to their relationship, but she had to know. "I'm not accusing you of anything; I just need to know some answers. Who were you buying a plane ticket for?" she retorted with all her strength.

He was shocked she knew and began to understand why she had her suspicions. Unfortunately, his feelings had already been hurt. He wondered how much she actually heard. "Do you usually go around eaves-dropping on my conversations?"

She hated it when he'd answer a question with a question, and he knew it. The cobra was about to strike when he continued.

"It was for *Paul*, all right?!"

"Paul?" she mumbled with surprise.

"That's right. Your louse of an ex-husband called me and asked how I felt about taking him in—seems he can't handle a teenager after all—so we discussed it and I talked to Paul about what was to be expected if he moved here and it was settled. The car was for him as a present of goodwill from me. I wanted to surprise you… Damn! I can't *believe* this!

I'm here bending over backwards for you and your son, as busy as I am with my work, and you're thinking I'm having an affair!" he stopped to catch his breath. "Debra, I cannot believe that you would think I would do something like this!" he yelled an octave higher.

"I'm sorry! But what was I suppose to think? All this going on and your working late when Robin doesn't—"

"That's what it's all about, isn't it? You've been acting oddly ever since he got married. What's the deal? Did you want Robin for yourself?"

"Don't be absurd!" she screamed. "He's like my baby brother and you know that!"

"Then what is it?" he asked, shaking his arms at her.

"It's…it's the relationship that they have—the way they always do things together, the way they talk to each other."

"Well, they *are* newlyweds."

"So that means you're supposed to stop talking to each other once you've been married over a year? When was the last time we simply sat and enjoyed each other's company? We always seem to have people over so we'll converse. Am I boring you?"

He looked at her and seemed to wake up from a slumber. He hadn't realized how they had lost each other. He began to wonder if he knew her at all. "No, no, baby. I love you."

"I love you, too, George. But I think we've got some work to do on our relationship."

George said nothing. He started to rub his left arm and Debra saw a change in his expression.

"George? What's the matter?" she asked with alarm.

He sat down. "I don't feel very well."

She noticed how he kept rubbing his arm subconsciously and that he was losing the color in his face. "I'm calling an ambulance."

"Why?"

"George!" she said pointing her hand to his arm. He looked down, not even aware of what he was doing.

He looked up at her with fear in his eyes as she dialed the phone. All he could think of was his father.

She quickly gave directions to their house. He was thankful she could handle a tense situation with a straight head. When she was done, she immediately came to him and said, "Don't worry, honey, you're going to be okay." He simply stared at her. "I'm so sorry, George. I am *so* sorry. I had no right."

"Well, I guess it did look funny."

"That's no excuse. I should have trusted you." Her tears finally came.

He began to get paler, and she began to get frantic. Fortunately, she heard a siren.

Robin entered the majestic old hotel clutching Shelly's hand for dear life. The memory of what happened there was still so vivid in his mind. She had no idea she had so emotionally scarred him that fateful day when she ran away.

He took her into the same sitting room that they were in when they had their argument and he sat her down in a chair and then sat opposite himself. He held her hands across the little table and looked into her bright, blue eyes. This time he saw no anger or fear, just love. He smiled at this reassurance and said, "I know you think it's a bit weird bringing you here, but I just wanted to try to erase that bad memory of this place."

"You can't erase the past, honey. Look what we just came back from doing."

"Ha. Yes, that's true, but I just wanted to put everything straight. I want you to know that as much as I want this baby, and love this baby, that with or without...*her* (she laughs), it is ultimately *you* that means the world to me. I was fine with the idea of it just being us. A baby wasn't a necessity, just an added bonus to something already terrific. Something that I seriously thought would never happen to me. There is no replacing you, Shelly Marie."

The words left him, and she reached over and took his glasses off. She saw that his words were true in his soft, brown eyes. She stood up and gave him a strong kiss. She sat back down and said, "I'm sorry I hurt you so badly."

"That's not why I brought you here. It was for *me* to make amends."

She smiled. "Have we wiped the slate clean now?"

He looked around, drawing in a deep breath. He gave her that odd, funny look he often gave her with a raised brow. "I believe so. The ghosts have been chased out of this lofty area and we can walk in peace through these hallowed halls."

"Ha! You make it sound like Oxford!"

"I almost went to Oxford," he said with a flippant tone.

"What happened?" she played along.

"I went to London instead to chase girls."

"Did you catch one?"

"N-no. A couple caught me, though."

"Oh..."

"I *did* get an education, however," he replied with a mischievous grin and a devious chuckle.

"I'm sure you did," she said shaking her head and laughing. "I'm sure you did."

They stood up to leave when Robin's cell phone went off. He answered it, and Shelly could hear it was Debra. She watched him turn pale and say, "We'll be right there."

"What's the matter?" Shelly immediately asked.

"George has had a heart attack."

"Oh, my God." Shelly was not only worried for George, but for Robin. A heart attack was always his biggest fear since his own father had died of one early in life. She never thought about George falling victim to one, and she felt a bit guilty about it.

Robin grabbed her hand once again and rushed her back out to catch another taxi. They got back to their hotel and packed their things quickly. Robin was really beginning to hate New York.

They took the next plane they could get back to Florida. He was quiet on the way, and Shelly did what she could to console him and assure him that his brother was going to be fine. Robin, however, wasn't convinced.

"Maybe if I hadn't been stressing him out so much, he wouldn't be in this situation."

"Honey, you're the least of his worries," Shelly said with almost a laugh.

"What do you mean?" he asked quickly.

Shelly had let the cat out of the bag, so she might as well tell him the whole story. "Well…remember when I fainted at dinner?"

"How could I forget?"

"Well, you weren't the only one who dropped a bombshell on me that night. Debra told me that she thought George was having an affair."

"What?" he asked with genuine surprise.

"Yes." She sadly nodded. "So, I imagine that they had an argument about that. You don't think he is, do you?"

He thought for a second and replied, "I'd say no, but I have no idea what goes on with him sometimes. Then again, he has been up to something, but I think it had something to do with Paul. I heard him mention him to his secretary."

"Debra's son?"

"Yes."

"Hmm."

"Wow… Yes, I really can't see him cheating on Deb, though. I mean, they're not the closest couple I know, but I've never seen them argue, either. I wonder what the issue really is."

"Do you think she has made an incorrect accusation and they had a fight?"

"Very possibly."

"I guess we'll find out."

Robin simply nodded and returned to looking out the window at the clouds below.

Chapter Six

They reached Miami very late that night, rushing to the hospital as soon as possible. They found Debra wide-awake in the cardiac care unit, alone. They greeted her and asked how George was.

"They're preparing him for surgery."

"What?" Robin asked with alarm.

"Yeah. He's got two big arteries that are blocked."

"Oh, gosh," said Shelly. "Well, we've got to believe that he's going to be okay." She held Debra with sympathy while Robin stood dumbfounded.

A thought finally came to him. "Where's Terry?"

"Oh, he and Rachel have been here all day with me. They went to the cafeteria to get Rachel something to eat since she hadn't had anything to speak of all this time."

"That's my Rachel," said Shelly with a little smile.

"Yes, she's been quite a comfort to me," remarked Debra.

"How long is the operation supposed to take?"

"About four to five hours. They don't have to stop his heart to repair that artery, so that's good, but it's all very complicated."

"What other artery is there?" asked Robin after a bit of thought.

"His carotid," she said with a motion showing where on her own neck.

"Oh," they both answered with surprise.

"Yes. They discovered that when they were examining him. In an odd way, the heart-attack kept him from having a stroke, since we had no idea he had a blockage there, either."

Robin stood with his eyes wide open. To imagine George a stroke victim floored him. Shelly gave a loving pat upon his leg to break his concentration. He looked down at her and snapped out of it. "Have you told anyone from work?" Robin stammered out.

"No, I figured you could," Debra replied. She was too tired to be apologetic.

"Of course." He went on to call their manager and others outside on his cell phone.

Shelly felt this was a good time to make her confession. "Debra, I hate to tell you this, but I let it slip to Robin about what you told me."

Debra looked at her with the saddest eyes she had ever seen her have. "I was wrong. I was so completely wrong. Oh, Shelly, what have I done?" she softly cried.

"You're not to blame for this," she stressed. "His heart was a time-bomb."

"Yes, and I set it off," she quickly replied.

"What was it all about, anyway?"

"Paul's moving in with us. The airplane ticket was for him along with the car—it was a peace offering, so to speak."

"You're kidding." Shelly's heart sank for her.

"Nope."

"My goodness." She realized how this must make Debra feel.

"What on earth made me accuse him of such a thing?" Debra cried, almost to herself.

Shelly really had no answer for her. They sat quietly for a while, until Rachel and Terry showed up. Rachel greeted Shelly with a kiss and asked Debra what was going on. Debra gave her report and Rachel waited a few minutes before asking Shelly how her visit went. Her news provided Debra with a good distraction. She and Rachel listened with interest to Shelly's account of the day. Both congratulated her and expressed their pride in her for doing such a brave thing.

"You know, I already miss him," Shelly said with regret.

"So you'll get to see him again—when?" asked Rachel.

"August, believe it or not. He's going to San Antonio."

"Fantastic!"

"I know. It was so weird—like a strange dream."

"But how wonderful, Shelly. I mean, you're so lucky you could find him and that he was receptive to you. He didn't doubt at all that you were his?" Debra asked.

"How could he?" she laughed. "I look just like him! Robin was freaking out. You know, turn me into a man in his fifties, and you have Fr. O'Connor!"

"You'd think in his profession he'd want to deny you, though." Rachel remarked.

"Well, I guess the truth is more important to him. He seemed quite happy to acquire a family, actually."

"Well, that's just great, Shelly. I can't wait to meet him," Debra said with her first smile of the day. She was genuinely happy for her.

"Really. I'm curious, too," Rachel said and then looked around wondering where Terry had run off to.

Terry had wandered off down the halls, having no interest in listening to women chat. George's heart attack seemed to hit upon a scar that hadn't quite healed. It had only been a few months since he had lost his own brother, and George was practically another brother to him. He felt panicky, and wondered how George was going to do. He strode slowly through the halls, almost without watching where he was going. He bumped into a man who was distracted with his cell phone. Both apologized and recognized each other's voices.

"Robin!"

"Hey, Terry." The cousins gave each other a hug.

"Sorry about George."

"Yeah, thanks. Well, it's a bit weird, I admit," said Robin as they both walked back towards the women. "Being the selfish brute that I am, I always thought I was going to be the one who inherited Dad's bad ticker. I never thought about it being George. He always seemed to be healthier than me."

"You never know about hearts. Sometimes it's just genetics. I knew a chap who could outrun anyone on the pitch, then one day—bam!—dead on the field—couldn't even be resuscitated. You just never know."

Robin gave a cold, blank look.

"But obviously George is going to be all right...right?" Terry quickly added.

"Yeah, I suppose so," he replied, still with his eyebrow raised. "Well, did the doctor have a good outlook for the procedure?"

"Yes, yes. Actually he was quite nonchalant about it all. Acted like it was an everyday occurrence."

"I guess they do this kind of thing all the time, what?"

"Probably so."

They made it back to where the girls were and they all sat down, surrounding Debra with support.

They played the waiting game, desperately trying to keep some sort of conversation going to keep their minds off of what could be happening with George. As time went on though, that became increasingly difficult. Debra became more nervous, going between blaming herself for the stress she put on her husband and George for not taking better care of himself in the first place.

Eventually, the doctor came out with the same placid expression he had before he went in. Everyone jumped up to listen to what he had to say.

"Well, folks, looks like he's going to be rockin' for a few more years," he reported with a smile. "He's going to be just fine. Everything went well—well, we had a little difficulty with the artery in his neck, but we got it."

Everyone gave a big sigh of relief.

"Yes, yes. He's going to need some time to recover, of course, and he's going to have to give up French food."

"It was my cooking as well," Debra lamented. "So what happens now?"

"Well, it will take some time to recuperate. You're looking at maybe a week here, then probably six weeks at home. We'll have a nurse show you how to take care of his incisions. We were very fortunate in that we didn't have to open his ribcage, but that only means that recovery time is less. He'll still go through all that's involved in taking care of his heart—eating right, exercising, you know, doing what he can to avoid this again. I take it he leads a pretty exciting life with world tours and such? Stressful, anyway?"

"It can be," she said softly.

"Well, he's going to have to take it easy for a while until he's properly healed. Plenty of good rest and relaxation."

Debra nodded.

"Good. Well, I'll have someone bring you some information and a little schedule I'd like for him to follow for a while. Obviously, he'll be on some heavy medications for the next few days. Does he exercise any?"

"Not really," she replied. "We have the occasional game of tennis, but that's about it."

"Well, his cardiologist will tell him all he needs to know about that. Now, if you'll excuse me, I need to get going. He's probably going to be in ICU for recovery and pretty doped up for a few hours, but they will allow visitors after a while."

Debra and Robin thanked the surgeon and then he was gone in a flash. The doctor's easy-going air did much to settle them down. Everyone sat back down with relief. Robin thought about the doctor's remark that he made in jest about 'world tours'. He certainly didn't want to get out of touring this way. He felt the urge to laugh at the irony, but he was too overcome with emotion that his brother actually was going to be all right.

A nurse came out later to tell them that visitors were allowed in twos. Debra begged Robin to come with her, so he did. She almost felt like a schoolgirl going to the principal's office. She came in to find him with all the appropriate monitors and hoses. It sunk in to her that it really had happened. Her husband just had bypass surgery.

She began to cry, and Robin rubbed her shoulders, trying to hold back his own tears.

She came up to the bed and softly said his name. He opened one eye and said, "Hi."

"Are you going to be okay?"

"Oh, yeah," he said with confidence.

"That's good… I love you."

He smiled. "I love you, too, dear." He breathed hard, for it hurt him to speak. But, being George, he had to get at least one joke out: "No more cheese soufflés, I'm afraid."

"No, dear," Debra said with a smile while clutching his hand. "But I can make one heck of a salad."

He smiled at her and then squinted at the sight of Robin. "Looks like…you're getting out of, uh…the tour after all."

Robin came up to him. "Yes, well, you didn't have to be so dramatic about it." This made George smile. "All the same, I'm damn glad you're going to be okay. Life would have been, uh…pretty boring without my big brother to kick around…or kick me around."

"Someone needs to help Shelly…keep you in line."

"Well, you've got a couple more visitors, and then we need to leave and let you get your rest." Robin said good-bye and escorted Debra out after she gave a take-care kiss to the patient.

Terry and Shelly came in and gave him encouragement, and Terry uncharacteristically did not joke, until George picked on him, that is. It was unnerving to George to see him serious about him, so he had to make him smile, even if it hurt. When they came back out, they asked Rachel if she wanted to see him, but she declined and sent her regards with Debra who went back to see him once more alone.

Debra gave her husband Rachel's good wishes and he remarked, "She's deceptively timid."

"Yes, she is." She could tell he needed to get back to sleep and that he was in pain. She wiped the hair back from his forehead and gave him a kiss upon it. "You need to rest, but let me say one thing: I am going to make up for all this. I promise."

He looked into her eyes, as if he were searching for something. He closed his own and breathed deeply. She leaned down and kissed him once more on the cheek. She got up to leave and he asked, "Debra?"

"Yes?"

"Goodnight."

"Goodnight, love."

It was Tuesday. Robin and Shelly were both frantically busy. Robin had chaos going on in his office trying to postpone the entire tour. Their manager had to put out an official statement about George. Robin would have preferred to keep it under wraps, but you can't cancel so many dates without good reason. This, of course, caused fans from all over to send their sympathies and well wishes. Shelly, however, was kidnapping Robin for a few hours for her first visit to the obstetrician. She was excited and didn't know what to expect. The two came into the doctor's office after the nurse got Shelly's history, vitals, and verified her pregnancy. They sat with nervous smiles on their faces until the doctor came in for their initial consultation. Dr. Hodges greeted them with a handshake and sat down.

"So, Shelly," he began, looking at her file, Debra Parker is your sister-in-law?"

"Yes, sir."

"So, you must be the other M.P.?" he asked, pointing to Robin.

"Yes. Yes, that is how I'm usually introduced—'the other M.P.'," he answered with a funny face and a gesture.

The doctor laughed at him with a hearty guffaw. "Well, pleasure to meet you and congratulations to both of you."

"Now," he continued, "I have been reading your history and you seem to have been through a rough time the past year or so." He looked at Shelly who nodded in agreement. "As I see it, there are three things we need to be concerned about, and we might as well discuss them and get them out of the way." Robin appreciated how he got to the point. "First of all, there's the ectopic pregnancy you had, let's see, last June?—we need to see if we can find out if there was a reason for that, or if it was a chance happening and also if it left any bad scarring, which should show up on the ultrasound."

"Secondly, you wrote here you just got over a bad flu?"

"Yes," she replied.

"Tell me about it."

Shelly went on to tell of how she contracted it in Japan and how close she came to dying. He listened with a grave face. Shelly then asked, "What are the chances that it harmed my baby?"

"Well, I really can't give you a number. How long was your fever very high?"

Shelly looked at Robin, for she had no idea. He thought about it and replied, "It was almost eight hours."

"Good grief, you poor thing." The doctor mulled this over in his mind. "Well…if there were any effects of this, we're probably not going to know until much later. I think it is important to not worry at this stage, for the chances of anything major happening will be minimal. I mean, there is a chance it could affect some developmental factors, but I still say slim."

"Now, thirdly: your age," he added delicately. This shocked Shelly, for she never really considered it. "You're about to turn thirty-six. That doesn't mean that much really, but risks that exist for any pregnancy increase as you get older. The one most people associate with maternal age is the risk of having a baby with Down's syndrome. Again, the risk is slim, but it does increase with age."

He looked at their once smiling faces and saw hopelessness. He knew he had better say something positive. "Shelly, I'm not trying to scare you. More likely than not, you will have a perfectly normal, healthy baby, but precautions are always good, and it's best to address these factors head-on. The fact you became pregnant is a miracle with so much going against you, so that was actually your worst hurdle."

"I think my herbalist had something to do with that," she said without thinking what it sounded like.

The doctor raised a brow in curiosity.

"I mean," she explained with a giggle, "she gave me all this stuff to straighten out my messed up cycle, and apparently it kicked my hormones into gear."

"Well, good for her! I have no problem with alternative medicine fused in conjunction with traditional. I do get nervous when some of my first time mothers insist on using a midwife at home instead of having their babies in a hospital. You never know what might happen. But of course, that's just me. Overprotective, I suppose. Anyway, what was I saying? Oh! So, there are precautions we simply need to take to make sure you deliver a healthy baby with the knowledge that we have."

"What precautions?" the couple asked simultaneously.

"I got that in stereo, didn't I? Well, we have to keep a close eye on your blood pressure, sugar levels, and you yourself can do the most good for your baby—make sure you come to your visits here on a regular basis, and you need to keep on a healthy diet and supplemental regimen. I'll give you a prescription for some prenatal vitamins."

"So I guess I shouldn't go to my herbalist any longer?"

"Well, I strongly suggest you let me know what she gives you, okay? We don't want you getting too much of some things, and there is always the chance there can be harmful side effects of others. I want to know *everything* that you take, all right?" he stressed.

"Yes, sir," she meekly replied.

"Let's not increase our chances of something going wrong, okay?"

She nodded.

"We also can run an amniocentesis sometime in your second trimester. That checks for Down's syndrome. We suggest it to mothers who are thirty-five and over. But, again, this is just precautionary, and you're only thirty-five at that. The more informed we are, the better prepared we are for any contingencies. Plus, it would be one less thing to worry about. But, it is up to you. I'll go over all the risks involved later. Now, I guess we better take a look at Baby."

He got up and led them to an examining room where Robin felt very uncomfortable. The doctor left to let her change. "Well," she said with a look at Robin.

"Yes. He doesn't beat around the bush, does he?"

"No, he doesn't."

"Everything will be fine… Um, you don't need me for this, do you?"

"Ha-ha. No, babe, I guess not."

"Good. I'm outta here. This place gives me the creeps!" he declared as he looked down at some implements.

"You wuss."

"Yes. Well. You have fun… Yech," he said as he passed by the scary-looking examining table.

She changed into the gown the doctor gave her and sat on the table thinking about it all. It was funny how she never considered her age a factor. This was the only time she felt older than Robin. It wasn't fair—men can be fathers well into their fifties—sixties, even!, but women, well, she was getting up there in that department.

The doctor came in and looked around. "Where's your husband?"

Shelly giggled. "He thought the place looked a little too mediaeval for him."

Dr. Hodges chuckled and leaned out the door to call a nurse in. He did his examination and reported to Shelly that all looked fine. "Now, I'd like to do an ultrasound and see what's going on with your uterus." He got his machine going and squirted rather cold jelly on her belly. He ran the instrument over her and studied the monitor intensely. "Well, my dear, it seems you have a pretty nasty fibroid not too far away from where you had the ectopic pregnancy."

"Is that what caused it?"

"It very well may have been. Sometimes they just happen, though."

"Is it going to hurt my baby?"

"It may cause some complication, but it's really too early to tell. It may, it may not… And there's Baby."

Shelly strained to see what looked like a simple little blob on the screen. Even though she could make nothing of it, she smiled with affection.

"He, or she, looks quite happy there… Everything else looks good except for that fibroid. At least you just have the one."

"There's usually more?"

"Generally speaking, it's not surprising to see more, but one is common, too," he replied as he wiped the gel off her stomach.

"Oh."

"Now, why don't you get changed and I also want to get a blood test done to check for anemia and such."

"Okay." Shelly would have preferred another exam to getting a needle in her arm.

After the nurse got her blood sample, the doctor came back in to give her a summary. He ran over her schedule of visits, gave her a copy of a diet and a prescription for prenatal vitamins. He did his best to figure out the due date with what information he had. "Also, just to be on the safe side, you may want to abstain from relations with your husband for at least until you're well into your second trimester. I'm a bit concerned about all your risk factors—just to play it safe, okay?" He looked at her with sympathetic eyes.

"Oh," she simply replied.

"Sorry."

"Understood," she said with a shake of her head. Whatever it took, she'd do it.

She said her farewell and thank you to the doctor, paid her bill, and found her husband waiting. "Are they done torturing you?" he asked with a grin.

"Yes," she said with a pout. She showed him where they drew blood.

"Ow."

"Uh-huh. But, I got to see the baby!"

"I didn't think they could so soon."

"Well…I mean, it was just a little blob, but what a sweet little blob it was!" she said, beaming from ear to ear.

He wrapped his arm around her and kissed her head, leading her out the door.

Once he helped her into the car, she decided to tell him the bad news. "Well, babe, I've got some not-so-good news as well."

"What?" he asked with concern.

"The doctor says we should abstain for a while."

"Ah, I was afraid of that."

"Really? It hadn't even crossed my mind."

"It hadn't? Well, you would think of things of more importance. I am a man, after all," he laughed. "For the duration of the pregnancy?"

"Oh, no. He said until the second trimester."

"Ah. When will that be?"

"For another month or so."

"So, when is the baby due?"

"Sometime in December. I'm afraid my cycle was so messed up, he's not too certain of the day."

"Oh… A Christmas baby."

"Yes. Our own special present."

"Huh. Wow."

"Yeah."

They looked at each other with silly grins on their faces, but then Robin's faded. "God, I hope nothing goes wrong." He said it quickly without thinking and immediately wished he hadn't.

"Me, too, honey. Me, too. I don't think I could handle it again…" She put a trembling hand on her forehead.

"Dearheart, we've got to put that past us."

"But, I can't forget, Robin. I'm never going to forget and to not wonder what that baby would have looked like, to be like…" She began to sob openly and he let her do so for a moment. Then he leaned over and lovingly held her in his arms.

"Baby," he found it difficult to talk and fought back his own urge to cry for her sake, "I'm not expecting you to forget. We're just not ever going to… I think what matters here is concentrating on this one," he placed his hand on her belly, "and making sure we do all we can to take care of him or her. Who knows? Maybe there was some fateful reason why we couldn't have the first."

"I thought you didn't believe in fate."

He smiled. "The longer I live with you, the more I do."

She took a deep breath. "You're right. I'm just being silly. What's done is done," she said as she wiped a tear from her eye.

He gently wiped the other eye and replied, "You're not being silly. You're being normal. You lost a baby, but now you have another who needs you and that's what you've got to focus on."

"Yes, yes, I know. It's hard to believe we're expecting one now."

"Everything will be fine, love. We just have to plod forward." He gave a gesture with his hand. "We've got to handle the challenges that lie before us with our usual spirit." He pushed her hair back, landing his hand upon her cheek and giving a kiss to the other. She couldn't help but smile with his sweet, confident face shining in front of her. All of a sudden, she was feeling quite blessed.

The couple was quiet the rest of the day. Not really depressed, but in deep thought. Robin had to go back to the office, but he really was of no use, and everyone sent him back home after a few hours. He spent the rest of the day with Shelly, curled up on his couch.

Chapter Seven

The day had come for George to come home. Debra had fixed up the downstairs spare room for him so that he wouldn't have to tackle the stairs. Terry stayed home that day to assist Debra with getting George settled in. She was very grateful, if not for the help, for the support.

George was happy to be home, even if it wasn't his bed. His energy was slowly coming back, but he was very sore and shaky from the surgery.

Debra caught Terry in the kitchen as she prepared George's lunch. "Terry, do you think you could baby-sit George for a few hours? I've got a big supply coming to the restaurant that I couldn't post-pone. I hate leaving him, but I really need to be there to check it all in and make sure I got everything I paid for."

"Well, right now he told me to bugger off," he said with a grin, pointing towards the bedroom.

"Yes, I'm afraid he's a little cranky. He gets like that when he's hurting, but I'll tell him to be nice to you."

"Okay then, I'll take care of Grumpy for you. I guess I owe him from when he baby-sat me."

"Bless you. Now, I've got his lunch ready—just give it to him whenever he wants it. He's starting to get an appetite again… God, this is just crazy," she said, slamming her hands down on the kitchen counter and startling Terry. "I wished I hadn't gotten this café—not right now, anyway."

"Everything will be just fine, Deb," he said, patting her back. "Don't worry or we'll have you in hospital next."

"Yeah—the mental hospital."

Terry laughed and she went to say good-bye to George and tell him to behave with his caretaker.

After she left, Terry came back in to check on George. He wasn't asleep, just lying there looking around the room vacantly. "Hey, you all right?" Terry asked as he sat down in a chair.

"Yeah, yeah. Bored."

"You want anything? Debra left you lunch."

"No, I'm not hungry… You know what I would like, though?"

"What?" he asked eagerly.

"Some of her lemonade. I don't know what she puts in it, but I'm addicted."

"Sure." He got up and stopped at the doorway. "Say, should you be having sugar?"

"Sugar's not bad for your heart, you idiot."

"What is?"

"Rich foods and annoying cousins."

Terry cocked his head. "How badly did you want that lemonade?"

"Sorry," he grumbled.

He chuckled at him and went to get his beverage. George knew he needed to watch his temper and be nice to the young man who was only trying to help. Terry brought his drink to him with a "Here ya go."

"Cheers," George said as Terry took his seat. "So how goes it?"

"With what?"

"Everything. Are you playing yet?"

"Just practice games. Real stuff starts in about a fortnight."

"Do you think you're going to like it?"

He shrugged his shoulders. "Yeah, but I'm beginning to feel old, though."

"Try having a heart-attack."

Terry gave him a sympathetic grin.

"Why do you feel old?"

"I think I'm the oldest. Me and one other chappy. These kids are straight out of schools, most of them, and here I am, about to turn thirty-one!"

"Can you still run as fast as they can?"

"Sure I can. Circles around some of them."

"Then don't worry about it," George stated simply. He could tell Terry felt better with this encouragement and asked, "How's Rachel?"

"Oh, fine, fine. She sends her regards."

"What is she up to?"

"Cranking out glass vases and such. She made a real pretty plate with a foil effect on it the other day that I really liked."

"I never thought you'd fall for an artist. Robin—yes, but you? No."

Terry simply smiled bashfully.

"So, everything is good with you two?"

"Yes, yes. Dandy," he said a little dryly.

"Well, that's good."

George smiled, knowing full well it wasn't 'dandy'. He could tell he wanted to get off the subject quickly.

"And Debra?" Terry asked, doing his best to switch the attention to George.

The question was asked in innocence, but George was unsure if it was. Terry had no idea of their fight, only that Debra was feeling unusually guilty for George's heart attack. "Well, fine, I suppose… What do you mean?"

"Well, she's getting that restaurant and Robin told me that her son is moving here, so I figure she must be feeling a bit bombarded with everything."

"Oh," he said with relief. "Yes, she's got a lot on her plate right now. She's gone from nothing to do to everything to do."

"Is that good?"

"Everything except this…I presume."

Terry picked up something else in his voice. "What do you mean, 'you presume'?"

George was unsure whether or not to confide in the young man or not, but it seemed only fair since he had picking his brains about Rachel lately. "Oh, just that she was getting a little stir-crazy in this house on her own. She needed something to keep her mind occupied."

"Oh, I see. Certainly, you're enough now."

George stopped to think what a responsibility he had become. How was Debra going to handle all this—her son, her restaurant, and now her husband? How much could she take? After the fight that they had, he had reason for concern about her stability.

"George?"

He was snapped back to reality by Terry. "Huh?"

"I asked if you wanted some more," he said, pointing to his glass. "What were you thinking about?"

"Debra… Yes, please," he finally replied, handing him the glass back with a shaky hand.

Terry took it, wondering what was really going on. He filled it up, wondering. He worried about George and Debra, but was afraid to ask too many questions in fear that it would give George good reason to ask more questions about Rachel. He certainly didn't want that. Their relationship was solid, but somehow he was sensitive and felt on edge talking about it. Best to change the subject, he thought.

He came back in with the filled glass and gave it to his cousin. "So, when does Debra's son move in? What's his name again?"

"Paul. After this school term—end of May."

"Pretty soon, then?" he said with surprise.

"Yes."

"Wow. Well, I guess I had better find some new digs."

"I don't see why. We have plenty of room."

"Well, I can't be using this as an hotel."

"No, really. I want you to stay."

Terry was genuinely surprised. George almost sounded desperate. Maybe he was worried about the stress the boy may put him through. "Well, all right… I wonder…does he like football?"

"I don't know. You should ask him. Remember to say 'soccer' though, or you'll get into something totally different."

"Ha-ha. That reminds me. I told someone the other day that I played football, and he asked, 'Oh, a kicker?' I looked at him like he was an idiot, but then I realized that *I* was the idiot."

George laughed, thinking how settled into America he himself was, and that Terry had a long way to go.

"Yeah," continued Terry, "that would be good for him—a good thing to take up his time. I could take him to some of the matches. Do you think he'd like that?"

"I'm sure he would."

"What's he like?"

"He's a very quiet boy. I think his parents splitting up has a lot to do with that. Of course, that just may be his countenance. His father is a bookworm—some scientist or other—and Debra's rather quiet in her own way."

"Well, Uncle Terry will bring him out of his shell."

George looked at him with raised brows and a grin, making Terry laugh. "Shells aren't necessarily a bad thing, ya know."

"Don't worry. I won't corrupt him." Terry gave George a big smile and was very happy that he could be of good use to George. He had always seen the hard, strong side to him, and now, within a couple of hours, he had seen his weakness. Not in the physical sense, but pertaining to Debra and Paul. He began to be more human to Terry, and Terry appreciated the fact that he didn't feel so intimidated by him. Maybe George wasn't such a beast after all.

They enjoyed chatting for a while about meaningless subjects and it offered a distraction for George from his present situation.

George eventually began to tire and Terry left him to rest. He decided to take this time to call Rachel, and went into the kitchen to do so. She was home preparing for another show, and the sound of his voice settled her frazzled nerves. "How are things?" he inquired.

"Oh, Terry, I just busted one of my best display lamps."

"Oh, no! Can it be fixed?"

"I don't know. I don't know anything about electronics."

"You broke it rather well, then?"

"Yes. That's me. I never do anything half-way." After Terry laughed at this, she asked, "How's George?"

"Fine. Getting back to his troublesome self."

"Ha, that's good."

"Well, whenever Debra comes home, I'll get over to your place and see if I can help you with that lamp."

"I didn't know you knew how to fix things."

"There's a lot about me you don't know," he purred. "Actually, I used to help Dad do repairs around the brewery."

"Oh, yeah. I guess you would've. I never thought about it."

"Well, I'm no genius, but I'm pretty good at rigging things, anyway."

"If you could rig this enough to last me through tomorrow, I'd be *so* grateful."

"Oh, really? How grateful?"

"Hmm… We'll just have to see…"

"Ha-ha. Well, I'll be over soon, my damsel in distress."

"Great… I'd love to see your face. I'm getting a bit crazy here, and I'm afraid it'll only get worse. See you later, then?"

"Yes, dearest."

She loved it when he called her that. "Okay, then. Bye," she said softly.

"Bye."

He hung up and sat at the bar, thinking. She was his world, which made him feel very vulnerable, but at the same time he felt an incredible empowerment—almost a high—from being with her. She made him feel whole, as if his life before was spent simply waiting for her. He laughed, for he couldn't believe he was thinking like this. He shook his head, got up, and fixed himself some of Debra's magic lemonade.

He sat on the living room couch, trying not to think too much. He looked at the glass and said to himself, "There really is something about this stuff." He gave a chuckle, finished his drink, and then lay down on the couch and took a nap.

"The bastards!"

Shelly ran from the living room to Robin's den to find out what the deal was. He only cursed like that when it was really bad, and her heart pounded at the sight of her husband pacing the floor with a fax clutched in his hand. "What is it?" she asked.

Robin continued his coarse language, but then stopped and quickly snapped the paper to Shelly. "Donnie sent this."

Their manager had sent over a copy of a famous tabloid's article about the band. It had libelously announced the demise of the band due to George's 'near death' experience and Robin's 'settling down to start a family'. Shelly studied the article very seriously until she saw a photo. She pointed at it smiling. "Look! I made the Inquisitor!"

Robin practically scorched her with his eyes.

"Sorry, I mean, this is awful."

"*Yes*, it is!" He quickly grabbed the phone to call his manager back.

Shelly left the room solemnly, but giggled once she got out. She knew it was a serious offence, but at the same time, no one believed that tripe. She also knew it was going to cause aggravation for the guys for the next month or so—unfortunate for George, for he certainly didn't need the stress, but for Robin…

A thought occurred to her. This may be the kick he needed to think about his job more seriously. He certainly didn't seem to want to lie down and accept defeat. He was ready to fight; he was ready to keep working. Shelly was so happy with this thought, she spun around in joy. She really didn't want him to quit because she knew he loved his job. She saw a different side to him when it came to performing. That was where his strength lie and she didn't want her condition to take him away from that. She didn't want him making any sacrifices.

She slowly walked back to see if he had hung up yet. She came back in time to catch him saying, "…and get Suzi to call Dominguez and have them put out a letter on our website, she doesn't have anything better to do… Yes, yes, I know… Well, tell Martin good luck is all I can say… Yeah, all right. Thanks."

He hung up and paced a bit before he realized he was being watched. He finally cracked a smile at her and she quietly asked, "Everything under control?"

"'Under control'? Yes. 'All right'? No."

"Well, I'm sure you've done what you can. Have you called George?"

"No… I suppose I'd better, though."

He picked up the phone and Shelly left the room. He paused before dialing. He stopped to think about how George may react. He knew he would explode. He wished he didn't have to tell him, but he knew someone else would if he didn't. Better himself than their tactless manager. He always meant well, but he tended to blurt things out.

He slowly dialed the phone and Terry answered. They chatted for a bit before Terry gave the phone to George. Robin gingerly explained what happened. George's reaction, however, was not what he expected. "Humph...tabloid rubbish. Oh, well. I take it Martin's handling it?"

"Uh...yes, of course," he replied with shock to unusual passiveness.

"Well, not much else we can do."

"No. No, I suppose not."

George took a deep breath and then asked, "So, when are you going to come visit your ailing brother on death's bed? Or are you too busy buying nappies?"

"Ha... Uh, I can come over now, if you like."

"Yes, do. Debra's still not back from the café and Terry's chomping at the bit to get out of the infirmary and back to someone a lot prettier than me."

"Yeah, sure," he laughed. "Shelly as well, or is she too hyper for you?"

"Oh, no, ow! Please tell her to come as well."

"You okay?"

"Fine, fine. Damn bandages on the neck. I need to shave."

"Oh... Well, you know, I've got Granddad's straight-edge—I can fix that for you."

"No thanks. I've had enough slicing for a while."

"Okay then," he said with a chuckle, "be around shortly."

"Great. Cheers."

"Bye." Robin hung up and hollered, "Shelly!"

"You rang?" she quickly replied.

"We're going to George's."

"Oh. Good."

Once at George's, they visited with Terry and George, cheering the patient up greatly. Terry eventually went into the living room to make some phone calls, leaving the couple to care for George. Robin began to feel uncomfortable with George lying there ill. It made him feel somewhat superior to him with his infirmity. He didn't like it. George was always the older, stronger one, but now his vulnerability was exposed. Shelly could feel an odd tension and broke it by asking, "Where's Debra?"

"Oh, she had her initial order of supplies coming into the café, and she had to be there to supervise." George obviously wasn't happy about it.

"Oh," she simply answered with a look to Robin. "Well, I'm sure she's glad to have you home finally."

"I certainly hope so."

"I'm sure she is. There are lots of women who would love to attend to you," she kidded, trying desperately to get him to smile.

"Yes, and she reminds me of it, too."

Not the reaction she wanted. She looked to her husband in desperation.

"You know, Debra really does care for you, whether you believe it or not," Robin remarked surprisingly.

George quickly stared at him and a flame lit his eye. "What has she told you?"

Shelly instantly interrupted Robin's reply by saying, "She confessed to me that she accused you wrongly of *something*, and I let it slip to Robin."

Shelly acted like she had no clue of what the 'something' was, but it made no matter to him. He was mad. George rolled his eyes in anger. "Great. She's made fools of us privately and publicly." He grumbled something under his breath. "I take it Terry and Rachel know, as well."

"No. No, I don't believe so," she answered nervously. "Please don't be angry at her, she just got confused—"

"Confused?! What about *faith*? I have *never* given her a reason to think me unfaithful." For the first time after his surgery, he showed excitement and it alarmed them.

"Of course not," Robin said defensively, hoping to calm him back down.

"I'm sure it really had nothing to do with you," Shelly said, patting him on the arm. "Sometimes women get unhappy about something and the man gets it."

"What has she to be unhappy about? She's got everything she could ever want."

"Maybe she missed her son or something."

"Well…there's just *no* sense in it, I say."

There was no reply to that. Robin tried to get him onto the subject of their work—equally irritating, maybe, but at least not as emotional. Shelly asked him if there was anything she could get for him. He simply replied, "Lunch." She went into the kitchen to see what she could find.

"Robin, are you going to be here a while?" Terry asked.

"Sure. Why? You need to go?"

"Yes. Rachel needs help with a lamp."

"Well, you are the light of her life," George joked. They were glad to see him warming back up.

"That shouldn't be a problem," said Robin. "When did Debra say she was coming back?"

"She said she'd be here by now, actually," Terry answered, looking at his watch.

"Okay, great."

Terry got up and said, "Hey, thanks, mate… George, you take care and keep getting better," he said, patting him on the shoulder.

"Of course."

"Ah! And here's Shelly with the magic potion."

"Good!"

"Well, uh… See you later, then." Terry was eager to leave the pensive atmosphere and return to his lady.

"Bye, Terry," they replied in unison.

They watched him leave and Shelly asked Robin "Is he okay to drive?"

"He hasn't been drinking."

"No, silly, I mean legally."

"Ah. Well, I showed him how to drive on the right side of the road and all that (not that it matters around here, of course), but I seriously doubt if he has a license yet."

"Huh, I doubt he had a license in England," George remarked. They had quite a chuckle from his little joke.

Terry showed up at the studio to discover a panicky Rachel running around. "Uh, hello, there!" he greeted.

"Oh, Terry, thank God you're here. Nothing's going right. Now I've lost my damn organizer, and I need to call the guy who's running this show and—"

"Hold on, hold on…come here." He took her into his arms and gave her a reassuring hug. She instantly melted.

"Mmm…God bless you, my love," she muttered into his chest.

"You, too, darling. I tell you, it's nice to be here with you. It's high tension at George's."

"Why?"

He shook his head quickly. "Something odd is going on with George and Debra, and now Robin and Shelly were giving each other dirty looks."

"Oh, my."

"Yeah," he laughed.

"Ugh! Where is that damn thing!" she exclaimed while making a mess of her work table.

"Wait, wait, wait," Terry softly demanded, gently grasping her arms. "Just for a second, sit down with me and breathe."

She relaxed and smiled. "I think I've forgotten how to!" She sat down with him on the little sofa and he held her hand.

"Everything is going to be fine. I'll fix your lamp and we'll find your organizer." He looked at his watch. "You have plenty of time!"

"I know, but I'm usually ready by now. I think I've rusty."

"Ha-ha." He wrapped his arm around her and pulled her chin up for a kiss.

She could feel the tension releasing from her body. She looked at him dreamily and sighed, "I love you."

He stared at her dark eyes with wonder. "I love you…so much." A sad look came over his face.

"What is it?"

"Oh, just the whole George thing. Life is so short—too short to be wasted in quarreling."

"Very true," she replied with a rub of his arm.

A smile grew upon his face. "So, you agree time shouldn't be wasted?"

"Yes," she answered with no hesitation.

"Then marry me."

"Wh-what?"

"You heard me. Marry me. Marry me and make me the happiest man on earth. We both know we're meant to be. Then I can concentrate on making you the happiest woman on earth!"

She paused for only a moment then squealed, "Yes!"

He laughed while he kissed her. "You had me worried for a second!"

"I had to let it sink in!"

She giggled and thought for a second. She snapped her fingers and pulled open a drawer on the worktable. There lay her organizer.

"Yay!" he said.

"No kidding!" she said with a loving smile. "Now, I *have* to make this phone call."

It was the next evening, and Rachel had settled into her 'show mode', as Shelly would put it. She was bubbly and personable at the art show and increased in her mood at the sight of Terry. She greeted him with a hug and kiss and asked about the bandage on his brow.

"Oh, we had a contest to see whose head was the hardest."

She giggled. "I take it you lost?"

"Oh, no. I won. You should see the other guy. I broke his nose."

She laughed and shook her head, putting her arm through his.

"So, how goes it?"

"I've already sold three pieces," she whispered.

"Terrific! How's your lamp holding up?"

"So far, so good. Thanks again."

"Don't mention it."

"Shelly called me earlier and said they'd pop by."

"Good. They need to get out more."

"Ha-ha."

"Did she sound in a good mood?"

"Yeah, pretty much."

"Good. I don't want them ruining ours." He hugged her tightly making her blush.

An hour or so had passed when Shelly came in with Robin. Salutations were exchanged. "You two seem in a better mood than when I left you yesterday," Terry quipped.

Robin rolled his eyes as usual, and Shelly replied, "There are bad vibrations in that house."

"So it seems," Terry replied. "Well, I'm glad you're out of your funk. It makes it easier for us."

"What do you mean?" asked Robin. He and Shelly noticed that if Rachel's smile were any larger, it would hit her ears.

"We've decided to get married," Terry said, beaming.

"Well, it's about time," Robin and Shelly said in unison and laughed.

"How do you do that?" asked Rachel.

"No congratulations?" asked Terry with disappointment.

"Well, of course!" said Robin. Shelly screamed with excitement, and hugged Rachel. She then hugged Terry while Robin gave Rachel a kiss on the cheek. "Well, when is it?"

"I don't know," Terry answered, and then looked at Rachel. "When is it?"

She thought for a second. "Probably June or July. Sound good?"

"Yeah," Terry replied. "We're going ring shopping tomorrow."

"We are?" Rachel asked with excitement.

"Sure! It's not official until there's a ring."

Rachel seemed quite pleased with this. The crew chatted for a while, and eventually the men trailed off from the women.

"So, you want to tell me what's up with George and Debra?" Rachel asked.

"Well, I'd like to, but we've already been warned not to. But I'll tell you this much: It's nothing major, just a misunderstanding between the two of them, and hopefully they can patch things up."

"Rich people always have marital problems."

Shelly looked at her with raised brows.

"Well, except for you two. You're perfect."

"Uh-huh. Well, you know, Terry isn't poor."

Rachel almost seemed shocked. "I never really thought about it."

"Yeah, he's pretty set up… Are you still going to marry him, now that you know you're doomed?"

"Six months with me and he'll be poor, too," she laughed with a wave of her hand.

"Ha-ha… So, what all have you sold?"

"That green fluted bowl, the red square dish, and that clear vase with the bubbles you like."

"Oh, cool. Congrats."

"How are you doing?"

"Doin' all right, other than I miss drinking," she lamented, looking at her plain punch. "But, I think my morning sickness is subsiding finally."

"That's good."

"You're not kidding."

"And how is Robin?"

"Fine, as you can see. Well, except for that mess with that tabloid," she said with a grimace.

"What mess?"

"Someone said the band split up."

"Oh, no!" she laughed.

"Yes. He was not amused."

"So, I guess he isn't quitting then?"

"Oh, no," she said with a smile. "I guess not!"

"You're happy about that?"

"Yes. He didn't want to quit. He's just encumbered by some guilt complex. I'm going to be fine."

"That's it! Put him to work!" she joked.

"Well, there's not a lot he can do now."

"Oh, yeah. George. Well, I guess he got his way after all."

"Unfortunately."

"How is he doing, by the way?"

"Pretty good, really. Grumpy," she laughed, "but otherwise, okay. Poor Debra had to go to the café yesterday for her first big shipment of goods, and it took longer than she thought it would. Boy, did he give her heck."

"He'll give himself another heart attack."

"Oh, he never raised his voice. Just grumbled at her constantly. He can be quite mean when he wants."

"I certainly wouldn't want to be on his bad side. He kinda scares me."

"Aw, he's a pussy-cat, really. I do hope things work out for them soon. I hate to see them so tense with each other."

"Makes you wonder, doesn't it? 'Bout relationships."

"Yeah. None of them come with guarantees, but you just have to do your best." She turned her head to see the approaching men. "But, between you and me…I think we did pretty darn good!" This made Rachel smile, and they both went to hug their respective loves with much gratitude.

The show went well, with Rachel selling two more pieces. Shelly remarked to her that her work had improved since Terry moved to America. Rachel, in true form, told her, "*Cállate la boca.*"

The following day Debra was able to stay home with her husband. He was no longer in a foul mood, but (more disconcertingly) was very quiet. Debra was so much in her own thoughtful mood that she really didn't notice his change. He was up and around quite a bit that day, turning the television off and on and generally being bored. He called Robin and their manager several times to the point of driving them crazy. Debra tried her best to make sure he was comfortable and wanted for nothing.

That evening, she helped him get ready for the night and sat down on the bed with him, asking him how he was feeling.

"Doing all right, I suppose... Appointment tomorrow, correct?"

"Yes, at ten."

He nodded.

She could feel the awkwardness of the situation. The tension seemed to grow the quieter it got. She had to ask something, and it was so difficult to ask. "George?"

"Yes?"

"Do you...do you think you can forgive me?"

He looked at her and saw the genuine sadness in her eyes. He didn't realize what she was going through. She wasn't the usual woman in that she kept her emotions to herself. How could he not forgive her? "Of course I forgive you. But...it may take some time to forget."

She nodded and hung her head down. "I understand."

He looked at her with pity and began to feel badly. Why did she accuse him in the first place? Maybe it wasn't all her fault after all. "Debra, I...I'm sorry as well."

This surprised her and she opened her black doe eyes at him. He felt something stir within him. He felt his heart pounding and was completely conscious of every beat, but it stayed steady. He was reminded of what that woman meant to him. He found himself tongue-tied.

"Sometimes I wish I had Robin's knack for poetry— for words. I'm the musician—the technician—and I can't always explain what I feel. I'm sorry for forgetting you—for taking for granted that you'll always be here, whether or not I pay any attention to you." Debra remained silent, shocked for what she was hearing. "Darling, I can't make it without you. I need you and yet I think about you as much as the very air I breathe. Is there a way to express something…to explain…" He shook his head with disgust at not being able to explain how he felt.

She caressed his cheek and said softly, "You just did." She leaned over and kissed him in what he felt was the first time in years.

Chapter Eight

It was a pretty Tuesday morning, and Shelly decided to pop into her studio while Robin went on a run. She sat at her drafting table and got out her sketchpad and flipped the pages to find a clean sheet. Upon doing so, she ran across the sketch she did of Robin after that first night they had spent together. She smiled at the memory, and couldn't believe it had only been a year since that had happened. This got her thinking. Was her mother right? Should she have hurried to have a child instead of enjoying being married first? There again, she certainly did not expect this to happen. When you're told that having a baby is a near certain improbability, it never enters your mind that it actually could be probable. Yet, she began to feel guilty. Did she rush Robin into this before he was ready? He seemed to be fine about it all. Also, she wasn't getting any younger (as the doctor so annoyingly reminded her), so it was probably a good idea to get on with it. Was having a baby going to put a complete and screaming halt to her art career? She began to feel it wasn't a good idea for Robin to leave her alone because she thought too much. She was over-analyzing the whole situation. She told herself to calm down. Of course she would paint again, she knew in her heart this to be true, and she did so want this

113

baby. The thought of it melted her. She was actually having Robin's baby!

She looked at her drawing again, lovingly going over a line with her pencil. She loved him so much and still couldn't believe that he picked her, when he could have had anyone. And now the fact they were having a baby really turned the fantasy to reality. The fairy tale had come full circle. The prince really did marry the servant girl and take her to his castle to live happily ever after. She smiled with the realization that a more important love had finally come before her artwork. She somehow felt a little more complete. Okay, a lot more. She had her own family. Not her parents or Robin's family—her own. This somehow also made her feel a little older. She was having to grow up and be responsible for someone else. What if it had been Robin who almost died from a flu or heart attack? How would she handle it? The thought made her cringe, and she wondered what made her think of such a thing. Truth is, she felt vulnerable. It's quite frightening to love somebody so immensely. What a snag life is! Which is worse—to not have anyone to love or to be a victim to love's enticing chains? She laughed at herself and admitted the latter is always the better. She prayed she'd never be alone again, and at that moment she heard a noise to discover her beautiful knight in shining armor (or rather, running shorts) had appeared at her door. She ran over to hug him.

"Oh, darling, I'm all sweaty," the knight pronounced with disgust.

"That's okay," she said, lavishing him with kisses, "I don't care."

"What's up?" he asked with wonder of all this affection.

"Oh, nothing. Just been thinking of how much I love you."

He chalked this up to hormones. "Well, I love you, too, dear." He smiled and studied her blue eyes. "You know what we should do?"

"No, what?"

"I'm going to shower up, and we're going to go shopping."

"Ooh! For what?"

"Well, we need a crib and all that for Baby, and you're going to need a new wardrobe."

"Ah, yes. In fact, I'm already wearing my fat pants."

"Ha-ha. There you go. We need to get you fixed up then."

"Sounds fun!"

She watched him regress back to the house and sighed with relief. He was happy, and his happiness was all that mattered in the world to her. Yes, this was good.

In the next couple of weeks Robin and Shelly managed to get the baby's furniture and other major necessities. Upon doing so, Robin came to the immediate decision that something had to be done about transportation. Rachel had all but kidnapped Shelly's little SUV, and all he had was his antique Jag and a manual Beemer that he hardly used and Shelly wouldn't touch, seeing how she knew nothing about a stick-shift.

"All right, my Shelly."

"What?"

"Now we're going to do some serious shopping."

"What have we *been* doing?" she laughed.

"Well, I'd like to know how you're going to get around town with the baby. Rachel's pretty much stolen your truck."

"Oh, yeah. Hadn't really thought about it."

"Anything come to mind?"

"I am *not* getting a minivan. I refuse."

He laughed at her refusal to follow the norm. She was still an artist and would never follow convention, no matter what may be considered the more practical thing to do. "Too conventional?" he laughed.

"Yes."

"Okay, then. How about a Hummer?"

"Now you're mocking me. How 'bout something in between?"

"Very well. Something nice and safe—big, but not too big, what?"

"There you go."

"Maybe something that parks for you, considering how you parallel park?"

"Thanks a lot! Well, at least I don't need that satellite thingy to tell me how lost I am," she said, giving him a sly look.

"Touché. Let's go."

They went to a large car sales that consisted of a variety of high-end sport-utility vehicles. Shelly laughed at the thought of her owning something nice and getting paint all over the interior, but she knew Robin was going to get her (and the baby) the best.

As they were being shown an interior with all its features by a very young salesman, Shelly felt the oddest sensation in her belly, and gave a surprised expression and laid her hand upon herself. Robin caught this from the corner of his eye. "What's the matter?" he asked with alarm.

Shelly smiled at him. "I think I felt a flutter."

"A flutter?"

"Yes. You know—the baby."

"You felt the baby move?"

"I believe so!"

"Wow!" He held her arms and gave her a kiss.

"I have to call the doctor," she said as she searched for her cell phone.

"Why?" he asked with curiosity.

"He said he may have a better idea of the due date when I began to feel it."

"Oh." He smiled watching her retreat to the show room to get out of the heat and make her call.

Shelly came back and announced that the doctor could not come to the phone, but that she left a message with the nurse.

They continued to shop, and eventually settled on a good-sized (but not huge) SUV in a deep red color. She followed him home in it easily, and thanked him for it when they arrived.

Once inside, she checked the answering machine to find a message from her doctor. He happily guessed her due date to be the 11th of December. She went into her office to consult a calendar, and Robin followed. "That's a Monday. How horrid."

"That's not bad. It shall be 'fair of face', as the old poem goes. Whichever day is wonderful, anyhow." He laid down his hand upon a table that was laden with mail. He looked down at them. "What's all this?"

She frowned and replied, "Oh, calls for entries."

He picked a couple up. "Entries to what? You haven't even opened these."

Shelly quickly gathered them up. "Oh, just to enter pieces for exhibits—no biggie."

"Well, why don't you?"

"Don't have anything." She stacked the letters neatly on her computer desk.

"Then paint something," he said cheerily.

Shelly started to show signs of frustration. "I just…I don't feel like painting, all right?"

"All right," he replied, throwing his hands to the air. Touchy subject, he thought, and wondered why.

"I'm just too distracted right now," she explained.

Robin began to worry, and watched her retreat back to the kitchen. He looked at the pile of papers here and there and pondered just how much the baby was going to affect her career. He went to find Shelly fixing some tea. "You know, whenever you're ready to paint after the baby is born, we can hire a nanny."

She softly laughed, but he was unsure if it was a good laugh. "A nanny. That's funny… No, I'm not going to have a child and then let someone else raise it."

"She wouldn't be raising it—just babysitting when we need to do something where we can't give her the attention she needs," he said defensively.

She picked up on the tone in his voice and looked him in the eye. "Very well…I'll think about it."

The next morning, Shelly kept her word and duly called her father in Ireland. He answered the phone himself and was quite surprised to hear that Texas accent once again. "Well, hello, my dear! It's grand to hear your voice, I do say. What can I do you for?"

"Well, I was wondering if you could put in a good word to your boss for George."

"George?"

"George is Robin's brother—Oh! I didn't tell you about him. He had a heart attack that same weekend we came to see you."

"No!"

"Yes. He's doing okay, but, well, let's just say there were reasons he had it, and it's just been very stressful around here."

"Well, I'm sorry to hear that, but *please*, don't stress out too much yourself. You are taking care of a little one. Don't put the weight of everyone's burdens upon your shoulders. You've got to pray about it and then let it go. That's what He's there for."

Shelly smiled. It's odd having a priest for a father. You're not sure in what mode he's speaking to you in. "Yes, you're right of course. It's just aggravating how everything happens all at one time."

"Ha-ha. Yes, it does seem to happen that way. I'm having to deal with a sick secretary, a broken fax machine, and a car that won't start meself!"

Shelly laughed. "Goodness! Well, I'll say a prayer for you, too, then!"

"Thank you," he laughed. "I certainly would appreciate it… Say, am I still going to get to see you in August?"

"As long as the doctor says it's all right for me to fly. We may have to fly you here."

"Oh, that'd be nice, too. I'm looking forward to it."

"So am I," she said honestly. "Well, I guess I'd better go."

"Yes, dear. I will put in our intentions for your friend at tomorrow's mass."

"Thank you, uh, Dad. No, no, wait, I can't call you that."

The man was very sad about that.

"Nope. I'll call you 'Papa' instead. 'Dad' has a bad connotation for me."

He cheered up. "That would be fine. Fine, indeed." He cleared his throat, which had tightened up on him, and added, "I'm glad I could help you, my dear. I'm always glad to help you."

"Good-bye!"

"Good-bye, dear. God bless."

As weird as it felt to call him 'Papa', she was glad she finally did it. Their talk had done much to calm her down, but she couldn't help but be distracted all day with thoughts of George and Debra. She got out a sketchpad and doodled.

The next day, George called Robin.

He took a deep breath and announced, "Well, Janice got us a spot on the Tommy Canales show."

"What? Oh, God," Robin growled with disdain.

"She felt it would help ease people's ideas of what's going on with us."

"When?"

"Next week—Tuesday."

"Are you going to be up to it?"

"Oh, yeah. I'm fine. Might have to borrow some of Debra's cosmetics to cover up my prison pallor, though."

"Ha-ha…" he laughed, but then let out a big sigh.

"What's up?" inquired his brother.

"Oh, just not looking forward to it, really."

George could feel the apprehension in his voice. The interviewer had a habit of getting very personal with his guests, and Robin had plenty that he didn't want to discuss. "Well, maybe he won't be so bad," George said casually. "He's calmed down a little in the past year or so. I think he got married."

"Someone actually married him?"

"Yeah. She's not from here."

"So she's never seen his show. That explains a lot," he joked.

"Ha-ha! Exactly."

"Oh… Say, doesn't Paul come next week?"

"Yeah, Thursday."

"Are you ready for him?"

"Yeah, yeah. Question is: is he ready for us?"

Robin chuckled and asked how Terry was.

"Oh, all right, I suppose. He plays his first real match tomorrow. Are you going?"

"Oh, yeah. It should be fun."

"Yes, a good break for everyone, except Debra. She can't make it, of course, but I'm looking forward to getting out. How's Shelly doing?"

"Oh, she's doing fine, thank you. She's stopped getting sick and dizzy all the time."

"That's good. Thought we were going to have to have her wear one of those bicycle helmets on a continual basis from all that fainting."

"Right?" he laughed. "How is Deb, by the way?"

"Crackers. You really can't have a conversation with the woman, she's so distracted." There was almost a note of hostility in the comment.

"I imagine so. When does her restaurant open?"

"A fortnight."

"Is she ready?" he chuckled.

"Can't say. I suppose one doesn't know until the day comes."

"Hmm. What's she going to do with her son while she's working? She's bound to have long days there."

"She's going to have him help her out there."

"That makes sense. I keep forgetting how old he is now. I haven't seen him for years."

"Yeah, you didn't see him last time he was here. You had gone to England."

"Oh, right." The mention of England had Robin's thoughts traveling off to the last time he was there with Shelly.

"Rob!"

"Huh?"

"I asked you if Donnie had told you about the numbers on the live CD over there."

"Oh, sorry, yeah, yeah."

"Funny, isn't it?"

"What?"

"Well, how that article in that rag ended up helping us instead of hindering."

"Yeah, no kidding. Everyone thinks it's our last recording."

"Maybe we shouldn't go on the telly and tell all after all. They'll stop buying it."

"Really. People will think *we're* the ones lying in the end—that we really are quitting."

"Humph."

"Well, you take care, and we'll see you tomorrow for Deb's opening. Can we pick you up?"

"Sure. They're not allowing me to drive yet, so that would be good."

"All right, then. See ya."

"Ta."

George hung up the phone and noticed thoughtfully how much more concerned Robin was for his well-being. It reminded him of just how close he came to the Grim Reaper, and it gave him a shudder. At the same time, though, it was comforting to know he cared. It was rare that brothers should be such good friends.

It turned out to be a warm day, and the evening sun blazoned across the great back garden of the Robin Parkers. Shelly had been in her studio desperately trying to get the creative juices flowing. She had managed to do a somewhat passable conté crayon drawing. She was on her way back to the house while she walked under the grape arbor, entranced by the cobblestone she walked upon. She ended up walking full-force into Robin.

"Hey there! You'd better watch where you're going!" He smiled down at her, holding her arms to steady her.

She laughed and apologized.

"What are you up to? Creating the world's next masterpiece?"

"No. Just desperately searching for my artistic side."

"Ah," he chuckled. He heard a noise above them and looked up, shouting, "Damn you, grackles! Shoo!" He reached up, banging at the trellis. He looked at Shelly and remarked, "Sometimes I wished I owned a gun—bloody grape buzzards."

Shelly laughed at him and studied his face. Little beads of sweat were beginning to appear on his forehead and she noticed how the summer sun showed up the faintest freckles along his cheek. His casual dress revealed his true personality and she knew that it was moments like this that made him seem human, and she adored that so much more than when he was pristinely dressed for the television with every hair in place and all flaws hidden by stage make-up. This was an odd thought considering what he was about to tell her.

"Well, guess what," he said with disdain.

"What?" She already didn't like the sound of it.

"We're going to be on the Tommy Canales show."

Shelly misunderstood. "W-Why?"

"To prove we're still alive and kicking."

"When?"

"Tuesday."

"Tuesday?! But, but, I've never…"

Robin knitted his brows, and then laughed. "No, dearheart…*George* and I."

"Oh!" she said with much relief.

"Although…"

"No way!"

"Ha-ha. No, I would never subject you to that."

"I can't stand that guy," she proclaimed with a disgusted look.

"I'm not crazy about him—he's a bit of an ass, really—but we need some publicity, and I don't think George is ready to make a trip to New York or L.A.. Orlando's not too bad."

"Well, I'm sorry for y'all, that's for sure."

"Would you like to go with us?"

Shelly thought for a second. She stopped to scare more birds away by banging on an arbor pole. "Nah. You and George can do some brotherly bonding."

"Mmm… Sounds fun with his cranky attitude of late."

"Ha-ha. It'll be fine. Come on," she grabbed his hand to take him to the house, "I've got some *cute* baby stuff to show you!"

"Oh, dear."

Chapter Nine

It was Saturday morning—Terry's big day. Oddly enough, Terry was calmer than others in his family—Debra especially so, for she was very concerned for her husband. This was to be his first real 'getting out' since his heart attack, and a sporting event at that! She was nervous about how excited he would get. She had seen him watching a game on the television—how was he going to handle a live game with his cousin playing? "Are you sure you're going to be okay?" she desperately asked one more time as she was walking out the door.

"Yes, yes, I'll be all right, love." He placed his hand on her back to help her out. "I promise to be a good boy."

"I'm sorry I can't go with you, but I just—"

"I know, I know. Go do your chef thing."

She paused at the door and looked at him. "I love you."

"I love you, too."

She was finally gone. George was left with an odd feeling. It had been so long since they said those three magic words, now they seem to say it constantly. It left him uneasy. Why does it take a death scare to make her say it? In all fairness, why did it never occur to him to say it either? He shook the idea from his mind and called Robin to pick him up.

The game was set to begin at 2:00. Terry went onto the field in his usual relaxed stride. Rachel got the crew box seats and was looking forward to having some down-to-earth fun with her friends. She hadn't been able to see Shelly in a while and chuckled at the fact she was beginning to show her pregnancy a bit. Shelly leaned over to George who sat next to her and said, "I've been instructed to monitor you."

"That isn't a surprise," he said nonchalantly.

"I don't know what I'm supposed to do if you do get carried away, though."

"Don't worry about me, Shell'. I'm solid as a rock and cool as a cucumber."

"Ha-ha. And full of similes! Well, as for me, I think it's great you're getting out and getting some fresh air."

"Yes, I agree. Mind you, I've been taking my little walks and sitting like the proverbial log at the pool, but this is definitely a good distraction. How can that be bad?"

"Right? But still, don't over do it, please… It is a shame Debra couldn't come."

"Yes, it is."

Her eyes were drawn from the field with the bitterness in his last comment. She looked at him, but said nothing; for it wasn't her place, but it was plain to see that it bothered him that Debra couldn't make the sacrifice to be there.

Rachel ended up switching places with Robin so that she was seated on the other side of Shelly. "I couldn't see with that stupid banner."

"Ah… You know what? I sure could use something to eat," Shelly said with a pat to the tummy.

"Hmm…I could use a hot dog, too."

"Robin, honey, why don't you get us something to eat?" Shelly hollered to her husband.

But, Robin was feeling quite lazy and was satisfied with his beer. "Uh…someone might recognize me."

"Not very likely with that hat," Shelly replied. Slightly perturbed, she looked at George knowing he shouldn't be tackling the steps.

Shelly drew in a breath and looked at Rachel. Rachel said dryly, "I know, I know, you're pregnant—fine, I'll go." She stood up and looked at the lot of them and said, "*Flojeros*." She walked off to get the food after Shelly gave her some money.

"What's that mean?" Robin asked Shelly.

"Just what you think it does." She snapped her head back, curls flying, back to the attention of the field. '*Lazies*' indeed, she laughed to herself.

"Humph," Robin grumbled. He slouched down in his seat and pulled his hat further down on his forehead. He wasn't feeling chivalrous that day and really didn't care.

Everyone was settled down (and fed) and was ready for some action. When the teams were introduced, Terry made a point to wave at his family. As the national anthem was played, the guys watched with humor as Shelly pelted out the words. "She sings better than you," George kidded Robin afterward. Robin looked at Shelly and wondered what their child would sound like. Would he get confused because his parents speak so differently, he mused. The game starting jolted him into present-day.

Rachel noticed how differently they were playing than when she saw him in England. The ball seemed to move in a fast, jerky motion throughout rather than the long lobs she had seen over there. But then the ball went to Terry, and there it went. She laughed at how much he stood out with his wild blonde hair and his three-quarter field length kicks.

The first half of the game passed by with no goals and everyone got up to stretch except Robin. Shelly looked at him curiously and came over to him and picked up his hat and discovered him asleep. "Was it that boring?" she asked with a giggle.

He came to and looked around. "What's up?" he drowsily inquired.

She laughed and informed him that it was halftime. "Go get me a soda," she commanded.

He slowly got up and did what he was told. George went with him risking both recognition and the steps, but he was eager to stretch his legs. This left the girls to visit for a minute.

"George seems pretty down," Rachel observed.

"Yeah. I don't know if it's because of what he's been through or Debra."

"What's up with Debra?"

("I do have a big mouth," thought Shelly.) "I think he was a little upset that she didn't come today."

"Well, she's got a lot to do." Rachel made no bones about it when it came to work. Terry had already learned that she works when she wants to and he can wait. Not that she put her work before him, but that she had been taught to be a responsible person and to do what was needed. Granted, Debra didn't have to work to put food on the table in her marriage, but Rachel couldn't help but have the work ethic that if you were going to do a job, you should do it well or you'll only be a nuisance to others.

"I don't know," continued Shelly. "I think they're a victim to bad timing. It's bad enough the heart attack and the café, but her son's coming, and I hope the poor kid doesn't feel like he's unwanted because of their distractions."

"How old is he?"

"Umm…fifteen or sixteen…something like that."

"Ugh. What an age. They're already having neuroses at that age—all he needs is grumpy, distracted parents."

"Really."

"How do you think Robin's going to do when your kid's a teenager?"

Shelly made a face and thought for a moment. She realized that when the child turned thirteen, he would be sixty-two! It jarred her a bit. "He'll probably lock himself up in his studio," she said with a glazed look.

"Wise idea. Make sure you're in there with him," Rachel replied with a final slurp of her soda. "And boys are such a pain. Least, my brothers were. They get all repressed and do stupid things, where as girls just want more clothes."

Shelly laughed at Rachel. "I thought Terry would mellow you out when it comes to men."

Rachel gave a sly smile, clenching her straw in her teeth. "Well, okay, they're not *all* pains."

"I thought so." Shelly felt she should make sure that Paul felt at home. She worried about the effect on George and Debra's relationship bringing him here. It was, in her opinion, rather going to bring them together or tear them apart.

The boys came back, and Robin dutifully brought Shelly her soda and also a candy bar. "Thank you!" she gushed. "How'd you know I wanted one?"

"It's about that time of day," he said with a smile. He touched her cheek and sat down beside her. He seemed to have woken up and she wondered what George might have told him while they were on their journey to the snack bar. He seemed to be very appreciative of her all of a sudden.

The game started back up and the team's new found energy perked up the lazy crowd. A score felt eminent. Back and forth the ball flew. They watched as Terry slid to kick the ball away from his opponent. The mood in the stadium changed as the spectators let out cheers and boos when a series of yellow flags flew for both sides.

"Lor', it's getting ugly out there," quipped George.

"And the masses were not happy," added Robin. "Hup! They got Terry!"

"What'd he do?" asked Shelly, who was completely lost. Rachel jumped up and started yelling Spanish epithets to everyone's amusement.

Robin explained the foul in a distracted tone, and then yelled out himself, "Aw, c'mon!"

Everyone watched with anticipation as Terry argued with the referee. When the ref gave the red card to him, the crowd went insane. Terry had been kicked out of the game. Immediately George and Robin stood up and started to leave. The bewildered girls got up after them. They followed the guys listening to their conversation until Robin remembered himself. He jerked around to find the girls and wrapped his arms around both of their necks. "Sorry, girls," he said. "You didn't want to see the end of it, did you?"

"No. I need to find Terry," answered Rachel before Shelly could say anything.

"That's what I thought," he replied.

They waited some time for Terry to come out. After a long discussion with his coach, a hot shower and seeing his people, he seemed to have calmed down quite a bit. He kissed Rachel with conviction with his hand behind her head, completely catching her off guard. He talked to them explaining to Shelly what a 'direct kick penalty' was. He felt certain he was set up and was relentless with his conspiracy theory. "They knew! They knew I was going to score before the game was over!"

"Ah! But did they know you were going to lose it with the ref?" asked George with his big brother tone. Terry simply glared.

At that time they heard the final buzzer. The game ended with no score on both sides.

"Let's go eat," George said with a smile. He enjoyed the game, anyway, and was ready to enjoy the rest of the evening as well.

Terry nodded with a hint of relief and Rachel took him to the truck, while the others went their way. Rachel was in the process of starting the vehicle when Terry grabbed the back of her head again and kissed her passionately. She enjoyed the kiss, and reciprocated. He then backed up and stared at her.

"What?" she asked with a nervous laugh.

"Thank you."

"For what?"

"For being you—for being this beautiful constant in my life. Life goes up and down, but here you are—just being beautiful. Don't ever change."

Rachel had no reply, for she had never had anyone speak to her like that before. She shyly turned the key to start the truck and smiled at him. He looked happy.

They went to Gioni's for Italian, and Shelly fulfilled her duty making sure George ordered something that wasn't bad for him. To assist him with his sacrifice, she also ordered the grilled chicken salad. He appreciated the kind gesture.

They had a good time at dinner, and by the end of it, everyone was laughing so hard at Terry's play by play of the game, that he stopped to ask George if he was all right.

"Oh, I'm fine. Great! Where as Shelly has gone into hysterics." They turned to look at her and found her face was almost as red as her hair and on the verge of hyperventilating.

"I'll be right back," she managed to get out. Rachel followed the giggling Shelly. "Geeze," Shelly laughed once they were in the ladies room, "I nearly peed in my pants!"

"Doesn't he kill you? Look, I'm crying!" Rachel exclaimed while wiping her eyes.

"You know, I'm so glad he moved here."

"Yeah, me too," Rachel gushed.

"I imagine so. He's a good guy."

"Yes, he is. I still can't believe he's going to marry me!"

"What did your parents say when you told them?"

"I haven't yet."

"Why not?" she asked with a laugh.

"I can't tell them over the phone."

"Oh, so you're going to go see them, then?"

"I can't with Terry playing now."

"Then bring them up here! We'd love to see them. At least, I'd like to see them again, and then they can meet everyone else."

"Yeah. I could do that, I guess."

"You're going to have to tell them sometime," she laughed.

"I know."

"Your parents liked him, didn't they?"

"Yeah, sure they did."

"So what's the problem?"

Rachel thought for a second. "The whole finality of it, I suppose."

"No going back, huh?"

Rachel returned the grin that Shelly was giving her. "Yeah, I guess so."

"There's always that hurdle. Just think about how much you love him, and it'll all fall into place."

Rachel opened her eyes wide and shook her head. "Yup. I've got to do it."

"Good for you! Congratulations."

When the girls came back to the table Robin told them that Debra was on her way. "Terrific!" Shelly replied. She was feeling quite celebratory.

"More wine, Rachel?" he asked.

"Yes, please," she replied, handing him her glass.

"None for you, I'm afraid," he told Shelly sympathetically. She replied with a pout.

"I feel your pain, dear," George told her.

"It's the beer I miss most."

"Yep, she's Irish," Robin laughed.

"I'm Texan, too," she laughed.

"Shelly, have you painted anything lately?" asked Rachel.

"Eh. I've done some conté, and a couple of pen and inks, but I don't seem to have the patience for painting. My concentration is *gone*."

"Well, just keep at it—don't get rusty."

"I'm taking to her to Italy to paint," chimed Robin.

"Oh, really? What a cool idea."

"It was Terry's, believe it or not."

The girls looked at Terry.

"Wha'?" he asked defensively. "Certainly you're not surprised I have a refined, sensitive side, do you?" he joked as he straightened the collar to his shirt.

"Sensitive—maybe. Refined—nah," Rachel replied quite comically.

Everyone laughed and Terry came back, "What was that you wanted for your birthday? A can opener?"

"Don't do that. That's what we were going to get her," George interjected.

Rachel was shocked by the joke. Certainly they weren't going to give her a birthday present, were they? She never realized her family could get any bigger, nor could it include members of a famous band. But there it was. She was marrying their cousin, whom they were very close to, so she was now related to them. She laughed at the fact that she, in an off hand way, was going to be related to Shelly!

They chatted for a while after eating when Debra finally came. "Sorry I'm so late, y'all," she apologized.

"Oh, we were going to leave you a note when we left along with some breadsticks," chirped Terry. Debra smiled back and kissed her husband. Shelly and Rachel studied George's expression. Up to that point, he had been having a good time. He wasn't mad, but had almost a sad look. It was as if the one thing he needed he couldn't have. The girls looked at each other with this same single thought, but then smiled at Debra when she said 'hello' to them.

She sat down and quietly asked George how he was. He replied that he was well and she took his hand and held it. He noticed with a chuckle that she smelled of produce. He was glad to have her at last.

They only stayed for a short while longer, and then everyone broke up to leave with Terry going home with Rachel.

Once at the studio, Rachel had him sit on the couch. "Terry, it's time we made this official."

"What?"

"Our engagement."

"I gave you a ring, what else do you want?" he laughed. "Ah! You want to set a date?"

"No, sweetie. Papa."

"Oh, Papa."

"*Sí, mí amor.*"

The young man shuddered at the thought of the burly man. He realized he actually feared him. He made a grimace, which made Rachel laugh.

"He's not as bad as all that… I think he liked you."

"Very well. Do you want me to call him?"

"I really don't think this is something you can do over the phone. I'd like to ask them up, if you don't mind."

Terry knew this had to be done. He would do the proper thing and ask for her hand. "Okay… Yes, of course. When?"

"I'll call them tomorrow to ask them to visit, so I'll leave it up to them. He'll need to take a leave of work."

"Yes, yes… All right. Sounds good."

She took his hand and smiled. "Are you okay?"

He cocked his head and smiled. "Okay? I'm going to marry the most terrific girl in the world. What else would I be?"

She shook her head. "Believe me, the pleasure's all mine." She kissed him and they began to get lost within each other. It got more and more difficult to tell where one began and the other one ended. Someone led the other up the stairs to the bedroom and they both fell into the soft bed where they continued to meld together.

Chapter Ten

The next day Robin called George.

"Hello?"

"Hello."

"Hey, Rob, what's up?"

"Wondering if you'd like to hook up tomorrow to discuss our plan of action before the disaster on Tuesday."

"No can do."

"Oh?"

"Doctor's appointment."

"Ah."

"Yes, once the great pop-star was all sex, drugs and rock-and-roll, now has diminished to doctors, drugs, and dietary requirements...with the drugs not being as fun as they used to be."

"But a sight less dangerous," he replied with a personal knowledge.

"Very true."

"No problem. How about today, then?"

"Sure. Debra's gone again."

"Already? It's only, what, 9:30?"

"Yes. Up with the hawks, eagles—some blasted bird."

"Chickens?"

"That's it. These Southern girls with their colloquialisms."

"Ha-ha. Shelly's got me saying things I thought would never come out of my mouth."

"Irritatingly infectious, isn't it?" George said almost venomously.

"Oh, I don't know. She makes me laugh," Robin said happily.

"Wait 'til you're married a few years, mate. It wears thin."

Robin recovered from this vile remark after a second then asked, "All right...who's coming where, when?"

"I'll come over there—sick of these walls—around, what, noon?"

"Sounds good. Maybe we can get Shelly to make some of her tuna fish salad."

"I never imagined her cooking for some reason."

"You don't cook tuna fish salad."

"You know what I mean, you silly git," he finally said with a glimpse of humor.

"See ya at noon."

"All right, bye."

"Bye."

Robin hung up, realizing things weren't as well as they ought to be with George, and felt guilty worrying about his brother's attitude instead of his well-being because of their interview Tuesday. He cared, naturally, but if George went on television with poison dripping all about, well, it wasn't a pretty picture to visualize. Robin knew he had to calm him down as best he could before that dreadful day. This may require a little under-handed assistance from Debra. She was, after all, the source of this bitterness, the least she could do was to come to his aid if needed. He felt this was a job he should delegate to Shelly.

He found his lovely lady already dressed and making her way outside. "Hey, whatcha doin'?" he asked.

"I have decided that today, I shall paint!" she said with a happy determination.

"Good for you! Hmm…"

"What?"

"Oh, nothing. You go right ahead, dearest. Good luck!" He leaned to give her a kiss.

"Thanks! I'll need it."

He watched her proceed to her studio, curls happily bouncing along. "Great… The one day I need her, she finally decides to paint," he thought. "Well, I suppose I must do this myself." He looked at his watch. "Just enough time." He quickly got ready and told Shelly that he would be back soon, that he had to run an errand but would be back for George at noon.

He drove to the Pavilion Mall, which was a conglomeration of beautifully architected strip-centers, all the while trying to think what to say. It wasn't his habit to interfere, but he knew that if something wasn't resolved, George might reach festering point at the interview in front of the world. Their interviewer had the knack to make you say things you normally wouldn't divulge and knew all your sensitive spots. He figured the best thing to do would just be honest with Debra.

He circled around until he discovered what was to be Debra's café. He came up and knocked at the door. Debra took her attention away from the hanging of a menu board to see her brother-in-law waving at her. She came over and unlocked the door, greeting him with a hug and smile. "Well, this is a pleasant surprise!"

"Yes, well, I come with a purpose… Is there a place we can talk?"

She knitted her brows and said, "Well, of course, Robin. Right this way."

Robin received many strange looks from the help as they went through. He wasn't sure if it was because they recognized him, thought him odd-looking, or were just annoyed by his interference of their work. Debra brought him into the cramped little office that was clearly meant for one-person occupancy.

"What's up, Robbie?"

He was struck blind what to say. "Uh…well… It's this way…"

"Is it that difficult?" she laughed.

He turned his brown eyes to her black. "Well, we have this interview Tuesday…"

"Oh, yes."

"And, well, George hasn't been in a very good mood lately…" Debra looked down with a guilty face. "Maybe you could have a chat with him? He may be a bit down about his appointment tomorrow." He knew the truth, but wasn't going to allude to it. He waited for a reply.

Debra felt trapped, and the small room wasn't helping. "I'm sorry this is affecting you, hon'… Uh, things have been a bit rough lately, and I'm not sure what to do about it."

"Frankly, I think he just wants a little more of your time," he replied carefully.

"The one thing I don't have."

"I realize that, but you can't put him on your back-burner right now—not after what he's been through."

Very unexpectedly to Robin, she began to cry. He didn't know what to do, and simply stood there with a shocked look.

"But what do I do? Give up the café? Tell my son he can't come? I can't *do* it all."

Robin snapped back to his duty. "Is there any way I can help? Or Shelly? Or even Terry? Delegate if you have to, Deb. He really needs to be your priority now."

Debra dried her tears and quickly went back to her professional mode. "Well…I guess Terry and Rachel could help with Paul, but they're getting married. They really don't have time to mess with him. You and Shelly have your hands full with the baby coming. It just seems so impossible."

"Debra! We can help. I mean it."

He only had slightly raised his voice, but it was enough to startle her. He was right, of course, no matter what else was going on, George needed to take precedence. "Okay, okay. You're right." She closed her eyes to release the last tears. "I'll do what I can."

"Will you talk to him tonight? Please?" The desperation was evident in his expression.

"Yes, of course," she replied.

"And I mean what I say. Shelly has already gotten the nursery ready. All that's left is a bit of decorating, but there's really not much else for her to do. Maybe she can polish some silver or something?"

Debra laughed. "I don't use silver here, but maybe she can lend a decorating hand to this place, too." She drew in a deep breath. "Well, I'll give you a call if I find something for her to do."

"Great! We'll both come."

Debra was doubtful that he would be much help, but appreciated the sentiment. She quietly said, "Thank you."

"No problem. Well, I must go now. George is coming to the house and we need to come up with a line of defense."

"That bad?"

"Oh, yes," as he reached for the doorknob. He looked to the floor and said softly, "There are *issues* I'd rather he not bring up."

"Yes, I can see that." She stood up from her chair and hugged him.

"Thanks, Deb."

"Thank you. I think I needed that little awakening."

He smiled and kissed her cheek. "See you later."

"Bye."

Robin left and she sat back down. She turned around towards her desk and laid her head down. Then, a knock on the door let her know she was needed back to work.

George's taxi showed up at Robin's on time. He came inside and looked around. "Where's Shelly?"

"She's working," Robin replied without thinking.

"What?"

Robin looked up. "Oh, she's in her studio."

"Ah."

"Have a seat." Robin led him into the living room. The men sat down and Robin looked pensive.

"So, what's the strategy?" George asked at once.

"I don't know," Robin drawled out slowly.

"I figure if we can keep him cut up, we'll be all right."

"Really depends on how he is that day. He's a moody bugger, and his mood sets the tone for the show."

"Disgusting. No continuity. Why are we doing this again?" he asked rather rhetorically.

"To prove we haven't called it quits." He saw the odd look on George's face. "We haven't, have we?"

George drew in a deep breath. "I don't know, Rob."

Robin began to panic. "You can't quit."

"Excuse me? Who was it that announced his retirement a couple of months ago with great determination?"

"That was a mistake, and it would be for you as well. More still, in fact."

"Why 'more still'?"

"If I had quit, it would be because something else is going to fill that void very soon. Whereas, if you quit—"

"I'd be sitting on my ass feeling sorry for myself?"

"Precisely," he replied, undaunted.

"Well…thank you for being so frank."

("I'm getting used to it," thought Robin.) "I should add that if you physically feel like you can't, well…"

"No, blasted, you're right. I guess… I guess I'm just a little scared."

Robin really felt overcome by seeing so many raw emotions in one day. "That's understandable. We'll just have to take it slow at first," he said with sympathy.

"Then pick up speed as we go along?"

"Yep."

"Very well. One trial at a time—first is Tommy."

"Yes," Robin grumbled. "I really don't want to discuss Shelly too much."

"I know… I'll do my best to not mention her at all."

"That's good, but I'm sure he'll bring up her expecting."

"We'll put it off as much as possible—keep him on the subject of music. The more we talk, the fewer questions he can ask. We'll say we've been working on tunes. Maybe he'll run out of time."

"Lying is very good."

"Well, actually, in my convalescence I have been doing some writing."

"Splendid! Who says you're ready to retire?"

George chuckled. "Can't stop the creative process—especially when you're bored to tears... I brought them along, by the way."

"Terrif'. I'll take a look at them in a bit."

"It's so refreshing not to hear 'take a butchers'."

"Terry's Cockney slang getting to you?" he laughed.

"Yes, quite."

"I hear he's going to do the engagement up formally."

George thought for a second. "Oh, you mean ask the father for her hand, and all that antiquated stuff?"

"Yes."

"How quaint! Imagine Terry being old-fashioned."

"I do. Whenever I get depressed about something I try to imagine Terry saying, 'Uh, Mr. Figer...Mr. Figger...Mr. Frogger...I, uh, could I possibly, uh...'"

"Ha-ha!"

The boys got a good laugh at their young cousin's expense. It was good for George to laugh.

They eventually felt that there was not much else they could do to prepare for Mr. Canales, so they went over to Robin's piano to play with the new tunes of George's.

Shelly eventually popped back in and greeted George with a hug and retreated through the kitchen. Robin got up to follow her in. "Darling?"

"Yeah, babe?"

"Do you think you could fix us some of your yummy tuna salad?"

"Sure!"

"Thank you so much."

"Not a problem. Whatcha been doin'?"

"We've been going over some music he's written."

"Fantastic! Nice to know he's keeping busy," she said as she got some ingredients out of the refrigerator.

"Yes, and we were going over some things before Tuesday. He's got an appointment tomorrow, so we won't have much of a chance to talk then."

"You do, too."

"Do what?"

She looked at him with a slightly hurt expression. "You said you'd go with me to my check-up."

"Oh, of course! I'm so sorry. Yes, of course I'm going with you, dearheart. I've just got so much on my mind right now."

"Everything okay?" she asked, concerned by his upset look.

"Uh, yeah… Let me know when you have it ready," he said, pointing to the tuna, "I'll come and get it." He gave her a quick peck on the cheek and returned to George. Shelly finished her salad, worrying about whatever he was worrying about.

It was nearly six when George was picked up by Terry who was on his way to see Rachel. He had left in a much better mood than what he came with. Working with Robin on music again made him feel he was back to the old routine.

He returned to his house and began to realize how tired he was. He reclined on his couch, almost shaking from his exhaustion. He took some deep breaths then started to worry about how stressing the next day would be and how it would effect Tuesday. He reckoned he should get as much sleep time as possible. He felt a nap was in order and soon fell asleep right where he lay.

Debra came home an hour later to find him out cold. She sat down quietly on the opposite couch and studied him for a moment. He seemed so at peace, she felt drowsy watching him. She looked at her watch and though that it was too early to go to bed just yet, and wondered what to do. She really wanted him to wake up so that she could visit with him. She was very concerned about how he was going to do the next few days, and even more concerned about how he and Paul were going to get along. She hoped her boy wouldn't put any undue stress upon him, but she really had no clue. A rush of guilt came over her for the fact she honestly didn't know her son anymore. He was no longer a child, and wondered how he was handling his teen years. Hopefully well—for George's sake.

She stood up, and in an unconscious act, knocked her knee against the coffee table. She quickly looked at her husband, who slowly opened his eyes. "Sorry," she apologized.

"Hello," he greeted her sleepily.

"How are you?" she asked softly as she squatted down beside him.

He slowly sat up. "Fine… How are you?"

"Tired, but fine."

"Busy day?"

"Yes, but I got a lot accomplished."

"That's good."

"What did you do today?"

George gave her a run-down of his day, and she listened attentively. This aided in waking him up. He then asked, "When is my appointment?"

She felt guilt once more for not knowing. "Uh, I'm not sure, but I have your appointment card." She went into the kitchen to find it and came back with it. "Two o'clock," she answered.

"Ah, good. I can sleep in."

"Yes, you need your rest. Just remember, it takes about forty-five minutes to get there."

"Oh, yeah."

Robin's little talk with her just kept replaying in her head, but she was caught not knowing what to say.

"Something wrong?" George broke into her thoughts.

"I'm sorry?"

"You were staring. Are you thinking of eating me?"

She laughed and sat back down. "No, I'm not that hungry."

"That's good. I may not be able to outrun you."

"You could tonight."

He began to study her, feeling a pensiveness emoting from her. He gave her a droll look and said, "Have a seat."

She didn't ask why, she simply got up and sat next to him. He raised a brow to look at her and she melted from his gaze. She was overcome with the emotion of it all, and she fought back the urge to cry. She had cried all the way home, and she had no desire to begin again. She knew she needed to talk, but didn't want to for fear of breaking down. To her surprise, he leaned over and gave her a powerful kiss and that was all it took. She did break down, and he was only slightly surprised. He said nothing, but pulled her to him. He closed his eyes, feeling her pain. He let her get it out of her system and he kept his cool. He just kept stroking her hair.

She finally settled down. She gave him a quick glance, but then turned away. She got up to get a tissue from the kitchen. He sat there for a second, shaking his head. He got up to find her. He stood behind her and finally said, "Why do you always run from your emotions?"

She didn't turn around, but shook her head. "I don't know what you mean."

"You know damn well what I mean." He waited a second and then turned her around to look her in the eye. "Why can't you admit you have too much on your plate right now?"

She looked down and softly said, "I...I don't know what to do."

Any anger he had was gone and all that was left was pity.

She looked up at him. "Tell me what to do, and I'll do it."

He was taken aback by the offering of another human's fate in the palm of his hand. He didn't like it. "If you want the café, you should keep it." She stared back at him. "Do you want it?"

"Yes," she didn't hesitate to say. This much she knew.

"Then keep it."

"But...but what can I do for you?"

He picked up his chin to look down on her. "I think you know what I need."

She nodded. She stepped back to find the telephone. She dialed it and waited. "Amy? Hey, can you cover for me tomorrow? There's something I need to do with George… Not much really, just the electricians… Well, there's that spot in the far end of the dining room that's out, and they're going to check the circuits… Okay, great. I really appreciate it… Sure, thanks, bye." She hung up and put the phone down on the cabinet. She looked at him and smiled nervously.

"Thank you," he said seriously.

She shook her head. "Thank you."

"For what?"

"For being so patient."

"Lots of changes, dearheart." He wrapped his arms around her waist.

"Are you nervous?"

"'Bout what?"

"Huh. This whole week."

"Oh, I don't know. I think it's the collective rather than any individual task."

"That's understandable. Sounds tiring to *me*."

"Yes. I'm afraid I'm going to run out of petrol by the time your son's here."

"I hope everything works out with his moving here. George, whatever happens, I'm on your side."

"Don't go saying that, Deb. There *will* be arguments. We just have to stick it out."

"Yeah."

George drew in a breath and looked around the kitchen. He saw Shelly's painting and thought of his brother. We all have our problems, he thought. He cleared his mind and asked his wife for something to eat. She happily obliged.

They went to sleep that night having bonded closer than they had in a long time. George felt whole once more, and Debra had her mind relieved of her anxieties. She was going to roll with the punches and accept things as they came and not before. She fell from consciousness with his words 'lots of changes, dearheart' ringing in her head. They both got their much-needed rest, preparing them for the next day.

It was earlier that evening, soon after George had left. Robin had chit-chatted for a bit with Shelly about how her art was coming along, and she happily replied that she had overcome her creative block. He watched her silently while she fixed herself a sandwich. He was feeling an overload of gratitude for his fair lady and eventually went back into the piano room. He sat down and began to play. At first, he tinkered around from one thought to another, but then settled down to a very somber tune. He began the song quite softly, increasing the volume as he progressed in getting lost in his thoughts. Before long, he was playing with intense feeling.

Shelly heard the captivating tune, and came into the room to watch. She knew she was seeing something both fabulously creative and embarrassingly raw in its emotion at the same time. She stood almost frozen in its spell until she felt a movement within herself that broke the spell. It was the baby. Whether it was upset by his mother's emotion or his father's playing, who knew, but he definitely wanted his say in the matter.

Shelly startled and held her tummy to comfort the situation. Robin's playing calmed down, and he landed the song softly at the end. He sat staring at the keys, almost in shock himself of what he had played. He felt his wife's presence and quickly turned to see her. He said nothing, but looked almost ashamed.

"Wow," she said quite seriously.

He gave her half a grin. "Didn't mean to disturb you."

She ignored the apology. "Where'd that come from?"

"Oh, well, the melody just popped into my head one day."

"What day was that?" she asked with a raised brow.

He averted the gaze, but confessed, "The day I thought I lost you… I had gone outside to think, and the air conditioning units were humming the tune to me."

"How odd."

"Yes… You'd think I'd have better things to do that day than to be picking up melodies from AC units."

"Maybe you were even more open to suggestion in that state," she said nervously.

"Yes… Yes, you're probably right."

"Robin, if…if I *had* died, would you have, uh…would you have gone back to your old habits?"

He knew exactly what she meant by that. It didn't take him long to answer back. "Very likely."

She stood playing with a curl of her hair, looking at the floor. "There are no promises in life, you know."

"Yes, I'm aware of that," he quickly retorted.

"But you have got to promise me that you'll never do that stuff again."

"I don't know that I can make that promise," he replied hopelessly.

She shook her head. "You don't think so? I think you can."

He got up and came to her like a scolded child. "You are my world, Shelly."

"Then you can make that promise to me. It's no longer just the two of us. If something should happen to me, there's still someone who would be depending on you."

He hadn't thought of that, and he felt bad for not doing so. "You're right." He stared into her big blue eyes and realized his life was never going to be the same again. Usually, that kind of thing scared him, but this time it was almost a feeling of reassurance. He finally was anchored to the ground—to reality—and he wasn't afraid. Instead, he felt he was home at last.

"So will you?" she persisted.

He stared hard. He knew he would have to keep a promise on this scale, and didn't want to be hasty because he was caught up in the moment. He slowly started to nod his head. "I promise."

She smiled warmly at this act of bravery. "Good."

He held her close and kissed her head. She let out a giggle, for the baby moved about once more. "What?" he asked.

"The baby kicked."

Robin laughed at her expression.

"He did that when you were playing, too."

"Humph. Everyone's a critic… Listen, you," he told the baby, "if I want to give your mum a hug, I most certainly will." He put his hand on her belly. "But don't worry, I love you, too." The babe wriggled around once again, and he could just barely feel it. "Hey, wow!"

Shelly burst out laughing. "He's talking to you!"

"I must be disturbing him."

"Oh, no. He probably already knows your voice."

He smiled and gave her a kiss.

"You ready to go upstairs?" she asked casually.

"A bit early for bed, isn't it?" he said, looking at his watch.

"Oh, I don't want to sleep," she replied with a grin.

"Yes, well, he'll probably have something to say about that as well."

"I'm sure he's happy his parents love each other so much."

"*That* is very true." He took her hand, kissed it, and led her up the stairs.

"Ya know, you ought to record that song," she said as they stepped up.

"Oh, I don't know."

"Too close to the nerve?"

"Yes, I'm afraid so."

"But there would be a lot of people who would appreciate it—some who weren't so lucky."

He stared at her with wide eyes. "Very well… I'll play it for George."

"It's really too good to waste."

He smiled. "Thank you." He knew he must think carefully about this first before he presented it to the world.

It was only a little after five the next morning when Robin was awakened by a clatter in the bathroom. He went in to discover Shelly unsuccessfully trying to get the diffuser to fit on her blow dryer, and then dropping it onto the floor. She had already showered and was a bundle of nerves. "What's up?" he drearily inquired.

"Can't get this damn thing to stay on," she replied as she continued to cram the aggravating object onto the instrument.

He took it from her and put it on but then placed the contraption on the lavatory. "What's wrong, dear?"

She looked nervously at him, assessing whether to tell him or not. "Well, I, uh," she stammered. She was practically trembling. "There was a little bleeding."

"Oh, God." He was suddenly very awake. She looked away, trying not to cry. "Do you need the doctor now?"

"No, no. I think I'll be all right until the appointment. It stopped, anyway." She turned to him so that he would hold her. "I'm so scared, baby."

He held her tight and said, "Everything's going to be fine. He'll be all right, dearheart. He'll be all right."

She cried, mumbling something incoherent into his chest.

He was still concerned, but her mumbling made him want to chuckle. "Darling, I can't tell what you're saying."

"Huh? Oh, nothing. Just…this may be the only child we will have, what a matter if we lose it, too?"

"Well, we just can't worry about something that hasn't happened yet, or may never happen. We've been told that already," he said in reference to her father. That seemed to be a recurring theme of late, and Shelly was tired of hearing it. She was tired of worrying.

However, the thought of that horrible ordeal repeating tore through him as it did her. He didn't want to go through that again, and he certainly didn't want to see Shelly go through that torment once more. He kissed her head and looked at her. He wiped her tears and asked, "Are you sure you don't need the doctor right now?"

"Yes…yes, I'm sure. I'm sorry to be such a bother."

"Well, this isn't your fault." He held her for a bit longer, slightly rocking her back and forth as he had done before. "Listen, you finish getting ready, and I'll fix us some tea and toast. How's that sound?"

"That sounds great," she said with her first smile of the day.

"Then so it shall be done," he said with a bow as he left the room.

He went downstairs and went into the kitchen. His mind was a blank when he got there. He dropped his head to the end of a wall cabinet, closed his eyes and took a deep breath. It's not easy being the strong one when you're worried to death yourself.

She eventually came down looking very self-conscious. She had finally broken down and put on one of her new maternity outfits. Her overalls just couldn't fit her anymore.

Robin saw her and lit up. "Well, you look very pretty." She gave him a grimace and he confirmed, "You do!" He came over and gave her a quick kiss. "You're more beautiful now than I've ever seen you. You're glowing. You have this wonderful aura of womanhood." He gave her a big smile.

"I don't know if you're being poetic or patronizing."

"Poetic, my sweet." He picked up her hand and kissed it. "You inspire me."

"You're really full of it, sometimes," she said, still doubtful.

"I'm serious!" he laughed.

"Well... Thank you!"

"That's better."

They ate their light breakfast and occupied their minds with the television before they left for their appointment. They arrived at the doctor's office, and this time she begged him to stay in the exam room with her.

"Please stay, Robin. I mean, you're going to have to get used to seeing them work on me if you're going to be in the delivery room."

This struck him. He never really gave it a thought. "I am?" he asked weakly.

"You'd better be! You have to be there so I can curse you out for putting me there in the first place."

This made him laugh, and he consented to stay with her in the exam room. Shelly's uneasy expression came back.

"Plus, I just need you here."

He caressed her hair back and kissed her.

They waited for the doctor in silence. Dr. Hodges eventually came in and seemed to be in a cheerier mood than the first time they met him. However, his mood altered slightly at Shelly's news of what happened that morning.

"Oh, dear. I should have said to hold off until I saw you again. Actually, it's not unusual this early on. I think, however, you may need to abstain a while still, considering all our risk factors. Sorry, but that's the way it goes."

"Well, we don't want any problems," Shelly said with her hands raised.

"No, certainly not," Robin stressed.

"Fine, fine. Okay, well, let's get you examined and my leech lady will get a blood sample... Uh, have you given any thought to whether or not you want to check for Down's syndrome?"

Shelly looked at Robin. "It's your call," he answered.

"I don't want to," she quietly said.

"Then you don't have to," the doctor replied. "That's why it's called an option... Well, go ahead and change and I'll be right back."

The doctor left, and Shelly prepared for her exam. "Are you okay about that?" she asked.

"I am if you are. If you don't think it's worth the risk, then I respect that."

"Would you feel better knowing, though? Really?"

"Well...I am the control freak, as you remind me so *very* often..."

Shelly bit her lip, unsure of herself.

"But if you don't want to, it's simply not an issue. It won't be done. We can cope with whatever happens." He laughed softly. "We always do."

She grinned. "Yes, that's true."

The doctor returned and did his exam. "Everything looks fine, Shelly. You seem to have a pretty low-lying placenta, in which bleeding can be triggered by intercourse, sneezing, any kind of strain, really. This should decrease as you go along, but, like I said, I think we need to play it safe—for a while, anyway."

"Of course," they both answered.

He looked at Shelly and smiled. "Now, you let me know immediately if this becomes something worse, won't you?"

She nodded. The doctor continued, reviewing everything he had said and making sure they understood. "Now, how would you two like something nice to listen to?"

Robin worried that the doctor was trying to get into the music business, until he saw him bring over a device and 'grease' it up. He put it on Shelly's stomach and turned it on. He moved it around a bit until they heard a rapid beat. Shelly immediately smiled, knowing what it was.

"What's that?" Robin asked.

"That's your baby's heartbeat," the doctor replied.

"Really? Wow. Now that *is* music."

"Yes, it is. Yes, it is."

Chapter Eleven

Robin looked at Shelly's smiling face and tears (of joy this time) rolling down her cheeks. It was one experience after another being married to her, and he wouldn't miss it for the world.

When the doctor was done with his patient, he sent the happy couple on their way to the nurse with the reassurance that all looked well. Shelly gave her donation reluctantly and left the office feeling tired, but relieved.

Once outside, she apologized to Robin.

"What for?" he asked with a puzzled look.

"One: for being a spaz. Two: for the restriction on our love life."

He laughed. "Well, one: it was only natural, and two: don't worry about it. Celibacy is not completely foreign to me." He made a silly face that made her giggle.

"It's just so unfortunate that I finally enjoy it, and now I can't have any. It's like having one bite of chocolate cake—it only makes you want more."

"Ha-ha. Oh, well, we do what we must. Let's go home and take a nap."

"Now *that* sounds lovely!"

"Well, Mr. Parker," the cardiologist concluded, "you seem to be recovering well. You must be doing pretty well on your new diet?"

"Unfortunately," George grumbled while Debra snickered.

"Well, it's a small price to pay. You just have to find healthy replacements to indulge in." The doctor was concerned. Physically, he was doing very well, but otherwise... He had seen George on television before. He always seemed to be a jovial, joking person, but he wasn't jovial now. "You know, George, there are people you can talk to if you're having issues about your situation. You're definitely not alone."

George took the hint that his sour disposition finally gave him away. He didn't know what to do, so he said nothing.

"Hold on a moment," the doctor said quickly disappearing only to reappear with a newsletter in hand. "This hospital has all sorts of support groups and private therapies... Maybe you'd like to look this over. Major life changes call for major readjustments, and no one is perfect. We all need a little help from time to time."

George took the paper, but remained quiet. He was afraid and confused, but wasn't used to opening up to anyone, except for maybe Robin. Even then, he felt Robin couldn't begin to understand what he was going through in this case.

He turned to look at his worried wife, who was only starting to grasp how this had affected him. He knew he was going to have to start relying on her, and wasn't accustomed to using her in that capacity. She had always been simply a nice addition to his life—a companion at most. For the first time, they were having to take life seriously, and he felt his love for her was being tested. He sensed he was being punished for taking things for granted all this time.

"Well," Dr. Epstein finally said, "keep up the good work, and keep walking!"

"Thanks, doc."

George and Debra took their leave with George getting to drive at last. They went along in silence until Debra noticed something. "Where are we going?"

"To the beach," he replied nonchalantly.

"Oh, why?"

"Because," he paused while he made his turn, "I want to enjoy you whilst I can."

Debra smiled a little to herself.

They got to a beach with pretty white sand and strolled along, for the most part in silence or in observation of the weather and wildlife. They found a nice, dry dune to sit upon and watch the waves. Eventually George asked, "Have I changed?"

Debra was genuinely scared to answer that question. "Anybody would in your case," was her safe reply.

George rolled his eyes. "Yes, in other words?" he asked rhetorically. "I don't want to go to a shrink," he groaned like that of a boy who didn't want to eat his vegetables.

"I'm not going to make you."

He could tell by the tone in her voice how she felt about it. A slight sense of guilt overcame him. "Tell you what; can you put me on probation?"

"Probation?"

"You know, can you give me some time to straighten myself out before you throw me into the loony bin? I know I've been an ass lately—"

"I haven't helped."

"Well...nevertheless...but, I just need time."

Debra grinned at his agreement and said, "Okay, then. You've got, say, three months, or we toss you in and throw away the key."

"You're being generous, but I'll take it and run... I do miss your French food, though."

"Well, I'm picking up some really healthy recipes."

"Really?"

"Yes, in fact, that is what my café is based on—healthy, delicious food."

"It's not going to be French?"

She shook her head. "No, babe. I'm not having a restaurant you can't eat at."

He was touched by the sentiment. Maybe she really did think of him more than he thought. "It'll be like old times," he mused.

"Yes, it will."

George took the hand he held and wrapped it behind his back as to put her in front of him. She was reminded of why she fell in love with him in the first place—that leonine attitude as he looked down at her. She saw that strength she hadn't seen in some time. He kissed her hard with his free hand behind her head. She felt herself swoon. He could still do it to her. Afterwards, he said softly, "I kind of feel we're starting over."

"Me, too," she agreed.

They walked around some more, and soaked in the sunset. They felt they were teenagers again, reveling in the simple things. They went home with smiles on their faces.

Both of the Parker brothers went to bed early that night to make sure they were rested and ready for combat the next day.

They took a private jet to Orlando that morning for an afternoon taping. They sat in their seats on the plane facing each other, but looking out their windows. Both were so distracted with their thoughts of home that their manager sat studying them, hoping to God they weren't going to go on television with those sad, distracted faces. "Hey! You two! Cheer up!" he hollered.

They both turned to smile at Donnie. "Bugger off!" they said in unison.

"There are my boys!"

They laughed and looked at each other. "You all right, mate?" George asked Robin.

"Yeah, and you?"

"Tired. Long day yesterday."

"Is all going well?"

"Oh, yeah. Doctor was quite happy... Wished it didn't take so bloody long, though."

"I hear ya. Doctors take forever. Took us an hour before we were even seen by a nurse."

"Oh, you went to the doctor as well?"

"Yes—Shelly's check up."

"And how is everything?"

Robin paused. He didn't feel like getting into the events of that morning. "Everything seems to be going well. We got to hear its heartbeat."

"Oh, how neat… You're rather enjoying this daddy thing, aren't you?" he asked, noticing the grin on his face.

"Yes, but I can't help feeling guilty."

"'Bout what?"

"Do you realize when he's twenty, I'll be seventy?"

George couldn't help but laugh for the funny face that he made at the remark. "Don't worry about it. You're the healthiest horse I know…apart from Terry, of course."

"Well…still. What if it's a girl? I'll be creaking down the aisle to give her away…"

"Ha-ha!"

"It's not funny," he pouted.

"Uncle Simon lived to be one-hundred and four. I obviously got Dad's ticky ticker in the family, so you'll be around long enough to torture the poor creature for quite a while yet."

"I have a feeling you will, too… 'Oh, God Dad! Does old Uncle George have to come over? I've got me friends here!'" he imitated the future teenager. George laughed and Donnie chuckled to himself catching this enactment.

"'Bloody old fool keeps leaving his teeth on the table!'" George finished for him.

"Poor thing, coming into this wretched family," Robin surmised.

"Oh, we're not that bad—just a wretched sense of humor."

Donnie leaned back to close his eyes. They were back to normal, he felt. The guys did seem a little more at ease.

George rested his chin on his arm to study the earth below while Robin looked around the cabin, bored. Presently he said, "Been a while since we've been in a plane this size."

"Hmm? Oh, yes. Nice little jet, this." George put his chin back onto his hand to stare outside again. "I like it— much more fun to fly... Flying...flying." He drifted off as if trying to recall something, and then apparently, he did. He raised his head with his eyes opened wide.

"What's the matter?" Robin quickly asked.

George was jolted from his thoughts. "Oh, uh, I just remembered something."

"What? You left the gas on?" Robin joked.

"Ha, no. Nothing."

Robin was quite sure it was something—something important, too. He found the change in his brother since his heart attack unsettling. It was as if he had a secret world he had to escape to where only people with the same experience could go. Robin didn't like this separation from him, for they had always been tight, but now George had something more in common with their father than he, who merely resembled him. He almost felt jealous, knowing George could truly feel for the parent they missed so much. On the whole, Robin was glad his heart was fine; he had a child on the way that needed him to be around. But still, he missed the old George.

They arrived in Orlando in good time. It was sunny and fair, but gloom was on their minds. Once inside the studio, however, the adrenaline started to course through their veins, giving them the spark they needed to deal with the notorious Mr. Canales. They had agreed to be as slippery as eels and Tommy was about to experience the Parkers at their best.

Taping had begun after a brief introduction to their interviewer. The syndicated program had a studio audience of primarily tourists of the area and they cheered loudly at the introduction of Parkers.

The boys came out and shook his hand. They towered over the 5'6" man, and he felt a little self-conscious. They took their seats and he welcomed them to the show. A couple of girls hollered out to the guys and in turn they chuckled and waved, causing more calls.

"Well, it seems you've got some fans in the audience today," Tommy said impatiently.

The guys simply smiled.

"So, you two have been pretty busy lately. Your *Live in New York* is doing great—being on the charts for a solid month now. A lot of people say this is your last album, is that true?"

"No, no. We're just taking an unexpected vacation, that's all," George replied.

"Yes. You had a bit of a scare there. Open-heart surgery, I believe."

"Well, actually they were able to do it without cracking me open, though, so that helped—recovery time, and all that."

Tommy winced a bit from the graphic description, being of a delicate temperament. He managed to ask, "Had you had trouble before?"

"No, not really."

"What triggered it then, do you know?"

"I didn't have time for the nervous breakdown that I so very much deserved. Your system has a way of telling you that under no uncertain terms that something's amiss."

"How much work was done?"

"I only had a little blockage in a vein in my neck that they had to scrape out," here, he showed his scar, "and they did one bypass on my heart, which resulted in them taking a vein out of my leg about here," he said with a motion to his calf.

Tommy really could have done without the details, and missed the opportunity of asking why George was under so much pressure by trying to recover himself. He could only think to ask, "All's well now, I hope?"

"Oh, yes, thank you. Running like a top. Just got a stamp of approval from the doctor yesterday."

"Good, good. And are you doing fine as well, Robin?"

"Oh, yes." He worried the next question was going to be about Shelly, so he averted his attention. "I run every day. I mean, I can't out run our cousin, but I can come close."

"That's right! Your cousin is playing," he paused to refer to his notes, "for the Miami Captains."

"Yes, he is."

"Terry…"

"Dunham."

"Ah, yes. He's creating quite a buzz."

"He has a habit of doing that," chimed George.

"Adjusting to America, is he?"

Both guys laughed. "Oh, yeah," they answered.

"It must be difficult to get used to another country, and Miami is a culture on its own accord."

"True," George agreed.

"But, he seemed to slip into it quite well," Robin added.

"Well, that's good. He's not married, correct?"

The guys looked at each other with a look of 'this is a safe subject'. George went on, "No, he just got engaged, though."

"Really? To a Miami girl?"

"Yes. Actually, she's Puerto Rican."

"Wow, well, that's great! He really did get into the culture, then?"

The boys looked slyly at him wondering if he meant any more than that. "Yeah," they both said slowly.

At this point, Tommy laughed, "Do you always say things at the same time?"

"What do you mean?" they both asked quite on purpose. This, of course, made the audience hoop with laughter, and the guys threw a wry smile back at them. George then said, "Oh, it's Robin. Annoying, isn't it? He does that with his wife all the time as well." George quickly blinked and turned to see Robin who stared back with an 'I'll kick you later' look in his eye. Naturally, here it came.

"Robin, how is your wife? I hear congratulations are in order?" Tommy asked with a great big smile.

"Thank you, yes, she's fine."

"You're expecting your first child—when?"

The audience clapped with happiness for him, and he managed to smile back. "December," he replied meekly.

"Just in time for Christmas!"

"Yes," he said with a bit more pride. He was trying hard not to look nervous.

"She had lost a baby before, correct?"

Robin held his breath, and George's heart broke for him, but Robin kept his composure. "Yes, unfortunately."

"Sorry you had to go through that. I had a family member with the same situation—tubal pregnancy, right?" He waited for Robin's nod. "It was pretty rough, but you're lucky to have another chance, though, aren't you?"

"Yes, we are." He smiled, even if he wanted to rip the man's head off.

"Well, congrats again, and hope all goes well."

"Thank you."

Robin could breathe again. It was over. Like a flash, all he dreaded had come and gone. That wasn't so hard after all, and only because the guy had had it happen to his own family. It still stung, however, and he missed the next question altogether for thinking about it all. The audience laughing brought him out of his thoughts, but he chuckled along anyhow, not knowing what he was laughing at.

"Do you see it that way, too, Robin?" Tommy asked.

He felt like a kid in school again, not paying attention to the teacher. George caught the subtle expression and came to the rescue. "No, he just sits and nods at Donnie—it's not worth the argument." Robin smiled at his brother as a thank you.

"Well, it's nice to know you're not breaking up. Isn't it, folks?" The audience clapped and hollered. "So when do you feel you'll be able to tour again, George?"

"Well, hopefully soon. We'll probably work it out in stages. I've learned not to push it."

"Good! I think everybody pushes themselves too much these days."

"True—especially Americans."

"Ah, yes. The great corporate cogwheel." The man noticed how quiet Robin had gotten and decided to stir him up. "Robin, are you all prepared for fatherhood?"

"I believe so. How does one prepare, really?"

"Ha-ha, yeah, you're right there. I haven't had to worry about such things, yet."

"You may soon though, huh? Just getting married and all that?" Robin was running on all pistons once more.

"Yes, well, we're in no big hurry there and we've got plenty of time."

"Oh, yeah, she's pretty young, what?" The audience laughed at the question. Robin was out for revenge, and George was loving it. He sat back with his arms crossed and big grin on his face.

"Ha, well, youngish," the man confessed. He didn't like being the interviewed. He refused to be upstaged, though. "Did you ever think you were going to be diaper changing at the age of forty-nine?"

"Nope," Robin plainly retorted. The audience chuckled again at his funny expression. He was not going to play coy, but instead went for self-mockery, which is a sure-fire way of undermining your enemy's tactics of making you look like a fool. "But I'm glad I'm going to get to!" More hoops and hollers.

Tommy gave up on Robin with his suit of armor, and threw a quickie at George. "You're just completely staying out of the baby business?"

"Oh, Lord, yes." (More laughter from the crowd.)

"Neither you or your wife have any children?"

"My wife has a son from her first marriage."

"And how old is he?"

171

"Sixteen."

"Ah, what an age. Does he live with you?"

"He will as of Thursday."

"You're kidding!"

"I kid you not."

"What made him move here?"

George hadn't prepared himself for that question, and knew he had to be careful. "Dunno, really. Probably thought Miami would be a nice change from Seattle."

Tommy laughed. "He probably figured there would be a lot more bikinis to look at."

George laughed and nodded. "I imagine that was a factor, indeed."

"Yes, and it wouldn't hurt to mention your step-dad's an M.P., either, huh?"

George just chuckled as a reply.

Tommy felt he wasn't going to get much more out of them (and he was feeling a bit tired of them as well). Fortunately for all three men, time had expired and he needed to wrap it up. "Well, guys, I want to thank you very much for coming up to talk to us for a while. Are you going to leave us with a song?"

"Yes, of course!" they replied in stereo.

He chuckled at them once more and announced, "*Live in New York—The Ministers of Parliament*—go out and get it everyone. It sounds great!"

"You actually listened to it?" asked Robin.

"Yes, I did. It's good."

"Thanks!" said the brothers. They shook hands with their host and waved to the applauding audience. They went to the stage and sang an old favorite and then it was over.

The boys wasted no time getting back into their little jet to get back home.

They sat back down in their seats just as they came, with Donnie chuckling to himself on his own. They looked at him and began to laugh. Soon, all were laughing including the young attendant, although she didn't know why; it just seemed like the thing to do. She brought them some sparkling water with a smile and retreated back to her station.

"Well, Robin," George began, still smirking, "I'll have to say I'm very proud of you."

"All in a day's work."

"You realize he'll probably never ask us back?"

"Oh, but why not?" he asked in a mocking sad tone.

"He doesn't like it when people ask *him* questions."

Robin's face turned dark. "Sodding, great ass. Who the hell does he think he is announcing such a thing to the world? Just because we're popular does not give him or *anyone* the right to delve into such a private subject. Why is it our lives are supposed to have no personal aspect? I can understand announcing births, deaths and marriages, but my God! That is *way* past acceptable. He has *no* right."

George was moved by the expression of his damaged feelings and regretted going to the interview. He couldn't comprehend what to say to him. "Absolutely," was all he could get out.

"Prat." He was mad and scared that Shelly would see the program.

"Complete prat," he agreed once more. George wondered if he was going to continue to go through the whole list of filthy names he knew. He wasn't going to stop him, either.

"But you handled him, mate. Beautifully!" He raised his glass to him.

Robin breathed and grinned again, clinking his glass to his brother's. "Tell me again all the gory details of open-heart surgery?"

"Ha-ha!"

"How'd you know that would get to him?"

"I've seen him on the telly a few times. Someone mentioned a tooth extraction once, and he looked like he was going to pass out."

"Ha-ha. You had him actually turning green! I loved it... Oh, by the way, thanks for the save."

"Don't mention it. I think I zoned out for a moment there myself. How anyone with such a monotone voice gets a talk show, I'll never figure out."

"Incredible... Idiot!" Robin added to his list of names. "Well, I'm glad that's over with."

"God, me too." George was taken over by an enormous yawn.

"Why don't you get some rest?" Robin asked with concern.

"That doesn't sound like a bad idea. You ought to do the same—you look shot."

"Yeah, I didn't get much sleep last night as much as I tried. Rough couple of days."

George reclined his seat as far as it would go, and almost immediately fell asleep. Robin followed suit, but as tired as he was, he found it hard to get that blissful state. It was going to take a while to wear off the amount of adrenaline that he had incurred.

That night, however, he finally slept like a baby, curled up with his wife, and all was right in the world once again.

Wednesday passed uneventfully. The only person who was full of energy that day was Debra. Her son was coming home, and she was beside herself. Not only was he moving in, but she hadn't seen him in well over a year. She couldn't wait to see how much he had grown and changed. She also couldn't wait to talk to him. She was unable to get out of him over the phone as to why the sudden urge to move in with her—not that she minded, but was concerned how things were between he and his father. Her ex-husband had made a terrible spouse, but had always been good with their son in the past. The man enjoyed having someone who depended on him—someone who was subordinate to him. The equality necessary for a marriage highly irritated him, but children were okay as long as they needed him for support. Debra figured Paul must be trying to gain some independence (as all teenagers do) and was locking horns with his father. She seriously hoped there would be no issues with George.

George could be very bull-headed and demanding, although not completely unreasonable. He was simply a perfectionist. Not so much in the obsessive-compulsive way, but in the desire to have everything running smoothly. Slacking was simply not allowed and anyone who worked for him had to pull their own weight. However, he was not into controlling anyone. In fact, he preferred not to be responsible for another human being's existence—hence, no children for him. He would leave that for people like his brother who was into responsibility.

She wondered if Paul had turned lazy. She rather felt he might have. She really, with all her imagination and what she knew of the two men, could not predict how they were going to get along living together. They always seemed very amicable during visits, but that meant nothing. Having Paul under George's roof was definitely going to be an experience for all.

She was a bundle of nerves, deservingly.

Thursday came whether she wanted it to or not. Although she stayed home, she was constantly calling the café to make sure the refrigerators had been repaired successfully. They had worked fine until the day before, and she took it as a personal insult because she wasn't there.

She and George arrived early at the airport. He sat inconspicuously wearing his sunglasses on a bench where he hoped he wouldn't be spotted. His features were more recognizable than Robin's, and he tended to attract more attention. His wife paced back and forth in front of him.

"We should have sent a limo," George grumbled.

"I am *not* bringing my son home by courier," she snapped.

"He probably would have thought it a hoot."

"No, he would have thought we felt we had better things to do."

"Well, at least sit down. You're going to create a ditch in the floor pacing like that. People with prams will get stuck in the ruts."

She had to crack a smile imagining women with their baby strollers getting wedged in the ruts she made in the floor along with anyone else rolling their luggage. She sat down obediently and received a kiss on the cheek for doing so. He patted her thigh and said, "You're not usually this nervous about him coming."

"He's not usually moving here."

"Gotcha." He picked up her hand and held it, patting it gently with his other.

They eventually announced the arrival of Paul's flight. Debra had succeeded in making George nervous as well.

The young man eventually came through with a small gym bag strapped over his shoulder. Debra was astounded by his height—he had surpassed her own. She quickly came to him and hugged him. "Hi, baby!"

"Hi, Mom," he answered with a smile.

George came trailing up. "Hello, Paul," he greeted with a big smile. He shook the boy's hand and he smiled back.

"Hi, George. You…you all right?" he asked nervously.

George laughed. "I guess it depends on what sense. If you mean my heart, yes, I'll be just fine, thank you."

The boy bashfully smiled back and they went off in search of his luggage. They inquired of his flight and his mother kept reiterating how much he'd grown. George looked at Debra and noticed a glow he hadn't seen in a long time. Paul was truly her pride and joy.

Paul, in turn, would just give her a sidelong grin. He had missed her as well. He found his bags and off they went to the house.

They got the young man settled in, and he studied his new room. He felt it needed a few posters to look like a proper dig, but otherwise it was definitely bigger than his old room. He was beginning to get nervous about the whole thing. Was it right to move here? He was unsure, but he knew one thing: he had to get out of Washington.

He came back downstairs after leaving his bags to find his mother in the kitchen. "Do you want something to eat, honey?" she asked.

"No thanks."

"You know," she began and looked around for George, "I'm sorry, but there's not going to be a lot of pizza and hamburgers in this house. You'll have to go out for stuff like that. You understand, right?"

"Oh, yeah," he said in complete agreement.

"We just can't have it around him, it's just too cruel. He loves pizza… And Paul, please be kind to him. I can't have him stressed at all."

He was about to give her a look of 'whatever', but saw the genuine concern in her eyes and realized this was no joking matter. "Okay, Mom."

"Thank you." She gave him a hug and a smile. "Lemonade?"

"Got any soda?"

"No."

"I guess I'll have some lemonade."

"Good choice!"

The boy took his drink and sat at the bar. He remembered being much shorter the last time he sat there. His mom came over.

"Honey, I hope you're going to be happy here, but realize that you are going to have to answer to George as well. He is your step-father."

"He's got to be better than the alternative," he said almost angrily.

Debra was confused. "What do you mean?"

"Ah, nothing."

"Well, obviously it's something."

He had a hard time keeping a secret from her, which drove him crazy. "Well…" he was unsure how she was going to take this, "Dad's got a new girlfriend."

"Oh," she simply said.

"Yeah. She moved in and she's a real…well, ya know."

"Oh," she said again, but longer. She didn't know how to react. "Is that why you wanted to move?"

"Pretty much."

"And at least with George you know what you're dealing with?"

"Huh," he laughed, "yeah."

She smiled and he smiled back with a guilty expression.

"Come on, let's go find Old Reliable."

As they entered the living room from the kitchen, George entered from the staircase.

"Hey, hon', watcha doin'?" Debra asked cheerfully.

"Taking drugs."

Paul's eyes lit up.

"Don't get excited. Just heart medication, none of the funny stuff for me anymore, mate."

Paul thought he was about to see George act like a real rock-n-roller, but was actually relieved.

"Well, are we going to dinner?"

"I thought I'd just make something here," Debra replied.

"Oh. Oughtn't we to celebrate his arrival, though? You're already going to have to cook Saturday as it is." He saw the look in her eyes of concern. "Don't worry about me, sweetheart. I've got this restaurant thing down. Let's feed the boy some Miami food and season him up!"

She laughed. She looked at Paul. "Are you sure you're not hungry?"

"Well…maybe a little." He really liked the idea of going out and seeing some sights.

"I thought so. Let's go," his mother said with finality.

The Parkers enjoyed their evening out. George and Paul felt like they were getting to know each other all over again. Paul noticed the change in George's demeanor from the last time he had visited, and George strove to learn more about the boy that he'd never bothered to before. They were a little more at ease with each other by the time dinner was over and all were looking forward to Saturday's party welcoming the young man to their home.

Chapter Twelve

The next day Robin had gone into the office to catch up on some paper work. He had had a long day Wednesday, and had taken off Thursday to recover. Shelly's hormones were in an uproar on Wednesday and to make matters worse, she did see the Tommy Canales show. Robin intentionally had not told her when the show was going to air, hoping she would forget and miss it. He should have known she was going to make a point to see it. The pain of watching her husband having to discuss their sad history tore her apart. It wasn't just the memory of the failed pregnancy, but seeing a flicker of the pain that they shared on his face. So, Robin spent the rest of the day consoling her and assuring her that this baby was going to be just fine and that *he* was fine.

Once in the office, he found Donnie and George's secretary amidst a pile of mail in the conference room, sharing with each other the best ones. "*What* is all that?" he asked, pointing to the mess.

"Fan mail," they both said gleefully.

"Good Lord. For us?"

"Well, yes. Who do you think?" Donnie retorted.

"That's how much we got for the whole of the '90's," Robin joked.

"That was a bad decade. But it seems that you are popular again," the man said with a grin. "Here is an outpouring of sympathy from people who are going through what you two have been going through, and they're anxious to support you and cheer you on."

"Here, read this one," Suzi said.

Robin took the letter and read about a woman who had both lost a baby and her husband had died from a heart attack. He found it odd how she could still manage to be so optimistic with so much sadness in her life. He looked at the pile once more and was overcome by the magnitude of the public's reaction. He certainly expected the onslaught of mail they received when George had his heart attack, but never considered that he would get any feedback about what he'd been through.

He sat down very slowly and quietly and the other two went silent at his expression. Suzi gave him her favorites, and Donnie gave him a couple that interested him. A few of them congratulated him and George for handling of the usually ornery host. He never was ceased to be amazed by the support of their fans. He wished he could write them all. He spent quite a while reading them and decided a formatted letter should be sent out to them.

He called for his secretary to come take a letter for him and the young girl quickly came in. She was a well-educated girl, but liked the old-fashioned way Robin went about business.

"Juliet, you're good at letters. Help me compose one for these people who have been so kind."

"Yes, sir."

Needless to say with Robin being the perfectionist that he was, it took quite a while to accomplish. The group picked out all the good letters and sent them out their replies. Donnie did notice, however, that Robin kept one letter to himself. He grinned and shook his head at how the group never forgot who put them at the top.

Robin went into his office to do his work, but before he left for the day, he grabbed a glossy photo of himself and his brother to take home. He stopped by George's house before going home.

"Here, sign this," he told his brother once he arrived at his house. He gave him the photo of themselves.

"Do you want me to write 'to Robin with love' or just simply my name?"

"Which one would I get more for on the internet?" he joked back.

"Fine—I'll sign your name… Who's it for?"

"A lady who deserves it. Read this." He handed him the letter of the lady with the bad luck in life but persevering personality.

"Wow. Poor thing."

"Yeah. So, I thought we'd cheer her up."

George happily signed the photo with relish and good wishes.

"So, how are things?" asked Robin.

"Fine, so far."

"Paul settled in?"

"Yeah, pretty much. Of course, he hasn't been here long enough for us to get into a fight yet."

"Do you think you're going to?"

"Oh, it's bound to happen—he is sixteen. Oh, he's a good lad, as kids go, but you never know when they're going to pop."

"You were definitely a champagne bottle when you were his age."

George chuckled with a recall of his youth.

"Where are they?"

"Where do you think?"

"Why didn't you go?"

George made an expression of no desire to go to Debra's café.

"Have you even been there yet?" Robin asked with a slight agitation.

"No."

Robin gave him a condescending look that left George feeling punished. "Do you see the restaurant as your enemy?" he then asked.

George answered his glare with his own. "Aren't we perceptive?"

"You're going to have to meet her halfway, you know," he said shaking his head.

George looked down to the coffee table, pursed his lips and let out a deep breath. "What are you doing right now?"

"Taking you to the café. Just let me call Shelly."

George nodded with concession. "Say 'hi' from Grumbleguts."

Robin found the phone and called his wife, letting her know where he was. He told her what he was about to do and she simply said, "Oh."

"Why? What's the matter?"

"Well, nothing."

Robin smiled to himself. He could practically hear her pout over the phone. "Do you want to come?"

"Could I?"

"Of course, my sweet. Be there in a moment."

The guys went to pick up Shelly and set off for the restaurant. Once there, they found Debra and Paul sitting at a table cheerfully chatting away while organizing the flatware. She beamed at the sight of her family, and smiled especially at George. She got up to greet them and introduced her son to Shelly. The boy seemed entranced by her unusual beauty. "Hi," he finally got out.

He then shook Robin's hand who dryly teased, "She's taken, and she doesn't have any sisters."

Debra went to hug and kiss her husband. He then realized how happy she was that he came. She took his hand and showed everyone around. She was like a kid who bought a toy store, bragging about all her wonderful appliances and gadgets. Everyone was happy for her whether or not they understood the complexities of professional cooking.

"I'm so glad you came!" she said to them. "In fact, Shelly, I was hoping to talk to you. I have a little business to discuss." She took Shelly back out to the dining room and left the others to mill around. Robin naturally started to tinker with things as he usually did. George and Paul laughed so hard when he accidentally turned a large juicer on, startling him greatly.

"Look at this wall," Debra directed Shelly with a gesture. "Now I could decorate it, but I rather had something else in mind."

Shelly smiled. "Yes?"

"Could you do a mural?"

Shelly raised her brows, bit her lip, and studied the wall. "I imagine I could. What would you like?"

"Oh, a pretty landscape, I suppose… I don't really have anything in mind, but I figure you would know what's best."

"How about a *tromp lóel*?"

"A what?"

"It's French for 'fools the eye'. Makes you feel like you're actually looking at a landscape, or such—three-dimensional, in other words."

"Oh, yes, I know what you mean. That sounds lovely!"

"I don't know that I can get it done by next week, though."

"Yes, I thought so. The idea only came to me today when we were about to hang up some prints. I thought it was a shame to simply cover it up with it being so large and plain. It almost looks like a mural belongs there. I don't know why I hadn't thought of it before."

"Unless…maybe… Where's your phone?"

"It's behind the counter over there. Why?"

"Because," she started as she went to the phone, "two paintbrushes are faster than one!"

Debra smiled, knowing whom she was going to call.

"Hey, Rach'! Can you help me with a project?… A mural for Debra's café… No, not that big… No, inside, inside… Well, you know she's opening up next weekend… Really? So they'll be here for the opening?… Cool!… Dunno. When can you start?… Well, yeah… Yeah, we're all here right now… Oh, I imagine so… Sure… Okay, bye."

"Well?"

"She's coming over. She wants to see your wall."

"Great! How exciting! Thank you so much, Shelly! I didn't know Rachel could paint."

"She dabbles in it. She's actually better than me when it comes to painting buildings and columns and such. She has more of an architectural eye."

Shelly went on to explain her idea and got Debra to give her some paper to draw on. Shelly felt a hand upon her shoulder and turned to see the smiling face of her husband. "What's up?" he asked.

Shelly explained to all the guys The Bright Idea. Then she mentioned that Rachel was coming over.

"Boy, we're going to have a proper party here in a moment," laughed George. He then came over to Debra and talked quietly about the place. Paul smiled and listened intently to Shelly's ramblings on what fun the wall was going to be to paint.

"Are you sure it's okay for you to paint?" Robin asked with concern.

"Oh, we'll be using acrylics and they're pretty harmless."

"That wasn't really what I was referring to. I meant all the getting up and down on ladders and such."

She looked at the height of the wall. "Well," she laughed, "I guess Rachel gets to do all the high stuff."

"You'd better make sure you have a good, long ladder then," he said with a smirk.

"Robin…" she scolded, but then laughed herself.

Rachel showed up after a bit with a bundle of items. She and Shelly got straight to it after Rachel said her hellos to the rest of the gang. They sketched and planned and measured and sketched some more. Debra watched with fascination, happily anticipating the great masterpiece.

The guys sat down at a table and George got out his cell phone. "Who are you calling?" Robin asked.

"Terry's missing all the fun."

"Of course! Everyone else is here."

"Yes, and he'll be coming home soon to no one. He'll feel so left out."

"Gee, you're so thoughtful, George."

"Yes, aren't I, though? I know our Terry. He'll think we're all conspiring against him."

Paul was happy at the news that Terry was coming. Debra had told him about George's footballer cousin, and was looking forward to getting to learn some professional soccer moves.

George hung up his phone chuckling. Robin turned with a smile. "Is he coming?"

"Depends," George said, still laughing, "if he can find his way here… Why he doesn't kick the ball the wrong way is a mystery. He *cannot* understand directions… Debra! You got anything to drink?"

She stuck her hands up with a grin. "The world's your oyster!" she hollered, laughing at the silly question.

"Lemonade?"

"Hmm… No, but I can make you some. That is, if the juicer is still working," she said with a smile at Robin, who in turn looked up to the ceiling in denial that he had been messing with the instrument. "Uh-huh, Mr. Innocent."

"Who, me?"

She laughed and asked who all wanted some. Everyone did. "Hmm… I need to make sure that's on the menu."

"Absolutely!" replied George.

Terry eventually made his way (after getting lost a couple of times) to the café. He knocked on the door to be let in and they all congratulated him for finding his way there. He grinned with embarrassment and came over to Rachel and gave her a peck, much to the confusion of Paul who didn't know they were an item. Terry inquired of the girls what was going on, and they explained their art project with enthusiasm.

He sat down with the other men and Debra brought him some lemonade much to his delight. "Well, guys, you're not the only ones to get on the telly," Terry boasted.

They all turned to listen and George asked, "Why? Did you get arrested?"

"No. They interviewed me for the sports segment tonight!"

"Hey, that's fantastic, babe! What channel?" Rachel asked.

"Uh, five, I think."

"You're not going to, you know, mention our names or anything, will you?" joked Robin, causing Terry to give him a dirty look.

"So, now that you're here, Paul, what are your plans for the summer?" inquired Terry. "Hit the beach, I presume?"

"Yeah, probably."

"Well, watch our for these Miami girls—they'll suck you in." He gave a wink to Rachel, who smiled back at the remark.

"No, no," contested Paul and shook his head with a big grin.

"Speaking of getting sucked in," chimed George with a mischievous smile, "I hear her folks are coming up so that you can be an embarrassment in three countries."

Terry gave and even dirtier look this time. He was getting picked on today, but he took it with an easy stride. "Her parents are coming Wednesday, yes."

"Great! We're all anxious to meet the people who brought our Rachel into the world."

Rachel smiled bashfully.

Robin turned to Rachel. "Where in the world are they going to sleep?" he asked, knowing full well the restrictions of the studio.

"In my bed."

"And then where are you going to sleep?"

"On the sofa."

"You can sleep at our house—" started all the Parkers.

"Heh, ole Tommy would have liked that," George added.

"That's okay, guys. Thanks, anyway. I come from a family of eight—I'm used to sleeping in tight spaces."

"That's actually a very comfy couch," Shelly said defensively of her little purple sofa.

"Yes, and they can always play air-hockey if they get bored," Robin kidded.

"I miss my air-hockey," Shelly pouted.

"Well, you couldn't make it very far over the table right now, anyway," Rachel said with a grin.

"Thanks for reminding me."

"Aw, you know you're beautiful, Shelly. Nice outfit, by the way," complimented Rachel.

Shelly studied her to make sure she meant it, and was satisfied she wasn't just picking. She still felt uneasy in her maternity clothes. "Thanks," she said with a note of uncertainty.

"I'm serious!" Rachel reaffirmed.

Robin laughed at the conversation that sounded like the same one he had with her only a few days ago.

The group enjoyed their little visit, but finally broke up once Rachel and Shelly finalized the plans of their mural.

"Don't forget everyone!" Debra hollered out while locking the door. "Eight o'clock tomorrow!"

"Rachel and I will probably come by for a little bit tomorrow to get this thing started," replied Shelly, but then in a lower voice asked, "Hey, will those girls be there?"

"What—oh, *those* girls. Ha-ha. Yeah, a couple of them may be."

"Good!"

"Nothing like rubbing it into some people's noses, is there?"

"Nope." She happily caressed her belly and said good-bye. As she left, Robin asked her afterward what they were talking about.

"Oh, just girl talk," she replied, proud of her play on words.

"You know, you are beautiful," he commented, thinking she may still be feeling insecure about her changing stature.

But, she was feeling rather satisfied with herself and simply answered, "You're not bad lookin' yourself!" She then gave him a little pat on the bottom, making him laugh and shake his head.

The next day, Shelly and Rachel came and did the basic outline for the mural in Debra's café. Debra sat and watched with amazement at the ease of how the two girls worked with each other. They barely talked as they drew mysterious, enchanting lines all over her wall. It almost seemed choreographed as they drew arches and horizons, straight lines and fantastic curves.

They finished what they had planned to do that day and were ready to go home and prepare for the party. They had accomplished a great deal and also happened to get Debra in a state of happy anticipation. She went home to arrange for her party in a joyful state.

If George was looking to get back into the groove of things, having a party was all it took. The Parker parties were infamous for the odd collection of characters that attended them, and this party was definitely no different. Terry brought a couple of his teammates, Rachel invited her friend Miguel and his wife, and Debra brought some of her employees to help and enjoy themselves as well, rounding out a grand mixture along with the band and their contemporaries.

Paul sat in amazement at the strange slew of people and had a growing feeling that he had been transported onto some peculiar party planet. Although there wasn't anyone there his age, he definitely was being entertained by all the funny conversations. His mother eventually beckoned him to help her. "Are you having any fun?" she asked doubtfully.

"Yeah," he answered without much feeling one way or another.

"Good, good. Take these out to that little green table by the pool, hon'."

The boy did so, and found an anxious Terry waiting for the next plate of surprises. "Oh, yumm! Your mum is fantastic, you know that?"

"Yeah," Paul answered timidly.

"Rachel! Try these!"

Rachel popped over and took one of the hors d'oeuvres and let out an 'mmm'. "These are terrific, aren't they?" she asked Paul.

"Yeah." He took one himself, smiled, and walked off.

He sauntered around until he found George and Robin talking to their manager and a couple of other record executives he didn't know. George called him over. "Donnie, this is my step-son, Paul. He just came to live with us. He's from Seattle."

"Wow, Seattle. Nice to meet you, Paul," said the quick-talking man. Paul said nothing, but gave a bashful smile and a nod while he shook his hand. "Do you think you're going to like Miami better than Seattle?"

"Yeah," he said with a grin.

"Good! Do you like music? Of course you do, you're a teenager. Well, we may have to put you to work, would you like that?"

"Yeah!" he said eagerly.

The man patted him on the back, and his mother called for him again. He begrudgingly left and was given another platter to take to where Rachel had joined Shelly and Miguel with his wife. The group was in a heated debate about a local artist and his controversial gallery display. "Oh, thank God!" said the ravenous Shelly. She took several of the shrimp delicacies and put them on her plate and then one more for her mouth. "Having fun, Paul?" she managed to get out when she finished her mouthful.

"Yeah," he said, nodding his head and looking around.

"Strange crowd, huh?" she laughed.

He smiled in agreement.

She quickly flicked back to her conversation of which he listened to until he realized he didn't have the faintest idea what they were talking about. Miguel's wife, Gloria, gave him a knowing look, seeing how she really didn't understand either.

Paul looked around once more, hoping for something interesting to listen to. He was relieved to see Robin talking to Terry along with Terry's mates. He went over to see what they were chatting about. He discovered the topic was soccer, but only after he remembered that they call it 'football'. All of a sudden Terry looked at Paul and asked, "Do you like to play?"

"Yeah," he said happily.

"Good! We'll have to get you out there and teach you a few things. Would you like that?"

"Yeah!"

The men continued their run-down of all the Premier League happenings. And although Paul didn't understand this conversation much either, he at least felt more at home around sports than arts.

Some time had passed, and quite a few people had shown up. Robin was close to the gate entrance to the pool area when an older businessman by the name of Johnson came in with his two tall, blonde daughters. Robin greeted them, but then glanced over to his wife. He could have sworn he saw a flame light in her eyes at the sight of the women. They were the same catty women who had once broken Shelly's heart by their petty talking behind her back. But, Shelly had quickly turned back to Rachel with a smile, enjoying their chat. Robin did notice, however, that Rachel peeped around to look at the women and seemed to be sizing them up. He knew disaster was eminent, but couldn't help but grin to himself anyhow.

George came up to greet the man and made a knowing glance to Robin at the sight of his company. George then begged Mr. Johnson to have a seat and a drink. The man went to sit down with a smile and George quickly apologized to Robin. "Sorry mate—had no idea."

Robin laughed. "Don't apologize to me. You're the one who's going to pay. One of those girls isn't going to get to leave here without at least a bowl of guacamole down her dress."

George squeezed his eyes shut, but then laughed. "Well, it wouldn't be a Parker party without something disastrous happening."

An hour had passed, and George was beginning to believe Shelly was going to behave herself, but Robin knew better. She was leading her prey into a false sense of security. He honed in on his wife like a hawk, he could feel something brewing as she walked with Rachel around the pool. They were getting closer to the Johnson sisters and he caught Shelly put her arm through Rachel's. "Here it comes," he said to himself. He shook his head as he watched Shelly clumsily trip on apparently nothing, catching herself on Rachel, but only after successfully propelling the sisters into the pool. Mission accomplished.

He and George ran to the pool to help the two girls out, trying desperately not to laugh.

"I'm so sorry!" Shelly exclaimed. "I'm such a klutz since I got pregnant!" She rubbed her belly remorsefully.

The women gave her a wicked stare and Robin said, "I'll pay for your dresses."

"Well, it's not *your* fault," said one, still with hope.

"Oh, well, actually it is," he said with a completely straight face. "You see, I'm the one who got her pregnant."

The shocked reaction of the crowd was broken with laughter. George couldn't hold it in any longer, and let out a great guffaw. The girls quickly got up, refusing any help (especially from Terry's friends) and commanded their father to take them home, which he reluctantly did.

Robin went to Shelly and looked down on her, trying his best to look serious. "Now, Shelly dear, that was *very* naughty."

"Sorry, I just couldn't help myself."

"I had a feeling you were going to do something like that."

"I notice you didn't stop me."

"Well, short of locking you in the closet, I didn't think it could be done." He chuckled and hugged her. "What am I to do with you?"

"I don't know, hon'. I don't know."

She then went to George and earnestly apologized. "I hope I didn't get you into trouble with someone important."

"Well, you probably did, but that was the funniest damn thing I've seen in a long time, so it was worth it." Then he laughed and hugged her. "Now, go behave!"

"Yes, sir," she replied with a smile. She did behave the rest of the night, and the party continued as if nothing had happened.

At one point, Robin sequestered his brother and asked him if he'd like to hear a song he had written. George replied, "Of course," and followed him to the white baby grand. Robin sat down and tinkered a bit.

"When was the last time you had this thing tuned?"

"Oh. You're supposed to tune them?" George replied dryly.

Robin went quite solemn and hoped he had drunk enough courage to allow him to share the painful song with him. He started the slow, enchanting tune which quickly captured not only George's attention, but also that of a few meandering guests. Soon, most all the company found themselves being drawn in by the stark rawness of the melody. They could tell that it was more than just a song, but a bearing of the singer's soul for all to see. The lyrics were vague, only enhancing its beauty by allowing each listener to claim his or her own meaning to it; but all, somehow, felt the memory of a loss. Broken hearts, deaths, and disappointments in life were relived in those few minutes, but with a clever twist in chords at the end, he accomplished a faint glimmer of hope.

He ended his song, but he was surrounded by a stunned silence. He quickly became embarrassed and looked around the room. Then, the clapping began. It grew into a fierce applause. He looked around for Shelly. He saw her clapping away with the rest of them, pausing to wipe a tear. He got up and came over to kiss her.

The crowd eventually dispersed, going back to their gaiety, but never forgetting what they witnessed. George came to

Robin after Shelly had gone back to Rachel and Debra. "Well, you really know how to put a damper on a man's party."

"Sorry."

George paused to study him. "Could you record that?" he asked with a slight reserve.

"What do you mean, 'could I'?" Robin was genuinely confused by the question.

"Well, I mean, if it doesn't hurt too much, it would be a hit."

Robin thought hard. George could sense the pain it took to sing it, for he could see it in his face, but he also knew a hit when he heard it, and Robin knew that to be true. Before he could answer, George continued.

"Look, I know where that song came from, so I understand if you don't want to do it, but you could think of it this way: Think of how many people could associate with it—how many could understand it and feel a bond with those same emotions. It may help them somehow to cope with their own pain."

Robin knew he was right. He looked at him and slowly started to nod his head. "Yeah… All right. I believe I could."

"Fantastic," George said sympathetically. "Now, I think you need another drink."

"Yes, I don't think that's a bad idea at all."

Eventually, George and Shelly (being the only sober ones left) found themselves making drinks for their friends in the kitchen. George studied his sister-in-law with interest. "You know, pregnancy really becomes you," he confessed.

She was startled by this observation and replied, "Why, thank you."

"It really does… I also think it's great Mum is finally going to get a grandchild. There was simply no hope with Tilly and me. She's all sea and soldiers, and, well, I just never put it on my list of priorities. Whereas, we all kind of knew Robin would be the one to settle down in the end, so I guess that kind of took the pressure off us two."

"It almost didn't happen," she said sadly.

"But it did! And I know you two—you would have adopted some orphans from a third world nation or something anyway."

"Yeah," she laughed, "that's probably true." She then asked timidly, "You never considered having children?"

"Well… It had crossed my mind, of course, but it just didn't work out." He shrugged his shoulders and continued to stir a drink thoughtfully. "I think sometimes if something is that important to you, it will eventually happen—kind of like our career. I never made it a priority to have a family, and it never happened."

"You were married before Debra, right?"

"I was never actually married, but I lived with a woman for, oh, uh, about five years, I guess. It was never that serious a relationship—we were really too young."

"Ah… Well, I guess you've got the opportunity now to show everyone what a great step-dad you can be."

"Huh. Yeah, I suppose." He replied with a look of embarrassment.

"Oh, I think you'll do fine."

"You really think so?" he asked doubtfully.

"Oh, yeah. I mean, you're so full of spirit and energy—that's just what kids feed off of. Who wouldn't get a kick out of having a famous musician for a step-father?" she remarked with a big grin.

"I suppose I do have that in my favor."

"Definitely!"

"You should have your own talk show, you know that? You'd put Tommy to shame."

Shelly gave him a giggle for an answer.

A moment had passed as he put ice in a glass with a distant look in his face. Then he quickly looked at her. "Shelly?"

"Yes?" she said with a startle.

"When you were so ill…" He stopped, unsure whether she was comfortable with this subject. But the fact was, he had the opportunity to ask his question, and he wanted to take advantage of it.

"Yes?" she asked with curiosity.

He looked at her and felt secure. "Did you, uh…did you ever have the sensation you weren't really there?"

"Oh. Like an out-of-body kind of thing?"

"Y-eah," he stammered out.

"Well…" She thought hard for a moment. "I remember being surrounded by a very bright light—but that could have been my eyes playing tricks on me because of the fever. Did you?" she asked eagerly.

He knitted his brows and knew he'd feel like an idiot admitting it, but he went ahead and did. "Yeah."

The pupils of her dark, blue eyes seemed to enlarge with this news. "Wow!" She answered with a childish relish. "Floating above and everything?"

He smiled nervously at her. "Yeah," he repeated. "I only just remembered the other day when we were flying. It was like déjà vu."

"Gosh."

They stood quietly for a moment, but then tried to talk at the same time, causing each other to shut up quickly. "Sorry, you first," he said.

"I'm glad you came back."

"Yes. And the same to you."

"Thanks… It's good to be alive, is it not?"

"Yes. Very."

He leaned down and gave her a hug.

"What are you doing, hugging my wife?" asked Robin who peeped around the corner.

"I told her how happy I am she suckered you into giving Mum a grandchild and getting the pressure off me."

"I'm sure Mum never expected you to take on such an undertaking, anyhow."

"That is probably very true. Which one of these is yours?"

Robin picked his drink and helped Shelly carry her load of beverages out. The crowd had begun to dwindle to a few good friends eventually and, as anyone who throws parties knows, that's when the real fun begins.

Young Paul was exhausted, but was determined not to miss anything. He was having way too much fun watching all these adults act in such an uninhibited fashion. The only people who were really sloshed were Terry, Rachel and his buddies. The friends were eventually taxied home, leaving Terry and Rachel to act as court jesters for the rest.

The party had migrated inside, as a summer shower had appeared from nowhere. The topic had turned to the grand extent of women's grooming and the total non-necessity (according to Terry) of it all.

"So you don't think men have any role in all the crap women have to go through?" questioned Rachel, standing above the seated Terry as if lecturing.

"Yes, absolutely. Women are always trying to one-up each other."

"So, you don't think it's necessary for women to shave their legs?"

"Well…"

"Aha!" she pointed.

"Legs are one thing—I mean, they are *right there* for all to see, you know. But, you don't have to frost your hair."

Rachel pulled a lock of hers to study with eyes that wouldn't focus. "You like my hair plain?" she asked, quite touched.

"I love the natural color of your hair. I love you just the way you are."

Everyone said '*aw*', embarrassing him.

"You mean I don't even have to wax my moustache?" She motioned her finger to her lip.

"Well, uh…" He gave up, putting his head into his hands and shaking it remorsefully.

Everyone broke out in uproarious laughter.

Rachel laughed and fell onto his lap, making the jet beads on her little black top fly. She gave him a big kiss and he came back whole-heartedly, causing them both to fall to the floor. The crowd was laughing so hard, and Shelly was about to lose it. It felt so good for them all to laugh like they hadn't done in so long.

Chapter Thirteen

The next week consisted of two things: Debra preparing for her opening (along with the girls attaining the completion of her mural in record time), and the arrival of Rachel's parents.

The couple arrived on Wednesday and her father was happy to find out Terry didn't seem to be a permanent resident at his daughter's studio—he had supposed that was probably true. She tried her best to entertain her parents even though she had so much work to do. Debra paid her handsomely for her share of the work on the mural, and she celebrated with a dinner for her parents and Terry at her favorite restaurant. She also felt that this was probably the best time to tell them the good news of their engagement.

It was Thursday when they all went out. Terry had never been so nervous in his entire life—even at the end of a championship match preparing to attack the final corner kick. He actually liked her parents, but her father somehow instilled a fear into his heart. The man was so completely different from his own father, and he was on uncertain footing with him. Terry was afraid that with one wrong move, he wouldn't allow him to ever see Rachel again.

The dinner immediately started off tense. Rachel had a feeling her parents knew darn well why they had been invited up, and it was just a matter of getting it over with. Rachel's mother sat with a nervous grin; her father constantly surveyed the room, trying to avoid looking anyone directly in the eye. He actually liked Terry, but was uncertain of his background and culture. He really had no clue how he would take care of his little girl.

There was no way Rachel was going to wait until after dinner. She wanted to get this over with. She took Terry's hand and held it on top of the table. For the first time her parents noticed the shiny ring she had avoided showing them until now. "Mama, Papa, we have something to tell you."

They waited patiently for the imminent news. Rachel looked at Terry as a cue for him to speak. He swallowed and looked at the couple directly. With a squeeze from Rachel's hand, he was given the strength he needed. "Mr. and Mrs. Figueroa, we have what I hope you'll think is good news." Rachel was proud he made it through the family name successfully.

"Yes, Terry?" her father replied seriously.

"We would like to ask for your blessing. We would like to get married." It wasn't exactly how he had rehearsed it, but there it was. He was happy he managed to get it out without embarrassment. He waited for Mr. Figueroa's reaction anxiously and then saw his wife's face smiling away. He returned the smile. Slowly, Rachel's dad began to speak.

"Well, Terry, let me ask you a couple of things first. I obviously expect you to take care of Raquel and I..." the man began to show emotion a this point, "I need to know if you're willing to do that—no matter what happens. Life is very unpredictable and things are not always going to be easy. You have to be willing to stick it out—to stick by her. Can you promise that?"

"Without a doubt in my mind, sir," he answered with no hesitation.

"I also want to know how you stand on marriage. Do you believe in the sanctity of it? I don't want someone marrying my daughter with the notion that if things don't go well you can always get a divorce."

"Well, sir. Let me put it this way: My parents have been married for forty years and I have seen ups and downs—more than you may think. I do believe in marriage, and I actually take it very seriously. I know I may seem flippant, but when it comes to certain things—the important things—I'm all but a joker. Rachel's the only person I've ever met that reminds me of the…the…" he thought hard for the proper words, "well, the *real meaning* of being married." He almost seemed to be losing patience and received another squeeze from Rachel's hand.

"Well, I'm very glad to hear that… Very well, you have my blessing."

"Thank you, sir." Terry shook the man's hand while Rachel squealed with delight and showed her mother her ring.

"Thank you, Papa!" She got up and hugged and kissed her father.

"Well, *mija*, I was losing hope of you ever getting married, anyway."

"Gee, thanks," she grumbled sarcastically.

"I'm so happy for the both of you," her mother said, beaming.

The tension was broken and gone, leaving the family to have a delightful dinner after all.

After they came back home after a scrumptious dinner Rachel made some coffee and everyone sat down at her little kitchen table to chat. Her parents began to really understand Terry and knew that only someone as unusual as he could satisfy Rachel's desire to be as different as possible from the rest of the family. She loved her family, but always had an insatiable thirst to discover the world outside Puerto Rico. She was really quite torn in a sense, but she seemed to have found a wonderful compromise in Terry. Here, the world was brought to her in the form of a happy-go-lucky European. He had the same zest for life as she did along with a sense of propriety. Both knew that they found what they had been looking for. Neither was going to settle for anyone who wasn't in their line of thinking—that life is something to be experienced, not simply tolerated.

"So, do you have a date set?" asked her mother.

"Not really, but soon," Rachel answered, smiling at Terry.

"*Where* are you getting married?" asked her father.

Rachel looked at Terry. "We haven't thought of that yet, but probably here in Miami." Terry agreed with a nod.

"What church?" her father clarified.

Rachel gave him almost a harsh glance because she knew what he was leading to. "I really don't know, Papa."

"Well, I would like to think you're going to be married in a Catholic church."

Before Rachel could reply, Terry surprisingly said, "But I'm not Catholic."

"Yes, but she is," he retorted.

"Well, that's something that Rachel and I are going to have to discuss with each other first."

"There is nothing to discuss—it's not a valid marriage if it's not in the Catholic Church," he said with conviction.

"Well, I'm sorry Mr. Figueroa, I'm afraid I disagree with you on that. I'll be damned if someone's going to tell me my parents aren't really married."

"That may be fine for them, but Raquel has been raised to respect the Catholic Church as the proper church of Christ, so that is where she is going to be married if she wants anything to do with her family!" He looked angrily at Rachel and went outside to smoke. Terry went out into the studio to cool off. Rachel stared at her mother who had been stricken speechless.

"This is ridiculous," Rachel said, slamming her hands down on the table, making her mother wince. She then went outside to talk to her father.

She came up to him, but said nothing. Instead, she stared at him with angry eyes and he felt practically a slight qualm of fear from the young woman. Even at her height, she could be quite intimidating.

She finally spoke. "Listen, Papa. I *am* marrying Terry; there is no doubt in that."

"Not unless it is in a Catholic church!" he interrupted.

As the two continued to argue, Mrs. Figueroa sat in the kitchen listening, unsure what to do. She understood both sides, and knew she was going to be placed in a difficult position soon. She decided to talk to Terry.

She went inside the studio to find Terry sitting on a stool at a worktable, slowly tapping a pencil on it over and over again. "Terry?" she timidly asked.

He turned his angry face to her, but then smiled at the kind lady. He found it difficult to be mad at someone who looked so much like the woman he loved. "Listen, Mrs. Figueroa, I'm so sorry about all this. It's not like I'm that staunch a Church of England goer, but I don't like being railroaded into becoming a Catholic. It's just not my cup o' tea."

"I understand, *mijo*. It's just, well, my husband has been raised to believe that the Catholic Church is the only way to go. I'm sorry. I hope we can compromise somehow, but I don't see how."

"Neither do I." His heart softened at her worried expression.

"Well, something will work out," she said as she placed her little hand on his arm. "If it is meant to be, it will be."

He returned her smile, but shook his head doubtfully. There was always something keeping them apart. He really considered taking Rachel away and eloping—get her before anyone could take her away from him again.

"And…Terry?"

"Yes, ma'am?"

"You can call me Blanca."

"Blanca? What a pretty name…and a sight easier to say than your surname, that's for sure."

She giggled coyly, but her laugh was destroyed by the entrance of her husband. "Blanca—*vente!*" She came over to him where he rattled off a million Spanish words per second with only a quick glance to Terry. Blanca simply repeated the word 'no' to him several times as a firm reply. The man threw his hands up to the air and went back outside. Rachel came into the studio.

"What did he tell you?" she asked her mother.

"He wanted to go to a hotel, and I told him no."

Rachel growled loudly, shaking her fists.

"Listen, Rach', I think I'd better go home," Terry said as he gingerly held her angry arms.

"Por qué—why?" She found herself so upset that she couldn't remember what language to speak.

"I think this needs to blow over a bit until we can think more rationally, don't you?" His words were soft, but his eyes were hard.

Rachel calmed down a bit and escorted Terry through the front door after he said goodbye to Mrs. Figueroa, leaving her to talk to her husband.

Terry paused in front of his car door and leaned back on it. He didn't know what to say and neither did Rachel. He looked wide-eyed at her, and she noticed his look wasn't of anger, but of determination. He grabbed the belt loops of her jeans and pulled her to him. He took one hand and gently caressed her face. He then slid his hand to the back of her head and held it to give her a long, hard kiss. She eagerly reciprocated. It was their way of telling each other that they were going to make it through this ordeal just like they had all the others. They kissed for a long while, but then Terry noticed that she was crying. He wiped her tears away and said softly, "Baby, it's going to be all right."

"You don't know Papa. He's always shoving his ideals down my throat. I'm sick of it!"

"That's what parents do."

"Yours don't."

"No, instead they turn a blind eye to their son who has a serious drinking problem and pretend that it's nothing.

Then when he turns up dead, they don't understand why. At least your parents care—maybe overly protective—but, well, I can see your father's point of view, but he still shouldn't be so black and white about the subject."

"See? God! We haven't got to discuss this at all—I didn't even know how you felt about it, and here he comes saying you have to do this or he'll disown me."

"He said that?!"

She stared at him without answering.

"Shit!" He started to take off back to the studio, but she held him back.

"No, no, babe. Don't believe him. He wouldn't. He would just make it hell on me, that's all."

"I can't believe this! You're twenty-nine years old, for crying out loud!"

"Well, babe, welcome to the Puerto Rican culture. We hold tight together, we love and support each other, and we constantly drive each other nuts."

"Yes, well, I guess it beats our indifference. I might still have my brother if we had been Puerto Rican."

"Who's to say, sweetie?" She rubbed his arm and realized he still hurt very badly from the loss of his brother. "Things like that happen all over the world."

He began shaking his head. "I don't need this!" he yelled out towards the house. "I've already got too much shit going on as it is."

She looked at him anxiously. "Well, what else is wrong?"

He gave her a guilty expression. He then looked away at the stars that were beginning to appear. "The season's off to a bad start, and with this being such a new team, well, it just doesn't look good."

"You mean, they may fire you?"

"That means, by next season, there may be no more team at all."

"Oh, Terry."

"Yeah."

He looked at her and marveled again at her beauty. "Whatever it takes, love, I'm not letting you go—ever again." He held her once more. "Whatever it takes."

Terry eventually took his leave, and Rachel returned to her parents and let her father know that she was not going to talk to him anymore that night, sending them to bed upstairs. She cuddled up on the purple couch and cried herself to sleep.

It was a quiet breakfast the next morning at the studio. A night's sleep had turned Rachel's father from angry and stubborn to sad and disappointed. Rachel, on the other hand, had gotten no sleep and was on the brink of screaming at him. He was conscious of this fact, knowing one word out of his mouth would provoke it.

The couple retreated outside and sat at the little patio table to drink their coffee while Rachel made a phone call from her bedroom. She needed to call Shelly. Shelly always knew what to do when it came to anyone but herself. Rachel was relieved at the sound of her voice. She gave her the run-down of the previous night and Shelly gave Rachel her sympathies.

Shelly thought for a moment and then a brilliant idea occurred to her. "Say, Rachel?"

"What?" she asked eagerly.

"I think I came up with a compromise."

"Oh, I hope so. What is it?"

"Okay, let me get this straight, first. Terry doesn't want to be Catholic and the Church won't marry you unless you go through all this, uh, rigmarole, right?"

"Yeah."

"But your dad is saying it's not valid unless a Catholic priest performs it?"

"Yes, yes," she said impatiently.

"Okay. Well, what if a Catholic priest marries you, but not in a church?"

"And what priest is—oh!"

"Uh-huh," Shelly happily confirmed.

"Do you think he would?" Rachel asked with excitement.

"I don't know, but I can always ask."

"So what—we'll have to go to Ireland?"

"He's going to Texas in August."

"You're kidding!"

"Nope."

"Where in Texas?"

"San Antonio."

Rachel went silent trying to imagine it. She laughed at the thought of exchanging their vows in front of the Alamo.

"So, what do you think?"

"Ask him."

"Consider it done."

"Shelly?"

"What?"

"I love you, you know."

"Love you too, hon'... Look, I gotta go. D'art has an appointment."

"Even your dog has a schedule?"

"Yes, he has to get his shots."

"Ah."

"Hey, how's Chuckie?" Shelly inquired of Rachel's guinea pig.

"Fine, thank you."

"What did your dad say about him?"

"Ha! He wanted to know why I have a rabbit with no ears."

"Typical."

"Yeah, then he bit him!"

"Who bit who?" she joked.

"You're funny."

"Okay, well, I'll see you later. I'll let you know what Papa says. Are you going to talk to them?"

"Terry's busy all day—game tonight."

"That's right."

"You going?"

"Don't know. Depends on Robin. I'd like to. We've been bad not seeing him. Are you taking your parents?"

"Yeah."

"Don't forget tomorrow!"

"I won't."

"Debra will probably call you, anyway."

"Yes. I'm sure she's told Terry a few times, too."

"Well, keep your chin up, okay?"

"All right."

"Leave it to Auntie Shelly."

"Okay, thanks, bye."

"Bye!"

Rachel plopped down face up on the bed, with some relief. Thank God for connections, she mused.

Shelly thought for a moment before calling her father. Would he agree to do such a task? Would she be taking advantage of his vulnerable state with her? She only knew that she had to do what she could for her friends, because they belonged together. That, she figured, is what she had to relay to her newly-found father.

She got out the long telephone number and nervously dialed. At the sound of his cheery voice, she somehow knew things would be okay. "Hello, Papa," she meekly replied to his answer.

"Well, hello, my dear! How are you?"

"Oh, I'm doing okay, how are you?"

"Fine, fine. What can I do you for?"

"Well, we have a bit of a predicament…" She then went on to tell him of the situation, and he sadly sympathized.

"Yes, I have seen this before, and it really can wrench a family apart."

"Yes, well," she took a deep breath before she dropped the question to him, "I was wondering…could you, by any chance, be able to marry them outside a church?"

"Ooh…well…" He thought quite hard about the matter. "Shelly, I don't think the Church would validate such an act. It really isn't valid unless you are in a church. They would definitely frown on me."

"Well, I don't think it would have to be registered *with* the church, just perform it as any other pastor would do it. As long as it was legal, that'd be okay."

He thought again. He sure didn't want to disappoint her, and he wrestled with the implications of getting caught doing a 'non-valid' wedding. "Well, when are they wanting to do this?"

"Well, we were going to bring the wedding to you. We thought maybe we could do it in San Antonio when you come."

"Ah…"

Shelly waited for an answer anxiously.

Fr. O'Connor really couldn't see the harm in it, and he felt for the young couple, who obviously did love each other. He relented. "All right. I'll do it."

"Are you sure, Papa? I don't want to get you into any trouble." She really did not want to be forcing him to do something he oughtn't.

But, he was the kind of man who, once he decided to do something, he followed through. "No, no. I'll do it."

"Oh, Papa, thank you so much. I can't tell you how this is going to help. I really appreciate it, and I know they do, too."

"Well, I'm glad I could help. I guess you'll let me know all the details soon?"

"Yes, sir. As soon as I can, I'll call you."

"Very well, then. I guess I should let you go."

"Okay, Papa. Thanks again and you take care!"

"Yes, you too, love."

They said their good-byes, and Fr. O'Connor sat wondering if he did the right thing. He knew very well he could get into trouble doing this, but how could he resist his daughter? He could tell she was earnestly concerned about her friends and wanted to make things all better. Was there anything really wrong about it? In the eyes of the Church, yes, but he really didn't know his own feelings on the subject. He thought hard the rest of the evening.

Shelly, too, had her own thinking to do. She was so happy he was going to help them, but she felt a twinge of guilt. She really did hope he didn't go against his beliefs for her sake. She hoped he was happy with his decision. She called and told the panicking Rachel her good news. At the sound of Rachel's scream of happiness, she knew she did the right thing.

Rachel took her parents sight-seeing that day, all with the silent agreement to not discuss the wedding. They had their fun and she successfully dragged them to the soccer match. Shelly had got Robin to come after all, and Rachel was relieved by the company.

The Figueroas enjoyed the game and she laughed at her father for cheering so loudly for Terry. She was so happy that Terry's team won that evening, and hoped it would help their chances of the club's longevity.

Rachel begged Shelly and Robin to go out to eat with them after the game. She felt their presence would help alleviate the chances of another argument and that maybe her father would be all right with Shelly's master plan.

They ate at an eclectic little restaurant downtown in which Robin knew the master chef. They managed to be seated in a cozy corner and had a delicious appetizer brought out with the chef's compliments. Rachel's parents were thrown off guard by all the poshness and were feeling quite spoiled, if not a little out of place. Rachel felt it was a good time to tell them of Shelly's idea. She looked nervously at her friend. Shelly had no problem tackling the job for her.

"Well, guys, I have a plan to get these two lovebirds married, and make everything okay with everyone." At this point, Rachel's dad lost his smile and Terry looked like he wanted to run. "As you may know, my father is a Catholic priest." She noticed the shocked expression on the Figueroas' faces. "Don't worry, he became a priest after he knew my mother and, in fact, he didn't even know about *me* until recently... Anyway," she said with some stress, "he has agreed to perform the ceremony for them when he comes to San Antonio in August. Now, as I see it, this fulfills the requirement of you, Mr. Figueroa, for the Catholic priest needed, and also for you, Terry, in that you don't have to join the Church. So, as long as the both of you are okay with that, I think this makes for a proper compromise."

Both men concentrated hard until Rachel's father spoke up. "How can I know that my grandchildren will grow up Catholic?" He asked this with almost sadness in his voice. Rachel got up and went over to him, laying her hand on his arm as she squatted down beside him. She spoke only to him in a low voice in his native language. He looked at her with concern, love and fear. Everyone finally heard him say, "*Sí.*" Rachel got up and kissed him and hugged his neck. She went back to her seat smiling. "Very well." He nodded his head. "Shelly, thank you *mijita*, I am happy with this—if you are Terry."

"Oh, you don't know, sir." He got up and shook the man's hand. He then hugged Shelly and turned to kiss Rachel. Everyone cheered. Rachel's mom was so relieved, that she began crying and got the hiccups.

"This calls for a toast!" exclaimed Robin.

"Here, here!" Shelly agreed.

"Go for it, Robin!" urged Rachel.

Robin cleared his throat and looked to the ceiling for the proper words. He stood up with his wine in his hand and began. "To Terry and Rachel: If ever there was a need for the proof of fate, here it is. A world apart—a culture apart—but yet deemed to be together as much as the sky and the stars. Some people fear the commitment of love, but others clasp on to love's chains with glory—such as you two have. Never forget what has brought the two of you together, for the memory of it will keep you inseparable. Never forget what it was like before you knew each other, for it will remind you of what life was like before love entered in. What you two have is so very rare. The two of you *are* so very rare, and it delights me so that you have found each other and found *in* each other the one thing that makes life worth living—finding that kindred spirit. Enjoy each other, revel in each other, and of course, love each other with all your hearts. To Rachel and Terry—many blessings!" He raised his glass and took a sip.

"Here, here! Congratulations!" erupted from everyone. The happy couple thanked Robin and then Rachel stood on her chair to kiss his cheek, causing laughter throughout the restaurant.

"Here, be careful. Andrew will kick us out," he laughed and helped her down. He sat back down and Shelly kissed his other cheek. "Boy, one speech, and I've become quite popular. I ought to do this more often."

"It reminded me of you," she said softly.

"It should. I thought of you while I was saying it." She smiled brightly at him. "Nice to be an inspiration?"

"Yeah," she answered bashfully.

They all had a scrumptious meal and Mr. Figueroa was put somewhat at ease. Terry, though, sat wondering what it was that Rachel told her father.

It was time for everyone to head back home. Shelly and Robin once more gave their best wishes and received thanks again for all the help. Robin helped Shelly into the Jag and took off. The rest slowly walked back to Terry's car with the parents trailing behind reminiscing about the wonderful meal they just had. This gave Terry the chance he'd hoped for; he asked Rachel about her secret conversation.

She slowly whispered her reply. "I told him that I hoped to fulfill his wishes, but that in the end, children will grow up to become their own people."

Terry waited for more, but she said nothing. "Certainly that wasn't all you said."

She flashed a quick smile to him. "I also said that I was meant to marry you, but that my heart needed his blessing as well."

"Oh." He thought on this a moment. "Rachel?"

"Yes?"

"How important is it for you to raise your children Catholic?"

She was afraid to answer, but knew she had to. "Well, it's important, but that's just me."

All he simply did was nod.

"Is that okay?"

"I certainly can't stand in the way of that level of dedication, seeing how I don't have any."

"Of course, they will only be half mine. How do you feel about it?"

"I guess I haven't given it that much thought," he said with a shrug of his shoulders. "I'd like to get married first before we have children."

She could sense he was getting tired of the subject, so she dropped it.

They arrived at the car and they all climbed in. Rachel studied Terry's face on the drive home and noticed no emotion whatsoever. She was puzzled as to how he really stood on the issue. Maybe it really didn't matter to him.

He dropped them off at the studio leaving Rachel with a kiss and a soft smile. She stayed up talking with her parents until they decided to go to bed.

Once she was alone, she picked up the phone and called Terry. He greeted her with a yawn.

"I'm sorry for calling so late, but I just wanted to make sure you were okay with everything."

"Well, yes, of course."

"You are?"

"Look…" he hesitated, took in a deep breath and began his explanation. "The thing is, my grandfather shoved religion down my father's throat, and he, in turn, wanted nothing to do with forcing the subject upon us. He had just had it with religion and, although he has his faith, he refused to be like his dad.

"I will not allow that to happen to my children, either— Catholic or C of E. I believe people have to find out for themselves. Now, don't get me wrong," he started before she could reply, "I don't have an issue with baptisms and church and all that—I don't even mind Sunday school—but I just can't stand it when people say, 'you've got to', that's why I got so angry at your father. I don't believe in that attitude, and I don't think the Lord does either."

There it was in a nutshell—the answer to all her questions. What could she say? She sat silenced and Terry asked if she was still there. "Yes, yes… I understand."

"Are you okay with that?" He was worried he had hurt her feelings.

"Of course." Her voice was warm and he felt better about it.

"It's not religion I have a problem with—it's the attitude. I'd love nothing more than to have our children as devout as you; I think that could only help them in life, but, I *will not* become my grandfather…or your father. No way."

"I don't think I could force anybody to do something they didn't want to. If I couldn't teach them the beauty of it and how to love God on their own, I would only consider it my own failure."

"Well, you can't put that kind of pressure on yourself, either. We can only do our best."

She liked the 'our' part. It made her feel she wasn't on her own on this issue. "That's true."

"So," he began in his usual flippant tone, "have we resolved this finally?!"

She smiled and said, "Yes," coyly.

"Good!"

She snickered and then quietly said, "I love you, Terry."

"I love you, too, you saucy minx."

So, their conversation ended on an amicable note, and the two slept better for it.

Saturday was Debra's day. Terry was happily driven by his fiancé with her parents in tow. This worked out much better than trying to find his way on his own again. They arrived at the café in plenty of time. In fact, Robin and Shelly weren't even there yet.

Debra, George, and Paul greeted them when they came in, but Debra immediately had to get back to work.

"She's doin' all right, eh?" Terry asked George as he surveyed the amount of customers.

"Yes, yes. She's doing okay. Of course, she'll have to be committed when it's all over," George laughed. He stood with his arms crossed watching Debra bounce like a ping-pong ball from one corner to another. It felt like old times to him, and he was in a very good mood—which surprised himself. He suddenly was distracted from his musing by his young cousin. "I'm sorry, what?"

"Where do you think we should sit?"

He looked about and replied, "Why not by Rachel and Shelly's art work? We can just pull some tables together."

Terry and Paul assisted him in doing so with Rachel and her parents helping with the chairs. All took a seat and got relaxed.

"You did this, Raquí? It's very pretty," remarked her mother, as she studied the mural.

"Rocky?" asked George with a laugh.

Rachel was embarrassed and explained the spelling and the fact it came from the way her baby brother used to call her that when he was a toddler.

"I like it. It fits you better than 'Rachel'," George replied.

"*Aye, aye, aye,*" Rachel grumbled with a shake of her head. As her face turned scarlet, everyone had a good chuckle at her expense. Robin and Shelly arrived at that time and salutations were exchanged and the couple sat down.

Robin made a quiet remark to Shelly about the mural and she replied, "We still need to do a little work on it, we simply ran out of time. Plus, we still need to put a protective coating of some sort on it, otherwise people will have it all biffed up with their chairs."

This got Rachel into the conversation and Robin sat bemused by all their artistic jargon. His brother nudged him in the arm and he was happily rescued by music jargon, which he spoke very well. George expressed his desire to start touring again, even if it were only a few cities. He felt it was necessary to follow up for their release of the live album in America with shows in at least the major venues. Robin was happy to hear his brother speak like this once more and he encouraged him to get the all-clear from his doctor.

Terry and the Figueroas chatted about yesterday's game, making the whole table quite animated. Paul listened with interest from one conversation to another. He was pretty sure they were all crazy and he was completely entertained. He was also pleased to see George getting back to his old self and his mother with such a big smile at working again. It was a relief to know things were good with them. He wasn't too sure when he arrived in Miami what exactly was going on with them, but whatever it was seemed to be improving.

The crew enjoyed their meal and Debra would sneak away to sit with them every once in a while. She was simply beaming from getting back to the insane grind of restaurant life. She was in her element and everyone was happily aware of that. Maybe, indeed, this was just what she needed. "Well, are you ready for dessert?" she asked everyone. She looked at her son and asked, "Can you help me, baby?" The young man agreed with a big smile.

Everyone watched the two leave and then Mrs. Figueroa asked Shelly, "So, have you picked any names out, yet?"

With a guilty face she replied, "Not really." She looked at Robin and said, "Have you?"

"Oh, I don't know. It's so difficult, really. There are lots of good names out there."

"I will say this," continued Shelly, "if it's a girl, I'd like to give her the middle name of Rose."

"Oh," started Robin, "for my mother" they both said. Everyone laughed as they stared at each other. "That's my mother's middle name," they both said in unison once again. "You're kidding!"

By this time, the rest of the table was laughing at this exhibition of their knack of saying the same thing at the same time quite hard. Then, Debra and Paul came out with a cake on fire. They encouraged them all to sing for Rachel as she died of embarrassment. She had been hoping that they wouldn't make a big deal about her birthday, but at the same time was flattered. They made her stand up and blow out her candles. "Speech!" they joyfully cheered.

"You people—I can't trust you." (Laughter from the table.) "Well, thank you very much, anyhow. Actually, I would like to give a toast instead of a speech. To Debra— congratulations on your beautiful new café. We wish you all the best and…" Rachel began to get self-conscious, "well, the food is really good."

She quickly sat down and everyone laughed and cheered, "To Debra!" raising their lemonades to her.

"Thanks, Rachel, sweetie," she replied, giving Rachel a peck on the cheek and a hug. "And now...presents! Terry?"

Terry got up to get the presents they all had stashed on the cart under the cake. Debra excused herself once again to take care of business.

Rachel noticed with curiosity that the presents seemed to be all large and odd-shaped, and as she opened them, they also followed a theme. Her parents gave her a snorkel set, Shelly and Robin gave her a wet suit, and George and Debra gave her an underwater camera, which Paul proudly delivered.

She sat laughing and shaking her head. "Are you trying to tell me to go take a dive?"

Then Terry gave her a card. She read the card, getting slightly flushed by what he had written, and then noticed a smaller card inside her envelope. She opened it to find a reservation for an exclusive resort in Barbados. "Oh, my God! Terry!" she exclaimed. She jumped up to hug and kiss him.

He laughed and happily replied, "Happy birthday, babe."

So, the evening ended on a fun note and the crowd wobbled home, full of good food and warm thoughts.

Chapter Fourteen

A couple of weeks had passed, and Rachel was going frantic trying to arrange everything. Shelly had planned (with some help from Miguel's wife) a bridal shower for her. Shelly was also doing all she could to help poor Rachel, and ended up having to call her own father several times. It proved to be a happy accident, giving her the opportunity to get to know him. She was beginning to learn he had a vicious sense of humor, which must endear him to his parishioners. She thought it odd how much he reminded her of Robin. She didn't know if it was because they came from the same portion of the world or if it was because you really do marry someone like your father. She had always taken it for granted that adage meant the one who raised you, though, which, obviously, Robin was nothing like *that* man.

Shelly had begun to get so engrossed in wedding plans and getting the nursery ready that she had very nearly forgot her monthly check-up was that Wednesday. She was excited about this one because the doctor said he was going to tell her the sex of the baby. She usually liked surprises, but this time she agreed with her husband that it would be good to know beforehand.

Robin, along with the staff, had very happily greeted George back to work Monday. The boys got busy making plans for a 'mini-tour'. They figured it would be practical to play some of the large cities, enabling them to get some good promotion of the album out there without jeopardizing George's health. Robin was also concerned about spending too much time away from Shelly. She was doing fine now, but would be well into her third trimester by the time they played these cities. But, the band was eager to get going on this as the album had been out for some time now. Everyone was way out of practice. The guys settled on the idea to start out west and work their way eastward. They would play Los Angeles, Las Vegas, Chicago, Dallas, and end in Miami. Both George and Robin were actually excited about it. Their lives of late had been in so much turmoil that it felt good to get back to what they knew so well.

Their agents had been sent off to set things up and the Parker brothers set up a practice schedule for the band. Robin was very cautious when it came to the amount of hours his brother was going to be working, even though George insisted that he was perfectly fine now. In reality, Robin also required a gradual easing back to work. He was still the proverbial mother hen to Shelly. The memory of her illness and brush with death still echoed in his mind with a most persistent clamor. She was healthy as she ever had been, of course, but he was still afraid that she might disappear if he turned away. He knew he was being paranoid, but her pregnancy added to her apparent delicate state making her seem vulnerable. He also knew that if he didn't alter this frame of mind it would make this tour unbearable. He was beginning to have that severed feeling again—being torn between Shelly and his work. Certainly he could handle a few cities? He knew what he needed to do; he just required some talking to himself or maybe someone outside the family who could be more objective. A guilty flush came over him. Shelly had been so good about going to her therapist, that she was given the okay to stop going. He, on the other hand, only went on an intermittent basis for a while and then completely stopped. He really didn't feel any desire to slip back into his bad habits, but he felt something a bit unresolved was lurking within his psyche. So much in his life had changed, that he was unclear where his priorities lay. Work, Shelly, George, the baby—he was feeling torn by so many sources where once his life was so clear-cut…and boring. He resolved to go to his therapist and see if he could get a brain adjustment. He made an appointment for Friday without telling Shelly. If he could only just talk to someone who didn't depend on him…

Wednesday came, and as busy as Robin was, he wasn't going to miss Shelly's appointment. They met at the doctor's office, Robin greeting the already waiting Shelly with a kiss. "And how are you doing?"

"Pretty good, and you?"

"Oh, great," he said sarcastically.

"What's wrong?"

He let out a sigh and looked around the room. "Our drummer's quitting."

"What? Why?"

"His wife is from Germany and she wants to move back because her parents are getting quite old. Her mother is not doing too well, I believe, and there isn't any other family around."

"Another Terry and Rachel, huh?"

"Precisely."

She thought for a moment. "Honey?"

"Yes?"

"What's going to happen with your mom? None of her kids live near by."

"Believe me, we have talked about it. We've asked her to move here, but she won't do it."

"Stubborn runs in the family, eh?"

He smiled at her, turning his head sideways.

"So what do you do now?"

"Hire another drummer who just *happens* to know all our music."

"Bummer," she remarked without hope.

"If it isn't one thing, it's another."

"My mother's favorite saying."

"Mrs. Parker?" asked the assistant.

The couple got up and went in to see the doctor after the nurse did her preliminaries. He was very happy to see them both and was pleased with Shelly's progress. He asked a barrage of questions and asked, "Okay, I guess y'all want to know if it's a boy or a girl?"

Shelly nodded her head eagerly and Robin grinned at her.

The doctor prepped up Shelly and the monitor and they watched with fascination as their baby appeared to them clearly for the first time. He scanned around saying, "Come on, little one, let us know what you are—they have to decorate!" The baby began to squirm until the doctor said, "Here you go! Well, looks like you've got you a little girl!"

"Really?!" Shelly asked with excitement. She hadn't told anyone, but she really wanted a girl. Robin's eyes remained fused to the monitor and he softly smiled. He was happy either way it went, just as long as it was healthy.

"Yep! I'd say that's a pretty positive conclusion… And she looks perfectly fine… Now smile!" he told the baby as he took her picture.

Dr. Hodges gave the printout to the happy parents. They looked at it lovingly and the doctor finished up with Shelly and told them to keep up the good work.

They were at the reception desk when Robin excused himself from Shelly. He ran back to find the doctor. Shelly checked out and waited for his return. Robin came back with a smile, scratching his cheek. Once they got outside she asked, "What did you ask him?"

"Well, I asked him if he thought if it was safe for us to…you know."

"Oh," she said with a grin, "and what did he say?"

"He said to try it and see what happens—that everything looks good and that you're doing very well."

"Really?"

"Yes. And then he gave me some dos and don'ts."

Shelly chuckled. "I guess you're not working late tonight?"

"Ah! But I am, I'm afraid. Practice makes perfect."

"Oh," she sadly replied.

He turned to look down his nose at her. "That doesn't mean I can't take an extended lunch, though." He raised an eyebrow and she giggled.

She took his hand and hurried to the truck. "Well, c'mon, then!"

He laughed and helped her in.

As they drove along, she started telling him what all she wanted to buy for their little girl, but then seemed to drift off in thought. Somehow, knowing the sex of the child made it more real to them. It was no longer just 'baby', it had its own identity—a characteristic. Robin wondered if she would inherit Shelly's red hair, whereas Shelly wondered if she would get Robin's beautiful brown eyes.

This caused them to be fairly quiet the rest of the way home—simply thinking and wondering what the baby would look and act like. Robin all of a sudden noticed the peculiar silence. "How are you?" he asked.

"Great," she said softly, looking at him with so much love it embarrassed him.

"Good," was his simple reply.

So they got home, and once inside he took her purse from her and set it on the bar. She looked at him with a nervous apprehension. She was a little scared, but he realized it and simply stood in front of her and caressed her cheek gently. He wanted her to be the initiator to make sure she was up for this. He got his wish. She stared hard into his eyes with her mouth slightly opened. She suddenly felt everything was going to be okay. She reached up, grabbing his neck, to pull him down. He kissed her hard and they both felt so alive. Up to that point, they had subconsciously been not only abstaining from sex, but anything more remotely passionate than a friendly peck.

She felt her knees go weak and she held onto him tightly. He smiled and led her upstairs. He helped her out of her blouse and he discovered that she was feeling a bit awkward about how her body looked. He smiled again to show how pleased he was and kissed her slowly down her neck. "You are beautiful, you know that?" he mumbled. She looked down and he picked her chin up. "I mean that. You've never been lovelier. You're full of life…just…" he actually ran out of words.

She believed him and took his hands to pull him onto the bed. She eventually forgot her worries and Robin remembered the doctor's directions. Needless to say, they reveled in being together again.

The sun was hot that afternoon, but they lay there in the cool air of the bedroom with smiles on their faces. "That was…nice," Shelly purred to her husband.

"Yes, yes it was… How are you?" he asked once again.

She thought for a moment to assess herself. "Good," she answered.

"Good!"

"Well, there is one thing."

"What?" he asked with concern.

"I'm starving!"

He laughed heartily, rolling back from his side. "Well, we'll have to take care of that!" He studied her and started to caress her belly with much affection. He gave it a kiss and, surprisingly, started to sing very softly. It made her so happy to see him so happy, and the baby reacted as well with a quick movement. Robin's hand was right where he could feel it and he exclaimed, "Hey! Hallo there, little one!" He kissed her stomach once more and noticed her scar from what seemed like ages ago. It was fading into oblivion, but he knew that it was something neither one of them would ever completely forget. This baby did seem to take the sting away from that sad memory. He kissed his sweet wife on the mouth and put his fingers into her soft red curls. She somehow didn't feel so unattractive when she was with him.

They stayed there quite a while, each enjoying the other's company without interruption from relatives, managers, doctors and other interfering people that had no clue what it was like to be them. They were feeling selfish, but didn't care if they were. They had a lot to ponder and a lot to enjoy.

Eventually though, they came downstairs to get Shelly fed. As she sat eating her lunch, he asked, "Are you still seeing Geri?"

She looked at him as a child with a homework assignment would. It had a been a while since she had seen her herbalist. "Actually—believe it or not—I'm going to see her tomorrow."

"Really?"

"Yes."

"Why aren't you looking forward to it? She's not making you drink that tea again, is she?"

She looked down at her plate. "Well, I haven't been too good with my diet."

"You don't need to diet. You look fine."

"It's not a weight diet; it's a health diet."

"Ah… Well, you're taking your vitamins, I know—I've seen you."

"I guess I could be worse, but I really do want to do all I can to make sure the baby's healthy."

"Well…don't get obsessive about it. You've been very good about walking and eating well from what I can tell. A doughnut every once in a while isn't going to hurt anything."

"Thanks…and thanks for walking with me, too."

"Oh, it works out fine. Walk with you, you go back in, and then I can run. Oh, and don't think you're not going to get back to running eventually, either, madam. After the baby's born, we'll get one of those fancy prams with the big wheels and take her along with us!"

"Aye, aye, aye."

He laughed but then got very quiet.

"What's the matter, honey?"

He looked up at her with his sad eyes and said, "I have an appointment with my therapist Friday."

"Oh," she simply replied.

He nodded.

"For anything in particular?" she asked with a squeak in her voice.

"Same old anxieties, I suppose."

"Too much going on?"

"Yeah." He watched her and could sense her fear. "Don't worry. I'm not craving drugs or anything like that. I just feel…torn."

"Oh." She didn't need to ask between what.

"So," continued Robin, "I thought I'd better nip that in the bud."

"Understood." She got up and kissed him. "Thank you for being responsible for yourself… Sometimes I think your sense of propriety is what I love the most in you." She smiled at him and then took her dishes in to the kitchen.

Robin remarked to himself, "If she only knew me in the old days!" He thought it odd that his 'sense of propriety' is what appealed him to her. What an odd quality to admire!

He chuckled and went to the kitchen to say good-bye before he got back to the grind of work.

"I'm sorry, Deb, but I don't have time to baby-sit," George said to his wife in a slightly heated tone.

"I'm not asking you to baby-sit. He's sixteen, for heaven's sake. You said you wouldn't mind if he came along with you to rehearsal."

"Yes, but I meant a different time. It's crucial we get a new drummer and get him ready for the tour. I *know* you understood that."

"Yes, of course, but I don't see how having Paul there is going to make any difference."

George took a deep breath and counted to ten. "Fine, fine!"

"Well, I'm sorry, honey, but I just don't understand why not."

"Because," he said with a hand gesture, "things can get ugly when we're under a lot of pressure, and I really don't want him to see that side of us."

"Oh." Debra was embarrassed for not thinking that George would be looking out for Paul's best interest. "Well, I guess he can stay home. It's just…"

"Just what?"

"Well, the poor thing gets so bored at the café. That's not to say he doesn't help—that he does—but it seems too much like punishment."

"Well, why don't you ask him if he'd like to stay at home? He's old enough to be on his own, and he'd probably appreciate it."

"You're right. I just want to make sure he feels welcomed and not abandoned."

"I realize that, but one day isn't going to kill him."

"You're right. You're absolutely right. I'm being silly."

He softened up a bit. "Look, maybe next week, okay? The next few days are going to be bloody awful, I know."

So it was settled, but George still went to work with frazzled nerves. He pondered just how complicated this being a step-dad was going to be. He had anticipated the issues he may have with Paul, but he hadn't really thought about how it was going to bring out Debra's protective side. He found it irritating, but not surprising. She was, after all, quite protective over himself, so of course it only would be worse with her own son.

He got to work Thursday to find his brother still bouncing around irritatingly happy. Robin had been showing off his first photo of his daughter to everyone who would talk to him and generally being a joyful nuisance. Even after a late night of rehearsing and having not much luck with drummer interviews, he was still on cloud nine. George grumbled a 'hello' to him and went into his office. Robin followed him in. "What's up?"

George turned his green eyes up to him. "Growing pains."

Puzzled, he asked, "What do you mean?" thinking it had something to do with his heart.

"You know, growing from a couple to a family. All I can say is, *be prepared*."

"Gee, thanks."

George softened his demeanor somewhat. "Ah…I know it's different in my case. You're not starting off with a sixteen-year-old."

"What'd he do?"

"Not him—his mother." George went on to explain the conversation.

"Oh. Well, it sounds like you got it all resolved."

"Yes, I suppose we did. Just bloody irritating to have to deal with this kinda crap first thing in the morning."

Robin felt sorry for him, but really didn't know what to say. "I guess this kind of thing will be common-place."

"Yes, I suppose so… Guess I ought to get used to it, eh?"

"Yeah," he laughed. "I'm sure I've got mine coming."

"For some reason, I can't see you and Shelly arguing."

"Why not? We do, you know."

"You're too much alike."

"We're *nothing* alike," Robin protested.

"Well, I mean in your thinking—your reasoning."

"So? You and Debra are not that *unlike*, are you?"

"Oh, yes, we are. We've always seen things differently. But, until now, we've always, well…"

"Got her to agree with you?" Robin slyly finished for him.

George put down his head and chuckled. "All right, all right… I get it. 'Get over it', eh?"

Robin smiled and asked, "Say, have you seen the picture of my daughter?"

George rolled his eyes and moaned, then he shooed his brother out of his office.

They had another late night and Robin woke up the next morning wondering why he was going to a therapist. He was in a good mood, and the memory of his brother and the pressures that he had been going through made his own seem trivial. Nevertheless, he got up and got himself ready for his appointment.

Dr. Vaughn greeted Robin with her usual cheeriness. She was one of those doctors who made you feel as if you were simply having a heart-to-heart with a favorite aunt rather than spilling your guts out to a psychotherapist. She let him have a seat and quickly got down to business. "So, Robin, what brings you here today?"

"I really don't know," he said honestly.

"Well, there must have been a reason. When you made the appointment, what was on your mind?"

He thought for a moment and wondered what the problem really was. "I don't know… I think I'm just stressed out. I'm feeling a bit torn between my family and my job."

She chuckled and said, "Well, that's a very common complaint, but I usually get that from my working mothers."

He smiled and laughed at her little joke. "Well, see, it's like this: My wife is pregnant and the band's about to do a tour, and, well, I don't want to leave her."

"How long will you be gone?"

"About two weeks. My brother just had a heart-attack, so we don't want to push him too much with anything any longer than that."

"And you don't think you can leave your wife for only a couple of weeks?"

As soon as she said it, Robin realized how silly it did sound. He didn't answer, but gave a look of confusion and fear.

"Is there another matter?" she continued. "Is she having difficulty with her pregnancy?"

"No, actually she just got a good report on her check-up the other day."

"Well, then?"

Like water just beginning to boil, the bubble of realization just came to Robin's mind. "Maybe…" he began, but then trailed off.

"Yes?" she asked gently.

"Maybe it's because I almost lost her, and…and I can't leave her." He began to get nervous and fidgety.

"What do you mean, hon'? She was going to *leave* you?"

"No, no. She had picked up a virus in Japan a while back and she…well, she almost died." He still found it difficult to say.

"Oh, I see. Well, I'm sorry you had to go through that, it must have been awful."

He felt his eyes getting watery. No one had ever told him how sorry they were that *he* had to go through that. He quickly dried his eyes and was embarrassed by his tears. The doctor simply handed him the tissues and smiled. "It's okay to be upset, you know?"

He looked at her without smiling as he held his glasses in his hand while he wiped his face. For the first time, she saw the eyes behind the glasses, and she learned more about him by gazing into those sad, expressive orbs than any listening to him before.

He put his specs back on, and then the barriers were back up.

"I think the problem is that you're still not done dealing with this trauma. Even though she survived, that doesn't take away all the pain you went through when you thought you had lost her. Your whole system shuts down when you believe you're going to have to deal with death, and then your brother's heart-attack not only scared you, but it opened up all those memories of what you had gone through with your wife... This was all in a short period of time, correct?"

"Yes."

She sighed and gave a sympathetic glance to him. "I think the first thing that you have to do is stop denying what you have been through. Admit that it was an emotional torture and that you have the right to still feel a bit shaken by it—that is a normal reaction. Secondly, what you're going to have to work on is trying to put it behind you. Your wife is doing fine now, and you need to focus on the future and the wonderful experience of being a father. Congratulations, by the way."

"Thank you." He smiled bashfully and thought for a moment. "So, you don't think I'm being paranoid?"

"Ha-ha. No, no, just overly concerned. She's gone from one fragile state to another."

"So what shall I do?" He wanted a direct answer.

"I can't tell you that, Robin," she said in a schoolteacher tone of voice. "If you honestly think that spending time away from her is going to affect your job, then maybe you're not ready to make that commitment... Tell you what. Let's do some visualization."

"Okay," he said doubtfully.

"Nothing complicated," she laughed. "I want you to close your eyes and imagine saying good-bye to her as you leave the airport to go on tour, and then describe what you feel."

Reluctantly, he did so. He was quiet for a few minutes. She noticed how he knit his brows and fidgeted with his hands. He quickly opened his eyes.

"Well?" she asked.

He shrugged his shoulders. "It wasn't nice, but I did it."

"You could get on the plane?"

"Yes."

"Then you probably can go through with it in real life."

A faint look of relief came over him and he stared at the coffee table. "Really?" he eventually replied.

"Yes," she said with a little giggle. His expression was priceless.

"So, I'm not a lunatic, then?"

"No, I don't think I'll sign you off just yet."

He smiled.

"Now that can be your homework."

"Huh?"

"Every day until you actually leave I want you to do that little visualization so that when you do leave, it should be easier for you to do so."

"Ah."

"Do you think you can complete your assignment?"

"Yes, I believe so."

"Good! Now, is there anything else going on?"

"No, but would you like to see a picture of my daughter?"

"Ha-ha. Sure, I would."

241

Robin said his good-bye to the doctor and left feeling relieved, if not a little bewildered. It was so blatantly obvious as to what the problem was, but he hadn't seen it. He was so full of ambivalence—anger, embarrassment, sadness, and frustration all plagued him. He knew neither the doctor nor Shelly could get him straightened out—only himself. He pondered all this as he drove to practice. Music, at least, was something he had no trouble understanding.

He came into work and searched for his brother in his office. There he found George talking to a familiar face. "Sam!" he exclaimed. The woman got up and greeted Robin with a kiss on the cheek. She was a tall, striking woman in her thirties with long, thick, blonde hair—a real Scandinavian beauty. She knew the guys from several recording sessions and loved her drums more than anything in the world. "Please say you're going to tour with us!" he begged, holding her hand.

"Well, I don't know. The studios keep me busy."

"But, but, we need you!" he pleaded. "You know our stuff, you know our tempers—"

"Boy, do I."

"Damn, she remembered," joked George.

"Come on, what do you say? It's only for a couple of weeks," continued Robin.

"Well…" She bit her lip and looked back and forth between their eager faces. "All right. You've got yourself a drummer."

"Great!" Robin thanked her with hug.

"Brilliant!" George added. "I knew she'd fall for you—they always do. I'm no good at begging," he sighed to his brother. He shook his head with a smile.

So the studio artist decided to go on the road with the Ministers of Parliament. The boys worked on quelling her fears of such an adventure, for she had never toured with anyone other than a few gigs around town. All was settled, and the paperwork was taken care of. Time to practice.

The band didn't get out until almost 11:00. George came home to discover Debra asleep already, but a light beaming from the kitchen. He went in to find Paul contemplating the contents of the refrigerator. "Gotcha."

The boy turned around with a jerk. He gave George a guilty smile and George flipped the kitchen light on. "Hey, George."

"Hullo. Anything in there?"

"She's got some sort of pasta salad—I don't know what's in it, though." He picked the container up and looked at it suspiciously. "Want it?"

"Sure."

Paul grabbed a few items to fix a sandwich with. He fixed his snack and sat down with George to eat. "Did you find a drummer?" he asked bashfully.

"Yes, thank God. A studio musician we've worked with before. She's dependable and she knows our material—too good to be true, really."

"*She?*"

George chuckled. "Yes—*she*. Just wait until you see her—she's fantastic. Believe me, I never thought a woman could get enough sound out of a set of drums, but she certainly can. I think she's been playing since she was in the womb listening to her mother's heartbeat," he replied comically with a gesture to his ear.

Paul got a good laugh out of this.

"Cripes," said George looking at his fingertips. "I definitely haven't been playing enough lately. A guitarist with soft fingers *won't* do."

"When did you start playing?"

"What? You mean how old was I?"

"Yeah."

"Oh, well, seriously, about your age, I guess."

"Really?"

"Yup. Have you ever tried to play guitar?"

"I've messed around with a friend of mine's, but I never had one myself."

"Would you like to see mine?"

"Sure!"

They finished their food and went into George's little studio. It had been off-limits to Paul until now and he stood in awe of the guitars, gold records, and recording equipment. George had him take a seat and got one of his acoustics out to tinker with. "Here, show me what you know."

Paul's eyes got quite large. George was one of the best guitarists in the business—to play the three chords he knew to him was extremely intimidating.

"Well…"

"Gotta start somewhere!"

He smiled and played the little that he knew. "That's it, I'm afraid," he then remarked sadly.

"No, no. That's good. It's better to know three chords well than six horribly."

Paul appreciated his input. George then grabbed another guitar for himself and showed Paul another chord to learn. The boy very patiently bent his fingers to capture the elusive sound and was thrilled when he got it. George went on to discuss the guitars he had there and the stories behind them. "The one you're holding I had for about, oh, eight years or so—just before I married your mother, actually."

"It sounds great."

"Yes, it does. Just goes to show that expensive doesn't necessarily mean better. It wasn't that much, yet has a sweet sound."

"Oh, really?"

"Yeah. It was only about six hundred dollars."

Paul laughed to himself that 'cheap' was a relative term. He continued to practice his newfound chord.

George studied him for a moment and then asked, "Would you like to have it?"

"What?" he asked in disbelief.

"One condition—you use it. I want to see you practicing on it continually." He looked at him to see if that was possible.

"Well, yeah! Sure… Thanks a lot!"

The young man seemed willing to learn, and this pleased George. They ended staying up for a while, talking until George couldn't hold his lids up any longer. They went to bed dreaming of lost chords.

By that following Tuesday, Rachel was about to pull her hair out. Trying to arrange a wedding in a town she was unfamiliar with (and Shelly only somewhat) and dealing with all the legalities of marrying a foreigner in a different state than her was driving her up the wall—never mind the usual details of where, when and flowers. She called Shelly in a panic.

"Hello," Shelly cheerily answered.

"Hi, girl."

"Hey, what's up?"

"Jesus. Do you know what kind of freakin' red tape I'm having to go through?"

"No," Shelly laughed. What?"

"Well, besides the fact I'm marrying someone who has just barely got his green card, I'm having to deal with a foreign priest. I think I'm actually going to have to have the J.P. there in attendance."

"No way, really?"

"Yeah. And, hey, where the hell is this La Villita you suggested?"

"Right downtown. It's an actual old settlement in San Antonio. Been there for Fiesta a couple of times. Could you get the church?"

"Yeah, believe it or not. It better be nice, or you're dead meat."

"You'll love it, I promise."

Rachel whimpered.

"You poor thing. Don't worry about it. Tell you what: You handle all the legal crap and I'll do all the decorations and reception and all, okay?"

"Really? You wouldn't mind?"

"No, of course not. It really is too much, isn't it? So, what's the date?"

"Uh…" she violently flipped through her day planner, "August the 26th."

"Okay, great!" Shelly glanced at a calendar and marked it. "Don't worry, hon', we'll make it work."

"You know, your dad's pretty cool."

"Yeah, he's a neat guy, isn't he?"

"Terry talked to him for quite a while on the phone the other night."

"Oh, really? Converting him to Catholicism?" she joked.

"I don't know. They were discussing theology of some sort."

"Men are all talk and no do."

"I hear ya. They can't just sit back and enjoy religion; they have to explain it, which, of course, you can't do." Rachel said with her own twist on the basics of theology.

"Ha-ha. Yep, that's true."

"Ah!" Rachel exclaimed out of nowhere and into Shelly's unsuspecting ear.

"Rachel! Don't scare me like that! I'm pregnant, remember?"

"Sorry. I just realized I've only forgotten the most important thing. Idiot!" she griped at herself.

"What?"

"My dress! I haven't even *begun* to look!"

"Oh, geds… Okay, well, let's go."

"You sure?"

"Yeah. I'll take you where I went."

"Bless you."

Rachel got home three hours later after wearing Shelly out looking at wedding dresses. She decided on one with spaghetti straps and a slight scoop at the neckline. It had beautiful, intricate beading on the bodice with only a faint beaded design on the skirt. She had to wait to have it altered for her little figure of which that was no surprise. With much relief, she plopped herself down onto her bed, kicking her shoes off. A noise downstairs told her that Terry had arrived. She got back up with a grumble, but smiled at the thought of him. She greeted him with a big hug and he swung her around. He stood gazing at her with an odd look in his eye. "What?" she had to ask.

"Have a seat." He escorted her to the couch.

She got nervous from his strange demeanor. "What is it?" she asked again.

He gave a chuckle. "Nothing bad. It's just that I have an important decision to make, so I needed to get your input."

"Oh."

"The owners had a chat with me today—"

"They fired you?" she asked quickly.

"No-o-o, silly. They complemented me very much, in fact. Said the team was about to be a failure before it even got going before I came along."

"So what's the problem?"

He sighed and answered, "They want me to coach."

"What?"

"Yep."

"Wow, Terry, that's great…isn't it?" The strange look on his face told her he was not completely happy about this news.

"Well, I don't know. I mean, I've always wanted to, but—and I guess this may sound a bit vain—but I don't know if I'm ready to stop playing."

"Well, I can understand that."

"You can?"

"Sure. It's like retirement."

"Exactly!" He was so happy she understood.

"And besides," she continued with a changed expression and a grave tone of voice, "your friends in England still want you to play with them."

Terry's smile faded promptly. He had no clue she knew and felt stupid for underestimating her intelligence. "Uh, yeah," he slowly drawled out.

"I thought so." She remained cool as a cucumber.

He put his head down and got up to walk around. He fiddled with some pastel drawings she had laying on the cabinet.

She studied him and then nervously asked, "You know what, Terry?"

He turned to her. "What?" he asked, as if waiting for his sentence.

"You do whatever you damn well want to do."

His eyes got large. He figured she'd finally had enough of his crap and it was over. "What...what do you mean by that?"

"I mean I shouldn't be standing in your way of having a good career. How many more years do you think you'll be playing anyway?"

"Pff...I dunno. Three. Five?"

"Well," she started, and then swallowed hard, "I think I can deal with that if we can come back home eventually. Uh, here, that is."

He quickly sat back down and put his hand on her knee. He was in complete disbelief of what he was hearing. "Do you *really* mean that? Are you quite sure?"

Rachel began to breathe heavily. "I can't live without you, Terry—we've already established that. Nor can I keep you from what you really need to be doing—that wouldn't be right. I love you and I can't stand in your way of something that some people only dream of. You'd resent it—me—for the rest of our lives."

"I wouldn't resent *you*."

"Maybe. But it would always be in the back of your mind."

"Why the change?" he asked suspiciously.

She looked down to her nervous hands. "Papa pointed out to me how selfish I've been."

"I wouldn't call it selfish. That's a bit harsh. You were just concerned about your family."

"No. He was right. They don't *need* me. I felt I needed them, but now you're my family."

"And I *do* need you," he said very seriously.

She smiled.

"Are you positive?" he sternly asked once more.

"Yes! You'd better not push your luck by asking me any more!"

"Ha-ha. Okay, okay." He stared at her and put his hand on her cheek. He couldn't believe the sacrifice she was making for him. He gave her a long kiss and then quietly said, "Guess I'd better make a few phone calls."

She smiled and gently nodded her head.

He went out to his car to get the phone numbers he needed and she retreated to the bathroom to cry a little and convince herself that she did the right thing. "This is right," she told the image in the mirror. "I know it is." Somehow, in the back of her mind, she knew that this was going to happen—or maybe she just felt a little guilty about the whole thing after her father's talk. She knew in her heart that he needed to be in England. More tears came when she thought of Shelly and missing watching her baby grow up. "No, no," she told herself, "this is what I've got to do. I can't live my life for all these other people. I'm going to marry Terry and we will be one, and we'll have our own family." The thought of having her own children—*his* children— pleased her. She managed to put on a brave face and went back down to listen to Terry talk to his friends in England. He was ecstatic—practically beaming. This convinced her that she had made the right decision.

She sat down, stunned at what she'd done. The first time that they had to deal with this issue, she debated with herself for days. She wondered why, all of a sudden, she was able to make this decision so quickly? The words of her father echoed in her head: *If you really loved him, you would move to China.* She then realized the reason for the change—her parents had given her carte blanche to do what she would with her life and it was up to her to carry out what she knew should be done. Terry was her world, and he would do anything for her as well, including moving to another country with no real hope for a good career. Her love for him had only grown since he properly proposed to her, so it was only right to make this sacrifice. As she continued to listen, she began to feel a warm feeling from within—the feeling that a wrong had been corrected. She felt redeemed for a past sin, and a genuine smile came to her face.

He hung up and looked at her with a big grin. He came over to her and took her hands to lift her up. He then put his fingers through her hair while staring hard into her eyes without smiling. "Rachel…my dear Rachel." He had a hard time finding the words, but finally said with an honest simplicity, "I love you."

He had said those words before, but for some reason they had so much more meaning now. He kissed her and held her so tight that she could barely breathe. Then he suddenly picked her up to where her head almost touched the ceiling and she looked down on him. She couldn't help but laugh.

He put her back down and asked, "May I take you to dinner?"

"Only if you promise to take me dancing later," she answered with a big smile. Terry's happiness was infectious.

"You've got it."

Chapter Fifteen

It was a week before the wedding. Debra was going insane trying to prepare her restaurant to run on it's own for a few days without her. She had promoted Amy to manager since she had shown such promise. Debra had originally thought she was going to have to miss the wedding, but Amy showed her that she could handle the ship without its captain. Debra had brought Paul that day to help in rearranging some stock items into a more easily accessible shelving unit. He begrudgingly came, even though he would have preferred to stay home and continue learning new chords.

Debra sat in her closet of an office duly entering her expenses when she heard a knock on the door. She turned to see the face of her produce supplier. "Well, hi Scott! How are you?" she greeted. There was almost a nervous tone in her voice. For some reason, the handsome man with black and silver hair always seemed to unnerve her.

"Just fine, Debra, and how are you?" he asked as he shook her hand, laying his other hand on their grasp.

"Fine, fine. Pulling my hair out like usual." She pointed her hand towards her unruly paperwork.

"Yes, there's always paperwork, isn't there?"

"Oh, yeah. Uh, what can I do for you?" She stood up, throwing her pen onto her desk.

"Well, actually, I just happen to be in the neighborhood and thought I'd stop by and see what *I* could do for *you*." He gazed at her with an odd smile.

"Oh! Well, uh, I think everything is fine, Scott. I think maybe we need to work on getting better Romaine, though. It's been looking pretty wimpy lately."

"I know, I know. We are working on that, in fact." He was looking down, but then turned his light blue eyes up to her, which made her even more nervous. He then asked, "Can I ask you a personal question?"

"Uh…not *too* personal." Her eyes were wide open while she waited with anticipation.

"You're married, aren't you?" he asked while looking at her ring.

"Yes, I am."

"Happily?"

"Well, yes."

He began to advance toward her, but she didn't have much of an escape route in the tiny room.

"You seemed to hesitate with your answer."

"Uh, no, no, no. I'm quite happy." She knocked the calendar off her desk.

"Well, if ever things don't work out," he picked up her hand and kissed it, "you'll let me know first, won't you?"

"Uh, okay." She swallowed hard as he stared at her and then he quickly turned to leave, putting his hand on the doorway as he exited the office.

She quickly sat down in a daze. "Wow," she said to herself. "What was *that*?" She shook her head and left the office to get some air. She was feeling quite flushed.

After several bouts of insanity from both Rachel and a steadily increasingly emotional Shelly, the wedding was underway. The Florida crew packed into a Streamliner jet. Rachel and Paul were thrilled to ride the luxurious little plane, but eventually slipped into their own thoughts. Shelly was just so grateful to have a place to lie down. Her doctor was wary about this trip on her, but in the end, he gave her permission barring the fact that she must be made comfortable at all times. She made no notice of her friend's unusual quiet demeanor, and kicked back and relaxed.

Rachel was happy though about the fact that Terry's family and a good portion of hers were going to make it. Seating would be tight in the little church, and she hoped everyone would still be able to fit.

They made it to San Antonio two days before the wedding. The entire party practically took over one of the smaller exclusive hotels downtown. Terry and Rachel met up with their respective families. Shelly, on the other hand, impatiently waited for the hour when she could call her father. He would be ending his retreat that day, so she still had another couple of hours to go. She had a humorous time of it though, watching Terry's parents meet Rachel's. She could hear Mr. Figueroa's voice booming across the lobby and then a faint whisper coming from Mr. Dunham in reply. As different as they were, they seemed to get along quite well. The mothers hit it right off, and were soon chatting about their children and what the future holds for them.

Terry's brother, Phillip, was at first a bit sullen, but the Parker brothers soon got him to feel at home. Terry was very happy he came and hoped the trip would cheer him up. He had gone on to work for his father at the brewery after all and was still feeling bad about the loss of his other brother. Terry knew he himself would probably have been the same if it weren't for the love of Rachel.

George and Robin were especially pleased about the person who came along with the Dunhams—their mother. They really didn't think she was going to make it, but she surprised them by showing up without a word. She actually wanted to see Shelly and know first-hand that all was well with her and the baby. She was so happy that she was finally going to get to be a grandmother after all this time. She had given up hope for her boys, and her daughter was even more doubtful.

She was welcomed with open arms by everyone and immediately inquired into George and Shelly's wellbeing. She was pleased to hear that all was well. She was amazed by how much Paul had grown. She hadn't seen him since three Christmases ago. George inquired as to which sea their sister was bumbling around in. She gave a lengthy explanation after which George suggested they all go to dinner.

Shelly had finally got a hold of her father and he agreed to get a taxi to downtown to join them. She was very anxious to meet him although she still felt so odd about it all. She really wished they had more time alone to get to know each other. There was still so much to learn.

The group split up with Terry and Rachel taking their families to a well-known Mexican restaurant, and the Parkers choosing the more discreet venue of an upscale restaurant on the River. Shelly's father made it, and he was very pleased to see Shelly doing so well.

They enjoyed their meal, and even though Shelly was concentrating on her father's funny anecdotes of his retreat, she was able to catch an almost defiant look on young Paul's face. She feared he wasn't thrilled having to come to some boring wedding with a bunch of goof-ball adults. She hoped he would have more fun when his parents would take him sightseeing later in the week.

The next day consisted of making sure all was ready for the wedding. Fr. O'Connor had a brief discussion with Rachel and Terry about the ceremony. This made them a tad nervous knowing that they finally were going through with it, but they held each other's hand with an eager anticipation.

The Parkers, in the mean time, played tourists. They enjoyed the river barge ride downtown, but Shelly and Mrs. Parker soon grew tired of walking up and down the steps of the beautiful River Walk. They eventually found themselves relaxing at the hotel café, watching everyone else tackle the steps.

Shelly had reserved a private dining room at an Italian restaurant for their dinner. Everyone piled in and it was a strange sight of the differences in the two families—not just appearances, but volume. Shelly happily soaked it all in with her artistic eye.

Terry seemed to be completely attached to Rachel. He was overcome with some sort of impending doom to befall them (as it always seemed to do with them), keeping him from finally getting to marry her. He wished it were all over, for this feeling was getting annoying.

The dinner began by a series of toasts given to the happy couple by Fr. O'Connor; Rachel's brother, Dominic; and Robin. George was asked before Robin, but he liked leaving the speeches to his brother. This time, Robin gave a much more light-hearted speech about the crazy temperaments of the young couple, and how they were destined to be together.

"You know," George told Debra, "I never think we have any Irish in us until I hear Robin make a speech." Debra gave a reserved giggle while their mother nodded in agreement.

The dinner was going along amicably until Mr. Dunham surprised everyone by raising his voice. The room silenced itself to listen to the heated debate between him and Mr. Figueroa. Somehow, Rachel's father made the grave mistake of bringing up the topic of religion. He was pleased that they were able to get a Catholic priest to perform the ceremony, but Mr. Dunham had casually deduced that Fr. O'Connor was there simply because he was Shelly's father. Of course, Mr. Figueroa then had to explain his point of view on the matter, and it escalated from there. Unfortunately, brothers began to get involved, and everyone else did what they could to silence the arbitrators, when all of a sudden a loud shout rose above all others, "Shut up!"

All eyes turned to see the pint-sized woman who managed to gain the silence necessary. Rachel stood, eyes aflame, staring at the two fathers as if she had murder on her mind.

"I have had it," she said quietly. "I have dealt with your attitudes, and we have bent over backwards to make everybody happy. And you know what? *I don't care anymore.* We are getting married tomorrow, and it is up to you if you want to be there or not. You need to grow up and put your petty differences aside… Geeze, you'd think we were of totally different religions, or something. We're *supposed* to be all Christians, but this sure doesn't sound like it. What do you think *He* thinks of us right now? Huh? I think you just need to get over it and be happy for Terry and me, because we love each other and we have come a long way." Tears suddenly built up in her black eyes, and Terry came over to her. "He came all the way to America for me, and I'm going all the way to England for him, but no distance is too long for us to be together."

"*Mija*, what are you saying?" her mother quickly asked.

Rachel looked around the room and let her eyes land on Shelly. "I mean, we're moving to England."

Her mother began to ramble in Spanish, and Shelly did her best to smile. She was proud of her friend for her commitment, but she really wanted to cry.

Eventually it was chaos, with half the room sad, and the other elated. Terry explained his new position, but came to Rachel's parents to comfort them with the knowledge that it would only be for a few years. Mr. Figueroa was sad by the news, but secretly, he was proud of his daughter for showing she knew her priorities.

Fr. O'Connor made sure to tell Rachel how much he admired her and her speech. "It's a very hard lesson for some people to learn. No one has the patent on how to worship God."

She smiled and hugged the man, but then excused herself to find Shelly. She looked around the room, but saw neither her nor Robin. She left the room and searched until she found them outside. He was holding her, letting her cry, and it tore Rachel to see it. But, Robin beckoned her over. "Someone here to see you, dear," he said softly to Shelly. She pulled away from him and dried her eyes to see Rachel. "I'll see you in a little bit," he said and went back in.

"I'm sorry," Shelly sniffed. "I'm very emotional lately, you know."

"No, I'm sorry, honey. I meant to tell you first, alone, but, well, this happened."

"That's okay… I'm very proud of you, you know?"

"Thanks."

"And I can come visit, too."

"Not any time soon, though," she said with a nod to Shelly's stomach.

"Yeah, I guess you're right," she replied as she lovingly rubbed her belly.

"Somehow, *amiga*, I think things are working out like they should."

"Yeah, I feel the same way, too… I can't tell you how happy I am for you and Terry."

"Thanks."

"You're getting married tomorrow!" she exclaimed. This caused the baby to give a kick, and Shelly flinched.

Rachel immediately got concerned and held onto Shelly. "Now, don't be having babies during the ceremony, okay? Reception—sure, no one will notice—but not in the church," Rachel joked.

"Okay," she laughed, "got it. No church."

They continued to chat for a while until they were beckoned back. They were grateful for their little bit of time together and it did them both good.

There were no more arguments, although the fathers had settled on the notion of 'agree to disagree', and rather avoided each other. This didn't keep Fr. O'Connor from chatting with them both on the fascinating topic of fishing. Fr. O'Connor, it seemed, shared Robin's knack for diplomacy.

Finally, enough wine had instilled itself into the guests and they went back to the hotel to try to sleep before the big day. Shelly couldn't have any of the lovely beverage, but she didn't need any, either. She was wiped out, and fell asleep once her head hit the pillow. She didn't dream at all.

The day had finally come. Terry found himself surrounded by various relatives while he tried to tie his tie. Not used to such a confounded thing, George came to the rescue with Robin arguing as to how it should be done. "Yes, well, this worked when you got married, did it not?" George retorted.

"I tied my own tie…didn't I?"

"You did not—you were too nervous."

Terry and Paul chuckled at their banter and Robin's memory lapse.

George managed to get the young man situated, and Terry looked in the mirror at himself. "I look like an idiot."

"You should've gotten a haircut," Robin observed.

Mr. Dunham caught the last remark. "Ah! Now, I've been telling that boy he needs to get that hair cut, but he won't do it."

"Yes. Repeatedly," Terry grumbled.

"That's Nick, too," added Mr. Figueroa about his son, who was within earshot. The young man rolled his eyes at his father.

"Well, at least grease it back a bit," suggested George.

"I've got some stuff." Robin went to retrieve some pomade from his room.

Terry went back to staring in the mirror. He found he couldn't stop grinning. He was surprised by his own happiness and the fact he really wasn't that nervous. He really couldn't think of a more natural thing to do than to marry the girl of your dreams.

Meanwhile, Rachel and her entourage had settled into the offices of La Villita's little church. They were located directly behind the actual chapel, and one could easily access the back door of the church from there.

The women had great fun decorating Rachel—she was like a little doll. In fact, her father's pet name for her meant 'little doll'. She was always his *muñequita*.

It was getting closer to the big event. The men had congregated at the front door of the chapel, the women outside of the rear of the building. Rachel couldn't help but peep in to see who else had shown up. Shelly took a glance in, too. "*What* is my mother doing here?" Shelly asked in a high-pitched voice.

"Oh, she came? Good for her! I'm surprised, really, but I'm glad she did."

"Rachel!"

"I wasn't *not* going to invite her. She only lives a couple of hours away, so I sure didn't want to be rude."

Shelly made a completely inexplicable face of panic.

Rachel's eyes popped open. "Shelly—do *not* tell me you didn't tell her about your father!"

Shelly stood shaking her head with her eyes wide open. "Oh, Jesus. No, no, no! This is *not* happening!"

"*¿Qué está pansando, mijíta?*" her mother asked quickly.

Rachel explained the situation in Spanish to her.

"*¡Aye, no!*" the woman interjected with a glance to Shelly.

"I'm so sorry!" Shelly explained. She quickly made her way into the chapel and accosted her mother. She was greeted with a hug. "Hi, Mom. Didn't expect you could come."

"Well, I was trying to surprise you."

"That you did. Look, Mom, can you come outside? There's something I have to tell you."

She looked at her strangely and said, "All right."

Shelly panicked again, for she didn't know which entrance her father would come through. She hadn't seen him in a while, but she figured he was with the men out front. She took her out the back just in time to run smack dab into the one she was trying to avoid. Everyone stood frozen and Shelly laid one hand on her baby and the other on her heart. She felt like one of the two was about to go.

"Jimmy," her mother barely uttered.

"Patty," he replied in the same manner.

Shit, Shelly thought to herself.

"You haven't changed a bit," he told Patty, unable to get his eyes off of her.

Patty began to cry and ran to the offices.

"Sorry, Papa," Shelly apologized, following her mother, "she didn't know you were going to be here, and I didn't know she was, either."

"Oh, dear," he lamented.

"Shelly!" Rachel yelled as she ran past her.

"I know, I know," she exclaimed with a gesture.

Her mother had locked herself in the restroom, leaving Shelly to talk to her through the door under the gaze of Rachel and all the ladies.

"Mom, *please* come out so we can talk about this. Rachel didn't know that you didn't know—"

"Know that my daughter was trying to trick me?" she hollered out.

"No! Mom, look, it's a long story. Can we please talk about this?"

"Shelly! It's time!" Rachel yelled.

Shelly began to breathe hard, so much so that everyone got alarmed. They helped her to a chair.

"Shelly, I told you—not during the ceremony," Rachel joked, but was really hoping that she was okay. "Uh, are you all right?"

Shelly continued to take deep breaths of air, and Mrs. Figueroa said, "I think she's hyperverlating."

The girls laughed and Rachel corrected, "That's *hyperventilating*, Mama. And yes, I think she is."

This made Patty come out of the protection of the restroom. "Is there a small paper bag around?" Everyone rambled through the wedding stuff until someone found one. Patty gave it to her daughter and coaxed her into settling down. "She used to do this when she was a teenager… Oh, Shelly."

Shelly kept breathing into her bag with tears in her eyes.

"Like, can I get married now?" Rachel asked in desperation. This made everyone laugh.

Shelly took her bag away and said, "I wouldn't dare stop you." She then told her mother, "Can we talk about this later?"

"Of course," she consented. She was still mad, but felt sorry for poor Rachel.

"Let's go see her get married."

"Okay."

The entourage made their way into the church with Rachel making the trek around the side of the church to the front. She found her father who proudly looped his arm around for her. She was nervous, but she was happy.

Fr. O'Connor stood at his position, ready for action, but couldn't help but avert his gaze to the general direction of Shelly's mother. He was glad she didn't leave, although she had every right to.

Terry had his brother as his best man. Even though they were never very close, he felt it was probably a good thing to do to help Phillip feel a part of his life and to remind him of the family that's left instead of constantly thinking of the family they had lost. He would have loved to have George and Robin up there as well, but there simply wasn't enough room in the little church.

Shelly managed to pull herself together to be the matron-of-honor. Her happiness for the couple helped quell the anxiety she had about her parents.

And then there was Rachel. At the cue, everyone rose to see her. Some were amazed just how beautiful she looked in her wedding gown. Her dark skin clashed against the white of her dress and her big, bright smile. Her black eyes were lit up above her round, blushing cheeks. She looked exuberant.

Terry gazed at her in complete disbelief that he was at the receiving end of her walk. She was coming to him and he felt himself quivering slightly. He was more nervous than when he was at a direct penalty kick in the last five seconds of a World Cup match. Finally, though, it was happening.

Mr. Figueroa gave his daughter a kiss and gave her away with a slight tug to the heart. Rachel and Terry found it hard to pay attention to the priest and could not stop staring at one another.

The ceremony went off well and included a lovely song sung by Rachel's younger sister, Damiana. Most guests were highly entertained by the mixture of accents including Puerto Rican, English and Irish. It was very amusing to hear Rachel say, "What?" a couple of times when she couldn't understand Fr. O'Connor. Terry would chuckle and make her embarrassed, but then she would giggle and go on with her lines.

Mothers were crying and everyone else was smiling when Terry finally got to kiss Rachel and they were introduced to the crowd as husband and wife by Father. There were great cheers from the company and they were issued out with applause and hugs. Once outside, photos by the score were taken and then everyone threw birdseed at them to the pigeons' great delight. They got into their waiting limousine to be taken to the reception hall. The reception was to be held at the hotel that everyone had booked at, making it convenient for everyone. They took their sweet time getting there, enjoying the pleasure of the grand car.

Shelly quickly went in search of her mother. She panicked when she couldn't find her, for she really wanted to talk to her and make things right. Robin found his wife in this state. "Darling? What's wrong?"

"I can't find Mom."

"You know, I was quite surprised to see her—"

"She didn't know," she said distracted as he followed her.

"What?!" he asked with surprise.

"Help me find her!"

"All right! Look, you go down that way, and I'll go down the street—and *please* be careful!"

Shelly quickly as she could went down the cobblestone pathways of La Villita to try to try to find where her mother had gone. She ended up on a street parallel to the one Robin had gone down. She surveyed the adjacent parking lot and saw her mother standing near her car. "Mom!" Shelly yelled. She went up to her panting and laid one hand on her shoulder.

"Shelly," Patty said with concern.

"Mom, we need to talk about this."

"Shelly, honey, go join your party. I'll call you later."

"But, Mom, I need to tell you something. I have to tell you why he was here." She waited to see if she would protest. "Look, yes, I did find him. But he came in handy, so to speak, for Rachel because her father was so bent on a Catholic wedding and Terry wasn't. He agreed to do the wedding and it satisfied them both. It was as if it was meant to be... And I had no idea Rachel had invited you, and she had no idea I hadn't told you about him yet. It was just a big, silly mix-up and I'm *so* sorry if you've been hurt."

Patty breathed hard until she finally said, "Okay. I'm not mad."

"Thanks, Mom… Now, is there any way you'll come with us?"

"No, no I couldn't." She shook her head quickly.

"Mom," she searched for the words to say, "the thing is, is that my father is now a part of my life. You will eventually run into him again. Very soon, I should think." She caressed her belly as a hint. "You might as well face him now."

Patty looked around with teary eyes.

"Besides, I'd hate to send you home on an empty stomach," she said with a grin.

She smiled back at her daughter. "Very well, I'll try."

"Thanks, Mom."

At that moment, Robin came rambling up and greeted the ladies, "There you are. Well, come along. There's a party to go to. Certainly you two ladies are going to dance with me, aren't you?"

How could Patty refuse that? They piled into her car and made their way to the hotel.

At the reception, there was a veritable feast, including some beautiful Puerto Rican dishes catered in by a local restaurant Shelly was lucky to find, making Rachel's family feel more at home. For the Dunhams and the Parkers, she was able to track down some proper British ale. The two cultures melded together just as readily as the food and drink.

Terry and Rachel took a moment to sit at their special table and relax. "I'm glad so much of our families were able to come," said Terry happily.

"Yes, I am, too."

As he looked out over the tables, he studied some of her siblings. "Now, Dominic and Damiana are the youngest, right?"

"Right. They're the babies."

"Who's the elder?"

"Huh?"

"You know, what order are they? Who's the youngest?"

"Oh! They're twins."

"What?"

Rachel laughed at his expression.

"You didn't tell me there were *twins* in your family."

"Ha-ha! Ah, don't worry, baby. It's not a family thing— it just happened."

"Really? Good. I'd hate to have to tell everyone I changed my mind." He watched her laugh with love in his heart. "But, uh, let's keep ours *singles*, okay?"

"Oh, you know I'll do my best!" She leaned over and gave him a kiss.

"Love you, Mrs. Dunham," he said seriously.

"I love you, too," she replied, desperately trying not to cry.

He smiled and poured her a glass of champagne.

Shelly and Robin escorted a nervous Mrs. Harrison into the ballroom. She surveyed the place until her eyes found the redheaded man she feared. He was chatting with Rachel's father as she turned to leave. "C'mon, Mom. Please?" begged Shelly. Patty looked at her daughter doubtfully.

"Why don't we have a seat?" suggested Robin. He led the ladies to a table, pulling the chairs out for them both. His own mother came up and greeted them.

"We've been wondering where you'd gone to," Mrs. Parker said.

"Oh, just got hung up… Mum, do you remember Patricia? You met at our wedding. My mother, Margaret," he then said to Patty.

"Oh, yes, dear." The women exchanged salutations and Mrs. Parker sat down with them. She was just what Patty needed, for they instantly began talking of their expected grandchild. Robin and Shelly exchanged glances of relief.

Eventually, George, Debra and Paul came to finish filling up the round table, and discussion turned to school for Paul and the upcoming tour.

"When exactly are you starting?" Shelly asked.

"September 15th," Robin answered.

"Oh, no," Debra groaned.

"What's wrong?" George asked.

"That's the weekend I'm going to that expo in Jacksonville."

"What expo?"

"That food service expo—I told you about it. They're going to have all the latest appliances and gadgets and things," she explained with relish.

"Oh… Certainly you don't need anything."

"I need some new refrigerators desperately. They're pitiful. I've had the repair people out there twice already. I think the owners before Jenny had put them in, so that makes them quite old. Besides, it's a fun thing to do. It doesn't hurt to keep up-to-date, you know."

"Okay, okay," he laughed. "Sorry I asked. Go to your expo. But I still don't see what the problem is."

"Well, that means Paul will be alone that weekend."

"I imagine he can handle a weekend alone." He smiled and gave Paul a wink. "But *nobody*," he added quite sternly to him, "is allowed in the house—or *anywhere* on the premises, for that matter." He knew he had to make it perfectly clear, so that there were no loopholes. "Got it?"

"Yes, sir," he dutifully replied.

George noticed Debra's expression. "*Really*, Deb."

"Okay, all right," she relented.

They all laughed to themselves about Debra's over-protectiveness and went on to discuss the details of the band's tour. George was obviously excited about getting back on the road and back to work. Robin found his eagerness contagious, and was also finding it easier to deal with the upcoming separation from Shelly. He still was going to miss her, though—but that he could deal with.

"So, Shelly, do you have the nursery all ready?" Debra asked with a big grin.

"I guess so," she laughed. This, of course, led to a barrage of questions from the mothers.

Eat, eat, eat. Drink, drink, drink. Talk, talk, talk. Everyone was having a good time—even Paul. He escaped to hang out with the twins. They were actually quite a few years older, but still kids themselves. They sat talking when all of a sudden Mr. Dunham's voice once again cut through the din like a knife. "I don't care what you say!" He looked around nervously from the attention he collected and quietly finished to Mr. Figueroa, "You can't catch a kingfish without a down-rigger." Everyone breathed a sigh of relief. Rachel and Terry laughed and got up to cut their cake.

As traditional, the best man was called up to give a speech. If Phillip had remembered this custom, he wouldn't have accepted his position. Public speaking made him nervous, but his family encouraged him to get up and toast the bride and groom.

He nervously took up a glass of champagne and cleared his throat. He didn't know where to start. He looked at his parents, and then at his brother. He saw the ecstatic look on his face and the glow on Rachel's. Her pretty smile warmed his heart and allowed him to speak. He concentrated on her happy expression and quietly started. "To Terry and his sweet Rachel: You have been blessed with something that has eluded many—a determined, strong and willful love. It is such a rare thing, and I am so happy for you for finding it. Terry, you have discovered this beautiful, rare gem of a lady who I can tell has captured your heart with her wonderful outlook on life. She's charismatic, dynamic, and has such an easy way about her that it will make it a cinch to spend eternity with her. How can one ever grow tired of that true, inner beauty?"

"Rachel, you on the other hand," he said sadly and paused to bring out a little laughter, "you have gotten a guy that I know will be true to you. He will take care of you and he will be there for you through thick and thin. He's a good man, my brother..." he trailed off a bit, as if fighting something on the inside. "I know you two will have a strong and faithful marriage. I give you my best wishes for a long and healthy life together. You set an excellent example of what it is all about. Complete devotion, really... Well, anyway, to Rachel and Terry—congratulations, and God bless."

"To Rachel and Terry!" the crowd cheered.

Phillip took a grateful swig of his drink and received hugs from the newlyweds. "Thanks, mate," Terry simply stated. He knew how difficult it was for him considering he himself was divorced. For some reason, the speech also seemed to bring out the fact that Jacob was missing from the family picture. It had crossed all the Dunhams' and Parkers' minds by the time the evening was over, and Rachel could sense it. It hadn't been that long since Terry's older brother had died, and this being the first big family occasion enforced the absence. She continued to smile at Phillip and tell him how glad she was he that came the long distance to be there. He became very grateful he did, too.

Then, Terry watched his cousins with curiosity—they seemed to be plotting something. They were chatting with a couple of employees who in turn disappeared for a moment then came back with large carts whose contents were covered with tablecloths. George made his way to the dance floor and clinked his glass to capture everyone's attention.

"Everyone! We've got a little surprise for Terry and Rachel. Whether they like it or not, we're going to play for them!"

"Yay!" they all cheered with laughter.

The guys set up a simple ensemble of microphones, keyboard and guitar. People got very excited, for there were several who had never heard them play live before.

They began with the song George had written for Robin and Shelly's wedding, and then sang a couple more. They were going to stop there, but then were urged on for a few more by the guests. Rachel was ecstatic—how many people get the Ministers of Parliament to sing at their wedding?

The guys were finally released from their duty and the DJ took over with some dance music. Rachel danced with her father and then he gave her back to Terry. After he did so, he felt a cigarette outside was in order.

People were beginning to mingle. Robin got his promised dances. Fr. O'Connor had intentionally left his daughter alone to be with her mother. He certainly didn't want to disrupt this sweet couple's reception with a row with his old flame. Patty realized this, and respected him for it, but knew the time had come to face him.

She stood up and made her way over to him. Shelly watched, biting her lip. "Want to go outside?" Patty asked once she approached him. The man nodded in agreement. Shelly held onto Robin's hand tightly.

They walked outside to the courtyard by the pool and sat down at a patio table. Neither of them knew where to start. "The wedding went well," she managed to get out.

"Yes, yes it did... Nice young people."

"Yes, Rachel's a sweetheart. A little gruff sometimes, but she's a good person."

"Yes, yes."

A moment of silence.

"You still live in Corpus Christi, then?"

"Yes, I sure do."

"Ah, good, good. Nice town."

"Yes, well, been there so long, I don't know any different."

He chuckled. "I understand that!"

"So when did you become a priest?"

"Oh, let's see, 1976 it was."

"Ah... Happy?" she asked with a slight crack in her voice.

"Oh… Yes, yes, it's been good to me—the priesthood. Feel I'm serving *some* purpose in this life, anyway."

"I thought all priests were required to answer, 'It's fantastic! I'm doing what I was called to do'."

"Ha-ha. Well, yes, indeed, that is the answer. I do feel I was called, but I didn't pay attention at first, so He had to keep yellin' for me 'til I listened."

Patty laughed. He was thrown off by the sound he never thought he'd hear again in his life. He gave a startled look and she asked, "What?"

"Oh, nothing, nothing. Just…never thought in a million years I'd ever see you again."

"Yes…it is strange, isn't it?"

"Patty…why didn't you tell me?"

She shrugged her shoulders and looked down. "I don't know… I was just in such a difficult position, you know."

"I can understand. I just wish…" He paused, trying to think how to put his feelings into words without sounding harsh—a very difficult thing to do sometimes. "I wished I could have been there for her."

Tears welled up in her eyes. "I know. I'm sorry."

"I'm sorry, too. I'm sorry you had to go through so much. I…I would've helped all I could." He nodded to convey his sincerity.

"You know, I think I knew that, and that's why I didn't say anything. I knew you were destined for greater things than me."

"I think God would have understood that I had responsibilities to attend to."

"Well…it's all water under the bridge now."

"Yes, true…true."

She looked at him for a second. "You can be there for her now."

"I'd like that very much," he said with his heart pounding. She smiled and he continued. "She's beautiful."

"She's got your red hair," she said with almost a laugh.

"Oh, yes, but that wasn't what I was referring to. I meant she's a beautiful person—so full of heart and spirit. She's going to make a fine mother."

"I don't see how. She didn't have much of a role model."

He smiled and said, "It's never too late to be a role model." She gave a faint smile and looked down. "She may have my hair, but she's got your eyes and the shape of your face." He ran a finger along her jaw before he even realized what he'd done. He snapped out of the spell he was under, and jerked his hand away. She said nothing, but for a moment, it was thirty-six years ago.

"I think we ought to get back to the party," she stammered.

"Yes, yes." He looked at his watch. "Time to go, I'm sure."

"What time is it?"

"Almost eleven."

"Already? Goodness."

They stood up to go, but he stopped her before going in. "Patty."

"Yes?"

"I'm glad to get to see you again."

She simply smiled and went in.

The time had come to relinquish the room to the cleaning staff. The party broke up with the majority of the folks going to bed and the younger ones finding a bar to continue their celebrations.

Shelly managed to get her picture taken with both parents, and then said goodnight with her heartfelt gratitude toward her mother for sticking it out. She gave a long good-bye and a multitude of thanks to her father with hopes of seeing him again soon. He hugged her with little to say. He was just so happy he could do this for her. Shelly then went with Robin to their room and chatted for a while, but finally went to sleep, both with a good dose of exhaustion. Shelly had good dreams that night.

Chapter Sixteen

The wedding crew had all gone home with the newlyweds heading off to their well-deserved honeymoon. They had given Fr. O'Connor many thanks and a sizable donation to take home with him. They were a very happy couple indeed.

It was time for everybody to get back to work. The Ministers of Parliament took care of the final details of their 'mini tour' and got in some good practicing. Debra was relieved to find her café hadn't burned down, and got busy preparing her son for school.

It was the evening before the guys were to set off to Los Angeles. George came home late from the office, finalizing everything and dragged himself upstairs to go to sleep. He noticed the light on in Paul's room. He came over to the door, and before knocking, heard a faint strumming of a guitar.

"Yeah?" the young man answered at the sound of George's knock.

George opened the door and asked, "What's up?"

"Not much."

"Up late."

Paul looked at his clock, not knowing the time. "Huh, yeah."

"Got those chords down?"

He smiled and remarked, "Gettin' there."

"You've been more quiet than usual lately. Dreading school?"

He instantly looked uneasy. "Yeah, I guess so."

George noticed the look of panic in his eyes. "Miss your friends in Washington?"

He looked down and answered, "Yeah" as usual.

"You'll make more… I'm leaving pretty early tomorrow, but your mother will be back around 10:00 a.m. the next morning. Do you know the routine?"

"Yes, sir."

"Yes, I imagine your mother has drilled it into you." Paul gave a quick grin. "I'm sure you're not going to miss working at the café, are you?" The boy simply turned his deep, brown eyes to him then looked away without a reply. George was beginning to feel there was something else on the boy's mind. "What is it?" he simply asked.

"What's what?"

"What's wrong?"

"Nothin'," he replied, messing with his guitar.

The way he answered told George that something was definitely wrong. "Are you mad at your mother for some reason?"

"No," he answered, still trying a chord.

George came over and held the neck of the guitar, preventing him from continuing his playing. "I don't like secrets," he said very sternly.

Paul still hadn't completely figured George out, and didn't know what all he might do. He looked up with large eyes and replied, "I don't like that producer guy."

"Producer guy?" His mind rambled over all the producers he knew.

"The guy who sells her produce."

George was relieved it was no one he knew. "Why? What does he do?"

Paul fidgeted and thought how to answer. "He…he hits on Mom."

Startled, George quickly asked, "How?"

"Ah, I don't know. He flirts with her."

"Does she flirt back?" he asked with a raised brow.

Paul shrugged his shoulders. "I don't know."

George had asked the question as a joke, but he didn't like his answer. "Well, how does she react?"

Paul desperately wanted to escape. Ratting on your mother just isn't right. He avoided answering, so George asked another question.

"Are they just kidding around, or did anything else happen?" The quick glance Paul gave told him something must have happened. "What?" he asked with his hands held up.

"Nothing, George."

"Obviously something happened," he retorted with a raised voice.

"Look, it was nothing." He was becoming desperate and George knew he'd better change his tactic or the boy would clam up altogether. He sat down in a chair opposite him.

"Paul, I understand you don't want to betray your mother, but just tell me what happened—it probably was nothing."

The young man calmed down and said, "I saw him kiss her hand."

George didn't know what to think. It could be innocent—it could not. "Were they in the café or outside?" he inquired, trying to get the whole picture.

"In her office."

He didn't like that. He knew how tiny that office was. He sat silently and Paul wondered what repercussions this was going to cause.

"George?"

"Huh? Uh…okay, yeah. Oh, I'm sure it was nothing, Paul, but thanks for telling me," he said in a reassuring tone.

"You won't tell her I told you, will you?"

George barely heard the question. "Oh…no, no. Don't, uh…don't worry about it. Look, I have got to get some sleep." He smiled and got up to leave. "If I don't see you in the morning, be good and I'll see you in a fortnight."

"In a what?"

He chuckled and realized Paul still had to get used to his English terms. "In two weeks."

"Oh, okay, yeah."

"Goodnight, Paul, and thanks."

"Sure. Goodnight, George. Have a good tour."

"Thanks. Keep practicing!"

He smiled once more and left. Paul sat on his bed wondering if what he did was right.

It was the next morning and Robin awoke before the alarm went off. He lay on his side staring at his wife, amazed by her beauty. Her rosy glow complimented her red locks that lay draped over her pillow. He barely touched her cheek and she woke up. She smiled without saying anything. "Good morning," he greeted.

"Morning," she hummed. "Tour day!"

"Yes."

"It should be exciting. You'll have fun."

He rolled his eyes as usual, making her giggle. "Oh, I suppose we shall."

"Well, honey, you've got to go and make lots of money—we're going to need a bunch of diapers!"

He lay back, laughing. "Ah, nappies…yes."

The alarm went off, startling them both. She hit it with a relish. "Nasty thing," she remarked with a yawn.

"Indeed."

They got robed and came down for breakfast. As she poured his coffee she studied him. "So…are you okay with leaving me here?"

He thought for a moment as he buttered his toast. "I believe so."

"Good."

"Just promise nothing will happen while I'm gone."

"Hmm…well, the living room may mysteriously turn yellow in a couple of days."

"Ha-ha. Well, that's fine, just don't do it yourself, okay?"

"Oh, definitely not. I abhor actual work."

He laughed and took a bite of toast. She still wondered, though, if he was really going to be all right.

But, time passes and he found himself saying good-bye to her. He was very quiet, and she proceeded to lavish him with kisses until he laughed. The taxi came to take him to the airport and he reviewed what his therapist had told him—a lot. Shelly sat back down on her favorite couch to have a little cry. She did well to control her emotions (and hormones) while he was here. Now she could let it out. She did so worry about him.

The band flew out to L.A. to (hopefully) find their equipment that had already been brought out by their trusty crew. Robin was too wrapped up in his own thoughts to notice his brother's demeanor. He had gotten used to George's quiet moments since his heart attack, and had chalked it up to having a near-death experience. He had no idea that there was another agitator at play with the man's mind.

Once safely in their hotel rooms, they called home to let everyone know that they had arrived. Robin had already called Shelly when he landed, but decided to call again. Shelly was relieved to hear him not panicky, but just excitable. He had gotten the touring bug, and things were beginning to feel right to him.

George called Paul and asked if he had heard from his mother. Paul replied 'yes' and wished him well. He then tried to call Debra on her cell phone. She didn't answer, but then she called an hour later, explaining her cell wouldn't pick up in the large expo building. She sounded happy and told him of some of the fabulous things she and her friend had seen. It was good to hear her voice.

The day was filled with preparations for the night's concert. They were only playing once in Los Angeles and then on to Las Vegas. George completely fed on the thrill of it all, whereas Robin was finding it hard to concentrate no matter how much he tried. He felt rusty. However, they made it through, and the concert went off with only a couple of small snags that would be worked out before Vegas.

The audience was very pleased to see them (especially George) and as soon as they began, Robin snapped out of his daze and became Robin the Performer once again. Somewhere midway through the concert, Robin sang the song he had sung at George's party. He got much the same reaction: a second of silence, then thunderous applause. As much as it stung him to conjure up those feelings and memories (especially now after leaving Shelly behind), he knew he had a potential hit on his hands. George looked at his brother and smiled understandingly.

Los Angeles and Las Vegas had come and gone successfully and Chicago was anticipated to do the same. They arrived at the Windy City with eager anticipation. Chicago had always been one of their favorite towns to play, and they made a point to stay right on the Magnificent Mile to enjoy the view. The grand hotel greeted them with a combination of open arms and decorum. They had an extra day to blow while the equipment made its long journey there, so the boys went shopping. They ended up at an exclusive old jewelry store right on Michigan Avenue. George looked for something for Debra (simple and elegant), and Robin looked for Shelly something (unusual and interesting) as well. Robin noticed, however, that George seemed to go off in a daze at times, as if recalling something. Robin helped him settle on some nice earrings for Debra, and continued his search for his own wife.

Task accomplished, they settled back into the hotel for their meal after locking up their purchases with the front desk. Robin called Shelly, so George figured he should call Debra. He called the café, where he presumed she would be. Amy answered and explained to George that Debra had stepped out, but that she'd tell her he called. He sat thoughtless for a moment, and then asked, "Did you enjoy the expo?"

"Oh, I didn't go with her."

"You didn't?"

"No, sir. I had to run the café."

"Of course you did," he mumbled.

"Excuse me?"

"Oh, nothing. Must have been someone else. I just could have sworn she said it was you."

"Nope. Not this time."

"Uh…when do you think she'll be back?"

"I don't know; she went off to see the produce supplier. We've been getting less than satisfactory goods, and I think she's about to ditch him. Don't know why she hasn't yet, to tell you the truth."

A flare went up in George's eyes, and if the girl could see it, she would have been afraid. 'The Producer', as Paul calls him. "Well, I'll try to reach her on her cell phone," he replied blankly.

"That's probably your best bet."

"Okay, thanks, Amy."

"No prob'. Good luck with your tour!"

"Thank you, Amy."

He waited a moment to calm down before calling. He dialed her—no answer. Figures, he thought.

So George stewed the remainder of the evening and the rest of the band could sense it. They would all ask what was wrong, but he was too embarrassed to tell anyone of his silly suspicions.

The group sat eating a nice dinner that night in a private dining room at the hotel. He was pleased to see his brother being his usual animated self. It seemed that getting back on the road did Robin a world of good. Once he got over his stigma of leaving Shelly, he was able to put on a top-notch performance as usual.

George sat casually eating his chicken piccata and looked up to see Sam. She was telling a funny story about a session she had once with an infamous band. He thought it was odd that he had never noticed the dimple on her right cheek when she smiled, considering how many times he had worked with her.

"Hey, mate, you all right?" asked Robin, leaning over to him.

"Huh? Yeah, why?"

"You've just been so quiet today. What's going on?"

"Oh, just confused about something."

"What?"

"Have you ever had someone accuse you of something only to find out it was because they were guilty of the same thing?"

Usually answering a question with a question drove Robin nuts, but his brother seemed genuinely concerned about something. Robin tried to see beneath the query for the root meaning. It immediately became clear he was talking about Debra, and his own heart pounded with the thought of George going through any stress again. "Uh, not that I can recall. Why?" he asked slowly.

George shook his head and smiled. "Hmm...no reason." It dawned on him that Robin had been told about Debra's accusation, and he felt he had better shut up—no need to drag that back up again.

Although Robin was his usual curious self, he knew not to ask George any more. He did notice, however, how George kept staring at Sam. Could Debra cheat on George? He really didn't think so. He thought about how George had changed so much after his heart attack—a bit more introverted. Somehow, though, he felt George's new knack for philosophizing was more because of Debra and her accusation. The sting still had not left and it was clearly evident. Robin knew George would feel justified if it were she who was cheating on him.

Robin spent a moment pondering all this, yet he still couldn't see Debra being unfaithful. Distant—yes, but she wouldn't cheat. He was beginning to feel he and George had fallen into some strange paradox in that their lives were constant magnets—one always opposite of the other. If one's life was going swimmingly, the other's was being plagued by tragedies. He was definitely grateful for his present blessings, but he worried about his brother and his stream of tortures of late. He worried about his heart.

George called once more before going to bed—he knew he would get no sleep until he talked to her. She cheerily answered and inquired how things were, so he replied and then asked, "You said you went to that expo with Amy?"

"Uh-huh."

"Well, when I called for you today, she said she didn't go."

A moment of silence.

Then, in a very non-cheery tone she answered, "I went with Amie Bautista, *not* Amy Hartford."

"Who's Amie Bautista?"

"She owns the bakery a few doors down. I've only mentioned her to you seventy times or so."

"Oh, sorry."

"What are you getting at? Why do you think I would lie to you?"

"I don't! I was just confused."

"Oh." She didn't believe him.

"Amy said you were about to drop your produce supplier."

"Ha-ha. Amy exaggerates," she laughed.

"Oh. So you're not unhappy with him?"

"Well, lettuce has been iffy, but it's just this season—no one is getting anything good there. Everything else is fine, and you really can't beat his prices."

"Oh. Well, that's good then."

"Since when were you so interested in my produce?"

"I'm always interested in your produce," he tried to joke.

"Very funny… Look, hon', I gotta go. I've got paperwork coming out of my ears that I've just got to get done by tomorrow—my accountant is coming!"

"Oh, of course. Okay. Well, then, goodnight, dear."

"Goodnight, George. I'm glad you called. Break a leg tomorrow!"

"Thanks."

"Okay, love you, bye-bye."

"Love you, too. Bye."

George sat on his bed confused as can be. He didn't know what to think. The bad thing was the fact he simply couldn't allow himself to be ambivalent. He had to be one or the other. He wanted to be desperately in love with his wife or leave her completely. He somehow felt they were just living a platonic co-existence. She said 'love you' just as she would to anyone else. He had to have that fire, and he wasn't sensing that she desired the same thing. How could she be so satisfied with their present status? Had she no heart (or maybe just not for him)? She was going to drive him crazy.

The next day, the M.P.s were at the auditorium doing the sound check. Robin noticed with relief that George was back to being the clown again. He was joking and teasing and genuinely having fun. He also noticed the fact that he was practically flirting with Sam.

The Chicago crowd greatly enjoyed their concert that night, and the band went backstage afterward to revel in the outcome. Champagne corks flew, and they basked in the moment.

George deftly made his way over to Sam. "You sounded good tonight!"

"Thanks! So did you. Actually, I don't think my bass is right. I think maybe something happened to it in transit. I tried tuning it, but it still feels funny to me."

"Then we'll have to get you a new one," he said casually.

"Oh, I'm sure it just needs working on," she said with hesitation. She saw no need in such an extravagance.

"Well, you still have two shows to do. Get another while we're in Dallas, and work on yours when we get home."

"Well…I guess I could get a temporary… I honestly think the front head is messed up, I probably just need to replace that."

"Ha-ha. Very well," he relented to her practicality, "we'll see if we can fix you up tomorrow."

"Good." She began to get a nervous feeling from him, and she couldn't understand why. She had worked with him numerous times before and never noticed anything, but this time he was definitely sending out signals. She also knew he was married. Was he still with his wife? She hadn't heard anything, so she presumed he was. He never wore a ring, so she couldn't tell from that. She always had liked George, but always saw him as an employer and nothing else. She studied him for a moment. She couldn't deny his handsomeness. He almost had a cowboy appearance with that wild look about him. If it weren't for that British accent, he would have been great for an old western movie!

"You're living in Miami permanently now, correct?" said the accent, zinging her out of her thoughts.

"Yes, I sure am."

"Miss home?"

"Mmm, yeah. Don't miss having to dig my car out of the snow… Miss my parents, but I think they're actually thinking of moving down themselves."

"Well, Miami is the epicenter for retirees."

"That's true! Strange combination of people there—present company excluded, of course," she said quickly and with a smile.

"Thank you. Robin on the other hand…"

"Now, George," she reprimanded, laughing. "I like your brother. He seems to be above it all."

"Conceited?" he genuinely asked.

"No! Ha-ha. I mean…aloof, I guess. You know, like he's thinking of more ethereal topics on a much grander scale than simple grocery store lists. Like that new song of his—wow!"

"Ha-ha. Yes, he is the philosopher. But he's really quite grounded. Mr. Practicality I call him. His aloofness is brought on by a crazy redhead who's about to have his baby."

"Oh! They told me his wife's expecting. How great! It's his first, right?"

"Yes, it is."

"Better late than never, I suppose."

George looked at her with a raised brow.

"Oh, sorry. I meant if you're going to do it at all."

"That's all right. I'm having my shot at parenthood learning to deal with a teenage step-son."

"Oh, boy!" So he still is married, she thought.

"Yes. But he's a good lad. Reclusive boy—keeps to himself."

"Those are the ones you have to watch!"

"True," he laughed. "Still, no worries quite yet."

She decided a shot in the dark was in order. "How's your wife?"

Instantly it appeared he had been stung by a grazing bullet. He looked down and quietly said, "Oh, she's quite busy—got a new café to run and, well, doesn't have much time for anything else."

There it was, she realized. Having to share his wife with her son and her job. He wasn't getting the attention he was used to. Nobody likes that. She certainly never did.

They continued to chat, and he continued to flirt. She saw no harm in that—probably felt some justification in it—as long as that was all he was doing.

"Hello, hello," said a familiar voice.

"Hey, Robin," the couple replied back.

He gave George a cold, suspicious look and then smiled at Sam. "What are you two conspiring to?" he asked only half-jokingly.

"Did my bass sound funny to you?"

"Well, actually I did notice a hum, but I wasn't sure where it was coming from. I figured George just forgot the words again."

She laughed, but then quickly apologized with an explanation of how she was going to have it looked at in Dallas.

Their bass-man came up and asked, "Robin, could you please explain—in complete detail—just how the hell I'm suppose to be playing that dirge of yours?"

Robin turned and looked down on the not-so-tall man and gave him a look. "It's not a dirge."

"Well, it sounds like one. C'mon!"

"All right, all right, Javi," he relented. He begrudgingly left to sit down with him and explain the complicated chords to his sad song. He regretted not being able to keep an eye on George.

Once he was done, he instantly searched for his brother and Sam. A portion of the people had already gone back to the hotel, and he realized they, too, had gone without a word. "Damn," he muttered. He had a bad feeling about this.

He and Javier packed it up and made their way back. He was walking down the corridor of the hotel when he barely caught a glimpse of George going into Sam's room. She, being the only girl in the group, had her own room. "George," he muttered again with deep regret. He hoped his brother wasn't making a big mistake.

He went into the room he was sharing with George and plopped down on his bed. He lay staring at the ceiling, wondering what George was up to. Maybe they were just talking. Maybe they were just having a nightcap. Maybe... He groaned and rolled over to look at the clock. It was already getting close to midnight. Shelly tended to stay up later when he wasn't around, so he called her and very gratefully heard the sound of her soft voice. Heaven, he thought...heaven, indeed.

George came into the room about 3:30. He laughed when he saw Robin asleep, still in his clothes, sprawled out on the bed with his cell phone lying near by. Then he frowned when he thought of how tight Robin was with his wife. They depended so much on each other, and he hated himself for being jealous of it. God bless 'em, he thought. He quietly got into bed.

The next morning, they were awakened by a phone call from their manager telling them to wake up and get on the road. Robin hung up the phone and laughed at himself for falling asleep the way he did, but then he saw George, and his smile faded. What all transpired that night? He proceeded to wake him and tell him to get cracking. George so did *not* want to wake up, but was coerced by a cup of coffee. Even decaf has its magic.

"What time did you get to bed?" Robin carefully asked him.

"Oh, I dunno. Three, three-thirty."

"Oh. Where were you?"

George looked at him knowing full well by the question that he knew the answer. He answered anyhow. "I was with Sam."

"Really?"

"Yeah. Just talking, you know."

"Oh. Okay," he replied nonchalantly.

"*Nothing happened,*" George growled. He knew what Robin was getting at.

Robin, though, was still unsure.

They made their way through the airline transit system from one horribly busy airport to another. Their only saving grace was that they got to have a private jet. George slept all the way (as did Sam), but Robin was going crazy wondering what had really happened. He had little relief in the fact that the two didn't make eye contact any more than usual. But then again, George was asleep most of the time.

He resolved to give George the benefit of the doubt, and tried desperately to believe him. He had no reason not to, really. It's just the way George had been acting lately that caused him to not know for sure what he was capable of doing. Oh well, he thought, on to Dallas.

It was ironic that they intentionally set the concerts apart by a couple of days to keep George from being too physically stressed, but then he ended up running around instead of resting on his off-time, anyhow. Why he felt he needed to go with Sam to get her drum looked at was anyone's guess.

Robin laid back on his bed in his hotel room pondering this when Shelly called, scaring him to death sobbing. She was practically incoherent and he feared something was wrong with the pregnancy. He calmed her down enough to get an explanation.

"I had the painters here today," she began.

Robin got very nervous wondering what they had done. "And?"

"Well, they were going in and out and...and they left the gate open."

"So?"

"D'artagnan got out and ran away before I even knew he was gone!" she cried and began sobbing again.

Robin lay back down again with a chuckle.

"It's not funny!" she exclaimed.

"I know, dear, but you gave me such a fright! I thought something was wrong with you and the baby."

"Oh. No, no...I'm sorry."

"It's okay, my love. You've just got to understand that I'm so far away, so I don't know what's going on—I can't see you, you know."

"But D'art!" she cried again. It was obvious that the dog had become very dear to her with him gone and provided a certain amount of protection and comfort.

"Yes, I understand. Did you call the authorities?"

"Not yet. I've been driving around looking for him and crying."

"Well, he's got his tags, call them and have them keep a look out. You stay home and take care of yourself. The dog may have meant a lot to you, but you mean a heck of a lot more to us, okay? We don't need you driving around in a state and having a bloody accident."

"Okay," she relented sullenly.

"Don't worry, dearheart, he'll turn up," he said with pity.

She sniffed a bit and then more quietly said, "I miss you."

"I miss you, too." He wished so badly he could give her a hug.

They were both silent for a moment when she finally said, "I guess I'd better let you go… Sorry to be such a nuisance."

"You're anything but a nuisance. You have every right to be upset, but don't worry too much, okay? I still worry about *you*."

She only now remembered what he had gone through to make this tour possible, and felt guilty. "I know…I'm sorry."

He then went on to ask her about the painting and give her some distraction from her worries. It was just nice to hear each other's voices and not think about runaway dogs… or runaway brothers.

The rest of the tour went on like this, with George acting unusual and Robin in the dark as to what was going on. But thankfully, their final destination was home. Dallas, though, proved to be a difficult show with the onset of a horrid thunderstorm.

The trip to Miami proved to be a turning point. George went from overtly jovial to sullen, and Robin the opposite.

At Robin's arrival, Shelly showered him with kisses and he held her dearly for quite a while. He noticed she had gotten a little bigger and asked how she was doing. Fine, she had replied, but better now that he was home.

He loved what she had done with the living room and expressed his gratitude for her adding brightness yet again to their home.

George, however, arrived at his house to find no one. "Some welcome," he grumbled to himself. He knew Paul was in school, but where was Debra? But then he heard her keys and his anger was quelled somewhat. He was dreading talking to her about his suspicions. As quick to anger as he was, he still didn't like confrontation. He wondered if he took his heart medicine that day.

"Hi, baby! Welcome back!" At the sight of her cheery face and beautiful brown eyes, he melted and started to forget all that had happened. She hugged and kissed him and he knew no other woman could give him that same feeling. "How was Dallas?"

"Oh, great. Well, except for that frightful storm."

"Oh, yes! I saw that on the television. Did it cause you any problems?"

"We were worried that the electricity was going to go out, naturally, and it made it quite an inconvenience for the road crew, of course."

"But you made it through," she said with a gesture.

"Oh, yes."

"Well, I'm glad you're home and safe. Are you hungry?"

He smiled. "Yes, actually I am."

She whipped him something up and gave him some of her magic lemonade and he began to feel quite normal again. Somewhere, though, in the back of his mind, lurked 'The Producer'.

The Miami show had gone off splendidly with their hometown giving them a warm reception. The guys were at ease and happy to be home. The tour, however small, was a success and really did the job of building up the Parker brothers self-confidences which had taken quite a beating of late.

Unfortunately, the time was soon for Terry to head to England. Everyone gathered at Robin and Shelly's for a farewell party and also to celebrate the Parkers returning home.

Shelly was in tears the majority of the day. She was so happy Robin was back, but knew that it would be soon for Rachel to leave. Raging hormones certainly didn't help the situation, either. Robin did his best to console her. He had calmed her down eventually, but when Terry asked where their dog was, Robin was back to the task.

Robin's parties, by contrast to George's, were usually quite calm and relaxing. He wouldn't invite just anyone, but he did invite the band and their manager. He felt a little funny inviting Sam, but wasn't going to offend her by not doing so. Certainly George would behave himself around Debra anyhow… Right?

Robin had Debra cater, as she knew how to put out a beautiful spread. Obviously Shelly was in no condition to cook or deal with caterers that she didn't know. Debra was more than happy to oblige and brought Amy and another young girl to help out so that she could enjoy herself as well.

As she brought things in, Robin studied her interaction with George. Things seemed no different, and she had no look of guilt that he could see. George, in contrast, watched her like a hawk. Robin couldn't tell if it was because he was mad, jealous, guilty, or just admiring her. He shook his head in confusion over the couple.

"What's wrong, honey?" Shelly asked.

Robin startled and replied, "Oh, nothing… I guess."

She gave an inquiring look.

He sighed rather sadly and said, "I'll explain later."

"Okay." She was in no mood to badger him.

The crowd lingered in what Shelly called 'the Great Hall' where the piano was. The party had been going on for some time, and Shelly had taken Debra and Rachel upstairs to see the nursery. George went outside with a couple of guys who smoked, but Robin stayed inside with the others, chatting to Terry and their manager, Donnie.

The girls loved the nursery and also gave rave reviews on the job she did in the living room. This cheered Shelly up quite a bit and they eventually made their way back down. They all came over to Robin and Terry and listened to their conversation.

"Well, I think you do need to do that, at least," said Donnie.

"Yes, yes, I know. We've already been making plans," answered Robin. "In fact, we've already booked the studio."

"Good, good… Yeah, it'll be a hit."

"As long as George is up to it. I still think he needs a decent rest."

"Well, if he'd stop chasing Sam all over the place, he wouldn't be so worn out."

Robin's eyes popped open.

"What do you mean by that?" Debra quickly asked.

Donnie had not realized she was there. "Uh, nothing." He knew he had a complete absence of tact, and preferred to shut up.

"What does he mean, Robin?" she asked sternly.

He had a hard time averting her gaze. He could never lie to Debra, and he really wanted to stay out of it.

"Well?"

He stood with his mouth open. He was at a blank what to say, and couldn't figure out how to get out of it in any way. She was gone like a flash to find George, and he dropped his head in failure. Then he hit Donnie on the shoulder. "Sorry," the man said regretfully. "I had no idea she was there."

"George," Debra said calmly as she opened the patio door. "Can I see you for a moment?"

"Sure, dear." The guys went back inside to leave them alone. "What's up?"

"I hear you've really been getting along with your new drummer."

He simply looked at her with no expression. "I try to get along with everyone."

"Do you *chase* them all around?"

His heart began to pound. His fight or flight instinct came out and he snapped back, "Kind of like you and the produce man?"

Her heart pounded in sequence with his now. "What do you mean?"

"Let's just say I've heard a few things."

"Nothing's going on with him."

"Well, nothing's going on with *her*."

She gave him a sidelong stare. "Is that the truth?"

"What is truth anymore, Debra? It seems to be a relative term lately. I think truth is what you want to make it out to be. Whatever is convenient and fits the bill." He came up right to her face. "Maybe, just maybe, you wanted *me* to be the cheater then it would pave the way for your own infidelity."

"I have *not* cheated on you!" she exclaimed.

He looked hard into her eyes. He believed her. He quietly replied, "And I *haven't* cheated on you."

She stood there, breathing hard. She wanted to argue, but began to get horrid flashbacks of their last argument and didn't want a repeat. But she had to ask, "Then what's going on?"

He looked down and then looked up to the clear sky. "I was enjoying her company. I enjoy talking to her. I swear to you that's it... And you?"

"He did make a pass at me. He told me if I ever divorce you, he'd be happy to take over."

George actually began to laugh. Then Debra began to as well.

"It does sound funny, doesn't it?"

He nodded. "Pretty much—yes."

"But I swear to *you*, that's all," she said seriously.

His smile faded. "What's happening to us, Deb?"

"I don't know. Why have we lost our faith in each other?"

He shook his head and shrugged his shoulders. "I really don't know why. Maybe we've just gotten too complacent and got scared when we realized we were taking each other for granted."

"That's probably true... Well, what do we do now?"

"Start over?" he said with a tired expression.

"Again?"

He remembered their talk on the beach and thought about what to do. "Counseling has seemed to work wonders with my brother."

Debra was ecstatic. She never thought he would ever agree to such a thing, much less be the one to suggest it. "Yes, let's do that."

He caressed her soft hair and stared at her big doe eyes. He leaned down and gave a strong kiss. She came back with much affection and he realized she was crying. She rarely showed emotion, and it really hammered it in to him what was happening. He held her tightly and whispered into her ear, "I love you, you know."

"I love you, too," she murmured into his chest. For some reason, it felt like they really meant it this time.

They stayed outside for quite a while with everybody wondering what was transpiring. Eventually they came back in, in time to share a toast to Terry and his new job. Robin and Shelly looked at Debra and could tell she had been upset, but she seemed to be getting along with her husband and they hoped everything had worked out.

Chapter Seventeen

It was a tearful day when Terry flew back to his homeland. Shelly, in particular, was crying her eyes out for she knew Rachel was close behind. Rachel had stayed to finish up and send off the last of their belongings to his parents' house until they could get their own place. She was completely wracked with nerves and was constantly on the phone to Shelly, if not over to her house.

Robin felt sorry for the both of them, but especially Rachel. He remembered how difficult it was back when he moved to America. Even though he had come into some money by that time, leaving home is never easy. Fortunately for her, their deal was to return to America after Terry had finished his years as a player. After that, he had told Robin, he would be happy to come back here and coach—even if it was for school kids. Truth is, Terry had gotten quite attached to the warm climate, and felt as if he had found his home amongst the palm trees and blue waters.

Shelly, on the other hand, would have little time to miss Rachel once the baby came, and in that Robin was somewhat relieved. Then he had an odd recollection of holding Terry as a baby when he was a young man himself, struggling to make it in the music business. How life has changed! If someone had told him then that years later that child would grow up to be married to his own wife's best friend, he would have thought that person crazy. The girls loved the fact that they were now 'cousins-in-law' and joked that they knew they were related somehow all the time. He thought about how Shelly was enjoying being related to anyone now. Used to be, she only had her mother and grandparents. Now, she had enough relatives to make her feel part of a large family—including a new father who was a good soul and somewhat made up for the original. Robin was definitely glad that the man who raised Shelly wasn't going to be around *his* daughter. He quickly realized that was a bad thought to think ill of the dead, but he knew he was just being protective.

He sat on the couch, trying to imagine what life was going to be like with their little girl, when Shelly came over. She sat down and snuggled up to him and he laid down his arm around her. Out of nowhere she said, "We really need to go to birthing classes."

He flinched, for he was dreading those words. Thoughts of watching horrid videos quickly flashed through his mind. He hung his head down in resignation. "Very well… I can't be one of those dads who stay out in the waiting room, passing out cigars?"

"Ha-ha. No," she replied adamantly. "Aw, it'll be all right, honey. You'll be just fine. You won't regret it, you know."

"Well…okay."

She rubbed his arm with a smile. "So, do you really like how I decorated? I tried not to be too feminine."

He looked around. "Yes, yes I really do like it. It's quite nice. Lovely drapes."

"Thank you."

"I presume you didn't put them up," he said with a look.

"No, actually Paul helped me out in exchange for money for guitar stuff."

"Good for him! He's really getting into playing, isn't he?"

"Yes, he is. It's good—gives him something to bond to George with."

"They seem to be getting along fairly well. Which, of course, is good in their present situation."

"Right?" she asked rhetorically in agreement.

They sat silent for a moment, thinking about George and Debra. Then Robin asked, "Have you talked to your father lately?"

"Actually, I called him this morning, but he wasn't home. I left a message on his machine."

"Ah."

At that point, the phone rang. "That's probably him now," he said.

"Ten to one it's Rachel," she laughed.

He smiled as she answered the phone and could tell immediately that she was right.

"Well, I'll be back after a while," she said after she hung up.

"More hand-holding?"

"Oh, yeah… Uh, Robin, dear?"

"Ye-es?"

"She wants to know about Chuckie."

He rolled his eyes. "Yes, why not?" he relented once more to baby-sitting the guinea pig.

"Thanks, honey," she kindly said with a kiss to his cheek. She knew she was pushing him today and felt sorry for him. "I'll be back soon, okay?"

"Do what you need to do, dearest."

"Bye, then."

"Bye. Give my regards to Rocky." He and George had gotten in the habit of calling Rachel that ever since they found out her parents' nickname for her was '*Raqui*'.

"Sure thing."

She left and he continued to sit on the couch. He eventually lay down upon the length of it, enjoying that sleepy time of day. He had just successfully dozed off when the phone rang again. He woke up with a curse and got the phone. "Hello?" he grumbled.

"Uh, yes… Is this Robin?"

He recognized the Irish accent and quickly woke up. "Yes. Hi, Padre. Sorry, I had fallen asleep."

"Oh, I'm sorry son. I'll let you go."

"No, no, that's fine. Need to get up anyhow."

"Oh, well then, how are you? Heard you did a tour?"

"Fine, thanks. Yes, we did a short one, but it was good."

"Oh, good, good."

"And how are you faring?"

"Oh, couldn't be better, thank you. Is our Shelly around? She had left a message for me to call her."

"Actually, she went over to Rachel's. The girl's on the edge of a breakdown preparing to move."

"Ah, yes, that's right. Well, could you tell her I called, please?"

"Yes, I certainly will."

"Thank you, son. Now, nothing's wrong with her, is there?"

"Oh, no, she's fine. In fact, she had some redecorating done while I was gone. 'Nesting', I suppose."

"Ha-ha. Yes, they do that, don't they? You're a kind heart to let her do as she pleases."

"Oh, I really don't mind. She's got quite good taste and she's more frugal than necessary."

"Oh, but you'd be surprised how many men get all riled up because their wives have moved the furniture around."

"Ha-ha. Well, I guess there are some things I'm a bit protective about, but all she has to do is look up with those big, blue eyes and I give in."

"Yes, ha-ha. She got that look from her mum. I think it must be hereditary. I remember once..." he trailed off. "Uh, yes, Shelly is a lot like her mum."

"Yes, she is." Robin felt embarrassed for the man, and quickly changed the subject. "You know, I haven't had a chance to say how grateful I am that you were able to marry my cousin and Rachel. It really got them out of a bad predicament."

"Oh, it was definitely my pleasure. I'm happy I could do it. You have a splendid family."

"Thank you. I'm sorry about that little blow-up, though."

"Tch. That's nothin'. You should have seen some of the things I've seen—and at funerals, too!"

"Ha-ha. I guess that's true. You probably have seen everything."

"Oh, goodness, yes."

Robin then realized with alarm it was Father O'Connor who had placed the call. "Oh, Padre, I suppose I had better let you go. I've kept you on the phone long enough."

"No problem, lad, no problem. I've enjoyed the chat. Just, please, let Shelly know I did call back, then."

"Oh, yes. No problem. She was just calling to say 'hello' anyhow."

"Ah, very good then. Well, you take care, the both of you, and God bless."

"Yes, thank you, Padre. You take care and we'll talk to you soon."

"Good-bye," they said simultaneously.

Robin hung up and sat pondering just how much history Shelly's dad had with her mother.

Two weeks had passed, and in that time the girls had given Shelly a lovely baby shower before Rachel had to give her sad farewell from her Miami family. Shelly, naturally, was devastated and knew she was overreacting, but it was getting more and more difficult to control those hormones. Even Debra shed a tear at Rachel's leaving, and the boys both kissed 'Rocky' good-bye.

It was late the night of Rachel's departure when George found Debra standing in the bathroom tapping something upon her finger. He looked in the mirror at her and saw a very distant look on her face. "What's the matter, dear?" he asked.

Startled, she instantly asked, "Huh?"

George smiled and asked again looking to see what was in her hand—it was her birth control pills.

"Nothing."

Father's Day

George raised a brow just as he had when her son said 'nothing' the same way. He took the pills away and noticed the packet was empty. "What's wrong?" he asked a little more worried.

She simply turned her eyes toward him, just as her son had. Uncanny, the similarities, he thought. She sighed and began slowly, "I'm supposed to be having my period now."

"And you're not?"

"Nope."

George didn't know what to think, but he definitely began to get scared. "Well, is it something to worry about?"

"It's not something to take lightly."

"W-well, you've been taking these, correct?"

"Yes, but that doesn't mean anything."

"I see... Are you saying you could be pregnant?"

"I'm not saying anything."

He saw the look of panic in her dark eyes and held her. Neither knew what to think. "Call the doctor in the morning," he said softly. She nodded.

An appointment had been set up for the next day. Debra passed one more day wondering. She could have gotten a test at the drug store, but she really didn't want to know. In fact, she tried desperately not to think about it and, instead, buried herself in her work.

That Thursday morning (after a nerve-wracking drive over), Debra came into Dr. Hodge's office and he greeted his long-time patient. "So, Debra, what brings you here today?"

"Well, my period hasn't come, so I thought I'd better get checked out."

"Ah! Thought maybe Shelly wasn't the only one in the family to be expecting, huh?"

"Well, I guess. I really don't think it's possible. I mean, I'm very good about taking my pill, and, well, I'm no spring chicken."

"Hmm. You're probably right, but you never know…you know." He squinted his eyes at her and said, "I take it you left a donation with the nurse?"

"Yes, sir."

"I'll be right back." He excused himself and came back after a bit to what Debra considered an eternity. He sat down and said, "Well, you were right. You're not pregnant," unsure of what her reaction would be.

She simply knitted her brows in confusion. She felt relief along with worry. "Well then, what is it?"

"Well…let me ask you a few questions first: Have you been having irregular periods for a while now?"

"Well, they've always been light. I've never had much of a period."

"Hmm. Well…do you ever get hot flashes?"

"I work in a restaurant," she laughed. "I run around, I cook, I clean…"

"Gotcha. Okay then, do you know how old your mother was when she hit menopause?"

The word scared her and she sat frozen. "D-do you think that's what it is?" she stuttered.

"It's a possibility. But there are other things it could be, too, but the chances are in its favor."

"But, am I the right age?"

He looked at her chart and replied, "Well, dear, you'll be 48 next month—that's young, but not too young, I'm afraid."

"Oh."

"So-o…can you remember?"

"No."

"Could you ask her?"

"My mother passed away about ten years ago."

"Oh. That's too bad."

"I guess I could ask my sister if she knows, but it's hard to get a hold of her. She lives in Germany."

"Ah. Military?"

"Yes, her husband, rather."

"Well, it doesn't matter too much; it just gives us something to go by. Heredity, and all that."

"Oh… What are the other possibilities?"

"Well, for one thing, it could be nothing—simply be an indication of impending menopause. Menopause isn't an instant thing—it comes on gradually which is actually called perimenopause. Menopause is the absolute cessation of your cycle. Also, it wouldn't be a bad idea to check a few levels and see if there may be something sinister going on, but I seriously doubt it."

"So, your best guess is menopause."

"Probably, my dear."

"I see."

"But it's not official until several cycles have passed without anything."

"Oh."

The doctor studied her for a second and said, "Debra, you know, this can be a very liberating moment in your life.

Some of my patients tell me about how they feared it, but then once it happened, they were thrilled with the freedom it gave them. No periods, no pills, no pregnancy…well, unless you opt for HRT, but still…"

She tried to smile, but any way she heard it, it still spelled 'old' to her.

The doctor could sense her thoughts, and added, "And again, it could be nothing. Next month could be a whole different story… Let's run some tests and see if they confirm if that is what's happening, okay?"

"Okay."

The doctor said his 'good-bye and take care' and left her to be finished up with the nurse and receptionist.

Debra decided to drive home instead of back to the café and did so in a daze. She had only to turn to go down their long driveway when she began to cry. Bawl, in fact. She told herself to not be ridiculous, and quelled her emotions as usual.

She pulled up to the house and dried her eyes. She saw that George was home and rather regretted it. She knew he would ask what the doctor said, and she didn't want to start crying again. She wasn't giving George any credit. He was concerned for her and she should have been grateful. But, stress is not always something you want to share.

She sat in the car for a moment to gather herself and then got out. She came inside the house and could hear George tinkering in his studio. She went to examine herself in the bathroom mirror, making sure she showed no signs of crying. She made the mistake, however, of examining too closely. She realized her youth had indeed passed her by, and that she was no longer the young cooking student with no worries except how to do a good Hollandaise sauce. Her first marriage was over as uneventful as it had come. But then there was Paul. She at least had him. Beautiful Paul—the light of her life. He was such a gem, and she was grateful that she at least got to have him. Was she making this all out to be more than it was? She shook her head and began to cry again. No matter how you look at it, it was a sign of getting older.

She heard a noise and discovered George watching her. He had the look of fear in his eyes. After all they had been through lately, he really couldn't imagine her pregnant, but presumed so by the tears.

She quickly wiped her eyes, and said, "Hi, honey," as cheerfully as she could.

"What is it?" he asked quickly.

She took a deep breath and went in to sit on the bed. He followed suit. She continued to wipe her face and said, "Well, I'm not pregnant."

"Oh." At first relieved, he then thought for a second to worry again. "Then what is it?"

"He thinks, maybe, it's the onset of menopause." She couldn't hold it in any more, and started to cry.

Shocked, he simply held her and stroked her hair. "My dear lady," he said with sympathy. He had been the patient for so long, it was odd that it was Debra with the health issue this time.

But, George remained nervous, for he didn't know what to say. He knew he couldn't belittle the issue by trying to give her the 'upside' of the situation. Instead, he felt showing his support was the wisest thing to do. "You know what, Deb?"

"What?"

"You're a strong woman. You'll make it through this, just like you have everything else."

She gave a slight smile.

"And you know what else?'

"What?"

"I'll be there for you."

She grabbed his neck and held on tight. He closed his eyes and gently rubbed her back. Even though he felt sorry for her, it felt good to be the one who was needed this time.

The following day, Debra was back to work (if not mindlessly) at her café. She brightened up at the sight of two familiar faces that came in for lunch. "Well, hello!" she said to Robin and Shelly.

"Hello!" they greeted back.

"What brings you to my humble establishment?"

"We're hungry," Robin answered honestly.

"Well, I guess that's a good reason," she laughed. "Do you want a menu?"

"I think I want your pasta special," replied Shelly.

"I'd like the roast beef sandwich," Robin added.

"And to drink?"

"Lemonade!" they said in unison.

"Ha-ha. Very good. I'll be right back with your drinks."

Debra dropped off the order to her sous chef and came back with their lemonade and sat down with them. "So what have you two been up to today?"

"We just got done with another check-up," said Shelly.

"And how is everything?"

"Great, thank you."

"Good!"

They both beamed a smile at her. "I've also got us signed up for birthing classes," added Shelly.

"Really?" she saw Robin's expression and laughed. "Well, Robbie, you're very fortunate that you're going to get to be there. You won't regret it, you know."

"Was Paul's father with you?" Shelly inquired.

Debra gave an odd chuckle and shook her head. "Oh, he tried, but Alex was never one to stomach things very well. He had to leave the second my water broke."

They laughed at this, and Debra thought back to that time, unable to fathom that it was almost seventeen years ago. Robin and Shelly soon realized that their hostess had left them for another place. "Deb?" Robin asked.

"Huh? Oh, sorry. Uh, let me check on your food."

"Okay," Robin replied with concern. He had noticed a wash of sadness seemed to come over the usually cheery lady. After she left, he muttered, "That was an odd look."

"Yes, it was," Shelly said nonchalantly. She was really too concerned about her upcoming meal, but Robin wasn't. He sat wondering what was bugging her.

As Debra prepared a salad in a daze while waiting for Robin's sandwich to be done, Amy called out to her, "Debra!"

"Huh? Yes?"

"There's a call for you!" Amy hated repeating herself.

Debra wiped her hands and went into the office. At the sound of Dr. Hodge's voice, she shut the door. "Hi, Doctor."

"How are you today?"

"Oh, fine."

He could tell she wasn't, but answered, "That's good," anyway. "Well, Debra," he continued, "your test results came back showing a change in your hormone levels, so our suspicions are probably right, but, thankfully, nothing else."

"I see," she answered calmly.

"I think it would be wise to make an appointment to talk about your options concerning hormone therapy and a few other things."

"Okay."

"You want to do that?"

"Uh, yes, but I'll need to call you back—I'm rather busy right now."

"Okay, Debra," he answered with a slight chuckle to her meekness. "Well, call back when you can, okay?" he stressed.

"Yes, sir."

The doctor said good-bye and gave his best wishes. After hanging up the phone, she sat at her desk with a million thoughts going through her mind, but then realized in a panic that she had forgotten Robin and Shelly. She quickly ran out to discover that Amy had already brought them their food and they sat enjoying it happily. They looked up to her and saw the emotion in her face. "What's wrong?" they both asked.

Tears welled up in her eyes and she quickly ran back to her office. They looked at each other as if asking, "Who should go?" Shelly chimed up, "I'll go."

She went to find Debra and softly knocked on her office door. "Debra? It's me, Shelly. Can I come in?"

Silence for a couple of seconds, and then, "Yes, hon'."

Shelly came in and shut the door behind her. "What's up?" she asked nervously.

"Oh, nothin'. Just being silly."

"You don't look silly."

Debra put her head down. "I just found out I'm about to hit menopause."

Shelly was overcome with unfounded guilt. She felt embarrassed to be so pregnant and laid her arms upon her stomach to hide herself.

Debra saw her expression and giggled. "Oh, sweetie, don't feel so bad—it's just that I feel so old all of a sudden."

"You're certainly not that!"

"Oh, I know, but…"

"It certainly doesn't help?"

"Yeah," she laughed.

"Did you want anymore children?"

"N-no. No, I don't think so. I mean, I never thought of it, really."

"Then you have everything to gain, then. No periods, no birth control, no getting crazy once a month…"

"I know, I know. I should be happy. This has all just snuck up on me without much warning, you see."

"Oh, okay… Well, gosh, Debra, I'm sorry."

"Oh, don't be. Just something I have to deal with."

"Well, just remember that you're still a hot, young chick and any guy would love to have you."

Debra smiled and gave a quick thought to her produce man.

"George is very lucky to have you," Shelly added.

"Oh, I don't know sometimes," Debra chuckled. She recalled some of the conversations with George and regretted them.

"Well, we all have our moments. I'm sure Robin wonders what the hell he was thinking when he married *me*."

"Are you kidding? He better thank the Lord for you every day. He was about to turn into a recluse when you came along."

"Really?"

"Oh, gosh, yes. You really have made him a whole person once again. He's happier now than…all the time I've known him, really."

Shelly smiled, but gave no response.

"Speaking of Robin, you had better go finish your lunch with him."

"Oh, yeah. The pasta's excellent, by the way."

"Thank you." They both stood up to leave. "And thank you for letting me cry and moan about my petty issues."

"It's not petty—and that's what friends are for!"

"Yes, indeed." She gave her a hug and Shelly left to go back to her lunch.

Later that day, Shelly sat watching television when Robin came back from the office. He had managed to get a little work done and caught up with some left over issues from the tour along with seeing George briefly about recording their next release. He came and gave Shelly a kiss on the cheek and noticed what she was watching. He made a slight grimace and she asked, "Oh, you don't like it? But it's a classic!"

"Oh, I don't have an issue with the movie, just those flying monkeys; they give me the hee-bee-gee-bees."

Shelly laughed. "Why?"

"Reminds me too much of an actual incident," he said with a chuckle. He came around and sat down next to her to tell her his little story. "I was at a fellow musician's home—no names, mind you—and he had this pet monkey—one of those skinny, jittery things, you know. Well, the bloody thing jumped up onto my chair and bit me in the arm for no reason whatsoever!"

Shelly broke out laughing. "What did you do?"

"Well," he laughed, "let's just say he did get to fly." Shelly held her belly as she laughed. "Then I asked my friend if the thing had had its shots." He watched her and figured he'd better stop making her laugh before she hurt herself. Then the phone rang, saving Shelly from disaster. Robin turned around to get it and greeted, "Well, hullo! How are you? Getting used to your new world?"

At the sound of this, Shelly quickly turned the television off and eagerly awaited delivery of the phone.

"Yes, of course. Here she is." He passed the receiver to her with a grin and walked off to the kitchen.

"Hello?" Shelly answered.

"¡Holá, chica!"

"Rachel, what's up?!"

Rachel immediately went into a series of epithets in Spanish of which Shelly only caught the majority of and then, "This place is *crazy*!"

Shelly laughed, "Why?"

"Well, for one thing, it's *huge*. There's absolutely no reasoning to the streets. I don't know how anyone finds their way home."

"Ha-ha. And that's different from Miami, how?" she laughed. "Has Terry let you drive any?"

"Are you kidding? He tells me I couldn't drive in Miami, what makes me think I can drive over here?"

"Well, he has a point…"

"Hey!"

"There again, you would be finally driving on the right side of the road."

"Listen, you. Just because I can't throttle you through the phone…"

"Ha-ha! But otherwise, how do you like it? How's everyone treating you?" she asked quite seriously.

"Oh, everyone is quite nice. Some of the other wives have taken me under their wing. I seem to be some sort of pet project. They got me to cut my hair."

"No!"

"Oh, not short, just at my shoulders."

"Does Terry like it?"

"No. He was pissed."

"Ha! I guess he's glad to be home, huh?"

"Yes, he is…and so is his family."

"And he's doing well. Robin's been keeping up with him."

"Yeah—it's a great team."

"Well, I'm glad to know you're doing okay."

"Yeah."

Shelly noted a bit of sadness in her reply. "What's wrong? Homesick?"

"Yeah, a bit. I miss being around people like us. Everyone's nice here and all, but just so different. Some of these women can be kind of stuck-up."

"Well, that was bound to happen—even here. You've moved into a new tax bracket."

"Yeah. I guess that's true. It's weird having money."

"Tell me about it!"

"And it's all your fault!"

"Guilty," she laughed.

"You're right, though."

"Have you found a place to blow glass yet?"

"No, not yet, but I'm getting there."

"That'll help when you do. You know, familiarity—be around people that like the same stuff you do, instead of conceited footballers' wives."

"Watch it. I am one now, you know."

"Yeah, well, truth hurts."

"Shelly!" Rachel laughed at this and felt much more at ease getting to talk to her friend. She caught up with what was going on with her old art gang and answered Shelly's many questions about her life in London.

"Well, I guess I'd better go," Rachel finally said.

"Yeah, go take care of Terry."

"Ha, yeah. He told me to tell you 'hello' by the way."

"Tell him 'hi' back. Hey, send me a pic of your new hair-do. Who knows when we'll see each other again."

"Oh, it may be sooner than you think," Rachel said with a sly tone.

"I certainly can't go anywhere. I feel like a big, ole beach ball."

"Ah, Shelly, you're beautiful. In fact, you should have your picture taken. Lots of women do that like in their eighth or ninth month."

"Or I could do like Carol Ann and make a mold of my belly."

"Yeah! That was neat. She covered it with that extra thick acrylic and a foil effect and stuck it above her fireplace."

"Robin would *faint*!" Shelly laughed.

"Oh, my gosh, yes! No, really though, you should have your picture taken—with Robin—all in white."

"Hmm…yeah, I like it. I'll see if I can get him to go for it. He's becoming very pliable of late."

"Really?" Rachel couldn't believe it.

"Yeah. You know, it's as if he's been freed from his own imprisonment. I don't want to sound too philosophical, but he is loosening up, slowly but surely."

Rachel listened to her and wondered if it wasn't Shelly who was the freed one. "So, I take it you're happy then?"

"Yes, I am. Although," she looked around to see if Robin was still in the room, "it's all just happening so fast, sometimes."

"That's how life works, sweetie. One minute you're arguing with one idiot foreigner at a dinner party, and then you're marrying him the next!"

Shelly laughed at this.

"*Ándale*, he comes now. What the—? What happened to you?" she asked Terry. Shelly heard some faint mumbling. "Jesus," Rachel returned to Shelly, "he broke his stupid nose. I'd better go."

"Ha, yeah, I guess you better," Shelly laughed. "Thanks for calling and take care of yourself."

"Same here, sweetie. Say 'bye' to the old guy for me."

"I will. Bye."

"Bye!"

Shelly hung up and went to find Robin to relay Rachel's good-bye and to tell him of Terry's mishap.

"Well, that was stupid," he laughed.

"That seems to be the consensus," she laughed.

"I shouldn't say 'stupid', I should say 'typical'. I don't believe that's the first time for him. He always has to straighten his nose out in the morning," he said with a demonstration.

"Eww! Good thing you never broke yours," she said, studying his profile.

"What do you mean by that?" he asked with a gleam in his eye.

Shelly laughed. "Just, you know, you're in show business, you don't need a crooked nose."

"Why not? Because it's so *big*?"

She giggled at his expense and he gave her a tickle.

"No, don't!" she screamed. "I'll pee in my pants!"

He instantly stopped with a funny expression, and she laughed at him. She gave him a big kiss and then kissed his nose. "I love your nose, Cyrano."

He looked at her doubtfully.

"No, really! I do! I love all of you."

"Oh? Would you like our child to have my nose?"

Shelly knitted her brows and he laughed. "Well, if it had been a boy—sure, but a girl?"

"She may, you know." He laughed at her biting her lip and added, "Don't worry. There are no big-nosed women in my family. Well, maybe my sister... Forgot what she bloody well looks like."

"You have a strange relationship with your sister."

"That implies that I *have* a relationship with my sister. She doesn't desire one. I've called her when Mum said she was home, but she never calls me. She lives in her own little world."

"So, she's never been married?"

"No. She had had boyfriends when she was younger, but her only lover is the sea."

"Do you think…" Shelly started with her thought, but then let go.

"Do I think what?"

"Well… Do you think maybe it was your father's death that made her follow his footsteps?"

Robin's face seemed to darken thinking back to that sad time in his family's history, but then he said, "No. That makes sense, but she had already enlisted when he died. It did pain her though, that she couldn't get back from her own tour of duty in time for his funeral."

"You're kidding."

"Nope. They let her go, but she just had a very hard time making it back from her destination, poor thing." He seemed to drift off, and Shelly tried to imagine the anger the young woman had when she realized she wasn't going to make it back to give her final farewell. She wondered if this might have caused some sort of jealousy between her and her brothers. Her mind rambled.

She walked back over to the couch to stew about this, and Robin followed. He studied her in her deep thought, and he asked, "Miss Rachel?" misunderstanding her expression.

"Huh?" she said startled. "Yes, I do," she answered, not knowing where this came from.

"Well, you'll just have to distract yourself with your other friends. Plus, you have Debra and George and…me," he added with self-deprecation.

"You have become my best friend, you know that?"

"And you, mine. In fact…I'm not sure I had any real friends before you, although I do rely on George quite a bit, but even he can get tired of my whining."

"You don't whine," she laughed. "What about Donnie and the band?"

"Well, I get along with them, of course, but sometimes they see me too much as their employer instead of a mate. I guess I don't come across as easy to get along with or something, I don't know. And in my position, you're never sure whether people are your friends for the wrong reasons or not."

"Oh. You mean you're never sure if they like you or your money?"

"Precisely. And, let's face it, a good chunk of our band is younger than us. They see us too much like smart old uncles, rather than someone they can confide in. I mean, there is Darius, our saxophonist, he's a smart old bird, but we have a communication problem at times."

"He speaks English."

"Not Queen's English, and I have a hard time with his accent."

"That's rich coming from you!"

"Well, what can I say… He is quite fun, though. We've come over to his house, and his wife cooks up some mean Caribbean food. Otherwise, not much in common."

"Well, you gotta know Rachel is your friend, anyhow, because she doesn't care about your money."

"I never thought she cared about any aspect of me," he laughed.

"Sure she does—at least once you made a respectable woman out of me." Robin chuckled at this. "I'm sure you still think it's odd she married your cousin."

"Ha, yes. Yes, I do. They seem to be quite happy, though."

"Yes, I think so, too."

"Boy, you never know about those relationships. Ones you don't expect to work do, and the ones you think are indestructible seem to show their weakness after a while."

"I take it we're the former?"

"Oh, but yes."

"And the latter?"

He looked at her and simply smiled.

"Ah. Do you think they're still having issues?"

"No, actually, they've been quite chummy lately. And, believe it or not, they've started going to marriage counseling."

"How ironic. We get to quit therapy, and they begin it."

"Yeah. Oh, that reminds me—they want us to come over this weekend. Is that okay with you?"

"Certainly! Sounds fun—been a while since we've done that."

"Great. I'll call George and tell him they will have company then."

Chapter Eighteen

The weekend came, and Robin and Shelly were preparing to go to George and Debra's when a dog's bark broke the silence. They stared at each other and then Shelly exclaimed, "It's D'art!" Robin looked at her doubtfully, but she quickly went downstairs with him close behind, paranoid she was going to do herself harm. She opened the front door and the red Doberman ran in like he had never left. Shelly gave him loads of hugs and kisses, and the dog reciprocated right back. Robin stood shaking his head.

"I knew he'd come back," he said happily. He leaned down and petted the animal that licked his hand with excitement.

"You've been very bad," Shelly scolded. The young dog put his head down for but a second, then continued to give her kisses.

"He looks starved," said Robin. He went into the kitchen to get him some food and water. D'art quickly followed and began to eat and drink ravenously. Shelly gave Robin a hug. Then they heard a squeal from an area near the patio door. "And what do *you* want?" he asked Chuckie the guinea pig. He went to the refrigerator and got out a piece of lettuce for the critter. "You know," he told his wife, "we're going to have to get two nannies—one for the baby and another for the animals."

Shelly giggled and let D'artagnan out into the back so that they could leave. He ran around, happy to be home. "We'll see," she eventually replied.

They were on their way, and Robin glanced over to his smiling wife. He felt the urge to talk about something, but was enjoying his wife's happiness too much to disturb her.

Once at George's, they were welcomed with open arms by the lady of the house. She seemed to be back to her old self, and George was clicking along on all eight cylinders with one joke after another. Debra had prepared a most exquisite meal of quail and veggies with mushrooms, and they all ate with gusto. Shelly had already dug into her food when she stopped and looked around. "Where's Paul?" she asked.

Debra smiled and replied. "He's on a date."

"Ah! Well, why not? He is a cutie. Is he getting all kinds of phone calls?"

"Lord, yes," George grumbled. Everyone chuckled, but then died laughing when George gave his impression of a young girl asking for Paul on the phone. "'Hi! Is *Paul* there?' 'Yes.' 'Could I please speak to him?' 'May I ask who's calling?' 'It's (whomever)' 'Very well'… I'm really thinking of just putting it on a machine, and then Paul can listen to the machine and screen his own calls."

"Ah, c'mon," teased Debra, "I know you like picking on all those young girls—I've heard you," she said with a heavy Southern accent.

George gave a guilty smile and wiggled his eyebrow.

"Shelly, have you heard from Rachel?" asked Debra. Shelly went on to tell her of her phone call.

"Poor Rachel," George said surprisingly.

"Really," Robin agreed.

"Could it be that bad?" Shelly asked him with concern.

"You're forgetting, sweetheart, that Terry's considered a superstar over there. It's like being married to…"

"You?"

"Worse," chimed George. "*Everyone* knows him over there."

"Ooh."

Robin gave a grimace in agreement.

"My poor girl. She'll never fit in."

"Nah. She just has to find her place. London's one of the most diverse cities in the world, she'll find some folks who are in the same boat as she. Besides, she's a resilient young thing, she'll make it."

"George is right," said Debra. "She'll let them know who's the boss." She gave a reassuring smile to Shelly who then smiled back. Shelly really wished she could be there to support her friend.

The evening went on with everyone giving their gratitude for the terrific meal to the chef. The men went outside to sit by the pool and chat about business while the ladies made themselves comfortable in the living room. They discussed the decorating going on at Shelly's and how odd it was that D'artagnan showed back up. Shelly eventually got very quiet and Debra asked what was wrong.

"Oh, nothin'," she replied with a smile. "Just feeling pregnant."

"Won't be long!"

Shelly's eyes got big and she let out a big sigh.

"Can I get you anything?" Debra offered.

"Oh, no. Just need to sit and not move." She rubbed her belly for a moment, and then asked, "How are you two?"

"Me and George?"

"Yeah." Being so pregnant and miserable seemed to give Shelly a legitimate excuse for being nosey.

Debra thought for a moment, looking around the room and then replied, "Good." She nodded and repeated, "Good."

"Good!" Shelly replied happily.

"Funny how you're humming along, not really paying attention, then *boom*, you crash, and then it takes you forever to get back where you started."

"Huh, yeah... My ex was an accident waiting to happen." She studied Debra's distant look for a moment. "Are you sure you're okay?"

Debra quickly looked at her. "Now, more than ever. He's breaking down his guard and learning to be human."

Shelly hesitated for a moment, but then commented, "Some would say the same about you."

Debra dropped her head back with a laugh. "*Touché*! That's so true. I'm learning that he can't know I'm upset about something if I hide it."

"Ha! Robin knows under no uncertain terms if something's bothering me."

"That's the difference between us and you two. You keep everything out in the open, whereas George and I are too much alike."

"Yup, exactly."

"But, I think the worst is over."

"And the produce man?"

"Oh, you heard about him? Why am I surprised?"

"Uh-huh."

"Ha... Well, he's gone."

"Sacrificed for the sake of your marriage?"

"No, for the sake of my Romaine!"

The girls laughed about this and then carried on the conversation to lighter subjects. Meanwhile, the boys were enjoying the cool fall air on the patio.

"So, did you see the figures?" George asked Robin.

"What figures?"

"On your song."

"It's not even on the shelves," he said doubtfully.

"You need to keep up, Rob. The numbers on the presale on the internet. People are going mad for it. You've hit a nerve, my friend."

Robin followed George into his den where he pulled out a paper and gave it to him. "Oh, my God," Robin muttered as he read it.

"I've told you not to call me that."

"This is incredible," Robin went on doubtfully.

"Yes, well, it is getting plenty of airplay—especially in the present situation." George sighed in thought of the current national news.

"I had no idea." Robin stared at the papers with a completely stunned expression. He felt a bit guilty for not paying attention to his work and being so preoccupied with Shelly. He was getting that weird sensation again of being torn in two, especially since the song was about Shelly. He felt like he was going round in circles.

"You know," George hesitated, "we really ought to play some more cities." He stood back, expecting a blow.

Robin jerked his head towards him. "You've got to be kidding, George—"

"I know, I know—the baby. But maybe afterwards?"

"I am not going to take off right after she's born and leave Shelly alone. Get real!"

"Fine, fine, but we really ought to do something to profit from the song whilst we can."

"Yes, well… No touring. Not for a while, least ways."

George made a face and then asked with disappointment, "Telly?"

"How about the music awards?"

"Yes, good. I'll call Janice Monday."

"Okay, fine."

George was just beginning to realize that Robin had more sense about being a father than he ever would himself. Maybe it was good that that job was left to Robin—it just was never meant to be for himself. He gave a quick thought to Debra and how that it wasn't an option anymore anyhow. He relented to the notion that it was for the best with, maybe, just a little disappointment. He noticed a wild look in Robin's eyes. "Getting nervous?"

A smile came over Robin's face. "Scared out of my mind, more like."

George laughed.

"She's got me taking birthing classes." He characteristically rolled his eyes.

"You're doing it for her? Ah, the miracles of modern medicine."

"No, you silly git. Breathing, and all that—and, Lord!—the films! Yikes!"

George laughed even harder at Robin's shudder, but then stopped and said seriously, "I think I'm jealous, you know."

"Really?" Robin was completely surprised by this.

"Yes."

"Why *didn't* you ever have any?"

"Messed up priorities, I suppose. I'm just now learning what's important."

"You always were a slow learner."

"Unfortunately."

"Well, you'll at least get to be an uncle finally."

They both heard a door shut nearby.

"And a stepfather," finished George. "Let's go bug him," he cheerfully suggested.

"Sounds fun."

The two men made their way to Paul's room and George knocked on the door. "Come in," the young man replied.

The two came in with mischievous grins and he greeted them with a bewildered look. "What's wrong?" George asked.

"Nothin'," he lied.

The brothers looked at each other and both said, "A girl."

"Okay, tell us all about her," Robin demanded as he took his desk chair and spun it around to straddle it.

Paul had to grin back at their flippancy and broke down and told them about the beguiling Denise. The guys listened attentively with smiles on their faces and complete empathy.

"Well, what you need to do is set yourself apart from the rest—make her know that you are special and that no other guy can take care of her like you can. Be the perfect gentleman," suggested Robin.

"How?" Paul asked with desperation.

"Hey, why don't you write her a song?" asked George.

Paul chuckled. "I've just learned my sixth chord, and I'm supposed to write her a song?"

"Sure, why not?" they answered in stereo.

"Shoot, how many chords do you need?" asked Robin. "Three, four?"

"You did one with two once, didn't you? Sounded like it, at least," kidded George to Robin.

"Well, I had to use the two that you knew," he quickly replied.

They both joked around like this for a moment until Paul was shaking his head laughing at them. "Look, I know it's second nature to you two, but I wouldn't know where to start!"

"Well, make a list of things you want to say—how she makes you feel," began George.

"Yes, and make it clear your intentions. That you'll treat her right and all that," added Robin.

"Hmm... I dunno," Paul said doubtfully.

"Here, let's see that guitar," said George. Before he knew it, the men were helping him write a simple tune to serenade Denise with. Paul was completely overwhelmed. How many guys his age have the Ministers of Parliament helping him write a song for the girl he's crazy about? What a treat!

They were getting close to finishing when Shelly waddled in. Robin stood up and came to her. "Hello, darling. Ready to go?"

"Oh, yeah."

He looked at her and noticed little beads of sweat upon her forehead. "Are you all right, dear?"

"No, not really."

They all looked at her with concern. "Well, let's get you home," Robin said with sympathy.

They took their leave with thanks for their dinner. Paul thanked Robin for his help and Debra wished Shelly the best and to call her if she needed her.

Paul was feeling quite happy about getting to know his step-uncle a bit better and really did hope his beautiful Aunt Shelly was going to be okay.

Robin looked at Shelly while driving home and asked, "Do you need to see the doctor?" He was getting nervous the way she was rubbing her stomach.

"No, no. I think I'll be fine."

"Well, don't hesitate to tell me if you do."

"I won't." She gave him a reassuring smile and caressed his arm.

But, around 1:00 Shelly couldn't stand it anymore. With a nervous husband beside her, she dialed up her doctor. The man groggily answered the phone, but got concerned once he knew that it was Shelly. He asked a barrage of questions and reassured her that it was nothing unusual. "How severe is the pain?" he asked.

"Ah!" she screamed as she got another pain.

"Ha, okay, thanks for the demonstration… Why don't you go ahead and check into the hospital and we'll take a look at you."

"Okay," she meekly answered. She certainly wasn't going to disagree.

Robin quickly got her to the hospital and Dr. Hodges showed up soon after. They got her checked in and set up in a room. Robin stood in a corner chewing his nails while the doctor examined her. "Well, Shelly, it all looks fine," he eventually said. "It's probably Braxton-Hicks contractions."

"Oh."

"You've heard of that, I take it?"

"Yes, like false labor?"

"Well, sort of. It's just your body preparing for the actual event. Testing the equipment, so to speak."

"Ah, okay."

"So, she's fine then?" Robin finally asked.

"Yes, as much as I can tell. But, with all her history, I think it wouldn't be a bad idea to have her stay overnight."

The couple looked at each other sadly, but said nothing. Instead, they thanked the doctor profusely for getting out of bed for them and he gave them a few encouraging words before he left. The nurses got Shelly into a room and prepared her for the night, while Robin sat in a chair, trying to stay out of their way.

Once the nurses were done and gone, Shelly caught Robin staring at her and said, "Don't think you're staying here tonight."

He grimaced and replied, "And why not?" His eyes were big and severe.

"You need to go home and get some proper rest. Last thing we need is you driving all groggy tomorrow."

"Do you really think I'm going to sleep either way?"

Shelly knew perfectly well what was going through his mind. "Well, the animals need to be fed in the morning."

"Damn the animals."

"No, no. It really won't do any good to stay here."

"It would make me feel better."

Shelly had no reply to this. "Come here."

He came over and sat at the foot of the bed. She took his hand and caressed it over and over again without a word. She wasn't smiling, and he felt so bad for her. He rubbed her belly and said quietly to it, "You let your mummy get some rest, do you hear me, young lady?" She couldn't help but laugh at that. He picked up her hand and kissed it slowly and softly, almost making her cry. He stood up, pulled her covers over her, gave her a kiss and settled into the chair to rest.

In the morning they were awakened by the nurse who checked Shelly's vitals. Her pains had subsided and all seemed well. The scare was over. She was to be released later in the day. They eventually brought her some breakfast, leaving Robin to scrounge for his own. He went down to the cafeteria, and in doing so, way too many flashbacks of the first time he was there came flooding back at him. It was the first time he had brought Shelly there which had originally seemed ages ago, but now seemed like yesterday. He shook his head and walked to the pharmacy to pick up a snack instead. He found a coffee machine and was satisfied with that. He sat blankly eating the sweet bread he bought, thinking about how different this time was compared to the last. He had already lost a baby, almost lost Shelly and his brother, and he really hoped that the next time he ever had to come here it would be to have this baby with no problems. Someone was always trying to die on him and he wished he could take the pain away from the people he loved and lay it all on him. He could handle if something happened to himself, but he didn't think he could stand one more incident like before.

After finishing his coffee, he purchased some flowers in the little flower shop there in the hospital. He took them to his lady, who cheerfully received them with many thanks. "Remember when you gave me that teddy bear?"

"Yes, I do."

"I still have him, you know."

"Yes, I know."

"He's in my changing room."

"Yes...and I noticed he has a very nice scarf now."

"Ha, yeah. Had to dress him up."

They sat quiet for a moment.

"Funny how different this time is," she said, reading his thoughts.

"Yes."

"I have a feeling everything is going to be all right."

He looked at her eyes and felt something stir within him. "You know, I think you're right."

"Yes, I usually am," she joked.

"Oh, my Shelly." He gratefully kissed her cheek, and she laughed.

The hours simply didn't go fast enough before she was released. When she was, he gladly helped her into the car.

"I guess I'd better fill up before I run out of petrol," he said as he noticed his fuel gage.

"Yeah, I don't feel like walking."

"Ha, I don't imagine you do," he chuckled.

After filling up, he went inside to get his wife something to nibble and himself a water. Shelly sat looking around and saw with exasperation that her ex-husband was filling up right next to her. What luck! He saw her as well and had too good of manners not to come over and say hello.

"Hi, John," she replied.

"Wow," he said when he saw her condition. "I guess congratulations are in order."

"Thank you." She smiled from his sincerity.

He was quiet for a moment. "I'm really happy for you."

"Thanks. Are you doing all right?" she asked, for she felt he wasn't.

He shrugged his shoulders. With a bitter look he answered, "Working on divorce Number Two."

"Oh, God. I'm sorry," she earnestly replied.

"What goes around, comes around, I guess." He knew she would appreciate that.

"Really?" she asked with surprise.

He nodded his head slightly. "Yeah."

Shelly didn't know what to say. When he had cheated on her, she wouldn't wish that on anyone—not even him.

John saw Robin coming back out and said good-bye to Shelly.

"Good-bye, John… John?"

"Yeah?"

"I really do wish you well."

"Thanks, Shell'."

He went back to his car and smiled back at her.

Robin got into the car and asked, "Wasn't that your ex?" as he gave her the snacks.

"Yes."

"Was he surprised to see you pregnant?"

"Yes, he was."

Robin got the car going and she asked with a philosophical look, "You know what's weird?"

"What, dearest?"

"How life is full of revenges we don't plan."

"How's that?"

"His wife cheated on him, and now they're getting a divorce."

"Oh, dear. Well, you know what they say—"

"What goes around, comes around," they both said, then laughed.

"*Exactly*," Shelly stressed.

"It's called *Karma*," he added.

They both sighed and felt so lucky that they were who they were. They both simply didn't ask life to take care of them, just to be kind to them. People who expect everyone else to cater to them are always doomed, and Shelly and Robin were certainly not in that category—not even with all the money they had.

He took her home and they took it easy the rest of the day. D'artagnan stayed by her feet until bedtime.

Chapter Nineteen

It was the next weekend, and Robin took Shelly out for dinner at her favorite restaurant. He figured she deserved it. They enjoyed the time together, and he mentioned the old studio. "I guess we should go check to see how Rachel left it."

Shelly rummaged through her purse. "I have the keys with me."

"Splendid."

"What are we going to do with it now?"

"I don't know. I guess we could always rent it out. It really ought not to be left empty."

"That's true."

"Then when Paul gets old enough, he could live there away from Mummy and Daddy."

"Oh, I bet he'd love that!"

"I'm sure he would."

So, after their dinner they made their way to Shelly's old home.

She stepped up the steps to the door holding his hand, and he held her back before she could go any further. She turned to look at him. He stared hard at her, soaking in her beauty in the full moon's light. His eyes were large as they took in this vision, and he slowly caressed her face. That place at that time brought back so many memories that were still so fresh in his mind. The past week seemed to be one, long flash back.

She looked at him and noticed an almost sad expression. "What's the matter?" she asked softly.

"Nothing…nothing."

She felt it, too.

"It's just…sometimes…" He trailed off, guilty for his feelings.

"It's all gone so fast," she finished for him.

"Yes," he quickly confirmed. "It's not that I'm not grateful for everything that has happened, it's just…I don't know, really."

"I understand. It's not simple anymore. We're not just lovers anymore, we're a family." She lovingly rubbed her belly, and he placed his hand on hers and stared at them for a moment.

"I don't want to fall off that high of falling in love with you," he said without thinking.

The remark scared her, and her heart raced. "It's bound to happen, you know."

He looked in her eyes and saw her fear. "Oh, no, Shelly dearest, don't think I'm going to stop loving you—just that I'll miss that initial magic we had. Heck, Mum and Dad always seemed to be deep in love with each other, and I have no doubt we will, too—of that I'm certain. I just somehow feel things are getting crazy and we haven't been able to enjoy each other."

"Yes, I know what you mean. We need to *slow* down."

He smiled and took the keys from her and led her inside. He flicked the light switch and the memories flooded back to them tenfold. They had not been there for quite a while, and what they just said had already begun to conjure up the time before their marriage.

They sat down on that sweet little purple couch to do some more talking. He took her hand in his—always amazed at how much smaller hers was than his—picked it up, and kissed it. "I've been thinking—yes, I know, dangerous thing to do, as you say. I really think we should get a nanny."

She rested her chin on her free hand and joked, "I knew it. You already want someone younger."

"No. Believe me, one woman is enough," he said with an exasperated expression. She giggled and he continued, "There are so many places I want to take you—so many things we should experience while we're young...well, youngish," he laughed. "There is this wonderful little village in the south of France near Monaco called Eze that I know you would just love. It's a medieval settlement with cobblestone pathways, and I can see you sitting outside painting it... I don't want you to forget who you are—motherhood should simply be an addition, not a substitute."

"You're very serious about this."

"Yes, I am."

She finally smiled and said, "Okay, we'll get a nanny, but that doesn't mean she'll be raising her."

"Absolutely not. *We* will do the raising." He ran his hand down the back of her head and asked, "So...are you happy?"

"Incredibly."

"Good."

"And you?"

"Ecstatic," he said with a great smile.

She laughed and kissed him. She looked around the studio and sighed. She got up to survey it all, and he followed.

"Miss it?" he asked.

"Sometimes."

"I can understand why."

"You can?"

"I'll always remember the first time I came here."

"I certainly do. You made me a nervous wreck!"

"I did?"

"Yes…and you fell in love with my little painting."

With a serious look, he replied, "That wasn't all I fell in love with."

She bashfully smiled and he gently lifted her chin and gave her a powerful kiss. She could feel herself go weak. He could still do it to her. He held her steady and laughed. He hugged her as best he could and they held each other in silence for a good while.

They eventually made their way upstairs to discover a small mess. "Aye, Rachel," Shelly griped. Robin was quite silent. She caught him staring at the bed. "What is it?" she asked.

He shook his head quickly. "Sorry—daydreaming."

"I know, we haven't had much of a love life lately. But, after the baby is born, it just takes a little more time then—"

"No, sweet, that's not it," he said impatiently. "This place has both good and bad memories," he said with his eyes quickly bouncing from one wall to another. He turned and went back down the stairs. She waddled her way down as quickly as she could. She forced him to look at her. He had an embarrassed expression.

"Tell me," she gently urged.

"I'm sorry. It's just…well, I remember so well having to help you up the steps and taking care of you after… And I had just been thinking about that the other day in the hospital, and…" he trailed off.

"Yes, I know, I'm reminded, too… Maybe we should go."

He looked around the studio once more, with his eyes landing on the couch. "Yes, maybe we'd better."

They were quite silent on the way home until Shelly asked out of nowhere, "Are you still debating about working?"

His eyes popped open and he shot her a quick glance. "How'd you know?"

"You're an easy book to read, Mr. Parker," she said with a grin.

Exasperated by the subject, he answered quite out of character, "Aw, Shelly, I'm so tired of it!"

She giggled at his funny expression.

"I just want to be the best father and husband that I can. *All my life* I have dedicated myself to my work—I would really like a change."

"Are you listening to yourself? You just answered your own question."

He got completely silent. He stopped for a stop sign and didn't move.

"Honey?" she asked.

He snapped out of it. "Huh?"

"It's a sign, not a light."

"Oh." He drove on for a bit and finally warmed back up. "You're right, of course."

"*I'm* not saying anything," she protested. "I think you've already made up your mind, and you're just fighting it because you feel guilty and scared."

Her Texas accent flared up, adding to her no-nonsense attitude. He knew she was right. "Yes, yes. That's very true. I'm scared witless."

She rubbed his arm. "You have every right to be."

"*So* many people depend on me."

"I know," she said with sympathy.

"Look, I'm not ready to do this—damn!"

She hurt for him, but he had to work this out on his own. "Well, maybe you should just take some time off after the baby's born and think about it later?"

He took a breath and thought. George wanted him to get back to work as soon as he felt he could after the birth of the baby, but taking a decent break sure sounded nice. To just not think about the subject of work for a while would be good, and then maybe he could get back to it later without any regrets. "That sounds good," he answered her without telling her of George's wishes. "Nothing like procrastination."

"Ha-ha. Yeah. Always works for me!"

Once home, Shelly realized that visiting her old studio not only conjured up memories, but her artistic way of looking at things. She intentionally let Robin walk a bit ahead just so she could observe him. It had been so long since she admired him for who he was instead of simply relying on him. She felt her blood move faster within her as she watched his graceful walk. She loved those long, beautiful legs of his and the way the moonlight reflected off his honey-colored hair. She studied his fine, slender fingers as he unlocked the door. He turned his head and looked up to her and smiled and it was as if she hadn't seen that smile for years. His deep, brown eyes closed softly as he gave her a gentle kiss. He held her hand as he led her in and she prayed that she would never forget this moment.

Where she was having such pleasant considerations of her husband, he was having more serious contemplations. He could feel she was in deep concentration, and for a moment saw a look in her eyes like one of his adoring fans. But the situation was different. This time, it was a woman—the only woman—who could make him feel likewise. She was the star—the once unattainable persona who, by some grace of God, actually fell for him. The reality of their love was completely mind-blowing to him, and he often tried not to think of it. How can another human being have so much control over another and why is it we crave that control so dearly? He didn't know the answer and knew he never would, but there she was—the sweet owner of his heart. The heart that was once all but frozen solid now beat fiercely and vibrantly for this simple lady. And now they were having a baby?! He shook his head, and without saying a thing, kissed her once again, then got down on his knees and gave a kiss to the baby. He hadn't done that since she first got pregnant, and it made her cry. Her sweet prince was there at her feet, handing his heart to her on a silver salver.

He stood up and stared at her dark blue eyes for a moment. He wiped away a tear with his thumb and softly smiled. "I think you need some rest, my fiery-headed angel."

She smiled and nodded, and he helped her upstairs.

Shelly fell asleep quickly, but awoke in the wee hours of the morning to find Robin gone from the bed. Actually, she wasn't sure if he ever came to bed. She lay there a moment trying to decide what to do. She knew she should get her rest, but she was so worried about her husband. She didn't envy the decision he was up against.

As she pondered these things, she could barely hear a piano playing in the background. She somehow felt she should leave him alone.

The next day, Robin and Shelly woke up quite late, but he eventually went to work, acting perfectly normal. She gave him a kiss good-bye and wondered how he did it. She was never any good at putting on a façade, but chalked up his talent to being a professional entertainer.

She couldn't stop thinking about him, and finally gave up and called Debra at her café. "Can you talk?" she quickly asked when Debra got to the phone.

"Yes! Let me get to the office… What is it?"

"Did George go through a mid-life crisis?"

Debra laughed and replied, "Who knows? He's always liked convertibles and young girls, so how can I tell?" Debra gave a laugh to herself and Shelly couldn't help but follow. It felt good to do so. "Why?" continued Debra. "Is Robin showing signs of it?"

"Well, I don't know if it's that or just having a baby."

"Mmm…probably the latter. What has he been doing?"

"Well, don't tell George, but he's still thinking of quitting."

"Well, Shelly, I'm not surprised. This is such a big change for him—never mind what all you two have been through."

"Yes, I know."

"And *you* certainly don't need to feel guilty about it."

"Well, I don't want him to change his whole personality because of me… I just wish I could help him with this decision. I feel so useless."

"No, you're not useless, and no, you can't help him, either. He has to work it out on his own. But, please, don't fret about it. He'll make the right decision, and he won't change his whole personality. If Robin is anything, he's someone who thinks things through. George is the spontaneous one. He does everything on a whim."

"Yeah, I can see that."

"Just support him and let him know you approve either way he decides, even if he does choose to quit," she stressed.

Shelly drew in a breath and replied, "Okay."

"But as for a mid-life crisis, I rather doubt it—or at least a full-blown one. He is probably going through a re-evaluation of himself, but that's because of all his new-found responsibility."

"Thanks to me," Shelly said almost bitterly.

"Ha-ha. Well, don't feel like one of those wives who break up bands. The band loves you."

"You, too!"

"How can you not love 'em? Well, okay, maybe I don't love *Sam*."

Shelly broke out laughing. "You're funny! But you know, she really is nice."

"Yes, I know," she said with almost a catty tone of voice.

It cracked Shelly up to hear Debra speak like that, and she couldn't help but to continue to laugh.

The two eventually ended their call, Debra being beckoned to get back onto the floor. Shelly found herself feeling better. So much so that she went to her studio and made a fantastic sketch of the fountain outside.

The month of November started to fly quickly by. Shelly and Robin celebrated their first anniversary with a quiet dinner at their favorite Italian restaurant. It wasn't much, but it was enough in Shelly's state. They got the precious alone time they needed and were able, if only for one night, to concentrate on that special bond that they were so blessed to have. It was a quiet night, but a good night.

The guys were also busy that month promoting their single as locally as possible. They did interviews, but were unable to get on the awards show, unfortunately. Nonetheless, the sales of the song proved to be one of their top songs of their twenty-five year history, and it brought on a resurgence of sales of their past albums. They worked frantically remastering some of their older works and getting them out onto store shelves just in time for Christmas, and Robin found himself deeper and deeper into his quandary. Shelly was getting closer to having the baby and George was getting more excited about touring, and it felt to him that there was a competition for his attention.

He was daydreaming as he left the office late one evening. He mindlessly made the turns it took to take him home. He thought about opening a bottle of wine once he was home to try and wash all the technical garbage out of his head when suddenly, what seemed from nowhere, a car rammed full-force into his car—and into him.

It happened so fast, he wasn't sure exactly what had happened, but soon realized he was in pain. He looked down at his left side and saw blood everywhere. He panicked, and dared not move. He prayed that someone would call EMS. Someone did. The pain got more intense, and he looked up and thought he was hallucinating, for he saw Samantha with a frantic look standing outside his car.

The paramedics, firemen and policemen had surrounded him. He couldn't help but start screaming for the pain. He began to feel weak and passed out. When he woke up, he was in emergency.

He vaguely remembered someone cutting his shirt off and people talking constantly, hollering out commands to each other. "Shelly," he managed to get out.

"Just relax, Mr. Parker, we'll get you fixed up," a man in green scrubs assured.

He looked around the room, then down at himself. He felt his whole left side was broken. He was unsure of the extent of the damage done to him and somehow knew that they had heavily medicated him. He had a hard time breathing, but yet he felt very calm and knew he should close his eyes. He coughed with a jerk, and then fell asleep.

The next time he woke up, he found himself in a hospital room with his arm being held up by a pulley rig. Intensely groggy, he could just make out the image of a crying Shelly beside him. He tried to wake up more to console her, but simply couldn't. The best he could muster was to smile at her. She kissed him profusely all over the right side of his face and he wanted to laugh.

Then, like a bullhorn, he heard George. "Hey, you all right, mate?"

Robin knitted his brows as a reply.

"Ha-ha. I guess that means 'Do I look all right?'" George joked. In reality, George was thrilled to get any reaction.

Robin felt himself drifting off again. He could still hear Shelly crying, but couldn't stay awake for her.

It was a day later. Robin woke up feeling like he'd been asleep for years. He was conscious now, and his mind was desperately trying to recall what had happened. He looked around and saw no one. He wondered what day it was. He looked down and saw his entire arm and shoulder wrapped up mummy-style along with bandages and tubes pasted around his middle. He immediately thought of Shelly. "My God!" he thought. "I hope this didn't put her into labor!"

He found the nurses' button and pressed it. Within a few minutes, a nurse came in and greeted him.

"My wife…is she okay?" he eagerly inquired. It caused him to go into a painful coughing spree, but anxiety overcame him—he had to know.

"Uh, yes, sir… She wasn't with you in the accident, though."

"No, I know…but she's…pregnant," he got out intermittently between coughs. "I need to know…this didn't upset her…too much." He was getting quite aggravated by the fact he couldn't get his words out.

"Oh, no, no," the nurse replied as she slipped the cuff of the blood pressure machine over his good arm. "She was upset, naturally, but your brother and his wife were here, taking good care of her."

"Good…good."

"Now, you need to take it easy, sir, and we'll get you fixed up. Try not to talk too much."

"What all broke? Why can't I breathe?"

"Oh, you got beat up pretty good, I'm afraid. Your ulna, your humerus, and your clavicle broke," she explained, pointing to the bones on his good arm. "I can't believe you didn't break your rotator cup, but it's a good thing you didn't."

"Why?"

"Very difficult to heal and it will give you problems later on, too."

"Three bones," he muttered.

"No, sir. Five. Two ribs as well."

Robin rolled his eyes and put his head back. "What happened?" he was dying to know.

"I believe someone ran a red light. That's all I heard." She mercilessly stuck a thermometer in his mouth and said, "You rest. Your family will be here soon. They've been here all day. They just went down to get something to eat at the cafeteria."

The cafeteria, he thought. How ironic he had just been here not long ago with Shelly and pondered their history of the cafeteria! He worried about how this was affecting Shelly. "What a time to have a wreck!" he griped to himself.

The nurse took down his temperature and studied his dressings. "I think we're going to have to change this one. Someone will be right in to take care of that." She smiled and left.

It wasn't five minutes when a man came in with a cart full of bandages of all shapes and sizes. He said, 'hello' and went to work.

Robin watched with curiosity as he took off the tainted bandages, and noticed with horror how bruised and cut up he was. He remembered what he looked like right after the accident and did his best to move his fingers to make sure they still worked. It hurt like hell, but they did. If anything kept him from playing piano, it would kill him. He thanked God for the use of his hand and the fact he wasn't dead, and fell asleep again.

In waking up again, he found the friendly faces he craved. Shelly came over and held his good hand for dear life. She gave him a kiss and he managed to ask, "How are you?"

"Shouldn't I be asking *you* that?"

"Oh. Well, with me…what's done is done. But…I've been worried…worried to death…about you." He was getting upset again that he couldn't seem to catch his breath.

She gave a heavy sigh. "Well, when they first told me, I had some rather bad cramping, but I think I'm okay now."

"Did you see…a doctor?"

"No, I'm fine, I tell you. You're the one who almost died on me!" She began to cry.

"Shh…I'm sorry, baby… I'm just…concerned, that's all… I just broke a few bones."

Shelly shook her head.

"Well, no, that's not *really* all," interrupted George as he put an arm around Shelly.

Robin gave a look of confusion.

"Your ribs broke and punctured your lung. It had collapsed."

His eyes got large and he muttered, "No wonder."

"But they say you're going to be fine," Debra reassured everyone. "They've got a tube in you helping your lung to expand."

"Oh, yes, you'll live," George tried to joke.

Robin looked at George and hoped this wasn't stressing his heart too much. "What happened?" he asked once more.

George made a funny face and looked at Debra. "Well, a drunk driver hit you—she ran a red light."

Robin was silent for a second. He then had a flash back of the accident and told George, "You know what's…weird? I could have…sworn I saw Sam…right after the accident." He coughed for a bit while George scratched his head with an odd expression.

"Well, that's the other thing."

"What?"

"She's your drunk driver."

"What?!" This caused him to cough quite a bit, and everyone tried to settle him down. "Where is she?"

With a bitter tone, George answered, "Out on bond and regretting like hell what she's done."

Robin swallowed and tried to breathe. "Well…that's a surefire way…to get fired… Try to kill your boss."

"Yes. And make him pay your bail."

"You're kidding." He took a drink of water from Shelly gratefully.

George chuckled. "Nope. She had no other recourse."

Robin looked at Shelly and motioned for her to get closer. He wiped her cheek, reminding him of the night they had gone to her old studio. "I'm going to be fine… Understand?"

She nodded and tried to smile.

Debra looked at George and he took the hint. "Hey, Rob, we're going to make some phone calls and let them know how you're doing."

"Okay."

He leaned down and hugged his brother as well as he could. It was a long hug, and George quickly left afterward to the hall. Debra followed suit with a hug for Shelly as well and followed her husband.

Shelly watched Robin in his silence until he asked, "What time is it?"

"Uh…almost 6:30."

"Where's the remote…for the telly?"

She thought it an odd request, but found the remote and asked what channel he wanted it on.

"Four. They're supposed…to have a bit about our single… It is Sunday, right?"

"Uh, yes." She figured it would probably be a good distraction for him, and turned it on.

They watched the entertainment program for a while, but the article they ran said only a little about the song. Instead, they spoke of the accident.

Shelly concentrated on Robin as he watched the program—she didn't want him to get upset. They then showed pictures of the wreckage, and she barely heard him utter, "My car." She knew he loved that old car, and now felt even sorrier for him. The sight of the bloodstained door seemed to make the both of them swoon a bit, and they sensed their hearts were beating at the same rapid rate. Naturally, the reporters also showed a photograph of Sam and explained the odd coincidence of the accident, adding to the stress on Robin.

The spot was then done, and he took the remote and turned it off. His eyes began to well up, but he said nothing. She didn't know what to say. She knew there were a million thoughts crossing his mind, and she had no idea where to start.

He turned to her suddenly. She leaned over to hold him, but between his injuries and her large belly, it was almost impossible. She couldn't help but let out a small giggle, and Robin couldn't help but smile. "We're a pair, aren't we?" he mused.

"Yes, we sure are."

"Well," he began. He blinked his eyes clear and tried to catch his breath. "I guess I'll be out of work…for a while… whether I like it or not. You said we needed…to slow down."

"The Lord works in mysterious ways."

"That He does." He went very quiet, but then suddenly closed his eyes and tried desperately to stifle the urge to cry. The mere thought of getting killed and leaving Shelly to raise their child alone jarred him like nothing else—never mind getting injured so badly that his career would be ruined. He never thought he'd have his own brush with death. Through George and Shelly's ordeals, he still felt invincible. It never occurred to him that just because he lucked out and got his mother's heart instead of his dad's, that doesn't mean that something—or someone—else might kill him. This made him ponder Sam, and in doing so, calmed him down. He wondered why she was driving intoxicated in the first place and what consequences she was going to have to face. He lay in pain with a half-deflated lung, but he still found it in his heart to feel sorry for her. She would probably go to jail. What a horrible situation.

He looked at Shelly again, who was holding on to his good hand tightly. "Oh, no," he groaned.

"What?" she asked.

"Your appointment's tomorrow."

"No, I cancelled it."

"Oh, you oughtn't."

"Well, honey, I don't know if you realize it or not, my husband's lying in the hospital looking like King Tut."

This made him laugh, then cough. It also made him curious to the extent of his outward damages. Unable to move his left arm he reached around with his right hand and felt about on his head. "What's up with my head?"

Shelly looked with sadness at the amount of dried blood and the tiny shards of glass that were still scattered about his hair. "Well, you have some pretty nasty cuts, but most are within your hair line, thank God. I couldn't stand it if your pretty face got harmed," she said as she picked out some glass. "Unfortunately, you've got a pretty ugly haircut right now, though, and you've lost your sideburn on this side."

He snarled his nose, and the funny expression did much for Shelly's heart.

"You're going to be fine, ya know."

He smiled and said, "Good."

A nurse came in and urged Shelly to let him get some more rest. So she kissed her dear man and they exchanged 'I love you's. Shelly came out to find George and Debra.

"How is he?" George asked.

Shelly didn't answer, but instead came to him to be held while she cried.

It was close to 9:00 in the evening when Robin woke back up. Oddly enough, the only one there was Debra. "Well, hello," she greeted.

"Hello," he replied sleepily.

"George took Shelly home. Poor thing hasn't slept since the accident."

"Good...good."

"Paul's here," she said cheerily.

"Really?"

"Yes, he went to get a—"

As if on cue, Paul entered, slurping on a soda.

"Hey, Paul," Robin greeted with obvious pain.

"Hi... How are you?" He felt a bit bashful, but came and shook his hand.

"I've been better." But then with an odd face, "I've been worse."

This made Paul smile. "Oh!" he began, and retrieved something from on top of the table, "I got you a card." He gave it to Robin, but then realized he couldn't open it very easily with one hand, so he opened it for him.

Robin read the funny card and laughed. "Thanks, Paul... Thank you very much." He smiled at the young man and remembered something. "Say, Paul... How's your... Denise?" he asked unsure of her name.

He smiled and looked at his mother. "I'm taking her to the homecoming dance."

"Splendid."

"Yeah," he replied with a nervous grin. He studied Robin, unable to believe this had happened to him. It wasn't that long ago Robin was in his room happily composing a song for his girlfriend with a big smile. Now he looked as if a part of him was missing, somehow. It made him uncomfortable to see him in such a vulnerable state.

Robin caught him staring and flashed a quick smile.

"Oh, sorry. Just can't believe… I'm really sorry, you know."

"I know," he said with kindness for the boy. He knew Paul wasn't one for words, but he could see the sadness in his face.

Debra and Paul visited for a bit, but then took their leave to let Robin go back to sleep—or at least sleep as well as he could.

The next morning, Robin's first visitor was the doctor. He greeted Robin and gave him his condolences for the bad situation he was in (considering this was the first time he caught Robin awake) along with his appreciation for his music. "Well, just thought I'd give you an update on your progress and let you know your options… I take it you're hurting more today than yesterday?"

"Yeah," Robin wondered.

"That's my fault. I wanted you a little more coherent for right now. Didn't want you falling asleep on me while I'm talking to you. After a while, we'll pump you back up."

"Glad to hear it."

"Let's see. Are you comfortable? Need another pillow?"

"Wouldn't hurt." Robin noticed the man's accent and asked, "Australia?"

"Got it!"

Robin smiled. Normally, he would have gotten into a conversation about his pleasant visits of Down Under, but he really was hurting and it simply took too long to get any words out. The doctor could tell this, so immediately went to work discussing in detail his damages and how they were going to fix them, including the physical therapy it was going to take to help his arm return to normal.

"Now, they're going to take another MRI of your chest here in a moment to check how that lung is doing, but…" he listened to his chest with a stethoscope, "I think you're improving."

"Good."

"Yes, indeed… So, you want to avoid pins in your collarbone if we can get away with it?"

"Yes… I have a hard enough time…with airport security."

"Ha-ha! Good point, good point. Unfortunately, it was an impacted fracture—the two broken ends of the bone were driven together," he explained with a motion of his hands. "But, we'll see what we can do."

"Doctor?"

"Yes?"

"What…what kind of shape will I…be in, in a month?"

"A month? Oh, yeah. Your pretty wife is expecting, isn't she?"

"Yes," he said with a little pride.

"Well, you'll still be bandaged up, but you'll be pretty mobile, if that's what you mean. Fortunately, you're in good shape for a man your age."

"I want to be able to help."

"Of course. Naturally. You'll still have your cast, but your lung should be back to normal. No lifting heavy objects, though."

"Not even the baby?" he asked with obvious disappointment.

"Babies aren't heavy," he laughed. "Just hold her with your good arm—you're a big man."

Robin went quiet thinking of the day he would be a father. The doctor adjusted the contraption that held his arm in suspension and made sure it was in the proper position.

"Well, Robin, like I said, they'll be x-raying you again and then they're going to give you your first real cast and bath and fed and all that and then I'll say nighty-night after I hook you back up to your pain-killers."

The doctor had a quick, humorous way of talking that brought a smile to Robin's face. "Thank goodness," he replied.

"Oh, you do have a couple of visitors first, but that's it for a while, okay?"

"Okay."

The doctor took his leave and was gone. The door then slowly opened up and a familiar face popped in like a gopher. "Hello, hello."

Robin grinned at his visitor. "Hello, Donnie." He was very pleased to see their clown of a manager.

The man came over and was appalled by the apparatus on his arm and how badly he was beaten up. "Goodness, Rob. If you wanted some time off, just ask."

"I've been trying to tell you."

He shook his hand, and he sat down on the chair next to his bed after peeping out the window. "I have something to show you."

"What?"

Donnie showed him the picture on his digital camera. "What in the world? Where's that?"

"Outside, buddy. They've practically built a shrine to you."

"You've got to be…kidding." The emotion made him cough.

"I kid you not."

Robin desperately wanted to get up to see, but felt like an animal in a trap.

"You are loved," Donnie teased.

"That's nice," he said honestly.

"Yes, I imagine so… Can I take a pic'?"

Robin made a grimace, knowing he looked like hell, but agreed to do so.

"Thanks. Need it for the archives, you know."

Robin then posed again with two fingers up and Donnie took that as well, laughing.

"You really couldn't have had this at a better time."

"I highly…doubt that."

"Everyone bought the CDs thinking you were going to the big bandstand in the sky."

"You're a blood-thirsty monster… You know that?"

"Yes, but I also knew you'd pull through. You always do."

"All I know is…I feel like shit."

"You look it, too. All the better to extract loads of sympathy from your adoring fans."

Robin laughed and then coughed. "God, Donnie, you're awful."

Donnie smiled. "Just trying to cheer you up… You don't mind if I sell this photo, do you? Maybe I should put it on our website," he said, studying the photo.

Robin put his good hand on his face.

"Hey, well, the doc told me not to take too much time, but I wanted to come by and give my deepest sympathies."

"I'm not dead."

"No, but that hair's going to take some time to grow back, especially with that receding hairline and everything."

"With friends like you—" Robin growled.

"I know, I know. Hey, really though," he said as he shook his hand again, "glad you're going to be okay." He was unusually serious with this comment, emphasizing to Robin just how serious this really was.

"Thanks...thanks for coming."

"Oh, yeah... Got to go find that triage nurse again," he said with a wiggle of his eyebrows.

"Good luck," Robin laughed. Donnie left and Robin was thankful for his short visit. Donnie always was good at cracking him up.

A knock at the door announced George. He greeted his brother and he asked his condition, and Robin explained what the doctor informed. George listened with grave interest and sat not saying anything until, "There's someone here to see you."

"Who?"

"Sam."

Robin's eyes grew large.

"I told her she needs to see you. I think it would be good for her. Are *you* up for it?"

Robin looked around the room, thinking. 'No' is what he felt like saying, but he knew it was best to get it over with. "I suppose so."

"Good." He got up and went out to the hall.

It took a couple of minutes, but eventually the woman came in. She stood frozen at the sight of what she had done to the man that she had always been fond of.

"Hello, Sam," Robin greeted without feeling of any sort.

She came over and began to tremble. She sat down in the chair and put her hand over her mouth. She was dumbfounded. She then began to cry. Robin averted his eyes. He knew she had to get it out. "I'm so sorry, Robin. I am *so sorry!*" she repeated over and over again. Robin was not in the mood for this stress, and wished for his pain relievers, but he knew she needed to go through this. She *could have* killed him—or someone else—a child even. Maybe this is the wake-up call she needed.

Fortunately, George was overhearing, and knew to come back in. He calmed the girl down until she could coherently say to Robin, "Forgive me."

He looked hard into her eyes. "I forgive you." He wasn't sure if he said it out of pity or to actually make her feel even guiltier. He just knew it had to be said.

George gave Robin an understanding nod, and exited with his arm around Sam. He was very glad that was over. He had pity for the girl, but pity wasn't what she needed right now. Later, maybe, he could have a decent chat with her when he was feeling better. Right now, he was already quite tired of this crazy morning. He tried desperately to forget Sam and concentrate on Donnie's visit. But, he had one more visitor before they came to take him to x-ray. A person he needed more than the precious air he had a hard time breathing.

"Hello," Shelly greeted sweetly. It was music to his ears after the pitiful sounds of Sam's laments. She brought some cheery flowers and sat them down where he could see them.

"Hello, dearheart… I can't tell you…how grand it is you're here."

She came over and kissed his cheek. She seemed rested, and gave him a beautiful smile. He held her hand and he could see the hope in her eyes. Maybe she could tell he was doing better.

They chatted for a while and he told her of all his visitors. She listened intently, and in the end simply said, "You poor thing." She always did have a way of getting to the heart of the matter.

The rest of her visit was on a lighter note. He complimented how pretty she was today, and she commented on the group of nail-biting fans that had collected outside. But when she caressed his face and held his hand—that was all he really needed.

As promised, his MRI was taken, proving his lung was doing better. With every bit of improvement, he could feel the difference. The pain, however, was a force to be reckoned with. After the staff took care of his basic needs, including a cast for his arm, they settled him in and happily doped him up again. He really did want to sleep the day away—it would not hurt his feelings at all.

He did manage to get some quality sleep through the afternoon, but the evening brought in several more visitors including the rest of his band mates. It proved to be a good visit, for it cheered him up immensely. They discussed the popularity of the single and the projects they had in mind, along with some funny anecdotes of other people's reactions to his accident. He went to bed feeling a little less pain.

Chapter Twenty

The next morning brought the doctor with a couple of male nurses. "Good morning, Robin!" he chimed with his Aussie accent.

"Morning," Robin replied. "Are these your lynch men?"

"More x-rays, I'm afraid."

"Keep it up…and I'll glow in the dark."

"Heh-heh. We've got to check that lung once more and see if we can remove that tube. Plus, we need to monitor those bones of yours. I'm still unsure about that collarbone, but we need to clear that lung before we think about surgery. We may still have to put in some pins, I feel."

Robin frowned, and the doctor instructed the nurses what to tell the x-ray technician. One nurse came over and took Robin's vitals, keeping him from being able to talk by sticking a thermometer in his mouth. He simply sat there, hoping they wouldn't have to operate.

"Well," the doctor continued, "I'll be back to discuss what we found."

"All right," he mumbled. The doctor took off as quickly as he breezed in. Robin noticed he seemed in a rushed mood today. Little did he know that the doctor had already worked five hours that morning, and had a long way to go still.

But, he did return as promised after they were done with Robin, and Robin knew by his sad look that the news wasn't good. "Well, the good news is, your lung is doing very well. Bad news is, your clavicle isn't. I'm sorry, Robin, we are simply going to have to brace it, or you'll look like the hunchback with a droopy shoulder."

Robin realized what needed to be done. He assented with a nod.

"It really is a simple procedure. Shouldn't be any complications."

"When can you do it?"

"I've already scheduled it for this afternoon."

Robin was shocked by how soon. He really must be concerned by it. "That's quick."

"Your bone is trying to heal, but incorrectly. We need to get in there and correct it."

"Very well."

"All righty. Well, we'll get you fixed up. I'll see you later, then."

"Thanks doc."

The doctor left and Robin mused at how everyone there was always telling him that they would get him 'fixed up'. Made him feel a bit like a car, which only led him to thinking about his poor old Jaguar.

The opening of the door broke his train of thought to reveal Shelly. "Hello," she sang softly.

"Hello, my dear." She was a sight for sore eyes.

"I have someone here to see you." She brought in a woman who instantly greeted him.

"Patty! I didn't expect...to see *you*!" he told his mother-in-law.

"Just felt I was needed," she replied with a shrug of her shoulders.

"Yes, well, that is probably true… Especially after I tell Shelly…my latest news."

"What news?" Shelly asked instantly.

"They're going to have to operate on my collarbone… They have to put pins in."

"Oh, no," they both moaned.

"But, my lung is doing better," he quickly said to relieve his wife.

"Well, that's good… When are they going to do this?" she asked.

"This afternoon."

"That soon?"

"Yeah."

"Well, I'm sure you'll be fine," Mrs. Harrison said with a reassuring smile. "You're a healthy young man."

"Ha. I'm not that young."

"You're younger than me, and I still feel fit."

"She's right, you know," Shelly agreed. "You run all the time, and you eat pretty well. You'll be just fine." She said this to reassure herself as much as him.

Robin had worried about being operated on for Shelly's sake, but it seemed she was okay about it. He felt some relief from his guilt. He realized now that he was the one who was a little afraid of being operated on.

He enjoyed his chat with his wife and her mother until they noticed how tired he was getting, so they took their leave to go baby shopping. He got to doze for a good bit until he heard a light knock on the door. "Robin?" asked a familiar voice that surprised him. The young woman's cheery face peeped in and her wide, bright smile was unmistakable.

"Rachel!" Robin exclaimed, causing him to cough.

"Hi, Robin!" she replied as she came in. She was overcome by his encumbrances. "Jesus! You look like shit!"

Robin couldn't help but laugh (and cough). "That's what I love about you, Rachel: Always giving me straight up honesty."

Rachel laughed and studied all the paraphernalia connected to the usually healthy man and the multitude of bruises on his face. She really was worried about him, and her smile faded.

Robin noticed and asked, "So what are you doing here?"

"I figured Shelly needed me."

"You're probably right," he said, echoing what he told Shelly's mother. He was glad she had a support system.

"I wanted to be here when the baby came, anyhow. Just thought I'd come early to see you."

"Well, I appreciate that."

"I'm very sorry this happened to you."

"Thank you… So, how are you fairing in London Town?"

"Eh," she replied without much enthusiasm. She looked down to the floor and studied her shoes. "I mean, it's neat and all, but I miss my old life sometimes… Is that wrong?"

"No, of course not—perfectly understandable. But sometimes…things happen for a reason. You had a *huge* change of life… You just have to find yourself in it." He coughed a bit for talking so much, but he wanted to ease her mind.

She watched him to make sure he was going to be all right and then asked, "You really are a poet, aren't you?"

He chuckled. "That's what they pay me for! You need to get into the art scene there and…forget the other footballers' wives."

She realized that Robin knew more of what goes on there than she ever guessed. "Yes, you're right… Hey! I'm supposed to be cheering *you* up!"

"Ha-ha. Believe me…it's nice to think of someone else's problems…for a change."

"Yeah, I'm sure you're not happy about the timing of this."

"No, I am not… But, like I said, things happen for a reason."

"Have you figured it out yet?"

"Yes and no. I know why, but I haven't…figured out the outcome."

"Well…let me know."

"That I will."

She was slightly taken aback by his honesty, but figured that people always get a bit introspective when they have a brush with death. She looked at him and commented, "Are those new glasses?"

"No—old ones. My good ones flew off in the accident. They were probably destroyed."

She shook her head. "Man, this sucks."

He smiled the biggest smile he had since the accident. "Rachel, I cannot tell you how refreshing it is…to hear the truth!" He stopped to take a breath while she gave a look of shock. "Everyone has been so sweet…and patronizing, and you deliver the truth…straight up, no chaser… Yes, *this sucks.* I've gotten myself completely broken…just at the wrong time, I've lost my car…that I love, and I've lost a good drummer." She gave him a look of confusion. "Oh, they didn't tell you… Yes, ironically the drunk driver…was our drummer."

Rachel burst out with a short laugh, but then apologized. "Sorry, I know—it's not funny."

He chuckled, but then drew in a big sigh. "No, but it is ironic, I'll grant you that."

"Well, my heart goes out to you, but you still better thank God you're alive at all, you know."

"I know. It just feels good to…wallow in self pity sometimes."

"Yeah, I know what you mean. I'm getting pretty good at it myself lately." There was a moment of pensive silence until she asked, "So when will they let you go home?"

"Oh, not for a while, I'm afraid. They want to operate on me today."

"Why?!"

"They're afraid my collarbone isn't going to heal right… so they want to put pins in it."

"Aye," she said with a worried face.

"My thoughts exactly."

"Well, good luck, Robin. I'll say a prayer for you."

"Thank you. I have reason to believe…your prayers work miracles."

"Ha-ha. No. It just depends if He says 'yes'."

"Ha. I see."

They went on to discuss Terry, Shelly and the baby, and things of a lighter note. He enjoyed the visit and it kept him from dwelling on the thought of his operation. As she was about to take her leave, she exclaimed, "Oh! Don't tell Shelly I'm here yet. I want to surprise her."

"Don't surprise her too much… She is eight months pregnant."

"Ha-ha. No, no, don't worry." She bent down and gave him a kiss on the cheek, rubbed his good arm, and wished him luck again and then she was gone.

A few minutes later, a nurse came to check on him and take his vitals. He watched for a moment and asked, "Will I be getting any lunch?"

"No, 'fraid not," she answered, checking on his IV. She left as quickly as she came.

He moped about the fact he was hungry, but eventually started to fall asleep again. He got to sleep for a couple of hours and when he awoke he found his dear Shelly sitting quietly beside him. "Hello, again."

"Hello," he replied with a groggy smile.

"The doctor said it wouldn't be long."

"Oh."

"Everyone's here—they're waiting outside."

"*Everyone?*"

"Y-yes. Aw! You know Rachel is here, don't you?"

He laughed. "Yes, darling. She came to see me earlier."

"Well, that's good, anyway."

He chuckled and studied her. He noticed how ragged she was looking—definitely not as fresh as earlier. "How are you?" he asked gravely.

"I'm ready to have this baby. Can you imagine carrying around all this weight?" she rubbed her belly.

"No, and you can't blame the bloke who's responsible… for your condition, because he's…laid up in bed looking quite pathetic."

"Yes, precisely. How irritating."

"Yes," he laughed. He reached out his hand for hers. She readily complied. "Don't think I don't admire you like hell."

This made her want to cry (as did a lot of things lately). "Same here. I really am so sorry you're having to go through this."

"I'll live."

"You'd better," she said quite seriously.

"Oh, certainly." Shelly was beginning to show signs of worry and he didn't like it. "The doctor said my lung is doing very well… Which is good, or I couldn't have the operation…and would end up looking like the hunchback."

"Ha. Yes, he told me. He said it was good that you're a runner."

"He said he'd rather see me swim, but I refuse to put a pool in—too dangerous."

"I guess we could put a fence around it."

"No, absolutely not. If I want to swim, I'll go to George's… I will not have any chance of endangering… our baby."

For some reason, Robin saying the words 'our baby' threw her for a loop. She could tell he was still excited as ever about the arrival of this child, and it elated her. Her heart pounded, and the baby kicked back a response. "Ooh!" she exclaimed as she held her belly with both hands.

"You all right?" he asked with panic.

"Yes, yes. Fine. Just a big kick."

"I'm beginning to think she's going to take after...her cousin Terry instead of us."

"You may be right!" she laughed.

The doctor interrupted them to talk to Robin before the surgery about the procedure, and they both listened with intent. The doctor made it sound routine (for him, it was) and it helped waylay their fears. The nurses came to prepare him and take him to surgery. Shelly gave him a kiss and her best wishes, then off he went.

The actual operation took only an hour, but the family had to wait at least two. Shelly was getting quite exhausted with the stress of it all, and everyone began to worry more for her than Robin. Finally, the doctor came out with his good news that all went well.

Once out of recovery, Shelly got to visit her groggy prince and thank God for his successful operation. Everyone urged her to go home for some rest with her mother demanding it. She and Rachel took her home while George and Debra stayed behind. Paul came as soon as he could after school, and was happy to hear that everything went well. The three of them went in to visit him, but didn't stay for long considering how out of it he was. He needed sleep.

It was several hours later when Robin woke up in excruciating pain. He buzzed the nurse who came within a minute. "Well, hello there," she said with annoying happiness. He simply looked at her with heavy breaths, and she said, "Hurting?"

"Quite."

"Okay. The doctor said you probably would be. I'll take care of ya."

"Thanks." It hurt just to utter a word. She shot something into his IV, and he felt a little relief immediately.

He only stayed awake for a little while, and then fell into a deep sleep for the rest of the night.

The next day brought a barrage of visitors, including several nurses and the doctor. Robin was starting to feel that he was never going to get any decent rest. But, the late afternoon came, and things slowed down. He fell asleep hard and didn't wake up until around 7:00. He discovered a sleepy Shelly relaxing in the chair next to him. He gazed at his lady as she closed her eyes and dropped her head back. He felt he was missing her final phase of pregnancy, and felt guilty. She was winding down. She was no longer preparing for her delivery day, she was almost upon it and it was only a matter of time. He was grateful that her mother and Rachel were here to comfort her and see to her needs. He also felt a bit bad about stealing her spotlight. People should be focusing on her.

He watched in silence and in thought until she opened her eyes and realized she was being stared at. She grinned and quietly said, "Hi, sweetie."

"Hullo."

"Been up long?"

"No, not really."

"How are you?"

"Much better, thank you. And you?"

"Fine."

"I didn't see you much today."

"Mom and Rachel took me for my check-up."

"Ah! Of course. And how is everything?"

"Great," she said without looking at him. "Just need to have her and be done with it."

"Ha."

"I think women have to be pregnant for so long so that you're not scared any more—you just want it over with."

"That's probably true. Good philosophy."

"Ha-ha. Thanks." She sighed and turned to smile at him. "Oh! Here I am being selfish—the doctor told me that as long as you're doing fine, they're going to release you tomorrow."

"Really?" he asked with excitement.

"Yep." A look of concern came over him, and she asked, "What's wrong?"

"Well, I don't want to sound like a baby, but, well, I'm afraid of being a burden to you."

"Nonsense. Mom and Rachel will stay with us for a while until we get into the groove of things. Besides, you will be happy to know that I finally broke down and did it."

"Did what?"

"Hired a nanny."

"You're kidding!"

"Nope. Rachel helped me find her—or rather Miguel did. She hasn't been here long, so it was perfect for her."

"You've done well without me."

"Please! Without Mom and Rachel, I would be in a pickle. Oh! That reminds me, heh-heh, Debra's fixing us all kinds of food to keep in the freezer, and she'll bring us the occasional sandwich tray, bless her heart."

"Ah! Pickle, I get it. Brilliant. Nothing like a change from hospital mush…to Debra's cooking. I probably would have healed a long time ago…if they had only given me some of her minestrone."

"And that lemonade!" Shelly laughed along with him. For the first time in a few days, normalcy looked like it was attainable. They both were so grateful for their friends and family.

Robin then looked down and muttered to himself.

"What?"

"Oh, just grumbling how I'm connected to everything. I'd love to get up and move around."

"Aren't you sore?"

"Oh, yes. But lying here is only making matters worse."

"Oh, I see."

"What *is* all this?" he asked with exasperation.

"Well," she said as she got up to look around, "this is your IV to your standard fluids and where they pump you up if you're complaining too much about pain," (he laughed). "This is…oh, never mind what this is."

"I can hazard a guess."

"Yes. This is," she ran her hand along a tube, "ah! The tube that's helping to release the air trapped in your lung— he said he was going to take this off today—oh, well. He probably figured it wouldn't hurt to leave it in one more day… Ew," she said with a snarl.

"What?"

"Not very pretty where it goes in." She continued her quest. "And this one is…oh, heck, you've got me."

"Ha. I knew I'd stump you eventually."

"Gimme a minute… I dunno. Looks like some sort of drainage pipe."

"Sounds like I'm more confusing than the sewers of London."

She smiled and wished, just for a moment, that he wasn't hurt and she wasn't so pregnant and that they were at his home in England. But the moment faded, and all she could think about was taking care of him. It was hard to believe that this bruised and frail looking man was usually the robust man who dragged her out kicking and screaming to go running with him. She knew it was just going to take some time and they would happily be back at their warfare.

He caught her staring at his bandages and joked, "I'm a mess, as you say."

"Yes, you are. All the same, I'm glad you're going to be all right."

"Oh, yes—right as rain." He saw how tired she was so he suggested, "You ought to go home and get some rest."

She was about to protest, but changed her mind. "Okay. If you say so."

"I say so," he mocked with a sympathetic smile.

She kissed him good-bye and goodnight. Robin fell asleep again only to dream that he was playing drums and couldn't get the beat right.

The next morning, he woke up with more spizz and vinegar than he had in a long time. A young intern came in whom he had gotten to know and said in a thick Indian accent, "Hello, Robin! How are you feeling today? You're looking much better; the color is coming back to your cheeks."

"Sure beats the black and blue of everything else."

"Yes, you do have some nasty bruising, but it will pass in time. It will turn all kinds of lovely shades before it is gone."

Robin laughed and had a flashback of one of Shelly's palettes.

The man had his chart pulled up on the computer terminal and said while perusing it, "You get to go home today, I see."

"Yes, thank the Lord."

"Indeed. It is much easier to heal when you don't have a bunch of nurses and doctors bugging you at all hours."

"Huh. Exactly."

"Well, let's see your incision, Robin." The man checked it out thoroughly with a penlight. "Only a slight oozing, but that is normal. We'll clean that up when the bandages are changed. Dr. Williams did an excellent job—there will be only a slight scar."

"Splendid."

"Yes, we must keep you superstars looking good." Robin laughed. The young man loved to tease him about his popularity, and Robin always enjoyed being treated like a regular citizen. "I will send a nurse to attend to this dressing… Okay, now did they explain about your follow-up treatments?"

"Yes, the doctor gave me a list."

"Yes, he is very good about that. Now remember, the physical therapy you will have is imperative to regaining your full range of motion. You were very fortunate that your rotator cup did not break, and we're still trying to figure out how you broke your clavicle without doing so, but I imagine you have a special angel watching you, yes?"

"No, I'm married to one."

"Ah, yes, she is a sweet lady. It is too bad you are so confined with the baby about to come."

"Well, they said she wasn't due for a few weeks yet."

"What? Oh, that is impossible. She is due any day now—that is for certain."

"How do you know?"

"You can tell by the position of the baby and the way your wife is acting. It will be soon!" he said with a hand gesture.

Robin's eyes got large, causing the doctor to laugh.

"Don't worry, everything will work out, I guarantee you. You are a blessed man, Mr. Parker, and your wife looks like a healthy woman. She will give you a healthy baby."

"Thank you," he said, feeling a bit patronized.

But, the young man was being honest, and took no heed of Robin's sarcastic look. He finished his chart filling, and shook Robin's hand with one of his large grins. "It has been a pleasure helping you, Robin. I wish you a speedy recovery and may everything turn out well for both you and your wife. Take care."

"Thanks. Good-bye, Doc." He left and Robin felt he was actually going to miss the permanently happy man.

He sat bored for a while until a large male nurse came in to change his bandages and detach his hoses. Robin watched with interest as he began to look more like a man and less like a science experiment. "Lest these chains be removed from me, I cannot become a man," Robin quoted. The nurse looked at him with surprise. "An old poem," he explained.

Robin chuckled guessing that the man was probably thinking, "Goofy Englishman."

"Well, there you are, Mr. Parker. Ready to go."

"Freedom is a splendid thing."

"Yes, it is, Mr. Parker. Yes, it is." He set aside his cart and some of the apparatus and asked, "Do you want to walk around?"

The thought of doing so without a ton of equipment attached thrilled him. "Oh, please." It was difficult to get out of bed without the use of his left arm, and he didn't realize how much movement of his collarbone was involved. He flinched in pain, but was determined to get moving. "Ooh." He felt the blood rush from his head as he stood up, and the nurse held him steady. He correctly deduced why they sent him the burly man. He held Robin up and urged him to walk.

He heard someone come in, and he hurt his neck twisting it to see who it was. He really didn't feel like having visitors when he was in such a vulnerable state, but this one he wanted.

Shelly was glad to see her husband finally up and around. "Yay!"

He smiled back as well as he could.

"How are you doing?"

"Eh."

She held up a bag and cheerfully asked, "Guess what I have?"

"Clothes, I pray."

"Prayer answered!"

"Bless you. I think that will help me feel normal more than anything else."

"It's good to see you up and walking." She sat in the chair and laid the bag on the floor.

The nurse asked Robin if he was going to be okay to which he replied, "Oh, indeed. Feels so good to walk upright again. I would like to freshen up, though." He hobbled into the bathroom and switched on the light. He saw his full reflection in the mirror with a gasp. Until then, he hadn't realized just how bruised up he was. "Oh, my God," he softly muttered to himself.

"What's the matter?" Shelly quickly asked.

"I had no idea how bad I looked."

"You hadn't looked in a mirror yet?"

"Well, I rather couldn't or wouldn't."

"Oh, I see. Well, you'll be fine. Bruises fade."

"Yes, they do," said the quiet nurse. He assisted Shelly in getting Robin dressed after he finished in the bathroom. They had difficulty rigging a shirt on to him, but did the best they could. Robin was grateful just to have a decent pair of pants on. He realized at that point what a hassle the next few weeks (or months) were going to be. He thought about this as he watched his nurse leave.

He sat down thankfully on the bed. "Have you met the nanny yet?"

"Yes, I sure have!"

"Oh, and how do you like her?"

"She's a sweet girl. Doesn't speak a ton of English, but enough for you."

"How old is she?"

"Not old—about twenty five or so."

"Goodness! That is young. Has she nannied before?"

"No, but apparently she practically raised her little brother and sisters."

"What happened to them?"

"Something about an aunt taking them over, or something—wanted her to have a better life, and all that... I haven't gotten the whole story yet."

"By working for us? Well, she'll definitely have a nutty life, that's for certain." He was happy about the fact he was finding it easier to breathe sitting up.

"Have you thought anymore about our life?"

His happiness faded and he looked around the room. "Well...I tell you. I really don't think I'm ready to throw in the towel."

"Good! What made you decide?"

"Look outside."

"Ah, yes. The Shrine."

"Ha. That's what Donnie called it."

"Your fans do love you, but it *is* ultimately up to you."

"Or not. It will be a while until I can perform again, anyhow... Are you okay?" he asked, noticing how much she was squirming about.

"I can't get comfortable."

"Come lay on the bed."

She didn't argue. She lay down with a huff.

"You're sweating."

"Well, it's hot in here."

"No, it's not. If anything, it's cool." Robin started to become very concerned.

"Really?" she panted.

"I think I'd better call the nurse."

He did so, and this time an older woman came in and was a bit perplexed by Shelly and Robin trading places. "Could you take a look at my wife? She's quite warm."

The nurse did so and replied, "We'd better get you checked in, and *you* checked out."

It was that same morning when George stopped at the office briefly, when he ran into Donnie. They greeted each other and Donnie asked about Robin and George explained that he should be released later that day. "Oh, that's great!" he replied. "Say, have you heard anything from Sam?"

"Actually, I was going to ask you if you had."

"Pff. I haven't the slightest idea. She was supposed to call me to let me know when her hearing was so that I could fix her up with the lawyer, but she never did. I've tried calling her repeatedly, but no answer."

"You don't think she bolted, do you?"

"I wouldn't think so, but people do strange things when they're under stress."

George didn't like the sound of this at all. "Maybe we should go see her."

"Go to her apartment?"

"Well, yeah."

"Okay...sure."

"Do you know her address?"

"Yeah. I took her home afterwards."

"After...oh."

The two men got in Donnie's car and quickly made their way to the pretty seaside apartments. They got out and looked around. "Look, her window is open," Donnie pointed out. Then the two men looked at each other and a cold chill passed over them both. They hurried to her apartment door and knocked. No answer. "Sam!" They both called out. Still nothing. "What do we do?" asked Donnie.

"Get the manager," George said with a shrug.

They found the apartment manager and explained the situation. She seemed unwilling to open the door until George finally said out loud, "We're afraid she may have hurt herself." The woman's eyes grew large and got the key. They made their way back up and she knocked one more time. This satisfied her and she unlocked the door. The guys felt uneasy about going in, but in they went.

Inside, newspapers were strewn all over the place—the vast majority having something to do about her and Robin's wreck. They shook their heads and really did not want to go any further in. "Sam!" they called. Silence.

The woman said, "We should check her bedroom." George ran in to discover Sam laying on her bed, her blonde hair cascading all over, and two empty bottles near by: one, whiskey; one, prescription.

Horrified by the sight, George simply uttered, "Oh, God."

Donnie reached down to feel her throat, only to jerk his hand back. "She's dead."

The landlady squealed out loud. George tried to remain calm, primarily for the benefit of his heart.

"I'll call the police," Donnie said.

George, in the meantime, tried to quiet the woman. "She was so young and beautiful," she lamented.

"I know, I know. But she, unfortunately, was not a happy woman," said George, almost to himself. He came over and sat down at the foot of the bed. He caressed her soft tresses one last time. He couldn't believe it. He shook his head and let a few tears come to his eyes, but he wiped them dry before speaking to Donnie again.

The police came, and the guys answered many questions. It must have been hours by the time they were done.

Tired and frazzled, George and Donnie made their way back to the office. They sat in Donnie's office talking to each other, trying to settle each other's nerves. Donnie was concerned about George's heart, and observed him as they chatted.

"Did she leave a note or anything?" asked Donnie.

"Not that I noticed."

"Odd, don't ya think?"

"Yes… You know what the worst of this is?"

"What?"

"I have to tell Robin, and I know him, he'll somehow blame himself."

"Do you want me to tell him?"

"Donnie, no offence, but you have the tact of a Pamplonian bull."

"Ha, okay, true… I'm sorry you're having to go through this—I know you were tight with her," he said as evidence of his lack of tact.

George quickly looked around the room. He didn't want to discuss the matter. He knew he meant well, but he really couldn't think about her too much right now. He was still trying to soak in the reality of what happened in the first place.

"Well, I'd better go and get this over with," George eventually said. He said good-bye to Donnie, and headed for the hospital.

He tried hard not to think too much, but he couldn't help himself. Memories of the tour flooded back whether he liked it or not. He remembered taking her to get her drumhead repaired; staying up all night talking to her; a long, intense (desperate, maybe?) hug; and a kiss that shouldn't have happened.

He had kept that kiss a secret, for he didn't want people to think the wrong thing. At that time, things were so rocky with his wife, and had he told anyone (including Robin) about it, they would construe that to mean he was ready to leave her. That simply wasn't the case. It would be something he would take to the grave, just as Sam had, especially since she couldn't defend herself now.

He began to feel this dreadful sense of guilt. Why didn't he notice she had a problem? Was he so wrapped up in himself and his petty issues that he couldn't see she was in trouble? First his wife, now his friend—was he ever going to learn how to see beyond himself and be responsible for others? It was a horrid thing to be so self-absorbed. Maybe it was a good thing that Robin was the one becoming a father and not himself.

He tried to get his mind off of his thoughts by thinking about the weather. It didn't help. The clouds were turning a depressing color of grey and the wind was howling—much like he wanted to. A song by some of his contemporaries moaned in sympathy for him on the car radio, compounding his angst. He snapped the radio off and pulled to the side of the road. He screamed and hit his hands upon the steering wheel. So many things were going through his mind. Was this fate's way of dealing with someone who could be a threat to his marriage? The thought was outlandish, but he somehow felt this was a slap in his face for his actions. He wondered if he had anything to do with her suicide at all. "Damn!" he exclaimed.

He sat and cursed until he got the worst out of his system and he felt the better for it. No more holding it in—he couldn't afford it. Maybe that was the reason Robin was the healthier of them, for he was always the 'emotional' one and never repressed himself. George thought it funny that he was learning such important things so late in life. He rubbed his face and tried to settle back down. He really was going to miss Samantha.

He got going again and finally made it to the hospital with a knot in his stomach. He came to Robin's room to find it empty with someone putting fresh sheets on the bed. "What the—? Where's my brother?"

The lady shrugged her shoulders. "Checked out."

Angry, he walked quickly through the hall to turn a corner and almost knock over Debra. "There you are!" she said with a smile. "I've been trying to call you."

"Oh," he answered with a confused look. "I think I turned off my cell phone when I was talking to the police."

"The police?" she asked with alarm. She stared hard at him and asked, "Why are your eyes red? George, have you been *crying*?"

He looked at her sweet face with his mouth agape. He didn't know where to start. "Come with me." He took her outside and told her the story of Sam.

"What?!"

He simply nodded.

"Oh, my God... Honey, I'm so sorry." She hugged him earnestly, for she knew that this was what he needed so much. No matter what she may have thought of the woman, she certainly never wished this to happen to her.

She held him for a while, both thinking how fragile life was. George took a deep breath and asked, "Now. Where's Robin?"

A big smile came over her face. "In maternity."

"What?" He couldn't believe his ears. They ran back into the building.

Chapter Twenty-one

It was at the point where they first wheeled Shelly into the maternity ward. Robin was beside himself with worry.

"Don't worry honey, I'm—ow!" Shelly exclaimed.

"*What*?!"

Shelly breathed for a bit, and then said, "Contraction."

"Are you in labor?"

"I don't know!" she cried. She began to panic.

"Try not to worry, dearheart, they'll take care of you."

"Yeah, right!" she hollered.

Robin gave a look of bewilderment. She hadn't barked back at him like that since the days of her medication for her messed up cycle and it took him a moment to realize that there were some serious hormones at play here.

The nurses were alarmed enough to get a doctor. She introduced herself to Shelly and asked what all she was experiencing. Shelly explained what she could and the doctor asked if she could examine her. Shelly said, "Of course," and the doctor took a look with a protective Robin near by.

"Well, it looks like your water broke and you're beginning to dilate. Hope you're ready for a baby!"

"What?!" both Shelly and Robin exclaimed. "Isn't it too soon?" asked Robin watching Shelly's frantic expression.

"Well, she looks full term, what did your doctor say your due date was?"

"Well," she looked at Robin with a guilty look. "He did say last time it may be sooner than we thought."

"Why didn't you tell me?" he asked with wild eyes.

She put her hands up. "Why do you think?" she said while pointing at his banged up body.

"Oh… Oh, God." He seemed to have lost the color in his face.

"Don't you dare faint on me!" she demanded, watching him swoon.

The doctor laughed. "Let's get you some water, Robin." A nurse took care of Robin, and they realized that he had just been released and urged him to take it easy, even to the point of getting him a wheelchair. They had no desire of having him fall and sue them for negligence.

"How am I supposed to take it easy?!" he exclaimed, causing him to cough ferociously.

His unexpected flare up took Shelly by surprise, for he never raised his voice like that before (that she knew of). "Everything is going to be—ow!" she tried to get out, but was interrupted by yet another jab of pain.

"Contraction?" the doctor asked as she and the nurse began strapping on monitors to Shelly. She nodded and it was duly noted.

Robin felt like passing out, but his natural curiosity kept him hanging on. He sat quietly in his wheelchair for a moment, bones throbbing in pain, but then got himself up to be by his wife and hold her hand. He had to be near her. His thoughts meandered to the rest of his family, so he decided it was time to make some calls. He told Shelly so, and did his best to give her a kiss. Between the bed and his ribs, it was almost impossible.

Shelly replied, "Yeah, I guess you had better let everyone know… Be careful of yourself, honey."

"I will." He dug out Shelly's cell phone from her purse and wondered momentarily what had happened to his own. Shelly sure had made him forget his accident for a blissful time!

When he got outside, the fresh air hit him softly on the face and he reveled in it. It helped to clear his mind. He saw some of the banners of well-wishes and old balloons that his fans had stuck on the bushes out front. He then set to his task. He called George first, but got no answer, so he called Debra. Debra said she would come down immediately. He called his house and got Rachel.

"Rachel? It's Robin."

"Hey, you're getting out?" she asked happily.

"Uh, well, sort of."

"What do you mean?"

He gave a funny chuckle, for it did seem ridiculous now that he thought of it. "Well, I've been released, but they checked Shelly in."

"Why? What's wrong?" she asked with alarm.

"Nothing's *wrong*—she's having the baby."

"What?! Shut up!"

Robin couldn't help but laugh, no matter how much it hurt. "It's true—she's ready to go."

"Okay, we'll be right there."

He went back in and told Shelly that her mother, Rachel and Debra were on their way and that he couldn't find George.

"Thanks," she replied thankfully, if somewhat distracted.

"Of course." He caressed her forehead and felt sorry for her. He sensed she wasn't mentally prepared for this, but knew not what to say.

"They're putting me in a room."

"Good, good." A thought came to him. He went through the numbers on her cell and she asked,

"Who are you looking for?"

"Just thought I'd give your father a ring."

"Ha. I didn't feel like programming all those numbers in, sorry."

"Well, we'll have to get a hold of him somehow."

"You should call your mom, too."

"Well, if I knew what happened to *my* phone, I would."

She stared at him and said, "Too much all of a sudden."

"Oh, yes," he agreed solemnly, but then flashed a comforting smile to his wife, who definitely was showing signs of fear.

"And have I even told you just how…how grateful I am you didn't get killed?" She started crying. "I can't imagine what it would be like to be doing this without you…"

"Lord, dearheart," he immediately said with all the pity in his heart, "it's all right. I just got banged up a bit—I was never in any great danger."

She closed her eyes and let the tears stream down her face.

"Oh, sweetheart, please don't cry," he begged, fighting his own urge to tear up as well. "This should be the happiest day of your life."

"I already had that when I married you."

He was speechless to hear such devotion. He bit his lip and wiped his eyes.

The doctor came back and interrupted their thoughts, which was probably a good thing. She checked Shelly's contractions on the graph of the machine, and said with a smile, "You're coming along well. Let's see just how dilated you are."

Shelly made a face as she checked, making Robin frown. He really did feel it was unfair that Shelly had to go through so much pain to have his baby. Thinking about pain only made his own amplified. He lightly rubbed his collarbone subconsciously.

"Two centimeters," the doctor announced. "Okay, Shelly, just keep it up, and you'll have this baby in no time."

"Have you called Dr. Hodges?" Shelly asked her.

"Yes, I did," she replied.

"Is he coming?"

"Yes, he said he would."

The doctor left for a while, and Shelly endured another contraction. It was killing Robin that he couldn't do anything for her. But he held her hand or caressed her, and that was all she really wanted from him.

Then, like a windy storm, blew Rachel and Patty in. There was much commotion as the two doted on Shelly and assured her that everything was going to be fine. Then, with a slight twinge of guilt, Rachel drew her attention to Robin. "Geeze, Robin, I'm sorry, how are you?"

He smiled. "Well, I'm not sure. I mean, I'm not stuck in my room anymore, but I'm still in pain; Shelly's about to have our baby, but she's in pain for that. So, I'm feeling very ambivalent right now." He began to cough and Patty gently patted his back.

"Well, the pain will eventually go away and you'll be left with a beautiful baby," she said with a beaming smile.

"Yes, and that's what I've got to focus on."

"How did everything go with your operation?"

"Fine, I think. Rather feel like…I've been mended by a carpenter rather than a doctor, though." He softly rubbed near that bone again.

They gave a chuckle and he felt it was probably a good time to leave the room and try George again.

He got outside where he met Debra. She gave him a hug and told him how good it was to see him up and around again. "So how are you?"

"I think I'm going to be fine."

"Well, that's good. How's your lung?"

"I only notice it when I get excited."

"Which is a lot lately?" she asked with a grin.

"Oh, yes."

"Well… How is she?"

"Doing all right for…someone who is writhing in pain, I suppose."

"Don't worry, honey. She'll forget it all after she has the baby."

"Do you think I will, too?"

"Ha-ha. Well, you'll definitely be distracted."

"Say…have you heard from George?"

"No, I haven't. Can't get a hold of him for some reason. He's usually pretty good about answering his phone." She shook her head with a look of confusion.

"Well, could you try again? I want to get back."

"Sure. I'll be right there."

Robin went back to tend to his wife, and it was at this point that George had turned up and had told Debra of his sad news.

She took him down the hall, but after he walked a bit, he paused.

"What's the matter?" Debra asked.

"I can't tell him. Not now."

"Honey, if you don't, Donnie will come and—"

"I know, I know." They began walking again. "Deb?"

"Yeah?"

"Can we take a vacation? You know—like a nice, long vacation?"

She was about to ask what was she to do with Paul and her café, but she saw the desperate look in his eyes and realized all she needed to do at this point was to agree. Everything else would work out. "Yes. Yes, of course, dear."

"Good. All of a sudden I am quite tired of it here."

Debra said nothing, but smiled sympathetically. Inside, though, she worried.

"Well, I won't tell him until afterward, anyway. Donnie doesn't even know we're here."

"Whatever you think." They were about to turn a corner and she asked, "Ready to become an uncle?"

He drew in a deep breath through his nose and put a smile. "You betcha."

"Always the performer," she thought.

Robin was very happy to see his brother and George in turn was concerned for both Robin and Shelly. Now it was time to play the waiting game.

Shelly's progression had seemed to hit a plateau. After a few hours, there was very little change. But, as worn-out as she was becoming, she could tell that her husband was fairing worse of the both of them. "Honey, you should get some rest."

"I'm not going anywhere."

"Why don't you go out to the truck and try to get a nap? Someone will get you if anything changes. I don't seem to be getting anywhere right now," she said with a bit of disgust at the situation.

He thought about it and knew he felt terrible. He couldn't see himself lasting much longer. "Very well…where did you park?"

Shelly explained and he took her keys, telling George and Debra what he was doing. They assured him that it was a wise thing, and that they would let him know immediately if something was about to happen.

He went outside to notice that the weather was turning around. "Must be a front," he mumbled to himself. Then, he swore that his eyes were playing up on him, for he recognized the young man coming toward him. He said nothing, figuring he was hallucinating.

The man looked up, and with a jerk he said, "Robin?"

His eyes weren't playing games after all. "Terry?" he asked in disbelief.

"Hey, mate!" he replied. He carefully hugged him.

"What on earth are you doing here?"

"Came you to see you, you poor begger."

"Well, that's a load of rubbish. You just want to make sure Rachel doesn't decide to stay here."

"Heh-heh," he said shaking his head. "Can't pull one over you, now can I? How are you? You look terrible, you poor thing. You got it quite bad, didn't you?" he asked, surveying the bruises, cuts and bandages. "Did they release you already? Are you having to drive yourself home?" He looked around for family, but saw none and was genuinely confused.

"Well, just as soon as they released me, they took Shelly in."

"Why? Nothing wrong, I hope."

"No. She went into labor," he chuckled, rather to himself.

"You're joking!"

"Nope. Right now, though, I'm so exhausted I'm going to see if I can get some rest in the truck."

Terry was very concerned for his cousin and followed him to Shelly's big red SUV and he helped Robin into the passenger side. He pulled up the lever to lay him back, surprising him with the seat going down suddenly.

"*Ah*! Terry…" he yelled, but then had to laugh, "do me a favor and *don't* help."

"Sorry."

"There is one thing you can do, though."

"You name it."

"When you get a chance, get some stuff to freshen me up a bit—I feel absolutely scummy. You know, something to shave with, a toothbrush, that kind of thing. They probably have it at the chemist's in there. I'm not going to scare my daughter when she comes into this world looking like a tramp."

"Sure, gotcha," he laughed. He really couldn't believe that Robin was actually (finally) going to have a child of his own. It seemed odd to him. He was always rather the unhappy husband or bachelor; now he was this happily married man and soon-to-be daddy. Weird, he thought. He wondered if he would ever catch himself in the same situation. He said, "Later," without really thinking, and then Robin stopped his leaving.

"Oh, hey, and get me some of the strongest painkillers you can buy over the counter, will you?"

"They didn't give you anything?"

"They gave me a prescription, but I'm not going to take it—they'll knock me out—and I'm certainly not going to sleep through my child's birth." He paused to cough a bit, and then continued, "Unfortunately, this weather is only making matters worse."

Terry looked around the cloudy sky and felt sorry for the man. "Okay, see you in a bit."

"Thanks a lot. I owe you one."

"No, you don't," he said shaking his head.

Terry left Robin to his uneasy slumber and trekked off to find Rachel and company.

Everyone was completely surprised to see him, and Rachel was absolutely beaming. He came and gave his best wishes to Shelly who, throughout it all, was pleased to see him. His jovial attitude was contagious, and it seemed to scare away some of the stress she was under.

Robin had managed to get an hour's nap when Shelly's phone went off in his pocket. He had forgotten he had the thing, and painfully wrenched it out with much cursing. He grumbled as to whom it could be disturbing him from his rest, and when he saw the strange array of numbers on the phone's display, he knew it must be someone from far away. "Hullo?"

"Hello! Is this Robin?"

"Well, hello, Padre! I'm glad you called."

"Yes, well, I just wanted to see how you were faring. Shelly had called me a couple of days ago to say you were in a nasty accident, so I wanted to see how you were. I read of it in the papers over here, but they didn't say much."

"Oh, I think I'm going to make it just fine."

"I was rather surprised you answered the phone."

"Yes, well," he chuckled, "Shelly's in no condition to answer it herself."

"Is she okay?" he asked with the same alarm as everyone else had that day.

"Oh, yes." He then took in a deep breath in order to repeat a story he felt he must have said already a thousand times. "Well, believe it or not, just as I was being released this morning, Shelly went into labor."

"Surely you're joking!"

"No, I sure am not," he laughed.

"Is she okay? I mean, it isn't too soon, is it?"

"No, no, she's just fine. Apparently she was due, and all this stress didn't help, either, I'm sure."

"Oh, goodness. You poor soul. The Lord isn't letting you rest, eh?" he laughed.

"No, Padre, that He isn't."

"Well, I do hope all goes well for her."

"Yes, I do, too… So, how does it feel to know you're about to be a granddad?"

The man was silenced by this announcement. Up until only some months ago he had no idea that he was even a father. Now, he was about to be a grandfather, and it dumbfounded him.

"You all right, Father?" inquired Robin.

"Oh, yes, yes. It's just amazing that's all."

"Yes. Some would say it was a miracle," Robin said with a glimmer of his usual sense of humor and also echoing the words of a doctor from a long time ago.

"Aye, yes. Ha-ha. Indeed. Hee-hee." The priest enjoyed this little jest. "Was Patty able to make it to be with her?"

"Yes, she is, thank goodness—and Rachel—they've been a great help and comfort to her. I don't feel like I'm much help as I am."

"Oh, I'm certain she's grateful you're there for her at the least. Let those who are experienced with this kind of thing take care of the rest."

"Yes, I suppose you're right. Debra is here as well."

"Did you say Rachel is there?"

"Yes—and Terry."

"Oh? And how are they doing?"

"Fine, fine. Being newlyweds, I presume."

"Ah, good then… You two seem to have more than the usual problems most newlyweds have," he remarked with an honest concern.

Robin hadn't thought about the fact he was still considered a newlywed since that quiet evening with Shelly on their first anniversary. "Yes, but hopefully—" he dropped off.

"Robin?"

"I'm sorry, uh…"

Fr. O'Connor could hear the pain in his voice and wondered if it was physical or emotional. "Well, I guess I'd better let you go and get back to Shelly."

"Uh, thank you, Father. I'll tell her you called."

"Oh, yes, do. I'll be praying for her and the baby."

"Thank you, she'll appreciate that… I appreciate that," he said in a soft tone.

"And also for you, too, lad."

"Thank you."

Robin went silent again. The father then asked him, "Will you call me later—or anyone—to let me know how everything went?"

"Oh, certainly, Padre," Robin said in his usual voice. "No problem."

"Okay then. Goodbye and take care."

"Thank you. You, too."

As he hung up, a rap on the widow startled him. It was Terry. He opened the door to hear him say, "Hey, I got the stuff you needed." He showed him what all he picked up and Robin gratefully accepted.

"Say, could you help me out?" Robin asked, trying his best to crank himself around.

"Me?" Terry asked with a grin.

"Yes, you," he answered and returned the grin. "Just be careful. I have two busted ribs and a newly repaired collarbone."

Terry helped him out and noticed how Robin was chilled by the cool air that the front was bringing in. "Here," he said as he took his jacket off and wrapped it around Robin. "Let's go!"

They quickly made it to the building just as it began to rain. It reminded Robin of another night so long ago when he ran from the rain with Shelly. He seemed to be surrounded by memories just in the past few hours, like some sort of rundown of the past year. Maybe it was some sort of way of fate saying life was never to be the same after this baby was born. It will all be different now. Between anticipating this child, the pain from his accident, and the odd weather, Robin felt like he was in some sort of time warp where everything had stopped but he kept moving. It reminded him of an old sixties music video. He had to laugh.

He left Terry to go to the restroom to try and spruce himself up a bit. It definitely helped his attitude and made him feel a little more normal.

He stepped out of the restroom feeling refreshed and ready to see Shelly. He passed the waiting room just as the evening news was on. Rather oddly, he heard his band's name mentioned. He turned to look at the waiting room's television in time to hear a report on how Samantha Hahn was found dead in her apartment today and had apparently committed suicide.

He was stunned. His time warp had turned into a nightmare where he couldn't wake up. The spot was over without much ado, and he turned himself around supporting his back upon the hall side of the wall of the waiting area. He turned his head up to stare at the ceiling, grasping for a decent breath, but then heard someone running up to him. He looked down to see George. The two men just stared at each other. George had heard the news coming from another television and ran around looking for him, hoping to God he wasn't catching this awful story in this way. Unfortunately, he had. "Come on," George simply said.

They went outside to talk under a metal awning. Robin sat down on the bench with his hand on his head, and George rocked back and forth on his feet nervously. "Why?" Robin muttered.

"I don't know… All I know is…is that we can't blame ourselves."

"I shouldn't have been so mad at her."

"Oh, for crying out loud—she could have killed you, Robin! I would have been worse than you. You at least forgave her. I would have had a hard time of doing that."

"But…I should have seen she had a problem—"

"Robin! Damn. You weren't in any condition to play nursemaid to her. Maybe *I* should have been, but—"

"But your brother was lying in hospital primarily because of her."

"Yes! Yes…"

"How did she…?"

"Sleeping pills and alcohol."

"Classic," he said, echoing George's remark to Donnie earlier.

"She was a classy lady."

Robin looked up at him for this remark and noticed he was shivering. He knew it wasn't for the cold, and worried for him. "Who found her?" he asked, sensing he knew the answer.

George got even more nervous. "I did."

Robin winced and began to cough. "Sorry," was all he could say.

"Donnie and I… We couldn't get a hold of her, so we went to her apartment and got the manager to let us in, and…there she was—lying there on her bed as if she were sleeping."

"Did she leave a note?"

"No."

Robin thought for a moment. All he could think to say was, "Oh, God."

"I know… Look, you need to get back to Shelly. We can discuss this later—much later, hopefully. You have a baby on the way."

"One life gone, another in its stead."

"Yes. Such is life."

Robin stood up and hugged George as best he could. George tried to smile and they re-entered the building.

As they returned to maternity, they discovered Paul had arrived with a young lady in tow. They were struck by her odd beauty, for her hair was so blonde it was actually white, along with ivory skin and the palest blue eyes you would ever see. Paul introduced Denise to his stepfather and uncle and she very bashfully said, "Hello." She almost seemed to be embarrassed by her striking looks, but the guys greeted her warmly and she shyly smiled back.

George talked to the young couple as Robin went on to discover Shelly walking the halls with Debra and Rachel. "What's going on?" he asked.

"I wasn't making anymore progress, so Dr. Hodges loaded me up with oxytocin and told me to walk."

"How barbaric!" he remarked with protective anger for his suffering wife.

Shelly looked at him and smiled. "Did you get a nap?"

"Oh, an hour, I guess."

"Well…better than nothing. Better than *me*."

"Your father called."

"He did?" This cheered her up.

"Yes."

"You told him the news, I guess?"

"Oh, yes. He's pretty excited."

She smiled. "Really?"

"Of course. You're about to make him a grandfather."

Shelly wanted to cry.

The girls then handed her over to Robin and he paced the hall with her. As he did so, he began to wish that all these people would leave. This seemed to be such a private thing between her and him, that it felt strange to have an audience for the event. He did, however, change his mind when Shelly went into a bad contraction. She leaned down, pulling him down with her. They both screamed in pain, causing everyone to rush over to release Robin from her grip. George and Terry took Robin, Debra and Rachel took care of Shelly along with her mother. The guys sat Robin down and actually watched his pupils enlarge with the pain she caused to his collarbone. They were worried that harm had been done, and constantly asked him if something was wrong. He just kept breathing hard and coughing, but eventually felt it was safe to say, "I'll be all right."

Once her contraction was over, she apologized profusely to him.

"You couldn't help it, dearheart… You gotta do what you gotta do."

Everyone smiled, seeing this as a sign he was truly all right. Shelly continued her pacing, but this time with her mom.

Time crept on, and she began to have her contractions steadily enough to satisfy the doctor. He certainly didn't want her to wear herself out to where she couldn't push. They prepared her for her epidural, of which she had anticipated for some time. She originally wasn't sure about medications, but now that she had gotten a fair dose of what the pain was all about, her decision was much easier to make. Patty helped her through the uncomfortable procedure, but Shelly was soon grateful. Robin was happy to see her slightly relieved, and wondered if he could have the same done to him.

After a while, the doctor checked her to see how she was doing. "Well, Shelly, you ready to do some pushing?"

"You don't *even* know!"

"Ha-ha! Okay. Let's have this baby!"

Everyone took their place. Robin's adrenaline coursed through his veins like a train, and Patty and Rachel stayed close by.

The doctor was pleased that Shelly was actually following his directions as to when and when not to push. Robin, however, was in complete disbelief of the miracle of it all. Earlier, Shelly had feared this moment, but now that it was here, she simply wanted to get down to business.

After a while of pushing, Robin got the best shock of his life seeing the top of his baby's head appearing into view.

"Here's her little head!" the doctor announced as Shelly let out a scream. He suctioned the child's mouth and nose out and told Shelly to push again. The baby came out like a breeze, and they laid the infant upon her mother. Everyone was crying and cheering. They wiped the baby clean and she sneezed. "Well, bless you!" replied the doctor. She then began to wail, causing more tears and applause.

Shelly couldn't believe her eyes. There she was—the most precious thing she'd ever laid eyes on. The little being that once lived inside of her was now wriggling and stretching and fighting for her first breaths out in the real world. Robin and Shelly let their happy tears flow as he strained to give his wife a kiss.

The doctor helped Robin to cut the cord, which was difficult for him to do, being naturally left-handed. The nurses took the baby up to clean and weigh her as the doctor finished up with Shelly. "Eight pounds, five ounces, and twenty inches," announced the nurse. They took her footprints and swaddled her up, giving her a little pink stocking cap. "Here, Dad."

"Oh, I don't know," replied a skittish Robin.

"It only takes one of your long arms. Look, have a seat." Robin found the chair, and sat down and then she gently placed her in his arm. He stared at her with wide eyes.

"Hello," he softly said. The baby looked back at him with his own eyes, trying to figure out who he was. "I'm your daddy." He wanted to say more, but the emotions were coming to him too quickly. He was blown away by what he saw. There was a pureness, a sweetness—a hopefulness. Suddenly, all that had been bad up to this point—the accident and Sam—seem to diminish in the magnitude of this incredible new life. She was perfect and they found relief in the fact she had no apparent defects. The scare was over. She had defied the odds—just like her parents.

With a flinch of pain, he leaned down to give his child a kiss. The nurse then gave the baby back to Shelly, who then gave her own kiss to her little one.

"I now know her name," Robin told Shelly as he got up to go her.

"You do?" she asked with a smile. "And what is it?"

"Joy."

Shelly began to cry again. "Yes… Joy."

Unaware of the pain, he leaned over, brushed back her hair, and graciously kissed his wife once more.

~~THE END~~

BIRTH ANNOUNCEMENT

Mr. Robin Edward Parker
and
Mrs. Shelly Marie Harrison Parker

Proudly announce the birth of their first child, daughter

Joy Rose Parker

On December 1st, 2006
1:00 a.m.

Weighing 8 lbs. 5 oz. and 20 inches long.

Please welcome our newest little band member!

Printed in the United States
By Bookmasters